MURDER AT CAPE THREE POINTS

MURDER AT CAPE THREE POINTS

KWEI QUARTEY

SOHO
CRIME

Published by
Soho Press, Inc.
853 Broadway
New York, NY 10003

Library of Congress Cataloging-in-Publication Data

Quartey, Kwei J.
Murder at Cape Three Points / Kwei Quartey.
p. cm
ISBN 978-1-61695-389-8
eISBN 978-1-61695-390-4
1. Police—Ghana—Fiction. 2. Married people—Crimes against—Fiction.
3. Rich people—Crimes against—Fiction. 4. Murder—Investigation—Fiction.
5. Real estate development—Fiction. 6. Petroleum industry and trade—Fiction.
7. Ghana—Fiction. I. Title.
PS3617.U37M87 2014   813'.6—dc23
2013038337

Interior design by Janine Agro, Soho Press, Inc.

Printed in the United States of America

10 9 8 7 6 5 4 3 2 1

To the people of Cape Three Points,
the land nearest nowhere

Money calls blood

—FROM AN AKAN PROVERB

MURDER AT CAPE THREE POINTS

THE SMITH-AIDOO AND SARBAH FAMILY TREE

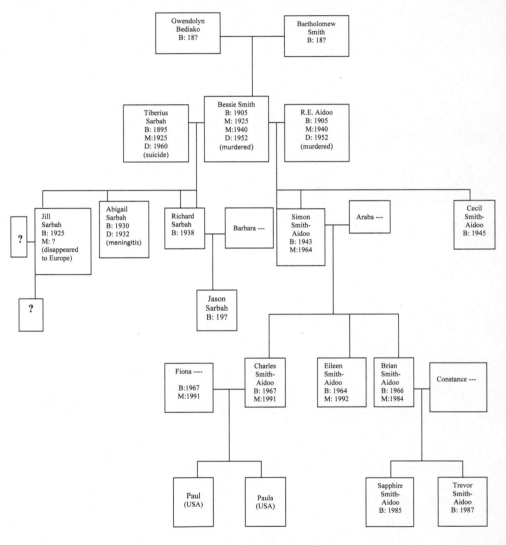

PROLOGUE

CAPE THREE POINTS, THE southernmost tip of Ghana, is beautiful and wild. Verdant forest covers the three finger-like peninsulas that jut into the Atlantic Ocean. Dizzying cliffs overlook the cyan waters. As waves strike the slate grey rocks and burst into gossamer spray, the roar of the sea crescendos like the sibilant clash of cymbals.

At dusk, the brightness of the sky melts and softens. The dying sun lays a wide band of gold across the sea. A full moon rises and imparts a silver gloss to the dark ocean, silhouetting fishing canoes gliding along silently like ghosts.

The forests and mangrove swamps of the coast are flora and fauna sanctuaries. In the Gulf of Guinea too, wildlife flourishes, but not without threat. Frolicking bottlenose dolphins and humpback whales would do well to avoid an alien creature in their midst. Afloat on powerful, squat limbs, its gangly crane booms resemble tentacles. From the derrick, its drill descends like a proboscis and penetrates the seabed to extract as much oil as possible. The creature is the *Thor Sterke*.

IN JULY, THE Equator dawn begins with a rosé blush expanding across the horizon. For the *Thor Sterke* crane operator who has worked graveyard, the lovely panorama is a welcome indication that his overnight shift is almost over. He struggles to remain alert as he lifts the last of the heavy loads from the supply vessel stationed at the starboard side of the rig. He brings up a large bundle of drilling equipment and expertly swings it around to the pipe deck, where two workers stand ready to guide the bundle to its assigned destination.

Over the next twenty-five minutes, the sun rises. High up in his cab, the crane operator has a 360-degree view of the seascape. A flat-decked supply vessel is approaching, a trawler is just visible to the south, and two fishing canoes are coming in from the southwest.

"Fuckin' fishermen," he mutters. Fishing canoes are not allowed within 500 meters of the rig. That's the rule, and yet they violate it all the time. They end up colliding with supply vessels, and their fishing nets sometimes snag on crucial rig installations.

He ignores the canoes as he begins another lift and sling, but at the end of the cycle, he watches them draw closer. Two fishermen are in the larger one, which is fitted with an outboard motor. After a while, the fisherman at the stern starts up the motor and turns the canoe north toward the shore. The smaller canoe is neither motor-powered, nor paddled. It appears to be drifting at the whim of the northeasterly sea currents. The crane operator thinks he can make out a figure in the canoe, but something is odd and still about the craft.

He puts a pair of binoculars to his eyes and searches for the canoe. He jumps with fright as a man's head comes into the field of vision. It is stuck on the end of an upright pole on the bow. Its mouth is open and the right eyeball has been scooped out. At first, the crane operator thinks it must be an extraordinarily lifelike mask and someone's sick idea of a joke, but as he shifts the field of view slightly, he sees the decapitated man sitting inside the canoe with ragged, bloody pieces of tissue projecting from the dark gorge in his neck.

The crane operator turns his head and retches violently.

Chapter 1

HOSIAH WAS ASLEEP. HIS little chest, wrapped in layers of gauze bandages, rhythmically rose and fell. His 24-hour observation in the Intensive Care Unit had passed uneventfully, and now he was on the step-down ward. Darko Dawson sat at his son's bedside keeping watch, frequently looking up to check the cardiac monitor on the wall.

He was thankful Hosiah was out of the ICU. It meant he was stable and progressing. Dawson had found the high-tech, intensive care environment overwhelming. To him, the array of machines wasn't so much a reassurance that every possible body system was under surveillance; it was a reminder that every possible body system could go wrong.

He was aware of a slight soreness in his own chest, as though he too had gone through Hosiah's cardiac surgery—sympathy pains for the boy who meant everything to him. Dawson felt relief and deep gratitude. He and his wife, Christine, had endured the agony of watching their son slowly deteriorate over the seven years of his young life. Hosiah had been born with a large ventricular septal defect, and his physical condition had progressively worsened as his need for surgery had become more urgent every day. Ghana's National Health Insurance Scheme only paid for the basics, like anti-malarial drugs. Open-heart surgery was not basic. The fee was far beyond their ability to pay.

Dr. Anum Biney, a forensic pathologist who had worked with Dawson on several murder cases, had called up his friend, the director of the National Cardiothoracic Center. Biney's personal appeal on Dawson's behalf had resulted in the approval of the operation for a nominal fee.

Dawson was off from work for ten days. It had not been easy to obtain clearance for temporary leave from the Homicide Unit at the Criminal Investigations Unit, CID, whereas Christine, who was a primary school teacher, had easily secured extended time off from work so she could be with Hosiah until he was well enough to return to school.

Christine had gone down the hall to the washroom. Dawson glanced over to the next bed where a four-year-old boy, also recovering from cardiac surgery, was sitting up in bed working on a coloring book. At the third bed, a nurse was attending to a teenage girl.

This hospital room was semi-private. In the adjacent ward, private rooms existed for those who could afford them. Everyone at this exceptionally well-equipped center had either money or good fortune. Located in Ghana's capital, Accra, where Dawson and his family lived, the center was the only one of its kind in the entire country. He could not help but think of the multitude of children in Ghana dying from congenital heart disease for lack of medical facilities.

Dawson occupied himself by reading the lead article in today's *Daily Graphic* newspaper. The headline was "Malgam Makes New Offshore Find." Malgam, a UK oil company, had been the first to discover substantial petroleum deposits off the coast at Cape Three Points in Ghana's Western Region. It had been producing oil at the rate of about 70,000 barrels a day. On an international scale, this wasn't much, but the plan was to increase it to 120,000 bpd over the next twelve months. Meanwhile, Malgam kept making new discoveries and appeared to be doing very well financially.

The oil find was changing the political and economic landscape of the Western Region, especially in the regional capital, Sekondi-Takoradi, the twin city about 180 kilometers west of Accra. Its unofficial name was now the "Oil City," and apparently, Ghanaians, foreigners, banks, insurance companies, and hotels were flocking to it. Since one visit to see his aunt when he was a teenager, Dawson had not been back to Takoradi, or "Tadi," as people affectionately called it. He could only imagine how much the city had transformed in that time.

Christine came back to the ward, looking lovely in a batik skirt and a kingfisher-blue top. Dawson could not count the number of times she had turned men's heads today alone. It always made him smile with pride and think, *Sorry, you can't have her.*

She sat down beside him, leaning on his thigh. "You can take a break for a while, if you like."

"I'm okay for now," he said, slipping his fingers into her soft palm.

Hosiah must have heard their voices. He stirred and his eyes fluttered open.

"Hey, Champ," Dawson said, smiling. He passed his hand gently back and forth over Hosiah's hair, cut low just like his dad's. The more the boy grew up, the more he resembled Dawson.

Hosiah's eyes lingered on Dawson's face first and then traveled to his mother's and back to Dawson's.

"How do you feel?" Dawson asked him.

"Good." Hosiah gazed around the room for a moment as he again familiarized himself with his surroundings. General anesthesia played tricks on the mind and the memory. "Mama?"

Christine went to the other side of the bed to be closer to him. "What is it, sweetie?"

"I'm hungry."

She exchanged a smile with Dawson. That was a good sign. She kissed Hosiah's forehead. "They're going to bring you something soon."

"How hungry are you, Champ?" Dawson asked.

Through his sleepy haze, a smile played at the corners of Hosiah's lips. He had a little game with his father. "I'm very, very, very, *very* hungry."

"Hungry enough to eat twenty balls of *kenkey?*"

Kenkey, made from fermented corn, was a staple particularly among the Ga people.

Hosiah began to laugh, then winced. "Daddy, don't make me laugh. It hurts."

"Dark," Christine said reproachfully.

"Sorry," he apologized sheepishly.

Hosiah turned pensive. "Daddy, did they really fix the hole in my heart?"

"Yes, they did."

"So, now I'll be fine? I can play soccer and do everything?"

"If the operation went the way it was supposed to and you heal up well."

"And how is my favorite patient?"

One of the nurses had arrived with Hosiah's lunch on a tray. She smiled at him. "Are you ready to eat something?"

"He's more than ready," Dawson said.

Christine and Dawson helped Hosiah to sit up. Dawson watched the boy's face to see how much discomfort he was having, but his son registered little. Over countless visits to the hospital, Dawson had observed just how tough sick children could be. Hosiah could take any injection or tolerate a large-bore intravenous catheter with barely a ripple of concern. Dawson, on the other hand, was afraid of needles.

The meal was light—two slices of tea bread with honey, and a bowl of Tom Brown, a popular cereal made from lightly toasted corn. Hosiah attacked it ferociously.

"Slow down," Christine said, laughing. "Breathe in between mouthfuls."

The boy took a rest. "When is Sly going to be here?"

"I'll pick him up from school later and bring him to spend time with you," Dawson said.

He had first met nine-year-old Sly on a previous case. For a while, the boy had disappeared, surfacing later as a homeless street kid. Neither Dawson nor Christine could leave him to that fate, especially after they'd learned that Sly did not even know who or where his parents were. They began adoption proceedings, and months later Sly was officially a Dawson. Two years older than Hosiah, he was protective of his younger brother and anxious to visit him in the hospital after school.

Dawson's phone buzzed, and he went out to the corridor to take the call. It was his junior partner, Detective Sergeant Philip Chikata.

"Where you dey?" Chikata asked in fashionable pidgin.

"I'm at the hospital."

"How is Hosiah?"

"Fine, so far. He's a strong boy."

"He is. Can I visit him tomorrow?"

"For sure, no problem. He'll be happy to see you."

"How long will they keep him?"

"They say he can go home on Tuesday."

"Okay." The sergeant paused. "Listen, my uncle will be calling you soon."

Chikata was the nephew of Chief Superintendent Lartey, Dawson's boss. Lartey doted on his nephew, who sometimes acted as a messenger between him and Dawson.

"What's going on?" Dawson asked.

"He wants you back at work on Monday."

Dawson's eyebrows shot up. "But I'm on leave," he protested, his voice sharpening.

"I know, but he says an urgent case has come up."

"Do you know what it's about?"

"Not exactly, but I know it's in Takoradi."

"Takoradi!"

"Yah. I wanted to let you know before he calls you, so you won't be too shocked."

Dawson heaved a sigh. "Okay. Thank you for warning me."

He ended the call and returned to the ward. Hosiah had finished lunch and gone back to sleep. At his bedside, Christine looked up from her romance novel.

"You don't look too happy. Who was that on the phone?"

Dawson sat down, reaching over to tilt her novel up so he could see the cover. "Honestly, what do these men have that I don't?"

"You wouldn't understand," Christine said enigmatically. "So, who called you?"

"Chikata. He says Lartey wants me back at work on Monday."

She stiffened visibly. "Why? For what?"

"A new case. In Tadi."

"*Takoradi!*" She put the book down and dropped her voice to a sharp whisper. "No, you can't do this. Hosiah needs us both right now."

"I know."

"Why does Lartey always do this?" She demanded furiosly. "What is wrong with that man?"

"You're asking me?" Dawson said gloomily.

"He's your boss, isn't he?" She snapped.

"He could be my twin brother, and I still wouldn't understand him."

"You can't go," Christine said, shaking her head vigorously. "You simply cannot."

She snatched up her novel. Dawson, sensing a looming crisis, said nothing. He was praying something would come up miraculously to change the chief superintendent's mind. However, when Lartey called within half an hour, Dawson had a sinking feeling.

"Massa," he answered in the colloquial but respectful manner of addressing a senior officer. "Good afternoon, massa."

"Afternoon, Dawson. How is your boy doing?"

Dawson stood up again to go outside the ward. "He's making a slow recovery, sir." He didn't want to give too glowing a report.

"Good. I need you to return to your duties on Monday."

"You gave me ten days off—"

"You can make it up some other time," Lartey interrupted briskly. "We have a petitioned case from Takoradi, and I've assigned you to take it."

"Please, sir, it won't be possible to leave Hosiah right now. He's still quite sick, and he needs me to be around for at least—"

"You have a wife, don't you? Now you listen to me, Dawson. Your solving that serial killer case last year doesn't suddenly make you a VIP. Your rank is still inspector, and you are still a junior officer. If you're planning to move up the ladder, may I remind you that you are up for chief inspector next year, and I will be one of the senior officers on the panel recommending your promotion?"

Dawson swallowed hard. Lartey had cut him down to size with a single swipe.

"If you're refusing to go to Takoradi," the chief superintendent continued crisply, "don't expect me to endorse your promotion. Instead, I will initiate dismissal procedures for insubordination. Take your pick."

Dawson shut his eyes for a moment and gritted his teeth. Promotion versus dismissal was hardly a dilemma. The chief was serious about his threats, and he had Dawson by the throat.

"Yes, sir," he said lightly, as if an unpleasant exchange had not just occurred. "What's the story, sir?"

"Do you remember about four months ago a fishing canoe was spotted from an oil rig off Cape Three Points floating around with two dead bodies inside, one of which was decapitated?"

"Yes. It was in the news for some time. The victims were a Mr. and Mrs. Smith-something, if I remember."

"Charles and Fiona Smith-Aidoo. She was a member of the Sekondi-Takoradi Metropolitan Assembly. He worked for Malgam Oil as director of corporate affairs. The canoe came drifting in full view of the Malgam rig. As if that wasn't enough, their niece, Sapphire Smith-Aidoo, who is a physician, was on duty on the rig at the time this all happened."

Dawson frowned. "What a bizarre story."

"It is. The bottom line is the murder is still unsolved, and the doctor filed a petition with CID Headquarters last month asking us to investigate, and the director general has approved it. Someone has to go to Takoradi, and I have decided it will be you. Superintendent Hammond is the regional crime officer in charge at Sekondi HQ. You're to report to him once you get there."

"And when am I to leave, sir?"

"Monday."

"Please, Hosiah goes home from the hospital on Tuesday. Can I leave on Tuesday instead?"

Lartey paused and then acquiesced. "Yes, all right—but directly after he returns home. There's no time to waste. I want this cleared up quickly. Understood?"

"Yes, sir."

"My assistant has left the docket in your desk at headquarters, so read it and get up to speed."

"I'll do that, sir."

"Chikata will join you in Takoradi on Friday. He hasn't done a case outside Accra, so I would like him to have some free rein. I expect you to give him the benefit of your experience."

"Of course." That was fine with Dawson. In fact, he would be glad to have the detective sergeant with him. He could be a handful, but Dawson was fond of him. When Chikata had begun working with him years ago, he had been cocky and incompetent, but he had improved so much that Dawson trusted him completely now.

"One last thing," Lartey said. "Dr. Smith-Aidoo works in Takoradi but has been in Accra the past three days. I told her to get in touch with you this afternoon after I spoke with you, so she will be calling to fill you in with the details of the case."

"Okay, sir."

"That's all, Dawson."

"Have a good weekend, sir."

Lartey grunted and ended the call abruptly. Dawson's heart was heavy. Now he had to face his wife and his two sons, one of them barely out of major surgery, and tell them he was going away. It would not go down well.

Chapter 2

THE SOMBER MOOD AT Hosiah's bedside was thick enough to chop into pieces. Dawson was despondent, and Christine was furious about the Takoradi assignment, but as Hosiah stirred and woke up again, they did their best to put away their glum frame of mind and keep their son in good spirits.

As Christine propped him up on his pillows, Dawson's phone buzzed, and the screen showed a number he did not know. His guess was that it was Dr. Smith-Aidoo, and he was right.

"Has Chief Superintendent Lartey briefed you about the death of my aunt and uncle?" she asked him, after mutual introductions. Her voice was as distilled and clear as crystal, and Dawson immediately liked it.

"He has," he said, "but, Doctor, I'd like to meet with you as soon as possible. Chief Lartey was very brief, so I will need to get more details from you."

"I was hoping you would say something like that. I'm eager to meet as well. I've heard about you—the serial killer case from a year ago made you famous."

"Thanks." He didn't like to dwell much on past achievements, so he moved on. "I should caution you that I might ask uncomfortable questions or things you've already gone over with the previous investigators."

"I expect that and look forward to it. I just want whoever did this to my aunt and uncle to be captured and brought to justice. Where are you right now? Can we meet in the next couple of hours?"

"I'm at Korle Bu. My son Hosiah has just had heart surgery."

"Chief Superintendent Lartey mentioned that. I understand Hosiah is doing well?"

"Yes, thank you, Doctor."

"God bless him. I'm so glad. I can meet you there. I assume Hosiah is in the Cardiothoracic Center?"

"Yes." He gave her the room number.

"Who was that?" Christine asked as Dawson hung up.

"The doctor I was telling you about." Dawson explained. "The niece of the victims. She's going to come here so we can talk about the case. You'll have to pick Sly up, and I'll stay instead."

She pressed her lips together with displeasure. It hadn't been long since Lartey's call, yet the case was already intruding, turning things upside down like a disruptive houseguest.

AN HOUR OR so later, Christine left to get Sly. With afternoon traffic building toward rush hour, it would be a while before they returned. As Dawson read a favorite Ananse comic with Hosiah to pass the time, his gaze shifted to the door where two women were entering. The first was the matron—the senior nurse—whom Dawson knew. She was buxom, but the other woman was tall, with fair, copper-colored skin. She wore a black trouser suit with a glimpse of an indigo blouse at her neckline. Her face was heart-shaped, and her head was crowned with luxuriant black curls. Tiny freckles dotted both cheeks like sprinkles of cinnamon.

"Inspector Dawson," the matron said, "you have a visitor."

He stood up. "You must be Doctor Smith-Aidoo."

"Yes." She smiled. "I'm very pleased to meet you."

They shook hands.

The doctor moved closer to the bed. "And this is Hosiah, the perfect patient I've heard so much about? How are you, young man?"

"I'm fine, thank you," he said softly and deferentially.

"Matron tells me you're a very brave boy."

He smiled bashfully.

"He is very good," the matron confirmed, beaming at him.

"Wonderful." Smith-Aidoo looked at Dawson. "Can we talk for half an hour or so? The matron will have her staff keep a special eye on Hosiah. They all adore him anyway."

"Sure," Dawson said. He ran his hand lightly over his son's head. "I'll be back soon, okay?"

Hosiah nodded. He wasn't troubled.

Dawson thanked the matron and followed Dr. Smith-Aidoo to a private room not in use. It was comfortably air-conditioned. Two chairs were available next to the neatly made-up bed. They sat down facing each other. She crossed one elegant leg over the other. He could not help staring at her hazel eyes. They were clear and bright, but he could see a certain sadness hanging within them like clouds marring the sun.

"I'm very sorry about what happened to your aunt and uncle," he said.

"Thank you. I'm grateful you're taking the case. To tell you the truth, I've been in Accra this week to personally pressure the director general of CID and Chief Superintendent Lartey. I didn't want to take the risk that the written petition would not be enough."

"As you see it, Doctor, what has been the problem with the investigation so far?"

"I have nothing whatsoever against Superintendent Hammond," she said emphatically. "I like him personally, but obviously he needs help. He has had four months and has made not even a single arrest."

"You're aware that there's no guarantee that I'll solve it either?"

"No guarantees, but I have faith in you."

"Thank you. You were very close to Charles and Fiona, Doctor?"

Her eyes softened. "They meant everything to me. My father, Brian Smith-Aidoo, is Uncle Charles's brother, but Auntie Fio and Uncle Charles really brought me up."

Not uncommon in Ghana, where the extended family's role is prominent, Dawson reflected, but in a murder case, it could be a crucial detail.

"How did that come about?" he asked.

"My mother is a schizophrenic," she said matter-of-factly. "By the time I was eight, she had become so violent that my father could barely manage her. She particularly picked on me. Once she almost strangled me, and on another occasion she fractured my forearm by twisting it." She winced, as if she were living through the experience again. "My father asked Uncle Charles and Auntie Fio if they would take care of me for a while. He kept my brother, Trevor, with him. Eventually he had my mother institutionalized at a psychiatric hospital in Manchester."

"Manchester? Why there?"

"It's her hometown. My mother is English. No way her family, or my father for that matter, would put her in the psychiatric hospital in Accra." She grimaced. "Have you ever been inside there?"

"Once, while on a case."

"Then you know how deplorable the conditions are. To say it's medieval would be too kind. After my mother was sent to England, Daddy wanted me back, but by then I was almost thirteen and so attached to Auntie Fio and Uncle Charles, and vice versa. They didn't want to give me up." She shook her head with regret. "I believe that's when the rivalry between Uncle Charles and my father started. Uncle Charles was protective and possessive of me. In the five years I was with him, Daddy didn't come around that much, and so my uncle asked him in effect, 'Where have you been all this time?'"

"Did you return to your dad?"

"Physically, but not in spirit. I was miserable with him. He didn't give me a fraction of the love and warmth that Auntie Fio and Uncle Charles had given me. By fifteen, I was acting out—misbehaving, smoking, and all that mess. I was at Accra Girls' High, and the headmistress told my father that if I didn't straighten out, she would expel me. Again, he turned to Auntie and Uncle for help. They took me out of boarding and made me a day student. Uncle Charles took me to school every single day and Auntie brought me home when classes were over, keeping me in check, and yes, I did straighten out."

"You must have," he said. "You're a doctor now."

She smiled, clearly glad that her fate had been shaped this way. "All due to Uncle Charles and Auntie Fio. And I tell you all this not to bore you with my life story, but to show why they were so important, so precious to me."

"I understand now. You said your father and his brother became rivals. This is a tough question, and I'm sorry to ask it, but I have to. Could your father have had anything to do with the murder of your aunt and uncle?"

"He doesn't have passion or courage for anything, let alone murder. Seems odd to put it that way, but there it is."

Doesn't think much of her dad, Dawson thought but then neither did he of his.

"How did he react to your uncle's death?"

"He was devastated. He went into deep mourning, as did I. This has been the most awful year of my life. Only two months before my uncle's murder, another tragedy took place. You should know about it because it might have some bearing on the case."

She slumped very slightly, as if a heavy load had been set upon her shoulders.

"Jason Sarbah is a name you will become familiar with," she continued. "After Uncle's death, Jason became the new director of corporate affairs at Malgam Oil. Uncle was Jason's first cousin—same grandmother, Bessie Smith, but different grandfathers. Bessie was first married to a Tiberius Sarbah, whom she divorced for Robert E. Aidoo, which is how the Smith-Aidoo surname came about. Bessie gave the hyphenated name to Simon, her only son by the second marriage."

"So, to get this clear in my mind," Dawson said, "Bessie and Robert Smith-Aidoo are your great grandparents."

"Yes, the Sarbah and Smith-Aidoo lines are connected through Bessie. Up until the time of his death, Uncle Charles worked for Malgam Oil as their director of corporate affairs. I didn't know Jason Sarbah or much about him until the end of February, this year, when he approached me. I had just finished my national service and joined a private clinic in Takoradi. Jason and his wife, Sylvia, had a sixteen-year-old daughter called Angela who was very ill. In spite of multiple visits to several hospitals in Accra and Takoradi, doctors couldn't figure out what was wrong. They were watching Angela die. She was severely jaundiced, so her eyes turned yellow. She was losing weight every day and having unbearable abdominal pain. He brought her to see me. By then, he was in a state of despair."

Dr. Smith-Aidoo's face mirrored the anguish of the scenario she was describing.

"How terrible it must have been," Dawson said. "The private clinic you mentioned—I assume it's expensive?"

"Very," she said, wincing. "It's part of a worldwide chain called International Medical Services, or IMS, with branches all over Africa. It's not a charity—doesn't even pretend to be anything else but a for-profit company. You pay with credit or hard cash and the patients are expatriates and well-off Ghanaians. I did an initial evaluation of Angela, which was moderately expensive but still didn't diagnose what she had.

"Jason was having difficulty coming up with the money even for that first medical work-up. I understand that at the time, he'd just started a real estate business that wasn't doing very well, and I don't believe his wife worked or made a lot of money. Angela was going to need a battery of tests and scans, but any movement forward depended on his paying for what had been done so far. Jason begged me to set up some kind of arrangement whereby his payment could be deferred. I asked the clinic administrator if that was possible, and her answer was quite firm. She said IMS doesn't give out free lunches, and anyone who thought it did was not welcome. Someone in the administrative office called Jason and politely told him that if he couldn't pay, he needn't bother to return. I was appalled, but only five or six years out of medical school and brand new at the clinic, I didn't feel at the time that I could argue on Jason's behalf, although now I wish I had."

She must be around thirty, thirty-one, Dawson thought, *graduating from medical school at a very young twenty-five or so.*

"And at around that time," she continued, "something else happened that I wish had turned out differently. Jason went to Uncle Charles to ask for a loan, but Uncle turned him down."

"Did he say why he refused Jason's request?" Dawson asked.

"He didn't see why Jason had to take Angela to the most expensive clinic in town. Jason tried to explain that he had been to several public hospitals, including Korle Bu at the very beginning of Angela's illness back in January. Uncle's advice was to take Angela back to Korle Bu and insist that they reinvestigate what was wrong with her.

"Soon after that, Jason accosted me one morning in the car park as I drove in to work, making an embarrassing scene. It was a combination of attacking me, saying I was letting his daughter die, and begging me for mercy. The security man had to escort him away.

It was horrible—still haunts me. By the end of April, I had heard nothing from him, so I called him. He said he was back at Korle Bu Hospital with Angela. They had done an exploratory laparotomy and found that she had hepatocellular carcinoma. It's very rare in children, and all of us had missed it. Angela was in hepatic coma at the time I spoke to Jason, and she died about ten days later."

"Oh," Dawson said. "I'm sorry."

She lowered her head and closed her eyes for a moment of pain that clearly still haunted her. "I am too. I failed Jason and his wife, and I failed their daughter. I could have made a stronger appeal to my administrator, or called someone at Korle Bu."

"Would it have made a difference in the end, Doctor?"

"Perhaps not, but the point is that I didn't try hard enough to save a girl who was the same age I was when Uncle Charles and Auntie Fiona rescued *me* from ruin. I wonder what that says about me."

With the last comment, she was almost talking to herself, and Dawson felt uncomfortable, as though he were eavesdropping. He had never witnessed such self-recrimination in a doctor. Like policemen, physicians rarely accepted blame for anything. He wanted to comfort her, or at least empathize, but he was afraid he might sound patronizing.

"Did Jason ever get back in touch with you?" he asked her.

"He didn't call me, but I reached him by phone once. I told him how sorry I was. All he said was, 'I hope it never happens to you,' and he hung up."

"Meaning, 'I hope you never lose a loved one like I have?'"

She contemplated. "Yes, I suppose so."

"Could he have killed your aunt and uncle?"

Dr. Smith-Aidoo took a breath and released a long, contemplative sigh. "It's difficult to accuse him while he has suffered the same kind of loss as I have, but . . ."

"The bitterness that comes with grief can be powerful."

"Yes. You read my mind." She shook her head. "But no, I can't in good conscience accuse him."

"I understand," Dawson said. "I was curious how you came to work on the Malgam oil rig. It's not a typical job for a physician, is it?"

"No, it's not. After Angela's death, I left IMS immediately with a bad taste in my mouth. I didn't want to have anything to do with them again. I was looking around for something completely different to do—a new environment to escape to, where I didn't have to hear all the talk about Angela and what had happened. Tadi is a small place. People gossip. Uncle Charles understood where I was coming from, and when he heard that a position on the Malgam rig as medic had unexpectedly opened up, he recommended it to me. I was overqualified since they usually use EMTs, but I was willing to take the cut in pay. In fact, I was glad to do it, maybe as a penance for the IMS tragedy. I pestered Malgam, and Uncle Charles added pressure. That's how I got the job."

"You must have really wanted it," Dawson commented. "Isn't that like the Inspector General of Police taking the position of a sergeant?"

She laughed. "I guess that's one way of looking at it. That didn't matter to me, though. I'm still an MD, no matter what."

"How soon after your uncle's death did Jason Sarbah take over as Malgam's Director of Corporate Affairs?"

"About two months. In September, the CEO of Malgam, Roger Calmy-Rey, met Jason at the funeral, and they talked. Jason's work history—first as a bank manager and then as a solo real estate agent—impressed Roger, and the story of the death of Jason's daughter touched him. He offered Jason a crack at the position, they interviewed him, and he was successful."

"Is it possible that Calmy-Rey gave him the job as a consolation?"

"Kind of a gesture of sympathy?" she asked. "I doubt it. Malgam Oil comes first in Roger's life. He's not going to jeopardize it by hiring someone unqualified. No, Jason is a very bright man. I don't doubt his abilities."

"Have you spoken to him since the time he told you on the phone that he hoped the death of a loved one never happened to you?"

"Months after the murder, we met once at an event in Accra. I told him I was sorry, and he gave me his condolences in turn."

Dawson saw there was a lot to think about here: Jason Sarbah had been anguished and angered by his daughter's death and probably still was, but he was also an ambitious man looking for a lucrative career. Was the murder of his cousin Charles a kind of two for one—get revenge and get his job? No, that seemed too neat, like an attractively wrapped box containing nothing.

Dawson became aware that Dr. Smith-Aidoo had been watching him ponder. "When do you return to Takoradi?" he asked her.

"Tomorrow. When do you expect to get there?"

"Tuesday afternoon or evening."

"I will call you Wednesday morning sometime."

They stood up.

"It warmed my heart to see your boy doing so well, Inspector," she said. "I think it's a good omen for the way the investigation will go."

Dawson hoped she was right. In his experience, omens were over-rated.

Chapter 3

ON SATURDAY AFTERNOON, AFTER Dawson had spent time with
Hosiah at the hospital, he rode his aging motorbike to CID Headquarters on Ring Road East. It was a seven-story, ailing building the
color of dirty sand. It looked no more significant than an old apart-
ment building. Its appearance didn't match its impressive name,
Criminal Investigations Department.

Except for the ground floor charge office where a certain amount
of chaos was standard, CID was quiet on the weekends. Dawson
took the narrow stairway to the fourth floor where he let himself
into the detective's room, greeting the only other person there, a
detective sergeant preparing for a big court case on Monday.

On most days, the room was stifling, but today a soft breeze came
through the louvered windows on either side. Only senior officers,
assistant superintendent, and above, got air-conditioned rooms.
Junior ones, from constable to chief inspector, did not. If Dawson ever wanted to have the high privilege of an air-conditioned
room one day, he was going to have to knuckle down, comply with
Lartey's orders and solve this case.

He sat at his desk to examine the Smith-Aidoos' case docket,
whose front cover was the standard appearance of all such police
records.

DOCKET
GHANA POLICE FORCE

Date of offense <u>Monday, 9 July/Tuesday, 10 July</u>
Complainant <u>Sapphire, Smith-Aidoo, MD</u>
Principal Witness(es)
    <u>Sapphire, Smith-Aidoo, MD</u>
    <u>George Findlay (Offshore Oil Installation Manager, Malgam)</u>
    <u>Michael Glagah (Safety Officer, Malgam Oil)</u>
    <u>Clifford Stewart (Crane Operator, Malgam Oil)</u>
    <u>Ghana Navy Service personnel</u>

Accused _____
Offense <u>HOMICIDE</u>
Victim(s) <u>Charles Smith-Aidoo, Fiona Smith-Aidoo</u>

He opened the folder and flinched. Front and center was a printed image of Charles Smith-Aidoo's severed head stuck to the end of a gnarled, wooden pole like a gruesome lollipop. It looked both real and unreal, like a botched waxworks beginning to swell up and melt in the heat. The mouth gaped. The left eye was partially open, and the right eye had been removed. Dawson imagined the murderer holding the head firmly while pressing and screwing it down onto the erected stake. He shuddered and began to feel nauseated. Cutting off a person's limbs was vile, but decapitation crossed a line into a realm of brutality that he could not understand.

Charles's headless body had been propped up against one side of the canoe's interior, dark irregular bloodstains around the neckline of his shirt. The murderer seemed to have mounted a display for maximum, sickening impact. Fiona Smith-Aidoo's body was stretched along the floor of the canoe behind her husband's. It appeared crumpled, more carelessly thrown—less staged than his.

Dawson had to stop looking at the photo. In his last case, a serial killer had disfigured his adolescent victims, but there, it had been the number killed that defined the horror. None of the individual victims had been inflicted with this degree of cruelty.

With relief, he turned to the next page, which was Dr. Smith-Aidoo's petition.

11th October

Dear Director General,

    It has now been almost four months since the death of my beloved aunt and uncle, Fiona and Charles Smith-Aidoo. Their loved ones, including me, are still in a state of shock and profound grief. As you are aware, they were shot to death in cold blood in July of this year. In addition, my uncle was savagely beheaded. The crime unit at Sekondi police headquarters, led by Superintendent David Hammond, has been unable to apprehend the perpetrator and bring him to justice. I hereby request CID headquarters to please review the case for any deficiencies in the investigation by the Sekondi detectives and either assist them or assume the investigation completely so that my dear aunt and uncle can finally rest in peace.

Yours faithfully,
Sapphire Smith-Aidoo, MD

Petitions to CID Headquarters could come from several sources; any citizen had the right to make a request for case review if he or she was unhappy with the investigation by a regional CID office. Not all requests had merit, however, and sometimes the assessment was that the region was doing just fine. The director general of CID made the final decision.

On the docket's second page, Superintendent David Hammond had written a brief summary of events.

    On the morning of Monday, 7th July, Charles Smith-Aidoo and wife, Fiona, traveled from Axim to Ezile Bay, a small resort area 8 km east of Cape Three Points, where they visited the owner of the resort, Mr. Reggie Cardiman. The purpose of the visit was business, which concluded at approximately 12:30 P.M. The Smith-Aidoos left Ezile Bay at that time, reportedly to continue on to Axim.

At 13:25, Mr. Cardiman was on the way to Takoradi when he came across the Smith-Aidoos' vehicle abandoned along the only road available to and from Ezile Bay (see attached Dixcove Police Diary of Action Taken). A search of the area yielded no clues as to their whereabouts.

At approximately 05:50 on Tuesday, 9th July, a small canoe bearing the corpses of Charles and Fiona Smith-Aidoo appeared at sea 60 km from Cape Three Points near the Malgam oil rig. Both had sustained gunshots to the head. Additionally, Mr. Smith-Aidoo was in a decapitated state.

The Ghana Navy Service (GNS) retrieved the canoe and transported it to shore, delivering the dead bodies to Effia-Nkwanta Hospital for identification and autopsy.

Dr. Sapphire Smith-Aidoo, the dead couple's niece, and her father, Brian Smith-Aidoo (Charles Smith-Aidoo's brother), identified the bodies at the hospital mortuary.

Dawson went on to the next section.

Police Report
Dixcove Police Station
Diary of Action Taken
Date of Report Monday, 7 July
Date of Incident Monday, 7 July
Reporting Officer Inspector Nana French

At 13:35 on Monday, 7 July, one Reggie Cardiman, owner of the Ezile Beach Resort, whom I know very well, called me on my cell phone to report that he was standing near a black Hyundai Santa Fe SUV with license registration WR-CSA-1 parked at the roadside about 9 km from the resort. The vehicle had its front doors wide open, but no driver or passenger was inside. Mr. Cardiman stated he had been on his way from the resort to Takoradi when he observed the vehicle. He further stated that he believed the vehicle belonged to one Mr. Charles Smith-Aidoo of Takoradi and his wife, Fiona. Mr. Cardiman stated that Mr. and Mrs. Smith-Aidoo had paid him a visit at the Ezile Bay during the morning of that same day and had eaten lunch in the restaurant there, leaving at approximately 12:30.

When asked how he was so certain that the Hyundai belonged to the Smith-Aidoos, Mr. Cardiman stated that he was familiar with Mr. Smith-Aidoo's personalized license plate bearing his initials, CSA. Mr. Cardiman stated he had stopped to look inside the vehicle when he came upon it at the roadside, but saw no sign of any driver or passenger. He further said that he had searched around the area including some of the roadside bushes but had not come across any person or persons. He then decided to report the incident to the police.

I asked Mr. Cardiman if he could please remain at the scene until my arrival. At 14:10, I took a taxi to the location, arriving at almost 14:45 to find Mr. Cardiman waiting by the Hyundai vehicle, which Mr. Cardiman stated had remained undisturbed during the interval in which I had been traveling from the police station. I proceeded to examine the exterior and interior of the vehicle. I found no signs of damage to the vehicle. I also did not find any evidence of struggle or foul play inside the vehicle. I searched the surrounding areas of the bush. I was not able to find anyone associated with the vehicle.

Dawson went next to the forensic report by a Dr. Hector Cudjoe, a pathologist at Effia-Nkwanta Hospital, Takoradi's largest hospital.

Seventh of July was the official date of death, but the time of death was a broader estimate of between 12:00 (noon) and 22:00 hours based on the degree of decay, which was not advanced.

Dawson looked at Charles's autopsy first. He had been fifty-two years old when he died.

PRESENTATION, CLOTHING, AND PERSONAL EFFECTS

Body: The body of an adult male arrives at the morgue in a bag in a decapitated state with the wrists tied behind the back with coarse twine. The severed head is also present. The body is clad in a cream-colored, heavily bloodstained tailored tunic with matching zipped trousers, a white, heavily bloodstained singlet, and white underpants. There are no socks or shoes. A gold ring is present on the left fourth finger. There are no other jewelry items.

Beach-consistency sand diffusely covers the right side and the posterior portion of the shirt. Clothing is also diffusely stained with dark material that might have originated from the bottom of the canoe in which the body was discovered. Limbs, torso, and genitals are intact.

Head: It has been removed in toto by sharp dissection at approximately the 6th cervical vertebral level. The right eyeball is absent, having been removed by sharp excision, and is not present among the remains brought to the morgue. This corresponds to a witness report and a photograph at the scene showing the enucleation on the right side. However, the left eyeball is intact. The victim's tongue has also been removed by sharp excision and is not recovered from the remains. Recovered from the victim's oral cavity is a bloodstained, old-fashioned pocket watch with a tarnished silver cover inlaid with a circular dark center that is most likely black onyx. On the inside of the cover is a crudely scratched message stating, "Blood runs deep," which appears to have been made recently, certainly within the last one month.

Dawson's eyes narrowed. Why the old watch, and what did the inscription "blood runs deep" mean? Along with the decapitation and the enucleation, it was simply extraordinary. He read on.

EVIDENCE OF GUNSHOT INJURY

Male victim, Charles Smith-Aidoo: A 0.5 cm gunshot entrance wound is present at the left temporal region 4 cm anterior to the superior portion of the helix of the left ear. Abrasions are present at the edges of the wound. Noted is a zone of soot measuring 2.5 x 2.0 cm in greatest dimension around the entrance wound. Patchy hemorrhage is observed in the tissues of the scalp and the skull in the temporal area. Extensive subarachnoid hemorrhage exists, with severe damage to the bases of the brain. Lodged in and recovered from the right ear canal is a copper-jacketed small caliber bullet. The direction of the wound track is rightward, backward, and downward.

Soot around the bullet wound signified discharge of the weapon at close range. Dawson pictured it. Maybe the murderer had made Charles kneel, gun muzzle pressed to his temple as Charles begged for mercy. It was a disturbing image, but the decapitation was even more disturbing. Dawson tried to read the graphic details of the severed arteries in the neck and the hacked cervical vertebrae, but he began to feel sick and stopped.

Warily, he turned to Fiona's details. She, too, was bound at the wrists behind her back. Her outfit was purple and pink with pink undergarments. Beach sand had soiled the clothing of both victims, suggesting that the perpetrator(s) had dragged both of them along the sand for some unknown distance. The pathologist's report also noted: *A large silver hoop earring hangs from the lobe of the right ear, but no corresponding earring on the left is present.*

She had sustained a gunshot wound to the right temple. The bullet had tracked across her brain to shatter the left cheekbone, where it had emerged. No bullet or fragments were present, nor did the report mention whether or not gunpowder stippling accompanied the entry wound. Had there been none, or had Dr. Cudjoe inadvertently omitted that detail? He had indicated the wounds on the standard schematic drawings always provided on a postmortem form. Photographs were not included with the documents, which was common. Most of the time, no camera was available, and in any case, the mortuary personnel, including the forensic pathologist, often took photos at a bad angle or in poor light.

Next to the name *George Findlay, Offshore Oil Installation Manager,* a telephone number had been circled, with a red arrow pointing to it. Dawson had no idea what an oil installation manager was. He was about to find out.

Chapter 4

GEORGE FINDLAY PICKED UP the call almost immediately. Dawson introduced himself and told him he was taking on the Smith-Aidoo case.

"I'm very glad to hear that," Findlay said. He had a light Scottish accent and a pleasant voice. "We need someone to solve it once and for all."

"Do you have a moment to answer some questions?"

"No more than about ten minutes. I'm at Kotoka Airport getting ready to leave for Glasgow."

"I'll be quick, then. By the way, what does your job entail as an oil installation manager?"

"I'm the most senior manager on the rig, ultimately responsible for day-to-day operations and safety of everyone on board. For example, that morning the canoe with the dead bodies drifted into the rig area, it broke everyone's focus on their jobs, and it was my responsibility to marshal everyone back to work. There could have been a breach of safety and security."

"I see," Dawson said. That gave him a clear picture.

"People were coming up to the pipe deck to see the spectacle," Findlay continued. "Eventually, Michael Glagah, our safety officer put a stop to that, but in the midst of all the confusion, Dr. Smith-Aidoo came up from the medic room to see what the commotion was about. The tragedy is that I had no idea that it was her aunt and uncle in the canoe, so I let her use my binoculars to get a better look. She stared for a wee bit and then let out a strange cooing noise, rather like a pigeon, and then she fainted. Fortunately, someone was right next to her to catch her. She seemed to recover somewhat a few seconds later, but she was still staring glassy-eyed as though in shock, and I couldn't understand why Michael took another look in the binoculars and said something like, 'Oh, my God,' and whispered to me that the corpses looked like Charles and Fiona Smith-Aidoo. He had met them before, but I had not."

"Do you think the display was aimed directly at her?"

"If so, it takes a diabolical mind to conceive of and execute something as gruesome and abhorrent as that."

Dawson could not have said it any better. "What happened next?"

"We took Dr. Smith-Aidoo downstairs to rest and radioed to shore for an emergency chopper to come in and take her back to the mainland."

"She will never forget that horrible day," Dawson commented.

"Never," Findlay agreed. "To see her beloved uncle decapitated . . . I can only begin to imagine how awful that was."

"What was Mr. Smith-Aidoo's role at Malgam? What does a corporate relations director do?"

"It's a delicate job of juggling government and public affairs, media relations, internal relations, liaison with the CEO and the board, response to external pressures, managing company image, and so on."

"Not easy, in other words."

"Not at all. I don't know how he did it."

"Do you think he made enemies?"

"Maybe he did; I don't know, but even if that was the case, I find it difficult to imagine *anyone*, enemy or otherwise, doing something this vicious and cold-blooded to him and his wife. From what I heard about him, he was well-liked."

"Still," Dawson said, "the job description sounds like every once in a while, he would have had to tell people things they didn't want to hear."

"Yes, I'm sure," Findlay said, "but companies like Malgam always try to stay on a positive note and make a favorable public showing—you know, refurbishing a school here or building a hospital there, repairing a stretch of road or roundabout, and so on."

Dawson heard the airport announcer in the background over the phone. "Sounds like they're calling your flight, sir. I appreciate your time. Have a safe journey."

BEFORE RETURNING HOME, Dawson rode the short distance from CID headquarters to a district of Accra called Osu, where his older brother, Cairo, owned a curio shop. Besides trying to stop by to see Cairo at least once a week, Dawson made it a rule to do his best to visit anytime he was going out of town. He supposed it was a kind of superstition that if anything happened to him on the road, Cairo would at least be able to look back and say that he had spent time with his younger brother, Darko, not long before he died.

Cairo had been a paraplegic since he was a teenager. In a tragedy that had occurred in just a few seconds but would affect him for the rest of his life, a car had hit him as he crossed the street on the way to buy some provisions. Flying up over the roof of the car and down the back, he had severed his spine and become paralyzed from the waist down.

In years past, he had relied heavily on the care of others, but the Cairo of today was fiercely independent, far from helpless, and doing very well for himself. His curio shop was located along the tourist trap, clustered around Oxford Street. It was packed with souvenir vendors, restaurants, hotels, nightclubs, banks, and telecom giants like Vodafone. During the global economic downturn, Cairo had fallen on a rough time, as had other merchants, but he had survived and trade had picked up again. Until only a couple of years ago, he had been single, but now he was married to Audrey, a gem of a woman, and they had one daughter.

The shop, Ultimate Craft, was air-conditioned and filled with the sweet smell of wood and leather goods. Recently Cairo had expanded, buying out the neighboring shop and annexing it. Georgina, his faithful store manager, greeted Dawson and told him his brother was in his office.

Dawson poked his head around the door. "Busy?"

Cairo looked up and grinned. "Darko, come in! Not really. I'm only pretending."

Dawson laughed and leaned down to hug his brother. "How are you?"

"Fine—just going over the books," he said, waving at the laptop on his desk. "You know how that is."

He was three years older than Dawson and had the same closely shaved hairstyle. They resembled each other in the face, but the physiques differed. Cairo, athletic as a boy before the accident, was now chunkier than his younger brother, although he had recently lost weight on the orders of his doctor.

He swung his lightweight wheelchair around to face Dawson as he took a seat. "So, what's up, little brother?"

"I'm off to Takoradi on Tuesday," Dawson said.

"Oh? What's going on there?"

"New case. Don't know if you ever read about the murder of Charles and Fiona Smith-Aidoo off Cape Three Points."

Cairo searched his memory for a moment and shook his head. "Doesn't ring a bell. What's the story?"

Dawson gave him a quick rundown, explaining that the case came to CID via petition.

"Hope it goes well for you," Cairo said sincerely. "You know we all like to have you right here in Accra. It's a pity you have to leave Hosiah right now."

"I know," Dawson said, shaking his head regretfully. "I hate it myself, but Lartey is in no mood to be messed with, and I'm coming up for promotion soon."

"Audrey and I will have Christine and the boys over at the house or drop in to see them," Cairo offered.

"Thank you. I'm sure she'll appreciate that."

There was a slight pause.

"I saw Papa yesterday," Cairo said quietly.

Dawson leaned his cheek against his knuckles and fixed his gaze at the floor. "And?"

"He asked for you."

Dawson grunted noncommittally, and Cairo cleared his throat awkwardly. "Darko, I know there've been hard feelings between the two of you, but he's getting old now, and he's not going to live forever. I'm just saying maybe it's time to not so much forget, but to forgive. He does love you."

Dawson snorted. "You don't hit the people you love, and whether

Papa used his hand or a cane, he hit me a lot. It was never the same for you, since you were his favorite, so maybe you don't understand, but I didn't deserve to be treated that way just because I was attached to Mama and a skinny boy who wasn't good at sports."

"I think I do understand, Darko." Cairo sighed heavily, rubbing the fist of his left hand slowly against the palm of his left as he contemplated this still unresolved family predicament. "Papa had a violent streak and he scapegoated you, that's for sure, but . . ."

"But what?"

"Isn't this something of a case of 'he who is without sin cast the first stone'?"

Dawson looked at him in surprise. "I have never once hit my wife or my kids, and God strike me down if I ever do."

"I know that," Cairo said reassuringly. "I'm not talking about your family. You are a caring husband and father, but you haven't been without violence in your *work*. A few years ago, especially up until the time you found out the truth about Mama, you were almost out of control—beating suspects up, losing your temper, remember?"

Dawson nodded reluctantly. It was true, and he wouldn't deny it.

"So, just give it some thought, little bro," Cairo said with a smile. "That's all I'm asking. You're a better person than years ago, so why not add reconciliation with your father to your achievements?"

Dawson took a deep breath and slowly let it out. "Okay, I'll think about it."

"Thank you."

They chatted for a while about less weighty things, and then Dawson stood up to leave. "I have to get going."

"Okay. I'll see you out." Cairo wheeled himself beside his brother to the entrance of the shop, and they embraced one more time.

"Be careful in Takoradi," Cairo said. "We want you back safely."

DAWSON RODE BACK to his Kaneshie neighborhood home at No. 10 Nim Tree. Cream-colored with olive trim, the house was very small, but it was far superior to the dilapidated police barracks where even officers above Dawson's rank stayed because they couldn't afford housing elsewhere in the city. He and Christine were simply lucky that their landlord was a member of her extended family.

The house was deserted since Christine was still out with Sly. Dawson sat on the sofa of the sitting room that adjoined the kitchen and looked through the docket. He made a couple of notes to keep the record up to the minute. He left the folder on the table as he got up to answer a knock on the door. His neighbor needed help unloading some building materials, so Dawson went next door with him and left the docket on the sitting room table. That would turn out to be a terrible mistake.

Chapter 5

ON TUESDAY MORNING, WHILE Christine went off to get Hosiah from the hospital, Dawson spent a few hours at CID tying up loose ends before he left. He was to take the State Transport bus to Takoradi, and he didn't want to start out too late. However, it was past noon by the time he was heading home on his motorbike, negotiating the clogged, asphyxiating traffic on Ring Road West.

When he finally got home, Christine's little red car was parked in front, meaning she had returned with the boys. He was eager to see Hosiah back at home from the hospital, and he could spend a little time with him before leaving, but the day was already getting old. At this rate, he might not reach Takoradi before nightfall on one of State Transportation's chronically late, lumbering buses.

Once inside the house, he sensed something was wrong. Sly was sitting by himself on the sofa looking forlorn.

"What's wrong?" Dawson asked. "Where are Mama and Hosiah?"

"In the bedroom," Sly answered, in barely a whisper.

Dawson put his hand on the boy's shoulder. "What's the matter?"

"She's angry with me."

"What happened?"

Sly bowed his head even further and wrung his fingers. It didn't look like the answer was forthcoming, so Dawson proceeded to the bedroom. On most occasions, these upsets were minor. *Maybe not this time*, he thought, as he heard Hosiah crying. He stopped in the doorway. Christine was sitting on the bed holding her son close as he whimpered and sniffled against her chest. For a panicky moment, Dawson thought perhaps something had gone wrong with his heart condition, but then they would have kept him in hospital, surely?

Dawson's appearance apparently unleashed a fresh round of tears from Hosiah. He sat on the bed next to his son, who promptly launched into his arms and held on tight. Dawson raised his eyebrows questioningly at Christine. He wished someone would tell him what was going on.

"On Saturday when you went next door," Christine told him quietly, "you left your docket on the sitting room table. Apparently Sly opened it and saw the picture, and today he told Hosiah about it and frightened him."

Dawson drew in his breath sharply and closed his eyes for a moment in the painful realization of what had happened. The cardinal rule was that his sons never see any autopsy or murder photographs.

He rubbed Hosiah's head gently back and forth. That usually comforted him. "*Shh.* It's okay. Are you scared?"

The boy nodded. Dawson shifted him to his knee so they were facing each other.

"Tell Daddy why you're afraid. You have to stop crying, though. Here, blow your nose."

He held a hanky to Hosiah's nose and he made a reasonable effort.

"That's better," Dawson said. He kissed him on the forehead. "Now what's wrong?"

Hosiah spoke haltingly as he fiddled with his father's fingers. "I don't want you to go to look for the *juju* man."

"What *juju* man?"

"The one who makes people's heads come off. Sly told me that's why you're going to Takoradi."

"I see," Dawson said. "You're scared that there's a *juju* man who might hurt Daddy?"

Hosiah nodded, his face beginning to crumple again.

"No, no," Dawson said, forestalling another teary performance. "No more crying. Listen to me. What Sly saw isn't because of *juju.* You know I catch bad people, right?"

"Yes, Daddy."

"Okay, so this bad man is just the same as all the other ones I catch. He's afraid of me, so he's not going to try to cut off my head. In fact, you know what he's going to do when he sees me?"

"What?"

"He's going to run away."

Hosiah looked at him with a glimmer of encouragement creeping to his face.

"And then you know what's going to happen while he's running away?" Dawson asked.

"What?"

"He's going to run right into the *kenkey* woman at the market and trip over all her balls of *kenkey*."

Hosiah looked at him for a second of bewilderment and then giggled at the unexpected, conjured image of the starchy, solid balls of fermented corn meal flying all over the place. "No, he's not, Daddy."

"He is," Dawson insisted, grinning.

"And then he's going to get all stuck in the *kenkey* balls," Hosiah laughed, his imagination sparked, "and the *kenkey* woman will say, 'Hey, what are you doing in my *kenkey* balls?' And then he'll have *kenkey* balls all over his body, and she'll make him pay for them, won't she, Daddy?"

"Yes, exactly right. And that will be the end of that. Then Sergeant Chikata and I will take him to the police station. What do you think?"

Hosiah nodded uncertainly once and then with more conviction. Dawson glanced at Christine, who was smiling but still looked concerned.

"Has he had lunch?" he asked her.

"He didn't have as much as he usually does."

"Are you hungry now?" Dawson asked Hosiah.

He nodded enthusiastically and Christine took his hand. "Come along. I'll get you some more to eat."

DAWSON RESTED HIS hand on Sly's shoulder and guided him outside to the backyard. The boy was shaking and Dawson knew why. A sound beating was the only kind of punishment he had known while in the care of his ill-mannered uncle. Now he was fearful that his new father was about to continue the tradition.

"Tell me what happened," Dawson said as they took shelter from the sun under an awning he had constructed a couple of years ago. "Start from the beginning."

His gaze shifting around guiltily, Sly recounted how he had come home with Mama on Saturday while Dawson was next door helping the neighbor. He had noticed the folder on the sitting room table and, without giving it a second's thought, had flipped open the cover. The picture of the severed head was the first and only thing he saw before he hurriedly closed the folder.

Today, after the boys had returned from the hospital with Mama and she was making lunch, Hosiah and Sly were talking about what time Daddy would be going to Takoradi. Sly had remarked that maybe he had already left because he had to keep it a secret that he was going to look for a *juju* man who was making people's heads get chopped off.

"He asked me what did I mean," Sly continued, "and I said I had seen that picture of the man's head on a stick in your papers. My uncle always told me that if you see someone with his head cut off, it means a *juju* man or a witch is punishing him for doing something wrong. So I thought you were going to Takoradi to find the *juju* man who did it. I'm sorry I made Hosiah cry. I didn't know he would get scared."

"He's not as tough as you," Dawson said, lifting Sly's chin to hold his gaze. "He's your little brother, so you have to think before you tell him certain things. Now I know your uncle used to tell you about witches and *juju* and all that, but you mustn't believe him. You remember last year when those people from Agbogbloshie were killed? *Juju* didn't make that happen. Murder never happens because of *juju*. It's just a man or a woman who gets so angry, jealous, or greedy, that he or she wants to kill another person. Understand?"

"Yes, Daddy."

"Now I made a mistake too. I'm not supposed to leave my work around the house because Mama and I don't want you and Hosiah to be looking at that kind of thing. I'm sorry you saw it, but you have to remember that when you see anything in the house belonging to Mama or me, you leave it alone. You don't go into our business unless we tell you to, you hear?"

"Yes, Daddy."

"Come here." Dawson brought Sly close and put his arms around him. "You know Mama and I love you and Hosiah both the same, right?"

He nodded. "You're not going to beat me?"

"No. That wouldn't make you learn your lesson any better, would it?"

Sly thought about that for a moment and then shook his head.

"You still need to do something, though," Dawson said. "You need to go to Hosiah and hug him and say you love him and you're sorry you scared him."

"Okay," Sly said happily, his zest for life restored. He made a dash for the backdoor of the house.

"But don't hug him too hard," Dawson added. "Remember, his chest is still sore."

Gazing at the door long after Sly had disappeared through it, a thought struck him and he smiled. The boy had more insight than he probably even realized.

IN THEIR BEDROOM with the door shut, Christine insisted that Dawson show her the picture that had caused all the trouble.

"Are you sure?" he asked. "It's terrible."

"I know it's terrible, but I have to know what we're dealing with."

Reluctantly, he opened the folder and extracted the photo. She looked at it for not more than a second, gasped, and turned her head away.

"Oh, Darko," she said furiously. "How could you leave something so horrible lying around?"

Dawson sat down heavily on the bed. "I don't know," he said hopelessly.

"You're usually so careful." She shook her head and grimaced. "That's Dr. Smith-Aidoo's uncle?"

"Yes, Charles Smith-Aidoo. He was the director of corporate affairs at Malgam Oil."

"Poor man." Christine frowned. "Wasn't there another oil company executive who was murdered not long ago? The one who was shot dead at his home?"

"You're right. Lawrence Tetteh, CEO of Goilco, the government's oil company. Shot execution-style in the head in June about a month before the Smith-Aidoos were murdered. They arrested and charged Tetteh's stepbrother, a guy called Silas. He's awaiting trial now. Some people think he was framed."

"What do you think?"

"There are still questions. Everybody agrees it was a professional job, but this Silas was definitely not a professional killer."

"Hmm. Well, regardless of who killed Tetteh, do you think the Smith-Aidoo murder could be related?"

Dawson gave her an impressed look. "That's what I've been wondering myself. Tetteh and Smith-Aidoo were both in the oil industry, both shot in the head, and only about a month apart."

"Who's handling the Tetteh killing?"

"Some kind of political monkey business went on at the top, and the Bureau of National Investigations took it over from CID. I know Chief Superintendent Lartey was incensed over losing the case. He doesn't get along with the BNI director. Anyway, I'm still going to keep the Tetteh murder in the back of my mind while I'm investigating the Smith-Aidoo case. One big difference between the two cases, though: the beheading."

Christine shuddered. "Why cut someone's head off and then display it on a stick tied to a canoe?"

"Sly said something that made me think. He said his uncle had always told him that when you see a body part severed, it means it has something to do with witchcraft or *juju*."

"And you, Darko Dawson, believe that a witch did this?" Christine said disbelievingly. "Come on, I know you better than that."

"No, I don't, but maybe the *murderer* wanted people to think so, in order to shield the real motive behind it. That's what I have to find out: the real motive."

Chapter 6

ON THE STATE TRANSPORT bus to Sekondi-Takoradi, Dawson squeezed in between the window and a large woman with no boundaries. Christine and the boys had seen him off at the house and Hosiah had been close to tears, which brought a lump to Dawson's throat. Christine was right. Brave as their son was, he needed his father to be with him right now. Emotionally and physically, he was still fragile.

Gazing out his window, Dawson tried to stop his brooding as the bus sped along the George H. Bush Highway. He turned his thoughts to his destination, the twin city of Sekondi-Takoradi. It was the capital of the Western Region (WR); Sekondi was the administrative section, while Takoradi was more commercial. Dawson's father, Jacob, had grown up in Takoradi and moved to Accra as a young man. In Accra, he met Dawson's mother, Beatrice, an Ewe woman. Although Jacob seldom if ever visited Takoradi these days, he still had family there, including a nephew called Abraham, or "Abe."

Dawson had called his cousin to ask if he could possibly stay with him while in town. The Ghana Police Service (GPS) was so unlikely to pay for accommodation or transportation costs that submitting receipts for expenses was a waste of time.

Abraham, who lived above his stationery store in downtown Takoradi, had told him that with his two teenage children at home, there was no space. But he had a better idea. He was remodeling a small family bungalow a mere ten minutes away. Hoping to profit from the boom in the hospitality industry spurred by the discovery of oil, he planned to rent the bungalow once he completed it. If Dawson didn't mind the state of incompletion of the place, Abraham had said, he was welcome to bunk there. It was an offer Dawson would have been a fool to refuse. When he had visited Takoradi as a teen, Abraham had been in his early twenties. It had been a long time since the two had seen each other, but that didn't matter. Family was family, and Abraham was more than happy to help.

On the open road, the bus passed Weija Lake on the right. It was the beginning of November, and although heavy rainfall was over for the year, the landscape was still verdant and rich. Deep green foliage covered the hills and hugged the roadsides. Soon, the dry season would arrive with its persistent Harmattan haze: fine particles of dust blown down from the Sahara from November to March.

Immediately after they'd passed Cape Coast University in the Central Region, the beach made its appearance on their left. The blue-green of the sea looked like a painting with the foamy white of the waves breaking at the shore, and the coconut palm fronds, atop spindly trunks that grew off vertical. It all looked freer and wilder than Accra's beaches. Dawson shuddered at the thought of swimming in the sea. He had not spent much time at the beach as a child, and he could barely swim. On the few occasions he'd ventured into the surf at Labadi Beach, he'd been frightened by the strong undertow.

After passing through the town of Sefwi, they went through a checkpoint and entered the Western Region. An hour later, they were on the final approach to Takoradi. Flame trees lined the roadside into town, reaching to form a leafy arch that would turn scarlet when the flowers bloomed. It was around 5:30, and the sun had become oblique and softer. They came to a roundabout called Paa Grant, the greenest and most luxuriant circle Dawson had ever seen.

Dawson dialed Abraham's number. It went through and a man answered.

"Abraham?" Dawson said.

"Darko! Are you around?"

"Yes, we're coming into the city now."

"Oh, wonderful!" Abraham's voice was smooth but dense, setting off a reaction in Dawson. Voices triggered his sense of touch—he could feel it in his hand or fingers, mostly on the left side, but as Dr.

Biney had explained to him, what was happening was entirely inside his brain. Synesthesia was the name of the phenomenon in which the stimulation of one of the senses leads to an automatic experience in another sense. Dawson, a synesthete, had vocal sound-to-touch synesthesia. He could never predict what might set it off—a voice as rough as sandpaper or as sweet as a musical instrument. Sometimes, it acted as a lie detector when a change in vocal tone set off his synesthesia, but it wasn't infallible. Good liars could sneak past Dawson.

He could recall experiencing it as far back as the age of two. His mother, Beatrice, increasingly noticed him staring at one or both hands, usually his left. The first time Darko ever said anything to her about it was when he was four. He told Mama that when his nursery school teacher was talking, it made "his hand tickle." She hadn't a clue what he was talking about then, but as he grew older, Mama came to learn that it was a real phenomenon even though she didn't understand it. She warned him repeatedly not to talk about it with others outside the close family.

"Why, Mama?"

"Because people might think you're a wizard, or possessed by spirits," she told him.

His brother, Cairo, was familiar with it, and Hosiah had a game in which he would make funny voices while holding Dawson's hand in the hope that he would feel something.

Abraham's voice was strongly triggering his synesthesia. He felt as though his left hand was massaging a handful of wet clay. When he was a boy, a potter had once pressed a clump of fresh clay into his hand. Darko had giggled with delight as he squished it through his fingers. As an adult, he still liked the sensation, and that Abraham had induced it confirmed that he was experiencing a positive connection with his cousin.

"I'll see you at the bus depot," Abraham said.

As the bus continued its route toward the STC station, Dawson made comparisons with Accra. Unlike his hometown, Takoradi had labeled its streets with clearly marked blue and white signs. Above each, in white letters on a red background, was a DO NOT LITTER warning. Dawson had the impression that people were at least in part taking heed.

In Takoradi, Ghanaian street names like Ako Adjei coexisted with British ones—Ferguson, Hayford, Kitson, and so on—a legacy of the British colonial occupation of Ghana from the nineteenth to the twentieth century. In the Central and Western Regions, the land of the Fante ethnic group, to which Dawson's father Jacob belonged, surnames of Dutch, Portuguese, German, and British origin were common.

Its air brakes wheezing and puffing, the bus pulled into the wide STC yard and parked. Dawson waited until his ample seatmate had heaved herself out and then alighted to pick up his bag. He looked around for Abraham, realizing he didn't know what his cousin looked like these days. He watched the crowd milling about.

"Darko!"

Dawson turned and saw someone hurrying in his direction. He was overweight, of average height. "Abraham?"

"Yes!" He shook hands and hugged Dawson. "How are you? It's good to see you! Welcome to Takoradi." His round face shone with delight. "Let me take your bag. I'm parked over there."

"Thank you. How did you recognize me so easily?"

"Have you forgotten your picture was in all the papers last year after you caught that serial killer?"

"Oh, I see," Dawson said, laughing. "Yes, I had forgotten."

They got into Abe's car, a yellow Toyota Corolla. Abraham talked continuously as they made their way through the center of town. He had an easy laugh and was quite funny. He drove aggressively, which surprised Dawson because his nature seemed otherwise easygoing.

"Traffic is heavy," Abraham commented.

"Not as bad as Accra," Dawson replied. He looked around at the vehicles parked in marked spaces along the curb. Good luck persuading drivers to do that in the capital. White, yellow, green, and pink buildings with square facades evenly lined the pavement. The canopied first floors were businesses while the second and third floors were residences with decorative balconies.

"So the oil business has really made a difference here," Dawson said.

"Oh, yes, both in town and out. New hotels, new houses, and new vehicles. Advertisements on the radio talk about offices being oil industry ready. We've become the Oil City."

"Yes, I've heard that."

"I hate that name."

Dawson smiled at Abe's obvious affection for his town.

"Here we are," his cousin said, pulling into a parking space.

His shop, Abraham's Stationery, on the corner of Ako Adjei and Kofi Annan Roads, was located opposite the Barclay's Bank in a congested commercial area where vendor stalls packed the pavements. Before he took Dawson upstairs to the second floor where he and the family lived, Abraham showed him the shop.

One assistant stood behind the sales counter and a second one was high up on a ladder getting something for a customer. The shop wasn't large, yet it was packed with every imaginable style, color, and size of copy paper, writing instruments, computer supplies, toner cartridges, and exercise books.

Dawson was impressed. "I like it. You have everything here."

"Almost," Abraham said. "I want to start carrying computers too, but I don't know where I'm going to put them."

"You've already outgrown yourself."

"Yes, that is it."

They exited the shop and went around to the rear of the building via a side alley.

They went up two flights of steps at the top of which Abraham's wife, Akosua, was waiting. She was about her husband's age, around forty. With an endearing dimpled smile, she greeted Dawson with the same elation that her husband had. Slim and straight, she was the physical opposite of Abraham, whose body was rounded off everywhere.

They had a cozy sitting room with a flat-screen TV, a small adjoining kitchen, and two bedrooms down a short hallway. After about an hour, Akosua announced that dinner was served. When she brought the dishes out to the table that she and their young housemaid had prepared, it was clear that they had put themselves out in the good tradition of Ghanaian hospitality. On a wide plate stood four smooth, perfectly shaped ovals of *fufu* brushed with a light coating of water to make them glisten. The *fufu* was made by strenuously pounding boiled *cassava* in a large mortar while adding water until it turned into a soft, glutinous mass.

Next to the plate of *fufu* was a deep bowl of steaming palm nut soup, its rich golden-red oil snaking languidly around succulent chunks of fish and turgid white eggplant. The sight and the aroma made Dawson's salivary glands contract so hard that they hurt.

Akosua brought a towel, soap, and a two bowls of water to the table. She waited for the men to wash up before she followed suit. The three ate traditionally with the fingers of the right hand only. Like many, Dawson would tell you he loved *fufu,* but in fact it was really all about the soup. It provided the heavenly flavor as well as the lubricant for a generous chunk of *fufu* to pass from the lips to the back of the throat and down the gullet in one smooth motion. He was famished and had to moderate his impulse to eat at high speed, especially a meal this sumptuous. He burned energy like a racehorse and was hungry punctually every four hours. Yet he had never been prone to putting on weight. Because he was tall and lean, people often underestimated his physical strength.

"So you have a big case here in Tadi?" Abraham asked Dawson after the silence that goes with the initial tasting of a meal.

"A family member petitioned CID Headquarters to look into the murder of Fiona and Charles Smith-Aidoo."

Abraham swallowed with a loud, glottal sound before exclaiming, "Hallelujah!"

Dawson smile. "You're glad about that, I see."

"Come on," Abraham said indignantly, leaning back in his chair. "Four months of investigation and no arrests, Darko? What is that Superintendent Hammond doing over there in his crime unit at Sekondi? I saw him once on TV making all kinds of excuses about lack of manpower and all that nonsense."

"It's not always all that simple to make an arrest," Dawson said gently, anxious to lower any grand expectations that he was going to wrap up the case in no time.

"That's true," Akosua agreed. "It's easy to judge from the outside. Still, it's frustrating to have a killer like that on the loose—someone who has done such a hideous thing to poor Charles and Fiona."

"Did either of you know the couple well?" Dawson asked them.

"Fairly well," Abraham said. "I went to the same secondary school as they did, but they were one year ahead. They were sweethearts

even back then, and they stuck together all the way through university and got married after that."

It didn't surprise Dawson that cousin Abraham had had contact with
two murder victims. Takoradi was a relatively small city, and personal
connections, whether direct or indirect, often went back as far as primary school. Ghanaians made it a point to mix with others in their
socioeconomic group and to "know" people and talk about them. Phone
numbers were exchanged and shared at the drop of a hat, and arriving at
a party with uninvited friends and relatives was quite the norm.

"What were your impressions of Charles and Fiona?" Dawson asked.

"He was a smart guy," Abraham said, "and he got close to the
right people. That was what he did in the oil business, but he was
influential and well-to-do even before oil arrived. As the CEO of
Smith-Aidoo Timber, he had contacts all over the Western Region.
He positioned himself to impress the circle of oil executives with
his smooth talk and his charming manner. He was really perfect for
corporate relations."

Without prompting, Akosua served more soup to both the men
and Dawson thanked her.

"What about Fiona Smith-Aidoo?" he asked. "Tell me about her."

"She was an attractive woman about town," Abraham said. "She
liked being seen in public—fundraising and so on. She was also the
first female chief executive of the Sekondi-Takoradi Metropolitan
Assembly—STMA. She displaced longtime chief Kwesi DeSouza,
which shocked many people, not least DeSouza himself. He thought
he was coasting to another term as chair. A rumor started—and some
people think Fiona was responsible—that he had embezzled a few
thousand from the STMA trust fund to build a new house on Beach
Road, one of the posh areas in Takoradi. De Souza and Fiona had a
strong rivalry."

"Do you think DeSouza could have killed her?"

Abraham grunted. "I've never been inside the man's mind, so I
can't say. He went on Skyy FM, one of our local stations, to deny
the embezzlement allegations and blast Fiona and others for trying to
destroy his reputation. He was obviously furious, but enough to kill?
I don't know."

They finished the meal and Dawson thanked Akosua for the

wonderful cooking. She cleaned up in the kitchen before rejoining the men in the sitting room.

"Akosua has her theory about what happened, and I have mine," Abraham said.

"Okay, Akosua," Dawson said. "Let's hear yours first."

"At the outset, only Charles was the target," she said. "The killer knew Charles was going to be down at Cape Three Points that day, but he didn't realize that Fiona was going to be with her husband. When this killer ambushed the vehicle, it took him by surprise that Fiona was there, and he had to kill both of them."

"You think one man handled two people and ultimately two dead bodies?" Dawson said. "He'd have had to get them into his vehicle, transport them, get them into the canoe, take them out to sea, and so on. That's a lot, even for a strong man."

"Good point," Akosua conceded. "Maybe two killers, then."

"I think they *did* know that both Charles and Fiona would be in the vehicle," Abraham said. "Someone had a contract out on both of them."

"A professional job," Dawson said.

"Yes."

"Why both of them?"

"Maybe a family rivalry."

"Interesting you say that," Dawson said. "Are you aware there was a vendetta?"

"I've heard that a generations-long enmity has existed between members of the Smith-Aidoo and Sarbah families."

Dawson was intrigued—Sapphire Smith-Aidoo had not mentioned that when she had been giving him her family history. "Where did you hear that?"

"I don't exactly recall," Abraham replied, "but back in the 1950s, the Smith-Aidoos and Sarbahs were competing in the timber industry. Maybe there's been bad blood to the present day."

"In other words," Dawson said, a smile playing at his lips, "Jason Sarbah kills Charles and Fiona in a modern version of the generations-long feud between the two families? And then on top of that, Jason gets to replace Charles at Malgam? It seems too convenient. You've been watching too many movies."

They all laughed.

"I've been wondering about how the murderer could get two bodies out to the deep sea," Dawson said. "Do you know anything about fishing canoes, Abe?"

"A little. I own a canoe myself."

"Oh," Dawson said, surprised. "What do you use it for?"

"About a year ago I began renting it out to fishermen who can't buy their own canoes. They're expensive, now that the price of wood keeps going up. I thought renting the canoe would bring in extra income, but it has been disappointing."

"In that case," Dawson said, "let me ask you something—maybe you know the answer. The Malgam oil rig is about seventy kilometers offshore, right?"

"Closer to sixty."

"Okay. Let's leave aside where exactly the Smith-Aidoos were shot. How would this canoe with the dead bodies get out that far? Can a fishing canoe go out sixty kilometers?"

"Oh, yes, easily."

"With an outboard motor, then? You couldn't possibly row that far."

Abraham was amused. "City boy, you don't row a canoe, you paddle it."

"Sorry. Paddle, then."

"Fishermen paddle out there all the time, Darko. Have you seen how strong these guys are? You are partly right, though, because in practice many fishermen split up the journey between paddle and outboard motor. Another alternative is use a sail."

"If someone wanted to steer the canoe to the Malgam oil rig, how long would it take?"

"Six to eight hours. The sea currents are predominantly northeasterly, so if you set out for the rig from, say, Cape Three Points, whether paddling or by motor power, you have to continuously compensate for the current if you want to arrive at the intended destination. Are you thinking that the dead bodies were transported to the rig deliberately to display them?"

"It seems too coincidental that Dr. Smith-Aidoo's aunt and uncle show up dead at the very rig on the very day she was working there."

It wasn't only that. Something else led Dawson to believe that a fundamental message invoking family ties was encoded in the bizarre scene of the canoe bearing two corpses: the old watch found in Charles's mouth with the inscription *blood runs deep*. He wasn't about to mention that to his two hosts, however. For security, some details were best left unrevealed even to relatives—perhaps *especially* to relatives.

"I think you're right, Darko," Akosua said. "It was like the murderer was boasting to Dr. Smith-Aidoo, 'Look what I did. I killed your aunt and uncle.' How terrible."

"Well, if that's the case," Abraham said, "whoever got the canoe there knew what he was doing because he had to slip by the fishery protection vessels that are on standby to enforce the five hundred meter no-go zone around the rig."

"No-go zone?" Dawson asked. "What's that?"

"It's the safe operating boundary around the rig to prevent collisions between vessels. It's standard all over the world, but some Ghanaian fishermen are convinced it's all a plot to prevent them from getting at the fish that swarm around the rig, especially at night when they're attracted to the rig lights. So to get at that bonanza of fish, sometimes the fishermen will sneak within the boundary and then their fishing nets get all tangled up with rig installations." Abraham shook his head and gave a dry, ironic laugh. "The classic battle between tradition and modernity."

Dawson agreed. That kind of conflict occurred onshore too. Recently, coconut palm farmers had been infuriated by the establishment of a new natural gas plant that meant the destruction of some of their farmland.

"I should introduce you to my fisherman friend Forjoe," Abraham said. "He's in charge of the canoe rentals. He can tell you even more about canoes and such."

An idea occurred to Dawson. "Does he keep a record of the rentals?"

"No, I do. When I collect my portion of the fees he's charged, I note it down in a book along with the fisherman's name. It's a little informal."

"Did you have any rentals last July?"

"I can check, but I don't think so. Business was very slow." Abraham stood up. "I'll fetch the book."

He disappeared inside briefly, returning with a notebook and sitting down next to Dawson. He flicked through the pages until he came to July.

"Nothing," he said, running a finger down the blank page. "Not a single rental the whole month."

"Any chance Forjoe could have forgotten to tell you?"

"I doubt it. He's very reliable."

"Is anyone else you know doing the same thing? Renting canoes?"

"I don't personally know anyone, but Forjoe will know. I'll call him tomorrow and then we can go down to the harbor."

"Good." Dawson paused a moment. "Did Forjoe know the Smith-Aidoos?"

"I don't think so. Why do you ask?"

"No special reason," Dawson said with a shrug. That wasn't quite true. In fact, a thought had struck him that Forjoe would have had perfect access to a motor-powered canoe that could transport two dead bodies out to sea. But maybe that was jumping ahead too far.

Chapter 7

ABRAHAM PULLED UP TO a wrought-iron gate set in a high brick wall inscribed with a sign that read CHAPEL HILL LODGE.

"I ran out of money," he said to Dawson as they got out. "That's why the building is temporarily stalled, but I'm hoping to finish everything by the middle of next year."

"Why did you call it Chapel Hill?" Dawson asked.

"That's the name of this part of town. The street we came on used to be called Chapel Hill Road, but it was renamed Shippers Road."

He opened up the padlocked gate, revealing a neat, square bungalow on a generous plot of land with a smattering of banana trees and two blooming jasmine bushes that lightly perfumed the night air. Abraham had not yet installed exterior lighting, but the street lamp on the corner provided a little illumination.

"It only has the primer coat of paint," Abraham said, unlocking the front door. "In the end it will be a sun-yellow color."

Dawson followed him in as he switched on the overhead light of the kitchenette to their left. It had a new house smell.

"I don't have the cupboards up yet," Abraham said. "But everything is connected and ready for use—stove, refrigerator, water . . ."

He lifted the tap handle and after a cough and splutter, water began flowing.

"This is nice," Dawson said, looking around. "It will be beautiful when it's finished."

"Thanks," Abraham said, smiling.

They went on into the small dining area, which was bare except for three boxes of unpacked materials in one corner. The recessed ceiling lights were in working order and missing only their trim.

"I will bring a table and two chairs for you to sit down and eat on," Abraham said.

"Don't worry about that, cousin Abe," Dawson said. "I can do without."

"It's no problem. I'll get them tomorrow."

The bedroom contained a wardrobe and a narrow bed.

Abraham snapped his fingers. "Oh, I forgot curtains for the window. I'll bring some tomorrow as well."

"The house is in better shape than I thought it was going to be," Dawson commented in appreciation. "I was imagining just the wood frame."

Abraham laughed. "No, not as bad as that. Are you okay with it? Sorry I don't have the AC connected yet."

"No worries at all. I appreciate this very much."

"Call me if you need anything—even tonight. I don't mind."

Once Abraham had left, Dawson hung his clothes up in the wardrobe and then remembered what he had meant to do earlier. Sly had unwittingly given him an idea about how witchcraft might have some connection to the Smith-Aidoos' murder.

Dr. Allen Botswe, a professor at the University of Ghana, specialized in African criminal psychology. His landmark book, *Magic, Murder, and Madness: Ritual Killing in West Africa,* was the authoritative text on the relationship between homicide and traditional West African culture, particularly in Ghana. Botswe had helped Dawson out during his last case.

He dialed the professor's number, but no one answered. He redialed, a trick that often worked, and this time Botswe picked up.

"Mr. Dawson! How nice to hear from you. I hope all is well?"

"Yes, thank you, Doctor." He got down to business. "I'm investigating a case in Takoradi of a murdered man and his wife who ended up in a canoe out by an oil rig."

"The Smith-Aidoos—the man who was decapitated?"

"You know about it?"

"Only the bare elements."

Dawson summarized the most important points. "My older son," he continued, "who accidentally saw the photograph of the severed head said he believed witchcraft or *juju* was involved."

"Possibly. Could I see the photograph?"

"I'll text it to you. Please call me back once you've had a chance to look at it."

"Yes, of course."

Dawson opened up the docket, took the clearest possible picture of the severed head with his mobile, and sent the image to Botswe, who called back a few minutes later.

"Gruesome," the professor said. "Some of the features here suggest a ritual killing, which is a murder committed in connection with the powers of gods, spirits, or ancestors. That often involves taking the victim's head, eyes, lips, tongue, breasts, genitals, or internal organs. Sometimes the blood may be drained as well. The sacrifice victim is often selected for his or her perceived purity or unspoiled nature—a child, or a virgin, for example. In that regard, Charles Smith-Aidoo doesn't quite fit the bill, but it still doesn't rule out a bloody ritual. Were any other body parts missing?"

"No, but I should have told you that an old pocket watch was found stuffed in his mouth with the scrawled inscription, 'blood runs deep.'"

"Aha," Botswe said, his tone changing from interested to intrigued. "Fascinating. The murderer might have been trying to invoke family ties, the old watch indicating generations past, maybe a vendetta, something terrible done to his family member or members, or to an ancestor. He is deeply embittered and vengeful. A human sacrifice aspect could be separate but related to the family issue. My feeling is you should look very closely at the Smith-Aidoos' family history, or one tied up with theirs—specifically ancestral tragedies or murders. When you do that, you may find the answer to this killing."

"Thank you, Prof. You have really helped."

"You are most welcome, Inspector," he said, smiling with his voice. "Please, do keep me posted."

As he hung up, Dawson reflected on what Botswe had said: *something terrible done to his family member or members*. Is that where Jason Sarbah came in? Did he blame Charles and Fiona for Angela's death and kill the couple for revenge?

Dead tired, Dawson took a cold shower, brushed his teeth, and fell into bed. In the morning, he would meet with Superintendent Hammond with a fresh mind.

DAWSON SAW THE neighborhood for the first time by the light of day as he emerged from the lodge. It had rained overnight, which surprised him because he hadn't heard anything and rain usually woke him up. It proved how tired he must have been. He locked the front gate behind him. Across the street was Stellar Lodge, a white, two-story hotel with a brand new extension. *Business must be good*, Dawson thought, although he recalled that the place had had some adverse publicity about a year ago after a hotel guest had been apparently electrocuted in the shower. Dawson wondered how one could engineer a murder that way. Not as gruesome as his present case, but certainly not a pleasant way to die.

He observed several 4x4 SUVs parked in front of the hotel. One pulled out with its Ghanaian driver at the wheel and a white man in the rear—probably an oil engineer.

He decided to take a short walk before hailing a cab so that he could get a good sense of the neighborhood. Within a ball's throw of the lodge, young soccer players were performing their early morning drills on a large green playing field that belonged to Hassacas, a local soccer team. He caught a slightly smoky scent to the air—someone cooking on firewood somewhere, but he couldn't tell from which direction. He passed a petrol station to the left, and a little farther along, a strip mall with a clothing store, a jewelry boutique, and a barbershop.

The morning had started out cool but had warmed up considerably by the time he arrived at Shippers Circle, a neat roundabout that Malgam Oil had recently refurbished. Taxis were ubiquitous in Takoradi; Dawson got one in seconds with barely a gesture. The driver, a bone-lanky man whose name was Baah, looked like he was eighteen but he assured Dawson he was twenty-four.

"How long have you lived here?" Dawson asked him.

"Since I born," Baah said, with a broad smile marred by crooked teeth. He added that he had only been out of Takoradi once in his life. His knowledge of the city and his love for it were obvious as he pointed out landmarks. Just beyond Paa Grant roundabout, he gestured to a thickly wooded area on their right.

"Dis place be Monkey Hill," he said.

"Why is it called that?" Dawson asked.

"Because plenty monkey dey." Baah said with a laugh. "They make sanctuary for them and plenty birds too. We should go there?"

"Okay, but later," Dawson said.

They passed a wetland area with a patchwork of glistening pools, woody plants, and swamp grass on either side of the road, and then Effia-Nkwanta Hospital, where Dr. Smith-Aidoo and her father had identified the bodies of her uncle and aunt. Next in quick succession were the high court, the men's and women's Sekondi prisons, and the pale green Sekondi Takoradi Metropolitan Assembly (STMA) building.

They turned in at a sign reading GHANA POLICE SERVICE, REGIONAL HEADQUARTERS, SEKONDI. SERVICE WITH INTEGRITY, and climbed a steep incline to a two-story pale yellow building with the signature GPS blue trim. The hill on which it stood gave a fine view past the corrugated metal roofs of old Sekondi to the blue Atlantic Ocean, the fishing harbor, and the naval base.

Dawson liked Baah, so he made him an offer to engage his services on a daily basis. They haggled a little and then came to an agreement on the price.

Dawson went directly to the Homicide Division on the first floor, where the front room was equipped with six desks, four of them with computers. No one paid much attention to Dawson as he came in except one of the men, who looked up at him over the top of his glasses.

"Morning. May I help you?"

"Detective Inspector Darko Dawson, from CID Headquarters."

The man jumped up to salute. "Oh, fine! Good morning, sah. You are welcome, sah. Superintendent Hammond is expecting you. Please, if you can have a seat. I will tell him you have arrived."

He went to a door a few steps behind him, knocked lightly, and then opened it.

"Please, Inspector Dawson is here from HQ."

Dawson heard the reply, "Show him in."

The sergeant opened the door wide and stepped partly into the room to allow Dawson to pass and then left, quietly shutting the door behind him.

Superintendent Hammond looked up as Dawson came in.

"Good morning, sir," Dawson said.

"Good morning. Please, have a seat."

He indicated the chair opposite his desk. His grey-peppered hair, which hadn't been trimmed for a while, was receding from his furrowed brow, where one especially deep crease cut sharply into the middle of his forehead like a canyon. The cold absence of a smile and his failure to make eye contact alerted Dawson that something was wrong.

"So," Hammond said with a tense, one-sided smile, "you're here to show us how to solve a case, is that right?"

"Pardon?" Dawson said.

"The Western Region has had thirty-four homicides this year," Hammond continued in a flat tone. "Headquarters won't give us a regional crime lab, we don't have enough crime scene technicians, and there's a hiring freeze. Our resources are stretched to the limit, yet we're expected to clear up all these cases in record time. Just four months on the Smith-Aidoo case and already Headquarters is breathing down my neck and sending a junior officer to supervise me."

Stunned, Dawson struggled to find the right words. "Sorry, sir, but Chief Superintendent Lartey has sent me here in response to a petition and in assisting capacity only, not to disgrace or embarrass anyone, sir."

They eyed each other in silence for a moment. Hammond heaved a sigh, as if he would rather not be bothered. "I see you have the docket with you. Do you have any questions?"

"Okay, thank you, sir," Dawson said, now uncertain where to start. "I met Dr. Sapphire Smith-Aidoo last week in Accra. She told me about Jason Sarbah. When you spoke to him, did he blame the doctor or her uncle for the death of his daughter, Angela?"

The superintendent seemed wearied by the task of having to explain all this to Dawson. "Sarbah didn't say that directly, but I know he is very bitter about the events that led up to Angela's death."

"Was he your prime suspect, sir?"

"At the beginning, yes, but his alibi is solid. The day of the ambush of the Smith-Aidoo's vehicle, he was working at his real estate business. Two other people in the office confirmed that."

Dawson had allowed his eye to stray as he tried to gauge what kind of man Hammond was. A folder with papers was in front of him, as well as a pen the superintendent had apparently been using to write some kind of report. His fingernails were medium long and cut square across, but like his hair, not that recently. His desk was piled with documents, but it was neither excessively jumbled nor chaotic. One drawer of a metal filing cabinet in the corner behind the super-intendent was half open. Dawson decided Hammond was probably smart enough, but maybe not meticulous. *He might be a little burned out too*, Dawson thought. *Or else I've burned him out because he's just so disgusted to see me.*

"What about a contract killing?" Dawson asked. "Sarbah hiring someone to do the job? Is that a possibility?"

Hammond appeared uninspired by the question and shook his head. "The signature—dumping these bodies in the canoe, the beheading, and all that, doesn't seem like a contract murder. It looks more personal."

"I see, sir." Dawson paused. This was not a conversation. It was a question and answer session in which one party was uninterested in talking to the other. "The pocket watch in Mr. Smith-Aidoo's mouth—what did you make of that?"

"It's a very old watch. We took it to a watchmaker and he told us it was made in England in the nineteenth century. We don't know if the killer was trying to communicate something. I asked Dr. Smith-Aidoo if she had ever seen her uncle with the watch, or knew that he owned one. She said no. Her uncle liked modern gadgets, nothing old like this."

Dawson nodded respectfully. "Still, it might have been some kind of family keepsake. Maybe the murderer is saying something about family generations."

"Yes, I know." Hammond barely raised an offhand palm off the desk and let it fall again. "But we haven't discovered anything in that regard."

"What about at Malgam Oil? Did Mr. Smith-Aidoo have any enemies there, perhaps?"

"We interviewed several people, including the CEO, Roger Calmy-Rey. He appeared to think very highly of Smith-Aidoo."

"Where is Mr. Calmy-Rey from?"

"I understand he's half Swiss and half English. He spends most of his time in England, coming to Ghana every so often."

"Is he in town at the moment?"

"I'm not sure. My ASP will know."

Superintendent Hammond fished around for his mobile, found it under a stack of papers, and called the assistant superintendent.

"Seidu, come downstairs to meet Inspector Dawson when you are finished. He has arrived from Accra." Hammond dropped the phone on his desk.

"And Mrs. Smith-Aidoo?" Dawson asked. "Did she have enemies?"

"The closest we could find to that was Kwesi DeSouza, whom she defeated in the STMA elections. He might have been bitter about that, but that motive doesn't seem to match the brutality of the murder. And if DeSouza disliked Mrs. Smith-Aidoo, why would he behead her husband? It doesn't make sense."

Someone knocked on the door and stepped in. He was younger than Hammond, short and stocky with a clean-shaven head and smooth, coal-black skin.

Hammond introduced him. "This is ASP Seidu. He's been working on the case with me."

Seidu shook hands with Dawson and took a seat.

"Inspector Dawson was asking if Mr. Calmy-Rey is around," Hammond told him.

"I believe he's still abroad," Seidu responded in a marvelous baritone. "I can email him to find out."

Dawson's phone vibrated, and he checked it.

"From Dr. Smith-Aidoo," he told the other two. "She wants me to meet her at the Raybow Hotel. Where is that?"

"It's not far from the Africana Roundabout in Takoradi," Seidu said. "It's not far from Shippers Circle."

"Thank you, sir." Dawson stood up. "I'll go there now."

"Okay," Hammond said. "We'll talk later, then."

Seidu rose from his chair with conventional courtesy, but Hammond stayed right where he was. As Dawson walked back outside, he reflected that the superintendent seemed to be stuck in resentment thick as tar. He appeared to be taking the intervention of CID

Headquarters as a personal insult. *There'll be little or no help from him,* Dawson thought. *In fact, he might be a hindrance.* Dawson would have to be on his guard and ready for a fight. He was up to it, but he would prefer not to have to do it.

Chapter 8

As Baah drove to the Raybow Hotel, he showed Dawson more evidence that the oil industry was profoundly affecting Takoradi. The skeletal necks of building cranes dotted the skyline. The sprawling Best Western Atlantic Hotel with luxury chalets and hundreds of rooms had superseded the old military barracks on Officers' Mess Road.

"What do you think of all this construction?" Dawson asked Baah. "Are the locals better off because of the oil?"

Baah sucked his teeth. "They say one day we will all see benefit, but I think they are telling us lies. Someone like me will never get any oil money. Only the *oburonis*, the white people, and those big businessmen and the ministers of parliament will get plenty money, buying Benzes and houses for their girlfriends. You watch. Just now when we get to the Raybow, you will see them—old men with young, young girls."

Baah, who lived in a section of Takoradi called Kwesimintsim, said that although his own rent of twenty *cedis* a month had not gone up, he knew of people evicted after their landlords had suddenly doubled or tripled their rent as higher paying customers arrived from other parts of Ghana and neighboring Côte d'Ivoire.

They turned into the driveway of the Raybow, a three-story, ivory-colored hotel with arched columns and a bronze *cembonit* roof. Baah pulled up at the portico entrance, and a uniformed doorman stepped forward to open Dawson's door.

"Morning, sir."

The doorman directed Baah where to park and then held open the entrance door for Dawson. He went into the lobby, which had subtle lighting, gleaming wood floors, and a spiral staircase to the left. He stopped at the receptionist counter where a young man and woman greeted him.

"Morning. I'm Inspector Dawson, here to meet Dr. Sapphire Smith-Aidoo."

The name on the woman's badge was Violet. She was pretty, with a baby-smooth complexion.

"Oh, yes," she said, flashing him an infectious smile. "The doctor is expecting you. Please, come this way."

Violet came around the counter and led him across the lobby, opening the door onto a wide patio with cream and sienna mosaic tiling. A white woman and her two children were dog paddling in the shallow end of the pool and a white man was turning a violent pink as he baked himself in the sun on a reclining beach chair. *So strange, white people and their constant sunbathing*, Dawson thought.

"The doctor is sitting over there in the corner, Inspector," Violet said, pointing across the pool to a restaurant area with a low thatched roof and open sides.

"Thank you, Violet."

"You're welcome. Have a good day and please visit again in the future."

If I weren't happily married, he thought, stealing a quick look at her derrière as she retreated.

He crossed the patio, and as he approached, Dr. Smith-Aidoo spotted him and waved from the far side of the restaurant, which was mostly empty. The waiters were standing around chatting.

"Good morning, Doctor," he said as he got to her table.

She smiled, and he was struck by how glad she seemed to see him. In a cream-colored trouser suit, she was luminescent in the sunlight reflected off the pool.

A male waiter who had been hovering in the background came to their table.

"Good morning, sir. Please, will you like to have something?"

"No, I'm fine, thank you."

"Please, Inspector," Smith-Aidoo said. "I insist."

"All right," he said, surprised. "Do you have Malta?"

It was his favorite drink. Non-alcoholic, rich with malt and hops, and deadly sweet.

"Please, we have two kinds," the waiter said. "Guinness and Schweppes."

"Only the original," Dawson said. "Guinness."

"Yes, sir." He went away.

"I've just been with Superintendent Hammond discussing the case," Dawson told her.

She leaned forward with eagerness. "What is your next step?"

"I'll be re-interviewing several people. They may not like that."

The waiter returned with the Malta, pouring it in a glass.

"Doctor," Dawson asked after taking the first delicious sip, "please may I ask what you have done with your aunt's and uncle's belongings at their home?"

"I'm still going through their documents, trying to organize them."

"Do you mind if I look through them?"

She shook her head. "Not at all. We can go now if that's convenient for you. I don't need to be at the hospital until after lunch, so we have some time."

"That would be perfect."

Something or someone behind Dawson drew Dr. Smith-Aidoo's attention, and he turned to follow her gaze. A middle-aged man in a dark suit was coming into the restaurant accompanied by a young, smartly dressed, full-figured woman.

"That's Terence Amihere," Dr. Smith-Aidoo said quietly. "Minister of Energy. Do you know him? The director of the BNI is his brother."

"Ah, I see," Dawson said. "I didn't know that. The BNI director and my boss are always at each other's throats."

A waiter showed the minister and the woman to a table that was quite close to Dawson and the doctor, and now Amihere noticed them.

"Doctor Smith-Aidoo!" he exclaimed, coming to their table. "How nice to see you!"

She turned on a brilliant smile for him. "Good morning, Mr. Amihere. How are you?"

"I'm doing well, by His grace, thank you. I hope all is well with you."

"Yes, thank you. Please, meet Inspector Darko Dawson from Accra CID. He's helping in the investigation of the death of my aunt and uncle."

"Oh, excellent." He turned to Dawson. "Good morning, Inspector." Dawson rose slightly to shake hands.

"Let me express my condolences to you once again, Doctor," the minister said. "Tragic, just tragic."

"Thank you," she said graciously. "Is your wife doing well?"

His face lit up. "Yes, by His grace, and we are both very grateful for your taking care of her so diligently."

She dropped her head slightly in a modest bow. "I was honored to do it, sir. What brings you from Accra to Takoradi?"

"We have a meeting with Malgam Oil, the STMA and some of the local chiefs this afternoon in Sekondi. I'm briefing my secretary prior to proceeding there."

Smith-Aidoo's eyes went very briefly to the secretary and Dawson thought he saw a twinkle in them. "I understand. Then let me not take any more of your time. You're a busy man."

They both laughed the Ghanaian laugh that could express so many things—pleasure, mirth, embarrassment, and even respect.

Dawson took in Dr. Smith-Aidoo's slightly amused look as she watched the minister rejoin his attractive young companion. He guessed she was thinking, *that's not his secretary.*

She returned her attention to him. "Shall we go now, Inspector?"

"Yes. I have a taxi, so we can follow you."

HER CAR WAS a deep, metallic blue Jaguar XF. Baah followed at a respectful distance, as if afraid he might accidentally rear-end the beautiful machine.

Dawson's phone rang. It was Christine.

"Hi, love," he answered. "How're you?"

"Good. How are things going over there?"

"Just getting started, really. How are the boys?"

She told him Sly was at school while she stayed at home with Hosiah, who was doing well. He was spending less time in bed and more time constructing his toy cars and rockets.

"There's a little problem, though," she said. "Sly had a nightmare last night."

"A nightmare? About what?" But Dawson knew already instinctively. "The beheading?"

"Yes."

"Oh, no." Dawson let out a long sigh. "Poor kid. I underestimated how much this was going to affect him. How is Hosiah reacting?"

"He seemed to be fine after you gave him the talk yesterday, but he heard Sly yelling out in his sleep before I did, so that has thrown him off again."

"I'm sorry, Christine. If only I hadn't been so careless."

"No point crying over spilled milk," she said briskly. "What's done is done. Now we have to fix it. Any ideas?"

Something occurred to Dawson. "What about you and the boys coming to spend the weekend with me? Seeing me alive and well will go a long way to reassuring them, don't you think?"

"Yes!" she exclaimed, her voice taking on new energy. "That's a wonderful idea."

"I'll ask Abe if it's okay with him for you to stay with me in the lodge. Don't tell the kids about our idea until I confirm with him."

"There's not much petrol in the car, though," she said, "and I'm low on cash until next pay day. I'll have to borrow a little money from someone. Mama can probably give me something. Alternatively, we can go there by *tro-tro* to save some money."

"No, *never*," he said in alarm. *Tro-tros*, the ubiquitous, privately owned minivans that transported the masses from point A to B, were often in a dangerous state of disrepair. Like his mother, who had had a mortal fear of *tro-tros*, Dawson saw them only as deathtraps. "Just get some cash, and I'll pay back whatever money you borrow when you get here."

Hosiah was waiting to talk to his dad. Dawson immediately detected the increased energy in his son's voice when he came on the line, and gone was the slight underlying breathlessness he had had before.

"When are you coming back, Daddy?" he asked.

"As soon as I can. You sound much stronger, Champ."

"Yes, I am. Soon I'll be able to play soccer again, won't I, Daddy?"

"Yes, I'm sure you will." He was going to tell Hosiah that he still needed to take it easy, but he had said that enough times. The boy was intuitive about his body and knew by now how far he could push himself.

Dawson ended the call as they reached the affluent neighborhood of Beach Road. After a few minutes, the Jaguar turned in at a gated entrance. Dr. Smith-Aidoo pumped her horn once and waited for the watchman to open up. He was a wizened little fellow, early sixties, dressed in a pair of shorts and an old orange T-shirt. With his knotted knees, bowlegs, and feet as broad as planks, he would likely remain physically durable well into his eighties, doing the same work he had done for most of his life. He saluted and smiled as they drove through and parked in the circular driveway.

"Wait for me, please," Dawson said to Baah. "I'll be here at least one hour."

"Yes, sir."

Dawson alighted as the watchman hurried to open Dr. Smith-Aidoo's door.

"Good afternoon, madam. You are welcome."

"Afternoon, Gamal," she said, getting out of the car. "How are you?"

"Please, I'm fine, Madam."

"This is Inspector Darko Dawson from Accra. He is here to help with the investigation. Answer any questions he may have of you."

"Yes, Madam. No problem."

"We will be here for about one hour. Wash the car, eh? Let's go inside, Inspector."

A luxuriant lawn with bougainvillea and hibiscus bushes flanked the maroon, two-story brick home on both sides.

"This is a beautiful place," Dawson said.

"Thank you. The garden is all Gamal's hard work. He's been with us for about fifteen years."

She opened up the front door. "It took me several weeks before I was able to face coming into the house."

"I can understand. Did your aunt and uncle have children?"

"Yes, Paul and Paula, my cousins. They're in college in the States. They went back about a month after the funeral."

She switched on the light in the hallway and turned on the air with a remote lying on a glass table. Polished mahogany in the hallway, marble in the sitting room with white leather armchairs and sofas, expensive paintings on the wall—for Dawson, it was both impressive and too much. A slightly recessed area held the dining room, and the kitchen was beyond that.

"I have all their papers in the study upstairs," she said, leading him up a spiral staircase to the second floor. "I might as well tell you that he left me some money as well as his house in Accra. Paul and Paula get this house."

"No other beneficiaries?"

"No. Nothing went to their siblings on either side." She stopped for a moment at the banister, looking down at the sitting room. "My uncle's mother, Granny Araba, was killed in a car crash in 1994. After the wake, I overheard Uncle Charles say something strange to Auntie Fio about a curse on the family. He said, 'First my grandparents and now my mother.' Later, when I asked him what had happened to his grandparents, he was evasive. Always made me wonder if there was some dark secret."

"Maybe the aspect of the grandparents goes along with the planted pocket watch," Dawson said.

She looked at him, puzzled. "What pocket watch?"

"I thought you knew," he stammered.

"Knew what? What are you talking about?"

"An old-fashioned silver pocket watch with a black onyx inlay was found with your uncle. Someone had scratched the words, 'blood runs deep' on the inside of the cover."

"What?" She looked baffled. "My uncle never owned anything like that. Where was the watch found?"

"In his mouth," Dawson said quietly. She recoiled. "I'm sorry, Doctor. To have to tell you that."

"Oh. No." She looked away, her expression between angry and revolted. "Why didn't anyone tell me about this? Why?"

He stayed quiet.

"Blood runs deep," she repeated. "What does that mean?"

"Referring to family ties, maybe? What about your grandfather, Araba's husband?"

"Grandpa Simon. He's alive, but demented, poor man—lives with my aunt, Eileen Copper, who is Uncle Charles's older sister." Smith-Aidoo's expression turned sardonic. "Auntie Eileen fancies herself the family researcher and genealogist and tries to come off as scholarly."

She might be very useful, Dawson thought. "Can I speak to her?"

Smith-Aidoo shrugged. "Sure, if you like. I'll text you her number."

"Thank you." He followed her the rest of the way to the study. He was hopeful that he would be lucky and discover something that would break the case open and neatly tie it up. Of course, it never worked out that way.

Chapter 9

THE CARPETED STUDY WAS stifling, but the doctor switched on the AC, and the room began to cool off. Dawson saw she had been making an effort to sort out her uncle and aunt's papers. Stacks of loose pages on the floor surrounded half-filled boxes labeled *STMA, Malgam, Personal, Legal,* and *Misc,* and the desk and file cabinet held more documents still.

"I apologize that it's such a mess," she said. "Superintendent Hammond and his guys looked through the paperwork, but as far as I know, they didn't find anything useful. Maybe you'll have better luck or a keener eye."

"Thank you." Dawson looked around the room, realizing something was missing. "There's no computer. Didn't your uncle use one?"

"He did have a laptop, which has disappeared. Hammond thinks possibly the killers stole it during the ambush."

Dawson nodded. That would make sense, but he made a mental note to ask the superintendent about it.

"There's something I want you to look at," she said, sitting down on the floor in front of the STMA box with her legs folded under her. He followed her example, sitting opposite her.

She picked through the box and extracted a folder, from which she selected a typed letter. "See what you think of this."

He read it.

15th February

Dear Madam Fiona Smith-Aidoo,
  I have received your letter from 5th February. I appreciate your can-did thoughts and agree how unseemly that these rumors arose. Based on your assurances, I believe you are an honorable woman who had nothing to do with the accusations. Regarding the radio broadcast in which I was involved, I apologize for and retract any inflammatory statements I made.
  As we move into a new year, I hope to preside as chief executive over one of the most prosperous periods for our beloved Sekondi-Takoradi, and I look forward to your support.

Yours faithfully,
Kwesi DeSouza

"Is this about the allegation that DeSouza embezzled STMA money to build a house?" Dawson asked.

"Yes," she said, looking a little surprised. "How did you know?"

"I have a cousin who has lived in Takoradi all his life and follows local politics, and I was talking to him last night."

"Ah, I see."

"He told me that Fiona and Kwesi DeSouza were rivals at the STMA."

"Yes, they were." She pulled a face. "DeSouza's a nasty man. He was expecting to be reelected for a second term as chief executive of STMA, but Auntie Fiona beat him solidly. He was stunned. And I was glad."

"Do you believe your aunt would have started the rumor about the embezzlement in order to discredit DeSouza?"

She shook her head vigorously. "Not her style."

"Did he show his resentment after losing to her?"

"Yes, of course he did," she said, as if it should have been obvious. "Things like being disruptive at meetings, coming in late, interrupting my aunt, and claiming she wasn't following various protocols. Mean-spirited, spiteful little man who couldn't stand the thought that a *woman*, if you please, had beaten him."

Dawson nodded. He knew a few men like that. "Did he ever make any threats to her?"

"Not that I know of, but there's no doubt he hated her."

"I understand he strongly criticized your aunt on that radio program."

"Criticize?" Smith-Aidoo lifted her chin slightly "No, Inspector Dawson—it was a tirade."

"Did he have animosity toward your uncle as well?"

"He did, because after the broadcast, Uncle Charles went to the STMA offices and lambasted him. DeSouza tried to hit back by saying, 'Just you try setting up a business in this town and see how far you get.'" She rolled her eyes. "Empty vessels make the most noise."

Dawson found her indignation attractive. "Do you believe that Mr. DeSouza hated your aunt and uncle enough to kill them in such a brutal way?"

"What do you think my very biased answer to that is, Inspector?" she said, a little mockingly, perhaps.

That's a yes, Dawson thought with a slight smile. He was eager to talk to DeSouza and find out for himself if he was as detestable as the doctor made him out to be.

"May I look through the rest of these boxes?" he asked her.

"Yes, feel free." She stood up. "I'm going downstairs to talk to Gamal for a moment, so help yourself. I'll be back in a little while."

"Okay, Doc."

He examined the other documents in the STMA box, many of them minutes of different meetings. One of them caught his eye.

MALGAM OIL: ENVIRONMENTAL IMPACT ASSESSMENT

Attendance Register
Meeting location: Raybow Hotel Conference Center
Date: 8th March, 2012

The attendees had signed in with their phone numbers, email addresses, and the organization each represented. Charles Smith-Aidoo had been present, with an environmental advisor from the

Malgam head office in Accra, a district finance officer, an engineer, Fiona Smith-Aidoo, Kwesi DeSouza, and Reggie Cardiman, owner of Ezile Bay Resort.

Dawson turned the page.

Mr. Reggie Cardiman (RC) stated that he was very concerned that he had yet to see a detailed plan from Malgam Oil on what specific measures they will take to protect the shoreline from destruction in the event of an oil spill. RC stated that Cape Three Points, where the Ezile Bay Resort is located, is a major nursing ground for marine turtles from August to March. Dolphins and whales also inhabit this area between October and December. Many birds feed in shallow waters at Cape Three Points, and their habitat is delicate.

In response, environmental consultant Hayford Nkrumah (HN) stated that Malgam Oil and the Ghana government were drawing up policies to delineate environmental measures and corporate responsibility in the face of oil exploration and production. Charles Smith-Aidoo (CSA), Malgam Corporate Relations Director, said he wanted to assure RC that a significant oil spill that would affect the flora and fauna of the shoreline was highly unlikely.

However, RC said that CSA's declaration regarding the small likelihood of a harmful oil spill was unsatisfactory, as oil spills occur regularly worldwide, citing the Gulf of Mexico disaster of 2010. RC stated that even discharge of ballast water from tankers could affect the integrity of the coastal environment. HN stated that the vast volumes of water in the Gulf of Guinea would dilute the ballast waters.

RC disagreed with HN's above statement, stating it was disingenuous and designed to allow Malgam to get away with polluting activities with impunity. Kwesi DeSouza requested that the meeting move on to the next item on the agenda regarding waste disposal at the hangars (warehouses) on the Ghana Air Force Base.

The box contained a lot more concerning the STMA. Dawson could spend hours on this. For now, he moved on to the Malgam box, which held policies and procedures, lists of personnel in Malgam, and available positions. The legal papers container included Malgam contracts and personal ones involving the Smith-Aidoo residences in Takoradi and Accra and some land in the Eastern Region.

He turned his attention to the bookcase against the wall by the window. A framed photograph of Charles and Fiona stood at an angle on one shelf. They were both well dressed for an obvious studio pose complete with misty borders. Charles appeared friendly, with a vanishing hairline and an expanding waist. Fiona looked intelligent and attractive; head tilted, she wore crimson lipstick and her hair was stylishly tucked behind ears that flashed pearls at the lobes.

Dawson examined the books. Oil, oil production, economics of oil production, rig technology, and one called *Environmental Impact: How the Petroleum Industry Affects Indigenous Peoples*. Dawson thumbed through the case studies: Nigeria, Ecuador, Norway, Equatorial Guinea, and the Gulf of Mexico. He supposed Ghana would be included in the next edition. He replaced the heavy book on the shelf and went to the window, where he stood watching Sapphire talking to Gamal as he finished wiping down the Jaguar, which looked as glossy as glass now. Baah was leaning casually against his taxi.

Dawson took down a box that had been thrown up on the top shelf and found a jumble of discarded items that people never knew what to do with—electronic cables, electrical outlet plugs, a damaged power strip, and two battered, old style Nokia phones. He switched on one of them. It still had a little battery life left. He went to the inbox and found five text messages to Fiona.

The battery of the other Nokia went completely out. He looked for and found the phone's charger, plugged it in, and connected it to the Nokia. He went to the log of received calls. They were from Fiona, Sapphire, twins Paul and Paula, and a few other names that weren't familiar. Dawson's guess was that the phone had belonged to Charles.

He came to one that made his scrolling finger stop.

Lawrence Tetteh, 020-156-4676, 19:46 27 Mar

Lawrence Tetteh, CEO of Goilco? Voice mail, a more recent addition to mobile service in Ghana, was not available on his phone. Dawson went to the log of text messages received and scrolled again.

He found three sets of messages received from Lawrence Tetteh, all on Friday, 4th May.

The first one said HOW R U

The second and third messages were:

DOING OK, NEED TO CHT WITH U IN PRSON

CALL ME WHEN U R IN WE CAN MEET

Of course, "prson" meant "person," Dawson thought, smiling at the way he had for an instant interpreted it as "prison." Too much time being a detective.

He went to the messages sent list and found the corresponding replies:

IM GOOD & U

WILL B IN ACCRA TUE

OK

He dialed 020-156-4676, and it rang repeatedly until it abruptly cut off without any kind of error message. He went through the phone's menu and found that the provider was Vodafone, which was good, since the company seemed to have an overwhelming presence in Takoradi. It should be possible to find out if this was the right Lawrence Tetteh.

"Are you okay, Inspector Dawson?"

He started slightly. Dr. Smith-Aidoo had returned. "Yes, thank you, Doctor."

"Find anything of interest?"

"Who owned these phones, do you know?"

"This was Uncle's before he got his iPhone. The other one belongs to Auntie Fio."

"Do you know if your uncle knew the CEO of Goilco, a man called Lawrence Tetteh?"

She shook her head slowly. "The name doesn't ring a bell, no."

Dawson wondered what Lawrence Tetteh had wanted to discuss with Charles. He had sounded serious and terse in his text. "In person" could have signified that he didn't want to risk speaking or texting about the subject on the phone for security reasons. Dawson checked his ruminations. Before he began all this speculation, he needed to find out if this was really the Lawrence Tetteh of Goilco. Neither "Lawrence" nor "Tetteh" was an uncommon name, and he wasn't going to embarrass himself by getting the wrong LT.

"Can I take the phones with me?" he asked the doctor. "I'd like to look through the calls and text messages. I would also like the STMA box. There's more in there that I need to look at."

"Yes, of course. Whatever you need."

"Thank you." He looked around the room again. "Please, Doc, don't forget to let me know if you come across your uncle's laptop."

"I won't forget."

"Do you mind if I look in their bedroom?"

He followed her out of the office to the master bedroom at the other end of the hall. A large mask on the wall by the bed startled Dawson. Made of matte blackened wood, it looked at him from dark triangular eyes set below a dome-shaped forehead and smiled at him with jagged teeth.

"What kind of mask is that?" he asked, moving closer to it.

"Interesting, isn't it?" She came up behind, and he became aware of her lingering fragrance. "Uncle told me it's a ceremonial mask from the Dogon people of Burkina Fasso."

"Was he particularly interested in the Dogon?"

"Yes, but he and Auntie Fiona simply liked to collect masks, as you can see."

He looked around. Several masks of various sizes hung on the walls. To Dawson, many were beautiful, but others were not what he would like to see late at night.

"Do you know what all of them mean?"

"Not really."

He looked at her. "Were your aunt and uncle superstitious at all?"

"No."

"Did they have any dealings with fetish priests or traditional healers?"

She laughed. "No, they were thoroughly modern, especially my uncle. Liked all the new gadgets—iPhone, i-this, i-that."

"They could still have some traditional beliefs," Dawson pointed out. "Many modern Ghanaians do."

"Not Uncle Charles, though." She appeared both puzzled and amused. "Their being mask collectors doesn't mean they were superstitious—or even spiritual, for that matter. Why do you ask?"

"I was just curious."

"Oh," she said, as it dawned on her. "I see. You're wondering if the beheading was related to some kind of . . . magical powers, or *juju*."

"Yes. I'm sorry to bring up the beheading again."

"It's okay, Inspector. You're doing your job."

She turned to gaze out of the window at the view of the back garden and the beach. Dawson looked around the room. The open closets were full of male and female attire. A magazine was open on the bed, as was a container of face powder on the makeup stand, and towels were hanging on the rack in the en suite bathroom. The place looked like it was in use.

"Is someone staying here?" he asked.

"No," she said. "I left everything exactly the way it was when they left that morning for Cape Three Points. Their bedroom isn't like the office—it's much more personal, and I can't bring myself to disturb anything. If you need to go through their effects, feel free."

"Just one thing I'd like to check," he said. "The pockets of his suits. Do you mind?"

"No, not at all."

She watched him do that, and Dawson felt intrusive performing this necessary evil. He found nothing and was glad in a way. Some secret item in those pockets could have been awkward for them both.

"Thank you, Doc."

She smiled. "You're welcome. Do you need to see anything more?"

"I think I'm fine for now."

He collected the boxes of documents from the office, and she accompanied him downstairs back to the taxi. He asked her to get in touch with him if she remembered or came across anything that might be important. As he and Baah left, Dawson called Jason Sarbah's number and left a voice mail explaining who he was and requesting a meeting.

He thought about the potential suspects so far: DeSouza, Cardiman, and Sarbah. They all had reason to hate Charles and Fiona, but under different circumstances and for different reasons. According to Dr. Smith-Aidoo, Mr. DeSouza, the chief executive officer of the powerful STMA, hated and resented Fiona for unseating him and hated her husband for his hostile visit to DeSouza after the radio "tirade" was broadcast.

Reggie Cardiman, the Ezile Bay owner Dawson had not yet met, was evidently in fierce opposition to Malgam Oil because of its potential threat to the survival of the flora and fauna of the sea and coast. Charles Smith-Aidoo, whose job it was to show his company in the best possible light, embodied the public face of Malgam, and for Cardiman, he would have been the most accessible and symbolic target for murderous wrath. The killing occurred not far from Ezile Bay and not long after Charles and Fiona Smith-Aidoo had left Cardiman. What had happened at their meeting? Perhaps it was acrimonious, leaving Cardiman infuriated and motivated to kill.

Jason Sarbah, too, could have had a strong motive to kill if he viewed Charles Smith-Aidoo, his cousin, as the person most responsible for the death of Jason's beloved daughter Angela. Charles had refused to help Jason out financially, and Dawson could imagine how much pain and fury that might have engendered in Jason. This hadn't merely been an appeal for assistance with buying something or paying the rent, this was a cry for help in saving a life. Charles's point of view was that there were other ways to solve the problem, but that could hardly have been any comfort to Jason.

What troubled Dawson most about these three as suspects was that he couldn't see any of them committing the crime without assistance. First, it would have been difficult for one person to handle two dead bodies. Second, someone knowledgeable about sea navigation would have been needed to take the bodies out as far as the Malgam rig. That was why Dawson was eager to speak with Abe's fisherman friend, Forjoe, who might have heard, for example, that a fellow fisherman had been hired for a "job" of some kind. Dawson would then simply make the connections. Who knows, he could be close to wrapping this case up in record time. *Stop that*, he scolded himself. It was exactly that kind of thinking that got him into deep trouble.

Chapter 10

ABRAHAM WAS ELATED AT the idea of Christine coming with the boys to stay at the lodge for the weekend. Putting down some extra bedding would not be a problem.

"Thank you, Abe," Dawson said.

"Don't thank me. You're flesh and blood, remember?"

That oddly reminded Dawson of the inscription in the old pocket watch. *Blood runs deep.*

In the afternoon, having reached Forjoe by phone, Abraham took Dawson on a trip to Sekondi Harbor along the coastal road. Dawson gazed at the seawall of large boulders along the route. Glancing farther out to sea, he saw the dark, squat shape on the horizon.

"Is that an oil rig?" he asked.

Abraham glanced over. "No, it's an accommodation barge for temporary workers who don't need to stay on the rig."

On their left, rows of faded old buildings appeared. Going up an incline, they entered downtown old Sekondi with its haggard British colonial buildings, including an ancient but still functioning post office. In the shadow of the seventeenth-century Fort Orange at the hill's pinnacle, the fishing harbor came into view with large and small canoes adorned with colorful flags and religious declarations painted on their hulls.

They parked near the marketplace and walked downhill through the maze of market stalls and over pocked, rocky terrain. Women and men carried pungent loads of fish on their heads in heavy, metal basins. To prevent an accident of equilibrium, they had to keep their

forward momentum, knocking to the side anyone who was unfortu-
nate enough to be in the way. Calling out "pure water" in a singsong
voice, other women head-carried bins of iced drinking water in plastic sachets that were a major source of the trash casually tossed into
the gutters of Ghana's cities.

Under a long shaded structure with open sides, both men and
women sorted through the fishermen's catches and displayed some
of the largest fish Dawson had ever seen. Abraham pointed out different ones as they walked along—grouper, swordfish, tuna, and red
snapper.

Just beyond that was the wharf where large trawlers were moored
and crowds of fishermen carried on a brisk and noisy business with
market women. Some of the women carted off their purchases on
their own heads, while others used a professional porter.

"See that guy?" Abraham said, pointing to a compact older man
who was moving off with a punishingly heavy bin full of fish on his
head. "He's about sixty years old—been doing this since he was a
teenager."

And all of it in the harsh sun, Dawson thought, wiping his drenched
forehead.

Abraham led the way to a quieter part of the harbor, weaving in
between shacks where mechanics were repairing outboard motors
and carpenters were building new trawlers. Compared to the area
they had just left, the vessels here were canoes of different sizes pulled
up on the shore or moored in shallow water with makeshift cloth
canopies for shade.

One of the fishermen, a densely muscular man of thirty-ish, was
darning his fishing net, a portion of it hooked over his big toe to keep
the net's tension as he deftly repaired holes and tears with a large
needle. His deeply black skin glistened in the sun.

"Clay!" Abraham called out.

The man looked up and grinned as he saw them approaching. He
put down the net and skipped out of the canoe.

"Abe, my brother! How are you?"

Abraham introduced Dawson as his cousin and asked Clay if Forjoe was around.

"I haven't seen him today," Clay said.

He called out to three fishermen on an adjacent canoe, asking them if they knew where Forjoe was.

"I think he went to the house," one of them replied.

Abe thanked them and went on with Dawson. At the top of the incline not far from where they had parked, they crossed the street to a ramshackle group of houses around a small compound. A teenage boy was washing clothes in a wide metal pan, and a woman was hanging them out to dry on the line.

"Good afternoon," Abraham greeted her. "Have you seen Forjoe?"

"He's inside," the woman said, pointing her chin at the door behind him. "Wait, I'll call him."

She wiped her hands and went to knock on the door, the top half of which was a large opening covered with torn mosquito netting.

A voice answered. "Who is it?"

"Some people are here to see you," she said in Fante.

"I'm coming."

It was too dark in the room to see anything from outside. Forjoe emerged from the gloom putting on a T-shirt as he came to the door. He smiled as he saw them.

"Abraham! How are you?"

They shook hands and Abraham introduced Dawson to Forjoe the same way as he had done with Clay. Forjoe was around 28, short and as solid as a brick house. He dragged over a couple plastic chairs and invited the two men to sit down while he took a seat himself on a nearby wooden stool.

"So what brings you here today?" he asked.

"My cousin wanted to meet you," Abraham said.

"Oh, is that so?" Forjoe said, looking at Dawson with interest.

"Abraham tells me you sometimes hire his canoe to other fishermen," Dawson said.

"Yes," Forjoe said, nodding. His expression was friendly. "Especially the young ones who can't afford to buy a new canoe. You know, now the wood is expensive, and the government doesn't allow certain trees to be cut. The fishing is tough too. Not so much fish in the sea anymore."

"Oh, I see," Dawson said. He had heard about the troubles plaguing the fishing industry. "It makes life hard, eh?"

Forjoe turned the corners of his mouth down. "Very hard." He looked at Dawson with curiosity. "Why? Do you want to hire a canoe?"

"Oh, no," Dawson said with a smile. "I just have a question, Forjoe. Last July, someone killed a man and his wife and took them out to sea in a canoe, all the way to one of the oil rigs. Did you hear about it?"

Forjoe's expression changed abruptly. "Are you a policeman?"

"Yes."

Forjoe shook his head as if to say, *I can't help you.*

Dawson was used to this kind of reticence. People became very uncomfortable and tight-lipped with police questioning, often afraid that they were under suspicion.

Abraham came to his rescue. "Forjoe, he's not here to make any trouble for you. CID sent him from Accra to help the Sekondi police."

"Oh, okay." Forjoe appeared to relax, although not completely.

"We think that late on the night of Monday, seventh July, after the killers murdered the Smith-Aidoos," Dawson said, "they put the dead bodies in a canoe and used a second one to tow it out to sea."

"Starting from where?" Forjoe asked.

Excellent question, Dawson thought. "That I don't know, but that Monday night, there was a full moon, so I'm hoping that maybe some fishermen might have spotted the canoes."

Forjoe frowned. "But you won't find any fishermen at sea late on a Monday, sir."

"Why do you say that?"

"Because we can't fish overnight. It's a taboo to fish on Tuesdays."

"Oh," Dawson said, flattened like an insect underfoot. He had forgotten that by ancient tradition, the sea is a goddess who must rest one day a week. Why it was Tuesday in most fishing communities along Ghana's coast, Dawson did not know.

Abraham looked at him ruefully. "He's right. I should have thought of that."

"On Mondays," Forjoe continued, "rather than going to sea, most fishermen concentrate on selling as much fish as possible from the weekend's catch. Monday is a big market day. We never miss it."

"So, no one rented a canoe from you on that day," Dawson said, disappointed and clutching at straws.

"No, sir."

"Do other people rent canoes?"

"A few."

"Please, can you ask around to find out if anyone took a canoe that night? It doesn't have to have been a fisherman who rented—anyone at all. If you hear anything, call me. I'll give you my number."

"Okay, sir."

A movement caught Dawson's eye, and he turned to see a girl of about nine years old hovering in the half-open doorway of Forjoe's dwelling.

"Hello," Dawson said, smiling at her.

"That's my daughter, Marvelous," Forjoe said.

Dawson saw how his eyes softened as he looked at her. Forjoe gestured at her to come to him. "Marvelous, *bra ha.*"

She approached and leaned against her father, shyly keeping her head down as he put his arm around her waist. She was pretty, with a heart-shaped face and the standard short schoolgirl haircut.

"Greet our guests, eh?" he told her.

She curtsied slightly and said, "Good afternoon," in barely a whisper.

"Are you feeling tired?" he asked her softly, passing his hand over hair.

She shook her head.

It was a question Dawson would not have expected of a parent to his nine-year-old child, and it was eerily similar to what he had often asked Hosiah during his years of suffering heart disease. In a flash, Dawson realized that something was wrong with Marvelous. Hours of sitting with his son in inpatient wards and outpatient waiting rooms had trained him to observe signs of illness in children. Here he noticed that while kids of this girl's age would normally have skinny ankles, Marvelous's own were puffy and so were her hands. She was retaining fluid for some reason.

"Okay," Forjoe said, his eyes still full of tenderness toward her. "Go and do your homework and get ready for school tomorrow, all right?"

She nodded, walked away with one glance back at her father, and disappeared round a corner.

"Your daughter is beautiful," Dawson said. "But is she okay?"

"She's okay," he responded, nevertheless appearing troubled. "Please, why do you ask?"

"Because you asked her if she was tired."

"You are right," Forjoe said heavily, as if reluctant to admit it. "The doctors say there is something wrong with her kidneys."

For Dawson, this struck home. Countless times, he had told people in response to their questions about Hosiah, *The doctors say there's something wrong with his heart.*

"Can they help her?" Dawson asked Forjoe.

He shrugged. "Anything they can do, my wife and I can't afford it. We are too poor. The doctors tell me that one day Marvelous will need a machine to clean her blood two or three times a week, but the cost of even one treatment is more than we make in one month. Or they can transplant one kidney from her older brother, but the cost of the operation . . ." He trailed off, shaking his head.

Dawson knew exactly what Forjoe was facing. It had been the same circumstance with Hosiah. Like Marvelous and her failing kidneys, the medical options available to Hosiah had been so costly, Dawson could never have afforded them without the benevolence of the Cardiothoracic Center. Even Jason Sarbah, a man of much more means, had run up against a monetary wall trying to save his daughter, Angela. Dawson's, Forjoe's, and Sarbah's stories were startling in their similarity, but not coincidental by any means. They pointed to the exploding health crisis in Ghana: modern diagnostics were detecting more and more chronic diseases in both adults and children, but the tottering National Health Insurance Scheme could not possibly pay for their treatment.

Dawson wished he could help Forjoe, but he would need to ask someone in the know when he was back home in Accra—perhaps when he took Hosiah in for a follow-up visit, he could ask a doctor if anything could be done for Marvelous. However, he didn't want to raise any false hopes by telling Forjoe that. For now, an expression of sympathy was about as far as he could go.

"I'm sorry," Dawson said. "I pray you will find a solution for your lovely daughter."

"Thank you, sir." Forjoe tried to shake himself out of his dark mood. "Everything will be okay. A certain man is trying his best to help me, and God will bless us."

Dawson stood up. "I'm grateful for your help, Forjoe."

"You're welcome, sir."

They traded phone numbers, and as Dawson left with Abraham, he reserved a space in his mind and put Marvelous securely in it. He wasn't going to forget her.

RETURNING FROM SEKONDI Harbor, they stopped off at Akroma Plaza Hotel for dinner. A visit to Takoradi was incomplete without dining at Akroma's legendary restaurant, Abraham told Dawson. It had been moved from its old, smaller location into a completely new section of the hotel twice the original size.

It was refreshingly air-conditioned, in contrast to their visit to the harbor. The hostess seated the two men in a nice spot with a view of the street. A quick glance through the seemingly endless menu revealed to Dawson that Asian, European, and American dishes were much more costly than Ghanaian ones. He and Abraham had a hankering for *banku*. It was only a matter of what to eat it with.

Dawson liked both *banku* and *fufu*, but some people were vehemently aligned with one and not the other. Both were presented as soft, pillow-smooth ovals, but their respective tastes could not have been more different. *Banku*, made from fermented cornmeal, had a sour and distinctive flavor, whereas *fufu*, derived from a freshly boiled starchy food such as *cassava*, was a blander affair that made no effort to compete with the soup with which it was eaten.

Abraham wanted grilled tilapia smothered in a spicy onion and tomato sauce. It was served whole, the head and all the bones included. Dawson didn't feel like dealing with the task of extracting tiny bones, so he went with okro stew instead. This was the ultimate explosion of taste, what with the prawns, beef, smoked ham, and herring in a dense mélange of eggplant, tomato, ginger, chili pepper, and okro, which gave the dish its slick mouth feel. Dawson agreed that it was one of the best he'd ever tasted—except his mother's, of course.

When Abraham dropped him off at the house, Dawson was pleasantly full but dying for a refreshing shower after the long day. Alas, the water pressure was low, and the flow from the showerhead was but a trickle. It was back to the old standby: a bucket bath. He came out of the bathroom feeling like a new man and pulled on a pair of shorts. A cool breeze blew gently in from the windows, lifting the curtains slightly. His phone rang.

"Hello?"

"Inspector Dawson?" His voice was rather boyish. "This is Jason Sarbah. I'm returning your call."

"Thank you very much, Mr. Sarbah. I'm investigating the murder of Charles and Fiona Smith-Aidoo," he said. "I would like to meet you for a few minutes to discuss it."

"Ah, I see." He paused. "Good. Perhaps we'll now get to the bottom of it. Did you have a time in mind to meet?"

"As soon as possible, sir."

"Let's see . . . How about two o'clock tomorrow afternoon?"

"Perfect, sir."

"Do you know where the Malgam offices are?"

"Yes, I do. I'll see you tomorrow at two."

DAWSON WENT THROUGH more of the papers in the STMA box. He came across three separate meetings for which the minutes described a sharp conflict between Kwesi DeSouza and Fiona Smith-Aidoo.

When he'd had enough of that, he put everything aside on the nightstand and sat back in bed. He had brought one of his mbiras with him from Accra, as he always did when traveling. It had two rows of graduated lengths of metal strips, sixteen in all, mounted on a handheld soundboard. When plucked, the strips produced notes similar to the sound of xylophone. Dawson's mother had given him one as a gift when he was ten, and he had played it sporadically into his teens, when he discovered he could make his own mbira with simple, scavenged materials—even old bicycle spokes. The instrument had a thousand-year history with the Shona people of Zimbabwe, who still made the most complicated of mbiras with twenty-three or more keys.

He rested his head against the wall as he practiced a piece he had composed the week before, a cyclical arrangement with intertwined melodies. After a few minutes of playing, it put Dawson in a relaxed and meditative mood, almost trancelike. It was the next best thing to smoking marijuana, and in his months of kicking the habit, he had increasingly relied on his mbira to relieve tension. In the "good old days," he combined smoking with mbira playing, a doubly heightening experience.

After half an hour, he became pleasantly drowsy. He reached out for the light switch on the wall to turn off the bare-bulb ceiling light and stretched diagonally across the bed since it was a little too short for him. He felt tired, but he couldn't sleep. His mind flitted over the events of the past two days like an undecided hummingbird. Instinctively, he felt that the Smith-Aidoo murder had greater breadth and depth than any of his previous cases. Two corpses in a canoe adrift around a deep-sea oil rig, a severed head with an excavated eye socket, a nineteenth-century pocket watch with a scrawled inscription invoking blood ties. What did it all mean?

Chapter 11

IN THE MORNING, DAWSON once again hired Baah's taxi services for the day. On the way to Sekondi-Takoradi Police Headquarters, the young driver, curious about the Ghana Police Service and the work of a detective, peppered Dawson with questions.

"So I think say you dey come to Tadi to investigate that man they dey cut off his head."

"Yes. Charles Smith-Aidoo. Did you hear something about it?"

"They say it be *juju.*"

"What do you think?"

He nodded. "It could be."

Baah's reference to the involvement of supernatural powers was the second one after Sly's. An idea struck Dawson. "Do you know any *juju* men in Tadi?"

Baah hesitated. "Many of them dey."

"Can we go to them?"

"I can take you," he said with a nervous smile, "but me, I won't talk to them. I fear them."

"No problem."

"So I should take you now?" Baah said, taking his eyes off the road briefly to look at Dawson.

"No—this evening, if we have time. If not, then tomorrow."

"Okay, sir."

THEY ARRIVED AT Sekondi Headquarters around 8:30. Superintendent Hammond was in a meeting with three of his detectives and

Dawson had to wait until they were done. Two detectives left while ASP Seidu remained behind.

"Good morning, sir," Dawson said as he came in, switching on what he hoped was a disarming smile.

"Good morning," Hammond said dully, barely looking at him.

"Morning, Dawson," Seidu said, more amiably.

"May I?" Dawson said, gesturing to an empty chair.

"Of course," Hammond said indifferently.

Dawson sat.

"Yes, Inspector?" the superintendent said. "Can I help you?"

The smile didn't work, Dawson thought. "Just wanted to report how things have been going so far."

"Go ahead, then."

Dawson related the events of the day before—his morning meeting with Dr. Smith-Aidoo and then the visit to her house.

"Seems she didn't know about the pocket watch inserted into her uncle's mouth," Dawson said.

"Of course she knew," Hammond said indignantly. "She has just forgotten because of the shock she was in. I told her about it myself."

Perhaps the superintendent was telling the truth, Dawson reflected, but he doubted it. How would Dr. Smith-Aidoo have forgotten that kind of lurid detail?

"Do you have anything else?" Hammond asked, resuming his aloof tone. "I have to get to a regional meeting."

He looked at his watch conspicuously, which Dawson ignored as he removed a document from his folder.

"As you already know," he said, "Fiona Smith-Aidoo had a rivalry with Kwesi DeSouza." He leaned forward and handed Superintendent Hammond the minutes of the acrimonious meetings. "I don't know if you saw this."

Hammond glanced at it and gave it back. "We questioned Mr. Kwesi DeSouza closely. He denied being on bad terms with Mrs. Smith-Aidoo or having anything to do with her death. Then we checked his whereabouts on the seventh and eighth of July. He has an alibi. We also looked into any possibilities that Mr. DeSouza could have hired someone. We have not found anything."

Dawson nodded respectfully. That sounded like some solid

detective work had been done. "Another name that came up in these meetings at the STMA," he continued, "was Reggie Cardiman, the gentleman who owns the Ezile Bay Resort at Cape Three Points."

"We already know about him," Hammond said, leaning back in his chair and irritably tapping the end of his pen on his desk. "He has lived in Ghana for almost twenty years—he even speaks Fante. He is crazy about wildlife and the environment and all that stuff, and he loves his Ezile Bay Resort. The village next to Ezile Bay is called Akwidaa. Various companies have approached the chief, Nana Ackah-Yensu the third, about buying land in the area—oil companies, real estate developers, and so on. Some have accused Ackah-Yensu of selling off tracts of land, although he denies it and says he wants to collaborate only with the government to develop that area."

Dawson leaned forward, happy to get this kind of information and wondering if the superintendent might be finally thawing out.

"Nana Ackah-Yensu told us that Malgam Oil wanted to build luxury villas in Akwidaa," Hammond continued, rocking back and forth slightly in his squeaky chair—a nervous habit, perhaps. "That's where the Ezile River joins the sea and a beautiful bay is formed, as well as some ruins of a German fort built in the seventeenth century. So, this is attractive real estate and the kind of scenery these tourists love."

"So, did Charles Smith-Aidoo go to the chief to talk to him about the villas?" Dawson asked.

"I was just coming to that," Hammond said, holding up his palm. "He approached the chief about the possibility of relocating Akwidaa either farther inland or farther east in return for building a new village from scratch with running water and electricity.

"Meanwhile, Smith-Aidoo went to Cardiman to tell him that if Chief Ackah-Yensu agreed to move, Malgam Oil would likely annex the Cardiman's Ezile resort as well, in order to build more chalets. Cardiman leases the land from the Akwidaa village so he would have no legal right to stop it."

"The prospect of losing Ezile Bay was probably terrifying for him," Dawson said. "It would give Cardiman a strong motive. Could he have followed the Smith-Aidoos and ambushed them on the road from Ezile?"

Hammond shook his head. "They left Ezile around twelve thirty, and we have confirmed that Cardiman did not leave for Takoradi until one o'clock. The Smith-Aidoos would have been long gone by then, and Cardiman could never have caught up with them."

"Maybe he had an accomplice who delayed them until Cardiman arrived."

"Maybe this, maybe that," Hammond said, with a sardonic smile. "We can't operate on maybes. At the end of the day, there is no evidence whatsoever that Cardiman was involved."

Discussion over, Dawson thought. He moved on. "I found an old phone in Mr. Smith-Aidoo's study. Were you aware of it?"

Hammond looked at Seidu and then shook his head. "No, we didn't find anything like that in his desk, and his niece didn't mention it."

"It was buried in a box of old equipment and cables," Dawson said.

"What about it?" Hammond asked.

"I saw some text messages from Charles Smith-Aidoo to a Lawrence Tetteh."

Hammond's rocking stopped abruptly in the forward phase and he almost hurtled off his chair. "Did you say Lawrence Tetteh?"

"Yes. I wonder if this is the same Lawrence Tetteh who was murdered."

"Why do you think that?" Hammond asked tensely.

"Could there be a connection between the murder of Tetteh and the killing of the Smith-Aidoos?" Dawson asked coolly. "That's the question I've been wondering myself the past few days."

Hammond squinted at him. "Do you have the phone with you?"

Dawson took it out of his top pocket and switched it on. He took the screen view to the text message section before handing it to the superintendent.

Seidu went around Hammond's desk so he could watch as the superintendent scrolled through the messages.

"Okay," Hammond said, but it came out huskily and he cleared his throat. "I see what you're saying."

"Shall I take it to Vodafone to see if they can trace the number, sir?" Seidu asked.

"No, I can take care of it," Hammond said. "I know one guy over there very well, and he can check it very quickly."

"Thank you, sir," Dawson said, pleasantly surprised by Hammond's apparent willingness to participate.

"Not at all."

Dawson stood up. "I'm going to look for Kwesi DeSouza at the STMA offices, sir."

"As I told you," Hammond said, his coldness returning, "we have looked carefully into his alibi already. Nothing is there. I don't think it's necessary to go back to him."

"Just routine," Dawson said lightly. "For my own records. You know Chief Superintendent Lartey—he scrutinizes every detail."

Hammond's cheek twitched, probably resenting Dawson's invoking a superior officer, because he couldn't very well challenge it.

"Also," Dawson said, "I think I forgot to mention that my assistant, Detective Sergeant Chikata, will be joining me from Accra to help with the investigation."

Hammond nodded. "Yes, Chief Superintendent Lartey has informed me of that."

As Dawson was leaving, he kept feeling he had forgotten something, and it was as he was opening the door that he remembered.

"One more thing, sir," he said, turning with his right hand still on the doorknob. "Mr. Smith-Aidoo's laptop was never found, is that correct?"

"Yes," Hammond said. "We believe whoever ambushed his vehicle also stole his laptop."

Dawson suppressed a wince as a quick stab of pain shot through the palm of his left hand. "I see," he said, catching his breath. "Thank you."

Dawson left stunned, because he knew decisively that Superintendent Hammond had just lied about the laptop. The timbre of his voice had changed, not in a way Dawson could consciously define, but enough to trigger his synesthesia and reveal that his superior wasn't telling the truth. The laptop hadn't been stolen. The question was, where was it, and what was Hammond trying to hide?

Chapter 12

THE STMA WAS AN old, two-story building painted an odd green and subdivided into three sections bordering the car park in a semi-circle. A blue-uniformed guard directed Baah to an available parking space. Dawson got out and entered one of the ground floor departments, where a woman directed him upstairs to Kwesi DeSouza's office. Marked with a sign that read CHIEF EXECUTIVE, it was the very last room at the end of the verandah. Dawson knocked and went in, welcoming the pleasant blast of cold from the air conditioner.

The secretary at the desk told him that DeSouza was in a meeting and Dawson could wait if he had a half-hour to spare. He sat down where she had indicated and used the time to check his phone, replying to a text from Christine asking how he was doing.

He also saw that Dr. Smith-Aidoo had sent him her aunt's number.

DeSouza's door opened. Two men came out laughing over a shared joke. DeSouza, burly, bespectacled, and shaved completely bald, was dressed in a short-sleeved white linen shirt with Ghanaian embroidery down the front. After shaking hands with DeSouza, the visitor left.

"What's next, Susana?" DeSouza said to the secretary.

"Please, there's someone here to see you."

Dawson stood up and introduced himself.

"Yes, sir," DeSouza said. "How can I help you?"

"May I speak with you for a few minutes?"

DeSouza appeared curious and wary. "Come in," he said, after a moment's hesitation.

He ushered Dawson into the inner sanctum and then shut the door behind them. It was even colder in there than in the front office.

Dawson chose one of the two chairs in front of the desk and DeSouza went to his on the other side. His office wasn't opulent, just comfortable.

"So, Inspector, what can I do for you?"

"I'm in Takoradi investigating the murder of Charles and Fiona Smith-Aidoo. CID Headquarters was petitioned to look into the killings."

"What, is this a different investigation from Superintendent Hammond's?"

"It's complementary to it, I would say."

"I've been questioned by both Hammond and his assistant, and now you want to do the same," DeSouza said in annoyance. "I'm tired of you guys showing up at my door in the middle of my work. I mean, what is it you're digging for? I didn't murder the man or his wife. This should be more than obvious to you by now."

"I apologize for the repeated intrusions, sir. I realize how irritating it must be, and that isn't my intention. However, I'm reviewing their investigation, and I have to be thorough. I have no choice."

DeSouza heaved an exasperated sigh. "All right. What is it you want to know?"

"Just to confirm, Fiona Smith-Aidoo succeeded you as chief executive officer of the STMA in April this year, is that correct?"

"Yes, yes. Isn't this information already in your files?"

"But once she was dead, the position reverted to you?"

"Look, after her death, I was designated acting chief from July to October, and then a special election was held and I was re-elected."

"Did you get along well with Mrs. Smith-Aidoo?"

"Oh, here we go again." DeSouza closed his eyes for a tortured moment. "There are all kinds of stories about the rivalry between Fiona and me, but it's much ado about nothing, and the notion that I might have plotted and executed her demise just to get this job back is just so ridiculous."

"You were on the radio—"

"Yes, I know. I was on that Skyy FM program, and I said this and that. Maybe I was a little heated, but it was theatrics, that's all it was."

He was theatrical—Dawson gave him that. "I was curious about this letter that I found among the Smith-Aidoos' belongings"—he opened the folder he had brought and took the letter out, sliding it across the table to DeSouza—"signed in your name. Did you write it?"

"Yes, I did," he said, with an impatient glance. "And what about it? In fact, rather than anything nefarious, this letter expresses my true sentiments. 'Based on your assurances, I believe you are an honorable woman' is what I wrote and what I meant."

"What lead to this letter being written?"

"Between January and April, Fiona was campaigning aggressively for the chief executive position," DeSouza said, sounding somewhat like he was explaining to a child. "At the time, some people accused me of raiding the STMA coffers in order to build a luxury home. I don't know where this blatant lie originated, but there was a rumor that Fiona was responsible."

"But you never had any evidence that the rumor was true."

"Correct."

"Is it possible that someone bore malice against Fiona Smith-Aidoo and tried to ruin her reputation by making it appear that she was creating the rumor?"

"I have no idea," DeSouza said, gesturing with impatience. "You're asking me an impossible question. I can tell you that I did confront Fiona about it. She was quite insulted by the notion that she was responsible for this 'gossip,' as she called it. Obviously, she wanted her objection and denial recorded in black and white, so she sent me a letter to that effect, and I accepted it and replied with this one."

"Do you remember where you were on Monday, the seventh of July, the day Charles and Fiona were killed?"

"Again, for the fourth or fifth time," DeSouza said, as if this questioning was torture, "I am here in my offices every Monday from morning till early evening. Every Monday night, I prepare for the IT class I teach at Takoradi Tech on Tuesdays. That Tuesday, we had an STMA meeting in the evening. When I got here, it was around five thirty or so, and everyone was there except Fiona. It was unusual for her to be late or absent. We were scheduled to debate the issue of Sekondi-Takoradi city planning in response to the influx of people into the area. We even had the director of the Ghana Tourist Board present as well."

DeSouza's phone rang, and he snatched it up, listened for a second, and then told the person on the line that he'd call him back. "So, yes—what was I saying?"

"The meeting," Dawson prompted him.

"Right—Fiona was very late. We waited a little longer and tried to reach her by phone, but after about fifteen minutes or so, I offered to chair the meeting and we went ahead. About an hour later, one of the STMA members got a phone call from his wife, who works at the Effia-Nkwanta hospital, saying that Fiona and her husband were dead."

"How did your colleagues react?"

DeSouza turned his palms up. "What do you expect? Disbelief. Shock. That doesn't even sum up the totality of what we felt."

"At that time, what did you know about the cause of death?"

"No one knew anything. The meeting came to a standstill and everyone was on the phone calling all over the place."

He stared at his desk for a while, evidently picturing the chaos and shock of that evening.

"Did Fiona have any enemies among the STMA members?" Dawson asked, allowing a pause.

"Not that I know of." DeSouza pressed his lips together. "I cannot tell you how to do your job, but the likelihood of finding anyone on the STMA with motive enough to kill not only Fiona but her husband as well is very small. Disagreements occurred, yes, but this is entirely normal on a board such as this. In fact, it would have been odd if we *didn't* have any divergence of opinion."

"Thank you, sir. You've been very helpful."

"Do you know what I don't get, Inspector Dawson?" he said, looking exasperated. "I don't understand why you don't target obvious suspects instead of coming here over and over to ask these tedious questions."

"Obvious suspects like whom?"

"Take the simple example of that madman Reggie Cardiman at

Ezile Bay," DeSouza said with a backward flap of the hand. "He hated Smith-Aidoo's guts. He was the one person who would suffer from some of the development plans that Malgam Oil had in mind, and Charles was driving those plans. Wouldn't you want to get rid of the man if you were Cardiman? And what about the rumor that Fiona was having an affair? Have you followed that lead?"

Dawson sat up straight. "An affair with whom?"

"You're investigating this case, and you don't know this?" DeSouza said in disbelief. "I have no clue with whom she was supposed to be having an affair, Inspector. That's for you to find out, for goodness' sake. And even if I knew, I wouldn't want to sully the person's name."

"Well, you've at least partially sullied Cardiman," Dawson pointed out dryly. "You might as well keep going."

Too late, he realized that the last comment wouldn't go down well.

"Are you quite finished?" DeSouza said icily. "I have work to do."

"Yes, sir," Dawson said, standing up. "Thank you very much for your help. Apologies for taking up your time."

DeSouza grunted and didn't get up. At the door, Dawson turned. "One other question, sir. Did you hate Fiona Smith-Aidoo?"

He gave Dawson a cold stare. "After all that we have said, you have the utter gall to ask me such a thing? I will not dignify it with a response. Please be sure to shut the door behind you."

Nice man, Dawson thought sardonically as he left. Not a pleasant interview at all. Nevertheless, what DeSouza had had to say was interesting. First, the chief executive had pointedly drawn attention to Cardiman's animosity toward Charles, which Dawson had already realized, and then he had remarked upon a rumor that Fiona had been having an affair, which Dawson was hearing for the first time. Spurned lovers are no joke, he reflected. Adultery was fertile ground for a vicious murder in any number of directions.

Dawson wondered about DeSouza's motive in planting these "suspicions," and it raised at least a soft alert in his mind.

Baah had been chatting with the security guard as Dawson approached. "Where now, sir?" Baah asked as they got back into the car.

"It's time for lunch. Can we go somewhere to *chop?*"

"I know a good place at Market Circle."

"Good. Let's go. I'm hungry."

Chapter 13

AFTER LUNCH, BAAH TOOK Dawson to his meeting with Jason Sarbah. The steel and glass Malgam building resembled its counterpart in Accra, but it was smaller. Baah drove up to the double gates at the entrance and waited for the armed sentry to come out and grant them clearance. Baah entered the large car park at the center of which was a circular lawn with perfectly tended grass and a rotating triangular prism bearing the Malgam logo on each face.

Dawson hopped out, signed in at the sentry box, and went to the entrance. The lobby was spacious and quiet with a small bubbling fountain in one corner, large potted plants, and a waiting area with low-set leather seats. Dawson stopped at the front desk where two lovely young receptionists were sitting.

"Good afternoon, sir," one of them said.

He liked her full red lips. Her manicured fingernails were the same color.

"Good afternoon," he said. "Inspector Dawson to see Jason Sarbah."

"Please sign in and take a seat. I will let his office know."

She called up while Dawson wrote down his information in the large logbook on the countertop.

"You can go up now, sir," the receptionist said. "Here is your temporary ID badge. Please wear it in plain view around your neck during your entire visit and return it at the end. Security will escort you up."

The security man released the barrier arm and held it open. The lift took them to the fifth floor and another reception area behind a pair of automatic glass doors.

"Please have a seat," the pretty but ice-cold receptionist said. "Mr. Sarbah will be with you in a moment."

Jason Sarbah came out a few minutes later. He was late thirties, athletic, of medium height and skin tone, dressed in a light beige suit and matching tie, clean-shaven, and very good-looking.

"Inspector Dawson?" He smiled, but barely. "Pleased to meet you. Come this way and we can chat."

He followed Sarbah down a carpeted corridor with glass-enclosed offices on either side. Printed boldly on Sarbah's door was his title: DIRECTOR OF CORPORATE RELATIONS.

The office was spacious. His desk was glass-topped. He had a leather sofa, a water dispenser, a mini-bar, a coffee machine, and a bowl of fresh fruit.

"Do have a seat," he said, indicating the chair in front of the desk and sitting down in his executive leather chair on the opposite side. "So. Sekondi police have put out an SOS to help solve the Smith-Aidoo murder, is that it?"

"Yes. A petition was submitted. As the detective assigned to the case, I do have to go over territory that may already have been covered by Superintendent Hammond, so I apologize in advance if some of my questions have been asked before."

He nodded and appeared very willing. Not a shadow or a frown passed over his expression. "No problem, Inspector. I'll try to be of as much assistance as I can."

"If I'm correct," Dawson began, "up until his death, Charles Smith-Aidoo had the job which you now hold."

"Yes, that's right. He had been Corporate Relations Director at Malgam for almost two years."

"How did your filling his position come about after his murder?"

"When the position for corporate relations director was first advertised, I applied for it and was interviewed. I didn't get it—Charles did. I met Mr. Calmy-Rey at Charles's funeral, and we chatted. He invited me here to talk some more."

"And then?"

"Well, when I told him I had been after Charles's position, he promised to talk to some members of his team. They invited me back for another interview, and after about a week, they offered me the job."

Dawson found the description bland—made for mass consumption and therefore unsatisfying. "You must have impressed them in some way."

Sarbah leaned forward slightly and interlaced his fingers on the desk. "Let's say that they challenged me at the interview. They asked me to be frank. They gave me some tricky scenarios and asked me how I would handle them." He lowered his voice very slightly. "I had a feeling that their test cases were not completely fictional, and in fact after I started work, I did find certain types of conduct that I wanted to change."

This sounded interesting. "For example?"

"You may have heard of Reggie Cardiman."

"Yes."

"Mr. Cardiman's resort is practically legendary in the Western Region. He brings in money." Sarbah made a tower with his fingertips. "So, in my opinion, you have to give him due respect and handle him with diplomacy. The way Charles treated Mr. Cardiman, telling him that a tentative plan was in effect to move him off the land on which Ezile Bay sits, is not how I would have approached it. There are other ways to perhaps sweeten the conditions, or offer alternatives. Is it any wonder Mr. Cardiman had no love for him?"

"Have you spoken to Mr. Cardiman yourself?"

"Yes, by phone. For now the decision is not to aggressively pursue acquiring any land on Cape Three Points, whether Ezile or Akwidaa. I'm sorry, can I offer you something? A soft drink, water?"

"Water, thank you, sir."

Sarbah rose and went to the bar.

"Did you know Mr. Cardiman before you started with Malgam?" Dawson asked him.

"By name only," he said, opening the small refrigerator and taking out a bottle of Voltic. "I've never even been to the resort although I intend to at some point."

He poured the water out in a heavy glass and handed it to Dawson.

"Me too," Dawson said, pausing to take a few sips. It was very good. Voltic had the market cornered in Ghana.

Sarbah returned to his desk, giving Dawson the pause he needed before tackling a delicate matter. "I know about the story of your daughter, Mr. Sarbah, sir. I want to offer my condolences."

"Thank you." Sarbah's eyes softened and saddened, demonstrating to Dawson how deep his feelings went.

"Angela must have been very dear to you."

"She was our whole world," Sarbah said softly. "We adored her."

"Did you—do you—hold Dr. Smith-Aidoo responsible for her death?"

Sarbah unconsciously fiddled with a pen on his desk. "The doctor could have helped us." His tone was still professional, but it certainly was not neutral. Dawson heard the emotion creeping into it. "She should not have turned us away like that. I don't know how she can live with herself, knowing what she's done. Doctors are supposed to heal, not harm."

"You were angry and hurt."

"I think you would be too."

"To make matters worse," Dawson went on, so as not to lose momentum, "when you went to Charles Smith-Aidoo for financial assistance, he turned you down."

"He made up some excuse that he had just invested money and that he didn't have any liquid funds."

"You didn't believe that?"

Sarbah gave a small chortle. "No, of course not."

"Were you close to Charles? Why did you go to him in the first place?"

"I wasn't close, but he's still my cousin, right?" Sarbah said, opening his arms. He had large hands. "If you are able to help a family member, you do so. It's the Ghanaian way."

"I don't know any polite way to ask you this question, sir, but . . ."

"Did I want to avenge Angela's death by arranging the murder of Charles and his wife?"

"Oh," Dawson said in surprise. "Well, yes. That was what I was about to ask."

"The question has preceded you." Sarbah smiled. "Chief Inspector Hammond has already posed it and received the same answer. No, I didn't kill the Smith-Aidoos. On Monday, the seventh of July, I was at my real estate office all day."

His eyes were looking sincerely into Dawson's, and he didn't blink.

"Do you still have the real estate business?" Dawson asked.

"Yes, I do."

"May I ask where it is located, and can you give me the name of someone there who can confirm your whereabouts on the seventh of July?"

"Sure. The name of the business is Sarbah Properties, and it's on the second floor in the Providence Building not far from here. You can speak to my manager, or anyone in the office, for that matter."

"Okay." Dawson stood up. "Mr. Sarbah, thank you for taking the time."

"You're welcome," he said, standing as well and seeing Dawson to the door. He hesitated. "Look, Inspector, I want this mess cleared up too, and it doesn't do me any good to do a dance of deception around you. So, if there's anything you think I might be able to help with, please call."

"I appreciate that sir," Dawson said. He was just about to leave when something occurred to him. "Actually, there is something you might help me with. I'd like to meet with Mr. Calmy-Rey for a chat. Can that be arranged?"

"Yes, of course," Sarbah said. "I'll set that up for you and give you a call."

As he took the elevator down, Dawson reflected what a breath of fresh air Sarbah was, compared to DeSouza. Sarbah was open and willing. He had a smooth texture to his demeanor. DeSouza was the opposite—as rough and lacerating as barbed wire.

Nevertheless, as different as the two men were, they were both still suspects with strong motives. In both cases too, however, it would be difficult to prove their involvement because they appeared to have good alibis. If either of them had paid someone to carry out a contract killing, it would be tough to make that connection.

For a while at least, Dawson turned his mind to something soothing and joyful as he thought about the family joining him in a little more than a day. Christine and the boys would leave for Takoradi on Friday afternoon directly after school.

He called her as he walked to the car. "Are you getting ready?"

"Yes. Sly and Hosiah are very excited about the trip. They can't wait to see you."

After hanging up with Christine, Dawson called Reggie Cardiman and introduced himself.

"Oh, thank *God*, Inspector!" Cardiman's voice was as deep and projecting as if he were using a megaphone. "At last we have someone competent to clear this nasty thing up."

"How do you know I'm competent?" Dawson asked in some amusement.

"Come now, Mr. Dawson. I know about your solving the serial killer case in Accra. You must come to Ezile Bay Resort. I would like to meet you for a good chat."

Cardiman's British accent incorporated heavy Ghanaian inflections. He sounded hearty and friendly, nothing like the impression Dawson had formed from the minutes of the STMA meetings.

"That's why I was calling, in fact," Dawson said. "When are you available?"

"I'm here all the time. Just let me know when you plan to arrive."

"My wife and two boys are joining me from Accra tomorrow, and they would enjoy visiting Ezile Bay with me. What about Saturday? We could leave Takoradi in the morning."

"That would be perfect. I'll be looking forward to your visit."

It was almost three thirty. Dawson wanted to add one more item to the list of the day's accomplishments. He called the number Dr. Smith-Aidoo had given him for her Aunt Eileen. She didn't answer the first time, so he tried again. This time, someone picked up the call.

"Hello?"

"Is this Eileen Copper?"

"Yes." The voice was husky and monotone.

He introduced himself and told her he was investigating her brother's murder.

"Oh, really." Now her tone was cutting. "Well, I live in hope that you'll rise above the mediocrity of the Sekondi Police."

Everyone taking a swipe at Hammond and his team, Dawson thought. "Then I'm sure you're eager to help. I'd like to come and talk to you this afternoon."

She hesitated.

"Around five," Dawson pressed, not allowing her to stall.

"All right, Inspector."

Good. He was thinking ahead and planning the next steps. DS Chikata would be arriving the following day, and Dawson was looking forward to it. Together, they could get a lot done much faster, clear this mystery up, and get back home.

Chapter 14

A GIRL OF ABOUT ten years old showed Dawson into a dark, stuffy sitting room with dusty stacks of papers, books, and folders. His nose tickled and he sneezed twice. The room had one window dirtied by the red dust kicked up from the unpaved road outside.

"Please, I will go and call Auntie Eileen," she said, her voice barely a whisper.

"Thank you."

He chose not to sit on either of the two white plastic chairs, and instead peered at some of the dusty documents on the floor—psychology and biology papers taken from journals, and books on herbal medicines. With interest, he picked up a book called *A History of African Witchcraft* and skimmed through a few pages.

"Inspector Dawson?"

He turned to see a thin woman standing in the middle of the room.

"Mrs. Copper?"

"That is correct. How do you do?"

They shook hands. Hers was as rough as a dead leaf. He estimated her age around fifty. Her unprocessed hair was speckled with grey, and she wore a simple throw-on dress with a brown and white Ghanaian print. Obviously, she chose not to support her sagging breasts with a bra.

She pointed to the chair behind him. When he sat down, dust puffed up from the cushion and irritated his nose again. He suppressed an urge to sneeze.

"First of all," he said, "I want to express my condolences for your brother's death."

"Thank you." She half smiled, but it was bitter. "If only expressions of sympathy could resurrect a person. Next to my husband, Charles was the most important person in my life. So, yes, I am stricken, but I feared this was going to happen."

"Why?"

She blew breath through her relaxed lips so that they made a soft, fluttering sound of weary disapproval. "You know how our fellow Ghanaians behave. People, even your own family members, would rather tear you down than cheer you on for your achievements."

"Were there family members who were jealous of Charles's success?"

"My ne'er-do-well brother, Brian."

"Could he have killed Charles?"

"Could he?" She smiled. "Of course he could. Brian is a failure who was jealous of Charles and hated the fact that Sapphire's uncle had more to do with her success than her father."

"Doctor Smith-Aidoo told me about that," Dawson said, nodding. "Her aunt and uncle essentially rescued her from self-destruction."

"Yes," Eileen agreed. "And put her on the path to academic success."

"But I'm curious about something," Dawson said. "Presumably Brian was jealous of his brother for a long time. What would trigger him to murder Charles? Why then and not some other time?"

"Ah, good question, Inspector," Eileen said, lifting her index finger. "Did Sapphire also tell you all about the death of Jason Sarbah's daughter, Angela, and how that made Sapphire want to leave the private clinic at which she had been working?"

"Yes, she did."

"So once more, Charles came to her rescue and got her that job working on the rig." Eileen crossed one leg over the other and smoothed her dress. "One day, Brian calls Sapphire to ask how she's doing. Remember that they don't talk to each other much—they're practically estranged from each other. Sapphire lets him know that she has a new job, and Charles got it for her. 'Why didn't you tell me?' Brian wants to know. 'What difference would it make?' Sapphire asks."

"Ouch," Dawson said. "That must have been hurtful."

"Oh, yes—so painful that Brian calls his brother and begins to berate him for influencing Sapphire's career while deliberately excluding Brian, which of course angers Charles, who ends up calling his younger brother worthless and a number of adjectives in Fante that don't even have an equivalent in English."

Putting himself in Brian's position, Dawson could feel the kind of distress, even fury, that the man must have experienced. It wasn't that Brian could have added anything to his daughter's career move, it was simply the principle of being included in her affairs. And Dawson immediately thought of what he had done to *his* father: excluded him from his life. He didn't call him or visit him. Cairo had asked Dawson to consider warming back up to their father, and Dawson was going to have to make a decision quite soon.

He forced his thoughts away from his personal affairs. "Your niece, Dr. Smith-Aidoo tells me that you're a dedicated genealogist."

Eileen looked pleased. "One of my many interests, yes."

"To a large extent, Mrs. Copper, that's why I'm here. Aspects of the murder signature suggested family and ancestry might have played at least part of the motive."

"Call me Auntie Eileen. Everyone else does, even when I don't ask them to." She laughed, more like a dry cackle. "What do you know so far about the Smith-Aidoos?"

"Not much more than a little background on Charles and his wife, you, Brian, and Sapphire. She told me that after your mother was killed in a car crash in 1994, and she overheard Charles telling Auntie Fiona that there must be a curse on the Smith-Aidoo family. He said something like, 'First my grandparents and now my mother.' Sapphire wasn't sure what to make of that."

"We have shielded Sapphire from some of the more brutal elements of our family's history." Eileen paused, her eyes to the floor as she apparently deliberated on how best to frame what she was about to say. "Inspector, we don't like to talk about family murder, madness, or marital infidelities, and we have plenty of that. The first half of our name, Smith, is from Bartholomew Smith, an

English seaman born around 1872. His ship docked at Takoradi for a few weeks when he met and fell in love with a Ghanaian woman and married her. After her death in about 1921, he returned to England with his daughter, Bessie, who got married there in 1925 to a Tiberius Sarbah."

Dawson's interest was piqued at that. Sapphire had told him that Jason Sarbah and Charles Smith-Aidoo were first cousins with a common grandmother, Bessie Smith. Now Eileen was going one generation earlier to Bessie's father, Bartholomew. This was the kind of family history Dawson was looking for.

Eileen rose and picked her way through some folders and documents behind her chair. "I have a photograph of her I can show you."

She brought out two manila envelopes, took out a picture from one of them, and handed it to him.

"As you can see, she was very beautiful," she said, dragging her chair closer to his.

He examined the photo. Despite the faded sepia tone of the period, it was clear that the fair-skinned Bessie with her dark swept-up hair and large expressive eyes had been a woman of extraordinary beauty. She was dressed in a white lace blouse and a long, layered, dark skirt with lace trim.

"I see what you mean," he said, turning the photograph over. "Lovely. What about pictures of Tiberius, her husband?"

Eileen shook her head. "I have never located any. It could be Bessie destroyed them or didn't keep them or pass them along, because in 1940 she and Tiberius were divorced."

"Ah, I see," Dawson said. It stood to reason that Bessie would then abandon mementos of her marriage to Tiberius. "Why the divorce?"

Eileen looked regretful. "Again, I don't know."

"Did Bessie remarry?"

"Yes—to Robert E. Aidoo, or 'R.E.,' as people called him. Not long after that, she and R.E. left England to settle in Ghana—the then Gold Coast. So, Bessie came full circle back home. I have several pictures of R.E."

From the second envelope, Eileen pulled out about a dozen photos that she handed to Dawson. She stood over his shoulder as he sifted through the pictures of Bessie and R.E. singly and together, and two children close in age.

"These are their kids?" Dawson asked.

"Yes. This is Simon, my father, and his younger brother, Uncle Cecil."

Dawson admired their style. The children were solemn and smartly dressed. R.E. was unsmiling but dashing in a dark suit, white shirt with a wing collar, and tie in every picture. He appeared inscrutable and proper.

"I understand your father, Simon, has dementia."

Eileen sighed. "Yes. He stays here with me, and I take care of him with the help of a house girl."

"Does he speak?

"Some days more than others. He mostly asks who I am—over and over again."

"Sorry. That must be difficult for you."

"At times, but he doesn't become agitated, and I'm grateful for that."

"Is Uncle Cecil alive?"

She made an offhand gesture. "He lives in the UK somewhere. He's isolated, and we don't communicate."

The fractured nature of the Smith-Aidoo family struck Dawson. On the other hand, Eileen appeared devoted to Simon. He felt a twinge of guilt as he thought of his relationship with his father once again.

"Do you know the span of these photos of Bessie and R.E. and the children?" Dawson asked.

"About ten years."

"Bessie looks happy."

"Yes, I believe she was very much in love with R.E. I have a love letter she wrote to him while she was still with Tiberius. "Would you like to see it?"

"I would be honored."

She extracted it from the folder with even more care than she had shown with the photos. The letter was a single sheet of paper that had darkened and become brittle with age. The writing was cursive and careful, as though Bessie had gone through several drafts before the final product.

21st July, 1939

My dearest Bobby,

Ah! You left me alone yesterday, darling, with the lovely ring to com-
fort me. I kiss it every passing minute, and now my lips are golden.
Thank you for your kindness. I will not let HIM find it. It will stay in
a secret place until I am rid of HIM and we are together.

All my night was sleepless, dreaming of playing with my beloved. Are
you feeling as if I am by your side, darling? God bless your thoughts for
me. I do not know what more to say but hope to write a long one next
time.

> *Good-bye darling*
> *A big kiss to you,*
> *Bessie*

"I like the old-fashioned language," Dawson said with a smile. "By 'HIM,' I assume she was referring to Tiberius?"

"Yes, evidently."

So, by at least 1939, and maybe even earlier, Dawson reasoned, Bessie had been having an affair with R.E. Obviously he had been a dashing, attractive man, but surely it would have taken more than that to drive Bessie into his arms? What had been going on in her marriage that had encouraged her to stray? Another thought struck Dawson. "What about children?" he asked Eileen. "Did Bessie have any with Tiberius?"

She looked up at him from the letter, which she had been studying. "Only one that I know of—Richard Sarbah. I was told he had at least one sister, but I haven't confirmed that. Have you met Jason Sarbah?"

"Yes, I have."

"That's Richard's son—Charles's cousin. Richard lives not far away in New Amanful, a suburb of Takoradi. On one occasion several years ago, I tried to approach him for more information about Bessie, but he said he couldn't help me. He seemed bitter and resentful—angry, even—and I know the probable reason."

She went to the window and looked out at the street through the dusty patina and then turned to face Dawson with a look of distress.

"R.E. and Grandma Bessie were killed in 1952, more than ten years before I was born. They were murdered—hacked to death late one night as they slept."

Dawson was shocked. "Oh!"

"A brutal, bloody killing, Inspector," she said quietly, with so much emotion that the murder scene could have been right before them. "I can show you some newspaper articles I got from the archives at the university library."

She picked through some boxes until she found three clippings from a daily paper called *Gold Coast Times*. In the first, the murder of Bessie and R.E. Aidoo, "who met their ruthless and tragic death while in slumber," was a front-page news item.

The second clipping detailed how Bessie's ex-husband, Tiberius Sarbah, had been arrested for the crime. The third announced that he had been released and charges dropped, due to insufficient evidence. A witness had retracted his original story that he had seen Tiberius commit the crime. The newspaper speculated that the witness, who was reportedly a minor, might have been one of the two now-orphaned children, Simon or Cecil, who were eleven and nine respectively.

All that was fascinating, but something else excited Dawson. "Do you see it, Eileen?" he said, turning to her in earnest. "Do you know what I'm thinking?"

"I believe I do, Inspector," she replied, her eyes widening as she caught his fever. "You're wondering if the butchery of Bessie and R.E. in 1952, and the massacre of Charles and Fiona in July of this year could be connected."

"They're too alike *not* to be," Dawson said. "A husband and wife brutally murdered in both cases. It doesn't matter that they are far apart in time."

She smiled widely for the first time, showing several missing teeth. "You must be a divine gift, Inspector. I tried to make that case to Superintendent Hammond. He was not impressed—dismissed it at once."

That's the way it often was in Dawson's line of business. What struck one detective as important could appear trivial, or at least coincidental, to another.

"The question is," Dawson continued, "how could those two cases, so separate in time from one another, be related? Have you ever asked your father what he remembers about the events surrounding the murder?"

"Yes. Even before he became demented, he refused to talk about it and told me to put it out of my mind forever."

"I see," Dawson said, watching Eileen. He hadn't quite known what to make of her in the first minutes of their meeting each other, but now he liked her. "What about Richard Sarbah?" he asked her. "You think he'll talk to me?"

She seemed optimistic. "Between your charm and your authority, he might."

"Charm?" He laughed. "Well, thank you. Where can I find Richard?"

Eileen gave Dawson a set of directions, which he wrote down in his notebook.

"Something else I was wondering," he said. "How did the hyphenated surname 'Smith-Aidoo' come about?"

"Ah, okay," Eileen said with a smile, "that part I can help you with. Bessie wanted my father and Uncle Cecil to have the distinctive name of Smith-Aidoo, rather than plain Aidoo, and to pass it onto successive generations. For every Smith-Aidoo, there are probably about a hundred Aidoos, so it does stand out. Or perhaps she wanted to show off her English ties or to render a lasting recognition of that part of her heritage. Another indication that she cherished the Aidoo part of her, but not the Sarbah."

"Yes, I see what you mean," Dawson agreed, reflecting on all Eileen had been telling him. Clearly she relished talking, thinking, and wondering about her family history. Not everyone did. Dawson himself was not well versed in the details of his own past.

"Can I meet your father?" he asked her.

"Of course you can."

As they walked to the bedroom, Dawson again caught sight of the textbook on witchcraft. He picked it up. "I noticed this when I came in. Another area of interest for you?"

She nodded. "Yes."

Dawson flipped through the pages. "Do you believe in witchcraft?"

"Yes," she said, cocking her head, "but it's like magic. Most magic is tricks. Only a rare instance is true magic."

Dawson thought about his investigation about two years ago in a village called Ketanu, where the death of a female medical student had been ascribed to witchcraft.

"What about Charles's death?" he asked Eileen. "Witchcraft?"

She shook her head. "No."

"Why not?"

She stuck out her lower lip in thought. "Too tangible," she said finally. "A good witchcraft death is subtle and mysterious—as if a physical hand never touched the victim. That's because the death takes place originally in the astral realm where the witches go at night."

Dawson nodded in understanding. He'd had his lessons on witchcraft in Ketanu. "What about human sacrifice?"

Now Eileen looked troubled. "Perhaps. They removed his tongue and his eye. Bad signs of ritual."

"You said 'they.' Who are 'they'?"

She stared at him. "Would you like to know what I honestly believe?"

"Yes, I would."

"Cardiman wants his business to continue to prosper without any external interference from the likes of Malgam Oil and so do the fishermen. I think he paid two or more fishermen to kill my brother. In murdering him, they chose to make it a human sacrifice, or at least make it seem so. I believe you will find the answer to this crime at Cape Three Points."

Chapter 15

EILEEN SHOWED DAWSON INTO the bedroom she shared with her father. Sitting in a rusty wheelchair behind a small table, he was a tiny man laid waste by dementia and immobility. He was completely bald, his scooped-out temples betraying how malnourished he was. The house girl was trying to persuade Simon, who was now almost toothless, to eat some *akasa*, a porridge made from fermented corn, but like a stubborn child, he wasn't having any of it.

He looked at Eileen and in Fante said, "Who are you? You can't build anything here, by order of the Sekondi-Takoradi Metropolitan Assembly."

"He was a land and housing inspector for the city," she explained to Dawson. "Papa, it's me, Eileen."

He stared at her, and for a moment realization appeared to dawn in his expression, but then he said, this time in English, "Who are you? You can't build a house here."

The caretaker held a spoonful in front of Simon's mouth and coaxed him. The old man opened his mouth, seemed to accept the *akasa*, but a few seconds later spat it out in a far-reaching spray.

"Oh, Papa," Eileen said chidingly. "What am I going to do with you?"

Unperturbed, she wiped her father's mouth while the caretaker cleaned up the table.

"He's been doing this spitting thing the whole week," Eileen said to Dawson. "Don't ask me why."

"Can you ask him what happened to his mother and father?"

"All right. I doubt he will answer, but here goes." She stood closer to him and spoke more slowly. "Papa, what happened to Mummy and Daddy?"

"I can have you arrested for building here," he said. "I have complete authority. Who are you?"

Eileen sent Dawson a rueful look. "Do you want to try?"

His efforts also proved fruitless as Simon gave him the same repetitive reply and then fell into silence.

She looked regretful. "Sorry. You won't get much, if anything, out of him."

"It's okay," Dawson said. "I understand." He was wondering if his father would get to this stage, and with another stab of guilt he realized that Jacob could well be approaching it without Dawson's knowledge.

Eileen accompanied him to the door. He thanked her for her time.

"Let me know if I can help any further," she said.

As he returned to the car, he noticed someone getting out of a battered Toyota on the other side of the street, and his blood went cold for a moment as he thought he was seeing the ghost of Charles Smith-Aidoo. He recognized him from the photograph in Charles's study. Then he realized that the man must be Brian, his brother. They were quite alike. He was walking at a hurried, agitated pace into Eileen's house. Dawson followed, and by the time he got to the door, she and Brian were locked in an argument. Dawson stood listening to one side of the doorframe.

"I don't say anything that isn't true, do I?" she said heatedly. "Just answer my question. *Do I?*"

"You don't have to spoil my name in front of my own daughter," he said sharply. His voice had a nasal, stuffy quality. "You told Sapphire that everything she has become is because of Charles and not me."

"Look me in the eye and tell me it's not true," she challenged.

"Of course it's not!" he shouted. "Why are you trying to destroy any little chance I have with her? I did what I thought was best back then."

"Best for you, not best for her."

Dawson heard the sound of a hard slap and Eileen crying out. And another slap in quick succession. He stepped into the doorway, expecting to see Eileen hurt by her brother's hand. Instead, the two were grappling with each other, arms intertwined and hands at each other's throats. She was taller than he was and quite possibly just as strong.

"*Stop*," Dawson said. He came closer. "Stop, or you'll both go to jail."

That distracted them enough for him to sever the grip they had on each other and separate them.

"She's a crazy woman!" Brian yelled, pointing at his sister as Dawson firmly pulled him back. "She's a witch!"

"And you are a fool," she jeered.

"You sit down here and don't move," Dawson told Brian. To Eileen he said, "Take a seat over there."

"You must be Inspector Dawson," Brian said dispassionately.

"Yes. What's going on here?"

"He slapped me, and so I slapped him back," Eileen said, almost casually.

"She insulted me," Brian said.

"And so you think you can just slap me like that?" She looked at Dawson. "I didn't even insult him. He's angry because when his daughter was here a couple of days ago, and we were reminiscing about Charles. We agreed that she owed everything to her uncle. "

Brian aimed a finger at her. "No, that's not all you said. You told her that I had just wanted to get rid of her, and that is not true. Why do you insist on saying that to her?"

Eileen turned to Dawson, almost as if her brother wasn't there. "Brian conceived Sapphire out of wedlock when he was barely nineteen—a mere boy. He fell in love with this raving beauty of an Englishwoman, Constance, some ten years older than he, and she turned out to be crazy. Brian was immature and couldn't handle parenthood, let alone a psychotic wife." Eileen opened her arms with her palms up, as if appealing to a judge. "So Brian asked Charles for help, and he took over Sapphire's care. That's the truth, and it's also the truth that he and Fiona shaped Sapphire more than Brian did. What have I said so far that is insulting?"

"But the way she's expressing it to you is not how she says it to *Sapphire*," Brian said plaintively to Dawson. "When it comes to her niece, Eileen does her very best to paint me as some kind of criminal. And why does she do this? Because instead of asking her to take care of Sapphire all those years ago when I was having so much trouble with Constance, I turned to Charles for help. That's why she resents me so much."

"Oh, that is not true," Eileen said, rolling her eyes.

"It's very true," Brian said quietly, leveling his gaze at her. "You know it is. And you became more and more resentful as the years went by because you were barren—childless to this day."

That was new information for Dawson. He wondered, had the infertility been her's or her husband's, or both? In Ghana, being childless was very troubling for a woman, her spouse, and the extended family. Rumors of a curse on the woman could rise quickly, and an older woman who had never had children often fit the profile of a witch because as the theory goes, she kills the fetus in her womb and shares it with the members of her coven. As Dawson had discovered in Ketanu, it could lead to isolation of the barren woman, threats to her life, and ultimately murder. Witch sanctuaries existed in northern Ghana, but the word "sanctuaries" belied their hellishness.

"I have made my peace with it," Eileen said curtly. "At least I don't have a daughter who despises me the way yours does."

With a kind of low whimper, Brian stood up again and began to menacingly approach her, but Dawson deflected him toward the door. "Let's go outside. Come on."

He took Brian out of his sister's earshot. He was shaking and hyperventilating, his face swollen with anger.

"Relax, man, relax," Dawson said, placing his hand on Brian's back. "Take it easy."

Just like his older brother, Charles, Brian had a bald patch beating a path through the center of his scalp with tufted hair on either side like the parted Red Sea.

"Why do you allow yourself to get so flustered?" Dawson asked.

"I don't know," he said with disgust. "It has always been this way. When we were kids, she teased and bullied me until I was sometimes in tears. And now she pounds it into me every chance she gets." He smashed his right fist into his left palm repeatedly. "'You're a failure, you're a failure,' over and over again."

Dawson noticed his slumped, resigned posture. "And do you think you're a failure?"

His eyes clouded and became moist, and he withered some more. "I may not be one, but I feel I have let my daughter down. I feel I've lost her and will never get her back."

"Not get her back from your older brother?"

Brian looked up sharply. "What do you mean?"

"Charles has rescued your daughter a lot. He saved her in secondary school and put her on the road to success. You were left out of big pieces of Sapphire's life while Charles took charge of her, and even in her adulthood, it has been happening. Earlier this year, it happened again. Charles got Sapphire a job on the Malgam oil rig, but neither of them told you about it."

Brian looked away, a slash of pain striking his expression. "He deliberately excluded me as much as he could. He put the knife in me, and he twisted it side to side."

Dawson paused, watching the spectacle of wretchedness before him. "You called him after you found out about Sapphire's new job," he said, "and when you tried to take Charles to task, he insulted you. Was that the last straw? Was that as much as you could take?"

"You're asking me whether I killed my brother," Brian said wearily. "Honestly, I felt like doing it. But no, I didn't."

"Where were you on Monday, the seventh of July, the day Charles and Fiona were killed?"

"At home."

"Where is home?"

"The Cocoa Marketing Board flats. I work for the CMB. I stayed home that day. I suffer from gout and was having a bad attack."

"Can anyone else confirm that you stayed home on both days?"

"I don't think so. I live alone."

"Do you own a pistol, or have you ever used one?"

"No," he said, looking startled. "Never."

"Did you hire someone to kill your brother?"

Brian pulled his head back. "Of course not."

"Do you know anyone who wanted him dead?"

"Any of the people who hated him, Inspector Dawson." He shrugged. "Environmentalists, fishermen and their advocates, all kinds of meddling NGOs in Ghana and from abroad—the whole bunch of them. Basically, anyone who hates the entire oil industry. Charles was one of its most public faces."

"What about a more personal vendetta against the Smith-Aidoo family as a whole?" Dawson asked.

"I don't know anything about that," Brian said, his voice weak.

"Do you know Richard Sarbah? The son of Tiberius Sarbah?"

"Sarbahs are all over the place in Takoradi, and whichever one that is, I don't particularly care. Are you done with me, Mr. Dawson? I'm sorry, but my gout is beginning to flare up. I have to get home now."

"Thank you, sir. Oh, one other thing—your phone number."

Brian supplied it and then limped away as his gout got the better of him. Dawson watched the troubled, confused man leaving.

Chapter 16

DARKNESS HAD FALLEN BY the time Baah and Dawson reached New Amanful. Its name spoke to its recentness as a suburb. Very little street lighting existed, and the brand new single-family homes and gated communities in the middle of untended, overgrown plots appeared as looming, bulky shadows. With its proximity to the beach, the suburb was prime real estate, but not all of it was new-fangled construction. In contrast, the original Amanful was an old fishing community clinging to the shore with its shacks, canoes, and non-potable water.

As they bumped along the unpaved road, Dawson fed Baah the directions Eileen had provided, but the house with a green gate that she had described as their final destination never materialized. They pulled up alongside a lone pedestrian walking toward the beach and asked if he could help. The man gave them another set of tortuous directions to the residence he asserted was Richard Sarbah's. Praying that the man was right, they set off again, and after one or two wrong turns, they found it. Baah pumped his horn twice. A man peeped out through the crack between the two halves of the gate and came out, approaching in the beam of the headlights and coming around to Baah's window. Dawson realized with surprise that the guard was Forjoe.

"Forjoe!" he exclaimed, switching on the car's interior light. "It's me, Inspector Dawson."

Forjoe peered in at him. "Ei, Inspector! Good evening!"

"You work here?"

"Yes, please," Forjoe said, smiling.

"Is this Richard Sarbah's house?"

"Yes." A worried look came to his face. "Is there any problem?"

"Not at all. I'm just paying a visit. Is he in?"

Forjoe hesitated. "He's in, but I have to check if he's available. Please, I'm coming."

He walked quickly back into the house, returning about five minutes later to open the gate so that Baah could pull into the front yard. The one-story house was a decent size with a white exterior tarnished by the red dust of the unpaved road outside. Within the compound, someone had been working on a water pipe in a deep hole underneath the wall that enclosed the property. A toolshed stood in the corner of the compound.

"Like I told you before," Forjoe said, as Dawson followed him in, "the fishing business is not paying enough these days, so I do extra work as a watchman. I've been knowing Mr. Sarbah since I was a small boy. He's a good man—something like an uncle to me."

"I see," Dawson said. "So is he the one you mentioned to me who is helping you with your daughter Marvelous?"

"Yes, please."

"How is she doing?"

Forjoe was visibly troubled. "Not so well, but I pray that God will continue to help us."

Dawson hoped the prayers were answered. He understood the kind of anguish the man was going through.

Forjoe showed Dawson into a dimly lit, stuffy sitting room.

"Please, you can have a seat. He will come just now."

Dawson chose a pair of old angular wooden armchairs with square cushions. They didn't make furniture like this anymore. Now it was all overstuffed sofas and chairs in imitation leather. He looked around the room. It was clean, if a little shabby. The building was obviously much older than the structures that now populated New Amanful. Some old family pictures sat on a bookcase, a small TV in one corner, a worn rug on the linoleum floor. The mosquito netting on the windows needed renewing.

He heard a soft sound and turned to see Richard Sarbah entering the room. He was of average height but exceptionally solid in the chest and shoulders. His hair was jet black, and Dawson thought he must dye it. If his son, Jason, was in his mid to late forties, Richard had to be in his early seventies, at least. On the other hand, he appeared youthful in posture, and his age was difficult to place from his appearance alone.

"Mr. Sarbah?" Dawson rose from his chair.

"Yes, please. You say your name is?"

"Dawson. Inspector Darko Dawson."

"Ah, I see." He had a slightly hoarse voice, but it didn't trigger Dawson's senses. They shook hands.

"Please, have a seat." Sarbah sat in a facing chair. "I don't usually accept visits from strangers, especially at this time of the night, but Forjoe tells me you're a friend."

"Yes," Dawson said, going along with it. "I'm investigating the murder of Charles and Fiona Smith-Aidoo."

His face revealed a flicker of interest. "So what can I help you with?"

"Jason Sarbah at Malgam Oil is your son, is that correct, sir?"

"Yes. Is something wrong?"

"Not at all," Dawson said pleasantly. "Just checking that I have the right Sarbah. As part of my investigation, sir, I've been looking into the Smith-Aidoos' and Sarbahs' past. I understand Tiberius and Bessie were your parents?"

"Yes."

"Your father was once accused of killing Bessie and Robert, is that correct?"

Sarbah closed his eyes and rubbed his brow slowly, as if he had a headache. "Please, Inspector Dawson, this is not a memory I enjoy discussing."

"I understand it must be painful," he said gently. He was going to be empathetic, but he wouldn't let Richard evade any questions either. "However it's important. I was ordered here by CID Headquarters to assist the Sekondi police with the investigation, so that's what I must do. Any details you can provide are much appreciated, Mr. Sarbah."

"And if I choose not to?"

Dawson remained polite. "Then there are one or two options. I can return daily to question you, which will become quite tiresome—for you, not for me. Or would you prefer to join me at the police station for interrogation?"

"Very well." He sighed. "My father Tiberius married Bessie Smith in England in 1925. They had two children—my sister, Abigail, and me. I never knew her because she died of meningitis in 1932, and I was born in 1938. Bessie and Tiberius divorced each other in 1940."

"By that time," Dawson said in a neutral a tone as possible, "your mother was already having an affair with Mr. R.E. Aidoo, is that correct?"

Sarbah looked resentful. "Yes, that is so," he admitted.

"I've been wondering," Dawson said measuredly, "what tore your parents apart and drove your mother to R.E."

"I don't know for sure. No one actually told me, and I don't remember. I was only two years old at the time, after all—too young to understand. In retrospect, irreconcilable differences and my father's drinking, perhaps."

"He was an alcoholic?"

Sarbah grimaced. "Yes. I'm not sure how severe it was at the time of the divorce, but in later years the alcohol became lethal."

"I'm sorry," Dawson said quietly. "R.E. and your mother had Simon and Cecil, your half brothers?"

"Yes, R.E. had returned to Takoradi with my mother and me in 1942. Simon was born in 1943 and Cecil in 1945."

"Did you get along well with your half brothers?" Dawson asked gently, fearing that he may be treading on sensitive ground too soon.

"Let's just say things could have been better and leave it at that," Sarbah said, tensely tapping the side of his thigh.

"What about Tiberius?" Dawson asked. "When did he come back to Takoradi from the UK?"

"In 1948."

"I'm sure he wanted to see you," Dawson said encouragingly.

"Of course he did. I was his son, and I wanted to see him too, but . . ."

Sarbah shifted his weight and Dawson waited.

"But R.E. and Bessie conspired to prevent us from being with each other."

Dawson could feel the bitterness that Eileen had ascribed to Sarbah. He had a seething anger. "Why do you think that?"

He shrugged, but it was unresolved pain he was expressing, not nonchalance. "R.E. and Bessie hated my father. I remember hearing how R.E. once humiliated Daddy in public—called him a 'drunken failure.'"

"How old were you at the time?"

"Twelve, thirteen—something like that. Two years before the murder. I presume you've been told about that?"

"Yes—1952?"

"Yes, sir. I was fourteen, Simon was eleven, and Cecil was nine. The three of us slept in the same room at one end of the house, R.E. and Bessie at the other. In the middle of the night, someone stole in through the screen window of their bedroom, butchered their bodies, and slashed their throats. Bessie screamed before she was slain, and Simon heard her. He woke me up and we ran to the room and saw it . . ." Sarbah shuddered.

"I'm sorry," Dawson said with feeling. "A child should never see anything like that. Cecil too?"

Sarbah shook his head. "I wouldn't let him go into the room."

"Good man," Dawson said approvingly.

"At first I couldn't understand what had happened," Sarbah went on, anguish on his face. "I saw blood, so much of it everywhere—on the bed, on the floor, on the walls—and then I saw my mother's eyes were still open, looking at me and begging me to save her. I'll never forget that. I saw red spraying from her neck, and I heard a gurgling sound and realized she was breathing through a gash in her throat. I remember saying, 'Mama' several times as I went to her and tried to lift her up in my arms, but her head fell back . . ."

Sarbah stopped talking. He was gulping down air in an apparent effort to control the grief that must have been as fresh as it had been that horrific night when he was only a young teenager. Dawson got up from his chair and kneeled down beside him.

"Take it easy, sir," he said quietly. "Take a rest. You don't need to finish it all right now."

Sarbah fell back in his chair and took three deep breaths, as if trying to calm himself.

"Would you like some water?" Dawson asked.

Sarbah waved that away. "I'm okay." He smiled wanly. "Now you understand why I don't like to talk about this."

"I do understand. I had no idea you had been through such a terrible trauma."

"The murder itself was only the beginning of the nightmare," Sarbah said, his voice even huskier than before. "You must be aware through your work, Inspector, how two or more eyewitnesses to the same crime can report completely different versions of what happened."

Dawson, transferring to a chair closer to Sarbah's than the original one, said, "I know the problem only too well."

"Well, there you are. What I saw was not the same as what Simon said *he* saw. Our parents' bedroom was dark when he and I got there. I believe I was in front of him—in fact I'm sure of it. He claimed I turned on the light, but I don't remember doing that. I thought *he* switched it on at the wall after I had already entered the room. In any case, the first thing I recall seeing then were the bodies of my mother and stepfather, but Simon reported to the police that he saw a man leaving through the window, the same way he must have come in."

"And he identified the man as Tiberius," Dawson said, taking an educated guess.

"Yes, sir. The police questioned us over and over. I swore, and still do, that I never saw anyone else in the room—let alone my father— but Simon insisted."

"Tiberius was taken into custody?"

"Yes, and interrogated for hours on end." Sarbah looked directly at Dawson. "He denied he had anything to do with the killing, and I believe him till this day. Lots of things about Simon's story didn't add up. Did he see the man holding a weapon—a knife or machete? At first he said a knife, but then he changed his story and it was a machete. What was the man wearing? Simon couldn't remember. Was the man bloody? 'Yes, I think so.' Why didn't your half brother, Richard, also see this man? 'I don't know.' His story was not holding up. Daddy didn't have a great alibi, but neither could the police place him at the murder site."

"The charges were eventually dropped?"

"Yes, but by then, the investigation had dragged on, and Daddy had been in prison for three or four months. He lost friends; he lost his job. When he got out, he was a crushed man. He drank more heavily than he ever had and ate almost nothing. I saw him lose kilos by the day and wither away. In 1960 he committed suicide by hanging."

In the gloomy room, Dawson could see Sarbah's eyes moisten and swell. "I'm very sorry to hear that, sir."

"In effect," Sarbah said morosely, "the accusation, the imprisonment, the disgrace all slowly tortured him to death, and I blame Simon for it because he falsely accused Daddy."

"Could it be that he did see someone in the room whom he misidentified?"

"No," Sarbah said, his jaw set like stone. "He deliberately made it up."

"Why would a boy make up a story like that?" Dawson asked.

"Spite," Sarbah snapped, as though the word was poison he had to disgorge. "He was a malevolent child who hated me and hated my father, not the least because R.E. had a running tirade against Tiberius that he let his children hear and breathe day in, day out."

In his mind, Dawson wondered instead whether Simon might have blurted Tiberius's name under suggestive police questioning. Tiberius was probably a fairly strong suspect at the time, given the public displays of antagonism between him and R.E. Sometimes a frightened child says what he thinks adults want to hear. Apart from that, Dawson knew of many cases in which one detective, particularly the most senior on the team, pressures his junior officers to focus on a particular suspect and either get a confession or a solid accusatory statement from an eyewitness.

"The murder was never solved?" he asked Sarbah.

"Never," he said, shaking his head slowly in sad disgust.

"Who then took care of you and your half brothers?"

"We were split up between R.E.'s siblings—I went to a sister of his, and Simon and Cecil went to a brother."

"What was your experience like with your step-aunt?"

Sarbah curled his lip. "I hated it. She treated me as if I wasn't there."

"Did you see your half siblings much after that?"

"Yes, but we didn't speak."

Dawson reflected for a while on this man's joyless life ridden with trauma, death, and neglect. No wonder he was angry. The question was whether he was angry enough to kill.

Sarbah stood up and went to the sideboard in his dining area and removed two framed photographs from the top of it.

"That's my father and me," he said, handing the first one to Dawson. "I was about six at the time."

The picture was a rather faded one in sepia. Still, the resemblance between Richard and his father was easy to see. Tiberius was squarely built with widely set facial features. He and his son were smartly dressed for the picture and showed the usual solemn expressions of the time. People didn't smile much for photographs back then.

Sarbah gave him the second picture, which was in full color and more modern in quality. "And that's Barbara, my wife; Jason; and me."

She was plump with a soft face. Jason, about nineteen in this photo, got his light skin was from her. Richard, well-built back then at around fifty, Dawson estimated, had evidently kept his strong physique and youthful features.

"That's nice," Dawson said, studying the photograph. "Do you have a lot of pictures?"

"Yes," he said, opening one of the sideboard doors to reveal a stack of photo albums. "All in there. Perhaps one day when we have more time, I'll show them to you."

"I would like that," Dawson said. He was thinking that much of the pictorial family history involving Tiberius, which Eileen so lacked, was probably all here with Richard Sarbah. "Is your wife around?"

"Barbara and I have been separated for years." Surprisingly, Sarbah chuckled. "No sympathy required. It was for the best."

"Besides Jason, do you have any other children?"

Sarbah's face lit up. "No. He's my only child. I'm proud of my boy and what he has done for himself. He's a gem."

That made Dawson think of Hosiah, then of Sly, and finally of children in general and what they did to a parent's heart and soul. "I heard about Angela, your granddaughter," he said quietly.

Sarbah stared at the floor, anguish in his face. "When she died, a part of me died with her. Jason was broken. I was afraid he might kill himself. I prayed to God—don't let what happened to my father happen to my son. I persuaded Jason to stay with me here for a while so I could support him and keep an eye on him. I would do anything for my boy."

"I admire you for that," Dawson said. "You might even have saved his life."

"But I couldn't save Angela's," Sarbah said sadly.

"Maybe no one could have saved her."

"There were people who could have," Sarbah said dejectedly, "but they turned Jason away."

"You mean Charles and Dr. Smith-Aidoo."

"Yes."

"Forgive me—I'm not trying to be offensive, but did Jason ever express a desire to take revenge on them?"

Sarbah dismissed that with a wave of the hand. "Not only is he not that kind of person, he didn't even have the strength. He was in deep depression. He wouldn't eat. He shed kilos the same way my father did. I was afraid."

"Both of you went through a terrible ordeal."

"As terrible as it was, life goes on. Have you spoken to my son?"

"I have. I can tell he is still in pain."

"He is. I feel for him."

"And maybe you were angry enough with Charles to hire two or three men to kill him?"

Sarbah snorted derisively. "If I ever decided to kill someone, Inspector, you can be sure that I wouldn't hire anyone to do it."

Dawson watched him carefully. "Mr. Sarbah, can you tell me where you were on Monday, the seventh of July and the following day, the eighth, when the bodies of the Smith-Aidoos were found?"

"That Monday Forjoe and I went to Tarkwa to look into buying some gold. We stayed overnight and returned Tuesday evening. Everyone was talking about the Smith-Aidoos when we got back. You're welcome to check with Forjoe about the trip. He'll confirm it."

Dawson stood up. "Thank you for your time, sir."

"Not at all. I'll see you out."

After Sarbah had said goodbye, Baah pulled out of the front yard.

"Drive slowly just a little bit and then stop," Dawson told him.

He got out and walked quietly back to the house, listening for a moment for any conversation between Sarbah and Forjoe. He heard none. That's what Dawson wanted—to talk to Forjoe alone.

"Forjoe!" he called out softly. "It's me, Dawson."

"Yes, sir?" Forjoe said from the other side. He opened the gate again a crack.

"I forgot to ask you something. Do you remember the day those people, Charles and Fiona Smith-Aidoo, were kidnapped and then killed? It was the seventh of July, and they were coming from Ezile Bay."

"Hmm," Forjoe said, considering. "Eh-heh, yes, I remember now."

"It was a Monday. Do you remember where you were that day?"

"Yes, I went with massa to Tarkwa. We were looking into setting up some gold business, and we came back on Tuesday evening. I remember because when we came back, everybody was talking about what happened."

Dawson nodded. "Okay, thanks."

He trotted back to the car, satisfied. Richard Sarbah was not on his list of suspects.

Chapter 17

AFTER DINNER, DAWSON PLAYED his mbira for a while until the electricity abruptly cut. He heard the drone of the Stellar Hotel's generators as they automatically switched on.

"Oil City, no lights," he muttered, sitting at the side of the bed. He had a strong desire to smoke some marijuana, or "*wee*," as it was popularly known. He wondered where one could get some in Takoradi. The wife and kids weren't around. This was a good time to do it. He growled at himself for thinking about it and then began to bargain with himself. If he smoked some *wee*, he might see things in this murder case more clearly. That's what had happened to him in the last investigation.

Stupid. He gave himself a mental slap across the face. *You are not going out to hunt for marijuana.* It disturbed him that he was even contemplating the idea. What he needed right now was some light, some noisy TV, and a couple of boisterous kids to keep him busy and banish these cravings. It was too dark, too quiet, and he was lonely.

His mind swung back to the investigation. Multiple locations were involved in the Smith-Aidoo murders. Dawson needed to see the site of the presumed ambush and kidnapping a few kilometers away from Ezile Bay. The killers might have shot their victims there, but he doubted that. He believed they had taken them to some secluded beach and murdered them there. That too, if Dawson ever found it, would become a crime scene. After that, they had been launched out to sea, ending up at the *Thor Sterke* oil rig sixty kilometers off-shore. Dawson would be able to investigate the ambush area when he visited Ezile over the weekend, and in time, he hoped to find the location of the beach from which the canoes launched. He propped himself up on his elbow. What about the perimeter around the Mal-gam oil rig where the canoe had drifted bearing the two dead bodies? It was analogous to a situation on land in which someone is murdered in one location and their body is dumped in another. Therefore, the area surrounding the oil rig had been a crime scene. The importance of thoroughness was not lost on Dawson. Neither Hammond nor any of his team had gone out to the rig, but as a good detective, Dawson felt he had to do everything in his power to get there, especially if he was one day to appear in court to testify against the Smith-Aidoos' murderer. Dawson had seen too many detectives go down in flames as the defendant's solicitor made a mockery of the fact that they hadn't familiarized themselves with the crime scene.

As Dawson drifted off to sleep, he thought eagerly about the next day, Friday. Chikata, his detective sergeant, would be coming up to Takoradi, and later in the day—best of all—Christine and the boys. Dawson could hardly wait.

AT 6:45 FRIDAY morning, Dawson received a call from Chikata that he and the driver were already on the road and should be in Tadi within two hours.

Oh, Dawson thought, *he has a driver while I got the cramped, smelly State Transport bus.*

"Very good," he said. "Do you have accommodations while you're here?"

"Yeah," Chikata said lightly. "My uncle knows one of the managers at Stellar Hotel, so I'll be staying there for free."

Dawson was stunned. While he had had to find his own accommo-dations, his junior officer would be staying in a fancy hotel? For *free*? This is the royal treatment you get when your chief superintendent was your doting uncle.

"I hear say some beautiful women dey," Chikata said, switching to his beloved pidgin.

"Maybe, but they are all escorts for the white oil engineers," Dawson said bluntly. "They're not interested in the likes of you and me. Anyway, you're coming here to work, not play."

"Yes, massa," Chikata said, humbly, but Dawson could hear the mischief in his voice.

It was past nine when he phoned Dawson again. The police drove notoriously fast, so it was no surprise Chikata had made such good time.

"I've arrived at the hotel," he said. "Room Three Eleven."

"All right. I'll be there soon."

Dawson walked across the street and went up the staircase to the third floor. Chikata opened the door to his knock and blinked in amazement. "Massa, how did you get here so fast?"

Dawson smiled enigmatically. "Magic. No actually, I'm staying right opposite the hotel on the other side of the street."

"Oh, I see." Chikata laughed. "You are welcome. Come in."

Natural light illuminated the room through a large window that looked out onto the landscaped grounds. Two large beds faced the widescreen TV, which Chikata had tuned to a movie channel. He had set his laptop on the writing desk. The whisper-quiet air conditioner high up on the wall had the room deliciously chilled.

"Enjoying life, eh?" Dawson said with a hint of envy.

Chikata laughed again. At twenty-nine years old, he consistently turned women's heads with his powerful build and bold, granite-chiseled facial features.

"Would you like a Malta?" he asked, knowing his boss's favorite well.

"For sure," Dawson said, brightening.

"I ordered some for you from the restaurant."

He got a bottle out of the mini-fridge and tossed it to Dawson, who caught it with one hand. Chikata took a bottle of water for himself. If he couldn't drink beer, he drank water.

"Okay," Dawson said, "turn off the TV and let's get started."

He sat in the desk chair while Chikata perched on the love seat in the corner to listen to the briefing. The sergeant had seen the now infamous picture of the impaled head, but he knew very few other details. At Dawson's account of his meetings with DeSouza, Chikata gave a one-sided smile.

"The most indignant guys are sometimes the most guilty," he observed.

"True," Dawson agreed.

He related his encounter with Hammond, warning Chikata to watch his step when dealing with the superintendent.

"Okay," Chikata said. "I'll be careful. So, what's next?"

"I want to go to Takoradi Tech to double-check DeSouza's alibi. Baah can drop me off there, and you continue with him."

"What am I going to do?"

"I've been looking at the family angle of this murder," Dawson explained, leaning forward. "Now it's time to find out whether traditional religious beliefs played a part—*juju*, witchcraft, ritual sacrifice, and so on. I want you to dig around fetish priests, shrines, and the like for any inside information relevant to the murder. In the past year, has anyone visited a shrine to ask for guidance for a problem for which the solution was to sacrifice Charles and/or his wife? And we want to know the significance of a severed head on a stake."

Chikata let out a mild expletive. "You go to Tech, but I have to go to these *juju* people? What kind of welcome is that?"

"But you're so good at that kind of thing," Dawson said, grinning.

Chikata looked thoughtful for a moment. "I don't think there's any kind of *juju* involved in this case," he declared.

"Why do you say that?"

He shrugged. "It's just my impression."

"Impression!" Dawson exclaimed. "You've just arrived on the case, you have been here barely one hour, and you're already tossing impressions around?"

Chikata threw his head back and laughed, showing a set of perfect white teeth. Dawson found a scrap of paper on the desk, balled it up, and threw it accurately at the Sergeant's head.

"I say no *juju* at all involved in this case," Chikata asserted. "You say yes. We'll see who is right."

•　•　•

CHIKATA'S CHAUFFEUR HAD had to return to his duties in Accra, so Baah would get to keep his post as driver for the detectives. He was waiting for them downstairs in the car park. After Dawson had introduced him to Chikata, he got into the front passenger seat and Chikata sat in the rear.

As they set off, Dawson called Jason Sarbah to ask a question. "Technically, the *Thor Sterke* oil rig is a part of the crime scene. How can I visit the rig?"

"That might be difficult," Sarbah said, after a short pause.

"Why is that?"

"A lot of regulations. For example, there can only be a certain number of people on the rig at one time. If you come on, we have to pull someone off."

"I see."

"And also, you have to get underwater training before you can step foot on the rig."

Dawson frowned. "Underwater training?"

"One goes to the rig by helicopter, so everyone has to go through HUET—Helicopter Underwater Escape Training."

Dawson felt a little faint. "Oh."

"Can you swim?"

Dawson's hearing had shut down as he broke into a cold sweat. "Pardon?"

"Do you swim?"

"Not very well. Well, not at all, really."

"You will have a life vest on, but you will still be required to know how to escape in the case of a submersion. If you want to proceed with it, I'll arrange a session for you and after you are certified, we can set up a date to fly you to the rig."

Dawson cleared his throat nervously. "Yes, all right. I suppose . . . I suppose I'll have to do it. Thank you, Mr. Sarbah."

He ended the call in near terror. *Underwater* training?

AS PLANNED, BAAH dropped Dawson off at Takoradi Technical Institute and continued on with Chikata. The buildings of the spotless campus were red with yellow trim on the end walls, and yellow with green trim along the classroom verandas. Dawson went upstairs to the main office on the second story of the administrative block and asked to see someone in charge of staffing.

"That's Mrs. Chinebuah," a receptionist said, and led him to an adjoining office. She knocked, opened the door, and looked in.

"Please, this gentleman has a question for you."

Chinebuah was a hefty woman in her early forties in a trouser suit with a short-style wig framing her round face. Densely packed into her outfit, she looked like she could take down two grown men.

Dawson entered. "Good morning, Mrs. Chinebuah."

"Good morning," she said pleasantly. "May I help you?"

"Inspector Dawson, CID. I'm making some inquiries."

She smiled. "Am I in trouble, Inspector?"

He smiled too. "Not as far as I know. I'm investigating the death of Mr. and Mrs. Smith-Aidoo."

"Ah," she said, shaking her head. "Sad." She took out several sheets of papers from the copy machine and straightened them on the counter.

"Did you know them?" Dawson asked.

"The man, yes. Not so much his wife. He was a strong supporter of TTI, both morally and financially."

"Really? So he was well-liked by everyone here."

"Someone donates money to your school, and you're going to dislike him?" She began to fold the sheets of paper. "We could hardly believe that this murder had taken place. Is there something specific you need to know?"

"You're in charge of staffing schedules?"

"Just one of my duties as an assistant administrator, yes sir."

"Mr. Kwesi DeSouza. He's a member of your staff, correct?"

"Yes," she said, pressing a button to begin a series of copies. "He's in IT."

"I understand he works on Mondays, Tuesdays, and Thursdays," Dawson said, watching the sheets of paper flowing into place with hypnotizing regularity.

"Yes, I believe that's correct," she said. "I can check for you."

"I'm interested in the dates of seventh and eighth July of this year."

She sat down with an air of efficiency, pulled her chair up to her desk computer, and went into the appropriate screen. "Let's see now . . . the seventh was a Monday. Yes, he worked that day . . . oh, no, sorry—he had to postpone the class until Wednesday."

Interesting, Dawson thought. DeSouza had not mentioned that. "Any reason given for the postponement?"

She was trying to remember. "Let me think. He called me about it . . . aha, yes, I remember now. He went to a funeral in Somanya, the Saturday before—that would be the fifth—and then some kind of family palaver arose, and he told me he couldn't be in on Monday, so the class was canceled and rescheduled to Wednesday."

"Is Mr. DeSouza here today?"

"He may be in the IT office marking exam papers, or else he could be invigilating an exam. The students are taking their midterms." She pointed out the window in the direction of IT. "Turn right where you see the electrical department and go straight."

"Thank you very much."

"You are most welcome." She looked concerned but not panicked. "Is everything okay?"

"Everything is fine. Just routine inquiries—nothing to be concerned about."

"Very good." She smiled and winked at him. "Then I won't bother to mention it to Mr. DeSouza."

OUTSIDE, DAWSON PAUSED to look at a bronze statue of a man in front of a piece of equipment on a tripod—a kind of mascot of the institute. The campus was neat, with well-kept grass and trimmed shrubs. Students, all in their early to late teens walked back and forth between classes in khaki and cream uniforms that reminded Dawson of his secondary school days. Women were evidently very rare here, and they seemed to be mostly assigned to the fashion design department.

IT's computer lab was holding an exam. Forty or so students sat at computer terminals under the watch of two monitors, one of whom was DeSouza. He saw Dawson standing outside the window. Surprise and then displeasure washed across his face. He held up a finger to indicate *wait*, whispered something to the other monitor, and then came outside.

"Good morning, sir," Dawson said quietly, not wanting to disturb the students.

DeSouza gestured that they should walk out of earshot and they moved away.

"Inspector," he said impatiently, "I'm in the middle of supervising exams. What is it you want?"

"I'm sorry to disturb," Dawson said cordially. "I won't take up too much of your time. I want to go over the seventh and eighth of July with you again. You said you taught a class on Monday, the seventh, and Tuesday, the eighth?"

DeSouza frowned. "Yes, I always do. What is your question?"

"I've just learned that you had your class on the eighth canceled and rescheduled to Wednesday, the ninth."

DeSouza shook his head. "Impossible."

"Not according to Mrs. Chinebuah," Dawson countered evenly. "You had a funeral on Saturday in Somanya? Does that ring a bell?"

Realization washed over DeSouza's face. "Oh. Yes, you are correct. That is what happened. It completely slipped my mind. Somanya is my wife's hometown. We went to her mother's funeral and after that, a family dispute came up and she couldn't avoid staying until Monday morning. I wasn't happy about leaving her in Somanya, so I thought it best to simply reschedule the class."

"And you returned to Takoradi with your wife around what time?"

"Around eleven, something like that," DeSouza said, glancing over to the classroom. "Mr. Dawson, I really must get back."

If he got back at eleven, Dawson thought, *he still had time to get to Cape Three Points, although it would have been tight.* "When you returned from Somanya, what did you do, sir?"

"I went to my STMA office for a few hours."

"Can someone confirm that?"

"Yes, Susana, my assistant—she was there."

Dawson would have Chikata check on that. "Did Superintendent Hammond or any of his people ask you about that Monday?"

"I don't remember," DeSouza said. "Why?"

"Because if you told them about your canceling the class that Monday, it seems odd that you forgot to tell me the same thing."

"I'm sorry if I forgot, Inspector," De Souza said, surprisingly apologetic. "Please, I must return to the classroom."

He left. Watching DeSouza, Dawson still had a feeling the man was hiding something.

Chapter 18

AT 6:20 SATURDAY MORNING, Dawson woke up to the sound of Hosiah and Sly moving around in the sitting room. Two grinning faces appeared around the door. He smiled at them, and they took that as their invitation to invade. They clambered on top of Dawson, bouncing and giggling while he tried to make them keep their voices down. They had arrived with Christine last night much later than Dawson had wanted or expected.

She was sleeping beside Dawson on the rather narrow bed. She groaned, lifting her head with one eye open. "Why do you boys wake me up like this every Saturday?" she complained bitterly. "If you want to play, go outside. Goodness."

Her head flopped onto the pillow, and she went back to sleep.

"Come on," Dawson whispered to the boys. "Let's go. And stop making noise."

He put Sly over one shoulder and Hosiah under his arm and took them writhing to the sitting room, where they had a wrestling match—two children versus one adult. Dawson marveled at how Hosiah's vigor was already returning to normal. Nevertheless, he kept the play to only fifteen minutes, at the end of which the kids declared victory.

"Next time I'll finish both of you off," he warned to their hilarity. "Okay, time to go and get ready."

"Where are we going today?" Sly asked.

"Cape Three Points."

Hosiah wrinkled his nose. "What's that?"

"It's the most southern part of Ghana. There's a nice beach there. Uncle Abraham and Auntie Akosua will take us."

Excited, the two boys rushed to the bathroom to wash up.

"There's a water shortage," Dawson warned them, "so use what's in the buckets and don't waste it, you hear?"

ABRAHAM DROVE HIS 4 x 4 Toyota with Dawson beside him in the front passenger seat and Christine, Akosua, Sly, and Hosiah in the rear. There was no room for Chikata, so he followed them with Baah in the taxi. Once out of Takoradi's city limits, it was thirty minutes to the turnoff at Agona-Nkwanta, where aggressive vendors swarmed their vehicle. Abraham didn't stop, turning onto the left branch off the central roundabout. They enjoyed the paved route for another fifteen minutes up to the right-hand junction to Cape Three Points. There, the dirt road began, winding ahead like a meandering serpent. It was potholed and bumpy in spots, but the Toyota handled it easily. On the other hand, trailing behind in the taxi, Chikata and Baah were having a rough time of it.

A left-pointing arrow indicated the final turn into Ezile Bay, a grassy pathway worn down by vehicle traffic. The two vehicles bounced over the remaining few meters and parked. Several small thatch-roofed, sandstone-colored chalets were scattered over a wide area, nestled among coconut palms, ferns, and trailing bougainvillea plants. Directly ahead, the aqua sea stretched to the horizon, rolling onto the off-white sand with soft wave breaks. Fishing canoes in the distance with their signature flags were clear silhouettes against a cloudless sky.

Hosiah hopped up and down with anticipation as everyone alighted. "Daddy, can we go in the water now?"

"Let's go to the edge and then Uncle Abe will go in with you later."

Sly walked alongside Hosiah, who skipped in the sand as he tugged and swung on his father's hand. He had no fear of the sea, whereas Dawson eyed the waves with some unease. He couldn't let his sons sense that, however. They went as far as the dissolving trail of the receding waves. Dawson guessed that the tide was low. Gleefully, Hosiah splattered the wet sand with his bare feet. Sly, who hailed from landlocked northern Ghana and was unaccustomed to beaches, was more restrained.

Dawson realized that this was the most serene setting he had ever experienced. Accra was hell, and Ezile was paradise. This place had no crowds or blaring horns, only a young white woman and a Ghanaian man having fun in the water. He was laughing as she wrapped her arms around his broad shoulders and her legs around his waist, pressing her crotch into his. Dawson shifted his gaze eastward about 500 meters to a village that was subdivided into two sections by a lagoon formed by the meeting of the Ezile River and the sea. He had done his homework and knew this was the village of Akwidaa.

"Okay," he said to the boys. "Let's go back."

They returned up the slight incline, and Hosiah scooped up a little sand and let it flow from his hand in the breeze.

"Daddy, did you catch the bad man yet?" he asked unexpectedly. "The man who cuts off people's heads?"

"No, not yet. Are you still scared he'll hurt Daddy?"

Hosiah's response was an uncertain shake and nod of the head— no, and yes.

"Anyway, Daddy can beat that man in a fight," Sly declared, executing a left jab and right uppercut. The boy still had the ways of the street in him.

Thanks for the confidence, Dawson thought with some amusement. "I'm only going to catch him," he said, putting an arm around Sly's shoulders, "not fight with him."

"Oh," Sly said, looking a little disappointed. He looked at Hosiah. "I'll race you to the coconut trees."

They took off, Sly holding back somewhat so that he wouldn't beat Hosiah by a great margin. Dawson rejoined Christine and the others near a set of chairs and tables in the shade of the coconut palm, where they had a perfect view of the bay formed by two forested promontories on either side.

"This is the life," Christine said. "I could live here."

"Me too," Akosua said.

"Fine," Abraham cracked. "When we depart, we'll leave you ladies both behind."

"Hmm," Akosua said. "Who's going to cook for you?"

A white man in shorts and slippers approached them at a leisurely pace. He was of average height with a rotund belly, a fiery head of red hair, and a hircine beard streaked with grey.

"Mr. Cardiman?"

"Yes, and you must be Inspector Dawson. Welcome, sir!"

His voice resembled paper clips rattling in a tin, which suggested to Dawson a man who enjoyed an unfettered, somewhat jumbled life.

"This is a beautiful place," Dawson said as he shook hands.

He introduced Chikata, the three other adults, and the two boys. Cardiman bent forward and playfully rubbed their heads.

"I'm sure you lads can't wait to get into the water, eh?"

"You are reading their minds correctly," Dawson said.

"Well, it's low tide and will remain so for a few hours yet," Cardiman said jovially, "so it's a perfect time to go in."

"My cousin can go in with them while we talk," Dawson said.

"Come on, boys," Abraham said. "Let's go and change."

Sly and Hosiah raced off excitedly in front of their uncle.

"Shall we go to my office, gentlemen?" Cardiman said to Dawson and Chikata.

"See you ladies later," Dawson said.

Lazing in the lounge chairs, neither woman was paying much attention to him.

A ROOM IN Cardiman's house served as the office. His desk, a muddle of papers crowding out two laptops, confirmed Dawson's first impressions: the man was a little scattered, but happy with it. Facing Cardiman, Dawson and Chikata sat down in a pair of cushioned chairs along the wall. A pleasant cross breeze passed through the two mosquito-screened windows.

"I know you are anxious to talk about the Smith-Aidoo murders, Inspector," Cardiman said.

"Did you know them well?"

"I knew Charles as well as I wanted to, but I met his wife only once, and that was when they visited me here at Ezile on that fateful Monday."

"What was the purpose of their visit?"

"Whenever Charles Smith-Aidoo was here," Cardiman said, leaning back and resting his hands on the promontory of his belly, "it was to talk to Akwidaa's chief, Nana Ackah-Yensu; myself; or both. Charles had a vision in which the two bays formed by the three peninsulas—the three points, so to speak—could become residential areas. Housing for low and mid-level workers in the oil industry would start some distance back from the beach and be built progressively inward. Luxurious chalets and mansions for rich people would be right on the beach."

Distress now passed across Cardiman's face like a shadow. "Have you seen the majesty of this place? A swampland with superb mangroves is just a short walking distance from here. Akwidaa is on the east side of the bay, and beyond that, you'll find the ruins of an ancient German fort. Later on, I'd like to show you the bay on the other side of mangroves—simply lovely. Unparalleled forest and wildlife thrive along the three peninsulas for which Cape Three Points is named. The oil companies are already destroying marine life and habitat, and now they want to add land to their conquests and get rid of Ezile Bay Resort. Over my dead body."

Or Smith-Aidoo's, Dawson thought. "I read the minutes of the meetings you attended at the STMA. You strongly oppose the oil people."

"What happens when multinational companies invade a developing country like Ghana to set up extractive industries like gold or diamonds, or oil?" Cardiman demanded, thrusting his hands out. "They *ruin* the country, that's what happens, Inspector. We all know about the chaos in the Niger Delta, where oil spills occur practically every day."

"Has there been an oil spill off Ghana's shores?" Chikata asked, and Dawson thought it was an excellent question.

"We had one just six months ago, and yet no one said a word," Cardiman said, folding his arms in indignation. "Not one word, gentlemen. No government announcement, nothing in the papers, and precious little on the radio. Can you imagine that?"

"How did you hear about it?" Dawson asked.

"I know one of the Malgam helicopter pilots who takes workers to and from the rig. He saw the sheen over the water surface. It obviously wasn't a large spill, but it was a spill just the same. I'm convinced that there's been more than one but I believe that there's been a hush imposed on the media. Fish populations are down, whales have been washing up dead on Western Region beaches—"

"Whales?" Dawson said in surprise. "Ghana has whales?"

"Oh, yes!" Cardiman exclaimed with a smile. "And dolphins and endangered giant sea turtles. They didn't teach you all that in school, did they?"

"No," Dawson said. "Although it's possible I slept through that class."

Cardiman laughed, the stern expression on his face softening a bit.

"Let's say a very large spill occurs," Dawson said, "who pays for it?"

"Malgam will pay for the cleanup, but that's as far as they're obligated."

"They wouldn't be fined?"

"No," Cardiman said, shaking his head with vigor. "Even worse, they don't pay restitution to fishing communities should their livelihoods be adversely affected. They can get away with murder, and that's not an exaggeration."

"And whose fault is that?" Dawson asked.

"Our government's, that's who!" Cardiman said, as if it should have been obvious. "A pusillanimous bunch who can't stand up to these multinationals or resist the money that gets deposited in their Swiss bank accounts, not to mention the all-expenses-paid jaunts to Europe."

"You're saying gifts in exchange for keeping regulations at a minimum," Dawson said.

"Do you think this lack of oversight of the oil companies is accidental?" Cardiman asked heatedly. "Don't believe it for a moment."

Dawson wondered if the man was being over-cynical, but he didn't know enough to challenge him.

"Where did Charles Smith-Aidoo fit into all of this?" he asked.

"Here's the problem," Cardiman said with authority. "Charles served two masters—Malgam Oil, and himself, and sometimes it was a conflict of interest. His duties to Malgam included presenting the best face of the company to outside agencies, and to the public. However, at the same time he was setting up moneymaking ventures for personal gain. So, for instance, while he's representing Malgam in their PR move to rebuild Akwidaa, he gets the bright idea that

Akwidaa should trade their beachfront property in return for electricity and running water at another location, and he's thinking about what's in it for him and his developer friend."

"What developer friend?"

"Peter Duodo. Savvy man—owns Duodo Enterprises in Accra. It's in the Price-Waterhouse Building near Kotoka Airport." Cardiman seemed to relish supplying information. "The two of them had some kind of informal scratch-my-back-I'll-scratch-yours arrangement."

"I see." Dawson was thinking about all Cardiman had said so far. "Do you think Malgam would really finance the relocation of an entire village?"

"Let me tell you exactly how it would go," Cardiman said knowingly. "Malgam officially collaborates with the government on the project to move the village back from the beach while allowing them access to the sea via the Ezile River and the lagoon. Malgam promises a certain amount of money to support pipe-borne water and electrification, on the condition that the government completes the housing. That's because Malgam isn't stupid, and the crafty devils know that the government will start the buildings, partially complete them, the village people will move in, and the Ministry of Interior will maybe put in a community tap at most, with promises of electricity to come. The MP gets a little pocket money from Malgam in return for the project dragging or coming to a complete stop."

Cardiman looked from Dawson to Chikata and back. "You follow? Okay, the opposition party comes into power four or eight years later, parliament defunds the project and it collapses. In the end, Malgam gains beachfront property to develop, they've paid a sum of money that's a drop in the bucket for them, the government hasn't spent that much either, and the people of Akwidaa are left with a less than half-finished village with reduced access to the shore, no electricity, and one lousy community tap."

"So now that Charles Smith-Aidoo is dead, a scheme like that is also dead?" Dawson asked.

"Oh, yes—for now," Cardiman said with undisguised satisfaction. "Not that I'm glad Charles is dead, but there you have it. The new man, Jason Sarbah, is not keen on all this development stuff, but don't be surprised if it all resurfaces at some point."

"What happened that day Charles and his wife came to visit you?"

Cardiman sighed, rested his palms on his knees, and collected himself for the account. "They arrived around eleven. Charles mentioned that they had come from a meeting in Axim that morning. Fiona sat at the beachside while Charles and I talked in the restaurant. He offered me a stake in a development along the Cape Three Points shoreline, including the Ezile Bay and Akwidaa locations. He showed me the plan, the expected revenue, the environmental impact assessment, and so on. And I said no. Full stop. No. I said I didn't want to lose this place at the hands of some faceless moneymaking venture. I don't operate this resort for money—in fact, I don't make much money from it at all. I do it for the love of it."

"What did Smith-Aidoo say to your answer?" Dawson asked.

"He accepted it, and we more or less left it at that. I had lunch with him and Fiona, and we parted on amicable terms." Cardiman smiled. "Look, I'm no fool, Inspector. I know you're looking for a murderer and that I was one of the last persons to see the Smith-Aidoos alive. So, yes, I accept that I could be a suspect, but let me assure you of one thing: Although Charles and I had fundamental disagreements in outlook, I did not hate the man. In fact he was really a nice, personable chap."

Dawson shook his head. That wasn't good enough. "It's not a matter of hate, Mr. Cardiman, it's rather his threatening the way of life you love. This place represents your very reason for living in Ghana, or am I wrong?"

"You are not, and I appreciate your clarity of perception, but . . ."

"Let's go over this again," Dawson interrupted, dissatisfied with the way the discussion was going. From the corner of his eye, he saw Chikata carefully watching Cardiman. "What time did Charles and Fiona leave Ezile Bay?"

"Around twelve thirty. I was due in Takoradi that afternoon, so I left at about one. I came across their vehicle at the roadside about twenty or twenty-five minutes later. The front doors were wide open. I took a look inside the vehicle without touching anything, I looked around, called out their names several times, but nothing."

"Did you see anyone in the vicinity or any sign of another vehicle?"

Chikata chimed in, to Dawson's approval. He wanted more of that from his sergeant.

"No one and nothing," Cardiman said firmly. "It's not a highly traveled road, as you yourself must have noticed on your way in. It's usually several miles before you see anyone else either in a car or on foot, and for the most part that's near the two or three villages along the way—women carrying firewood and so on."

Which makes it a very convenient place to kill someone, Dawson thought. "Do you own any firearms, Mr. Cardiman?"

"No!" He looked baffled. "Come on, Inspector. I didn't kill the man any more than you did. How could I have ambushed their vehicle if they left at twelve thirty, and I left almost thirty minutes later? By that time, they would have been close to the Agona Junction. I couldn't possibly have caught up with them."

Dawson admitted to himself that Cardiman was right. He took a few minutes to jot down notes in his book and then looked at Chikata. "Did you have any more questions?"

The sergeant shook his head.

"Would you do us a favor, Mr. Cardiman?" Dawson said. "We'd like go to the spot you discovered the Smith-Aidoos' Hyundai and look around a little bit."

"Certainly. I can drive you there right away."

Chapter 19

DAWSON OBSERVED THAT RESORT ownership must not have been treating Cardiman too badly. He owned a late edition Land Rover SUV, which he drove at breakneck speed. Dawson sat beside him with Chikata in the rear.

"I know every centimeter of this road," Cardiman said, swerving violently to avoid a pothole. "At the height of the rainy season when everything turns to mud, it's bloody awful."

"Is this the only route to and from Ezile by car?" Dawson asked him.

"The only civilized way, so to speak."

They passed a creek into which several laughing kids were jumping from the bridge overpass. The children waved and cheered as the Land Rover sped past.

About twenty minutes later, they had reached their destination. The thick vegetation came right up to the sides of the dirt road, so Cardiman let the two detectives down first before pulling over into the bush and out of the way. He heaved himself out of the Land Rover with a grunt and joined them.

"So their vehicle was right about here, where we're standing," he said, indicating a stretch of a few meters on the same side he had parked.

It was hot and eerily quiet, but Dawson gradually became aware of birdcalls piercing the silence. He looked up and down the road. The spot was situated directly after a slight incline and a particularly rocky and potholed section, which meant the Smith-Aidoos would probably have had to slow down a little bit as they approached, making it easier to flag them down. Who, besides Cardiman, knew that the Smith-Aidoos would be on the road from Ezile?

The dense bush at both sides of the road seemed impenetrable. Dawson approached what looked like a gap or clearing in the vegetation and started to make his way inside. Chikata followed.

"Where are you going?" Cardiman asked.

"I don't know," Dawson shot back.

Underneath the tangle of plants, the ground dipped down sharply and Dawson almost lost his footing. Chikata had the benefit of his slip and didn't make the same mistake. It wasn't easy going, but once they'd reached a clump of banana trees, the bush cleared somewhat. They searched the ground, looking for anything that the murderers might have left behind if they had made their way into the bush with Charles and Fiona.

"You're thinking the murderers brought the Smith-Aidoos in here to kill them?" Chikata asked.

"I was entertaining the idea," Dawson replied, "but seeing how difficult it was to make our way in here, I'm beginning to doubt it. Can you imagine dragging two dead bodies out back through that bush?"

"It would be tough—and a waste of time, too," Chikata observed. "Better to flag down the vehicle, get the Smith-Aidoos out at gunpoint into another vehicle, and get them outa here as quickly as possible."

"I agree," Dawson said. "Anyway, we're here, so we might as well check for any cartridges, or even a murder weapon. That would be a real stroke of luck."

"Do you suspect Cardiman?"

"If his time frames are all correct, and it seems they are, then he couldn't have taken part in waylaying the Smith-Aidoos. Again, just like DeSouza and Sarbah, the only way he could have been involved is if he had a partner."

"But then he could simply have had them shot at the roadside and that would be the end of it," Chikata pointed out, standing akimbo. "Why have them loaded into a canoe and taken out to sea and all that palaver? Doesn't make sense."

"Amazing how nothing ever seems to make sense, isn't it?" Dawson muttered, bending down and lifting the fronds of a fern. Low-lying plants in a forest were of special significance to him. In the Ketanu case two years ago, the victim was found dead in a thicket with a shrub partially concealing her body.

As expected, they found nothing—not even any signs of disturbance of vegetation. Abandoning the "murder-in-the-bush" theory, they came back, dusting twigs and leaves off their clothes.

"Anything in there?" Cardiman asked them.

Dawson shook his head absently, looking around again. In the distance he saw towering kapok trees with long, straight trunks topped with branches shaped like a fan or umbrella. Much closer, about 200 meters along the road in the direction they had been traveling, Dawson noticed another tree of some size, this one not as tall as a kapok. Its sturdy, widely spread branches, resembling multiple tributaries of a river, overhung the roadway somewhat. He guessed it was a mahogany. It was well situated to function as a lookout for vehicles coming along the route, provided one climbed high enough. He took a photograph of the mahogany with his phone, several snapshots of the Hyundai and surroundings, and the red dirt road in either direction.

"Thank you, Mr. Cardiman. I think I've seen all I need."

As they drove back, the three men were silent until Cardiman said, "I'm concerned about something. I didn't express it before, but a thought has crossed my mind more than once. Could one or more fishermen in Akwidaa have committed the murder? Maybe they didn't want the village to be moved to another site, especially since it's sacred ground to them. Perhaps they would want to get rid of Charles for that reason."

It was interesting that Cardiman was expressing the same suspicion that Eileen had. On the other hand, maybe Cardiman was trying to shift suspicion away from himself, Dawson reasoned. But he admitted that he did not suspect the resort owner of lying.

He went with Cardiman's idea to see where it would go. "What do you suggest?"

"Let's pay a visit to the Nana of Akwidaa," Cardiman said. "I have a bottle of gin in the back. He'll expect something from you."

• • •

CARDIMAN HAD TO switch to four-wheel drive to climb a steep hill, and when they reached the crest, the beach again appeared in the distance.

"If you go up that way," he said, pointing to another branch in the road, "you'll reach the lighthouse, where there's a splendid view. If you have some time, I highly recommend a visit before you leave Cape Three Points."

"How far is it?"

"Just fifteen minutes or so from Ezile."

He coasted down to the village and stopped at its edge in a swirl of dust.

To Dawson, born and bred in a frenetic city, village life seemed to move at a snail's pace, or to not move at all. It was peaceful, but how did the residents live without electricity and running water? Not that Accra didn't regularly have power and water failures, he thought wryly. That was almost worse, in a way. These villagers didn't worry about electricity cuts because there was no electricity to be had. No expectations, no disappointments.

As they entered the village, about a dozen children ranging in age from two to eight came running out to greet them jubilantly. "Mr. Cardiman!" they shouted, dancing around him, tugging at his clothes and putting their arms around him.

"Hi, kids!" he said, beaming and ruffling their heads.

"How are you?" several of them asked repeatedly, practicing their limited English.

"I'm fine, thank you," he said. "Now line up, come on, come on, you know the drill." Cardiman winked at Dawson and Chikata. "Got them trained."

Giggling and jostling, the children got into the semblance of a line, and Cardiman gave each of them a handful of sweets from the plastic bag he was carrying. They took off shrieking with delight, and Cardiman and his two companions continued through the village toward the shore. Some of the houses were of brick, others were wood frames filled in with mud. Dogs, goats, sheep, and chickens wandered freely. They didn't bother anyone, and no one bothered them. Everyone knew Cardiman it seemed, acknowledging him as he passed by. He took care to greet each of them. *Good village etiquette*, Dawson thought.

"We're coming to the chief's house now," Cardiman said.

It was a square brick home whose faded blue paint appeared to have run out before the work was finished. One side of the corrugated metal roof was sagging. The front door was ajar. Cardiman knocked. A skinny man in his early fifties came out.

"Good morning, Yao," Cardiman said.

"Good morning, sir."

"This is Inspector Dawson and Sergeant Chikata from Accra. They have come to pay respects to Nana Ackah-Yensu. Is he in?"

"Please, he has gone out."

"Any idea when he'll return?"

"Please, I think he will come back soon. You can have a seat."

Yao gestured to two plastic chairs in the corner of the porch. Dawson and Cardiman took the seats, Chikata remained standing, and Yao hovered indecisively.

"Please, I will go and call him to come," he said, as if it had just occurred to him.

"Thank you, Yao."

He set off.

"He's a relative of Ackah-Yensu's," Cardiman explained. "He's a really sweet man, just a little slow mentally, that's all."

They waited almost forty-five minutes before the chief arrived. He was a scrawny man in his early sixties, dressed traditionally with yards of richly patterned cloth wrapped around his body and thrown over one shoulder, and he wore it well.

The three men rose to greet him. Dawson presented him with the gin, which Ackah-Yensu graciously accepted.

Yao brought the chief a chair, and he sat down opposite them.

"So, Mr. Dawson and Mr. Chikata, what is your mission here today?"

Speaking in Fante, Dawson told the Nana that apart from his hearing about the esteemed Akwidaa village and wishing to pay his respects to the Nana, he was on business, investigating the death of Charles Smith-Aidoo and his wife.

Nana Ackah-Yensu nodded and smiled and then paused for a long time. "Yes," he said finally, rubbing his palm slowly up and down his thigh. "I knew Mr. Smith-Aidoo well, and I was very sorry to hear of his death."

"Nana, I understand he visited you on a few occasions?" Dawson asked.

"Yes." He didn't volunteer anything further.

"Please, Nana," Dawson pressed, laying on a thick coat of deference, "can you tell me the nature of his visits?"

"Hmm," the chief said, as though considering a choice of ingredients. "Well, the first time he came here, he told me that his company, Malgam, wanted to help some of the villages on the coast of the Western Region, and he asked me what the needs of Akwidaa were, and I told him, you know, just like so many villages in Ghana, we need electricity, and we need running water. It's simple. No mystery about it. He said he would talk to his people and return."

He hitched his cloth more securely onto his shoulder. "About two months later, Mr. Smith-Aidoo came back. He said Malgam was going to join the government to provide us with electricity and water. They were making plans. I was very happy. I told him that the next time he comes, he has to meet with all the elders of the village, and he said okay. Then after a few weeks, he met with the elders and me. He brought us all kinds of fine gifts, we poured libation, and then we started the meeting. The elders were eager to know the details of the plans Mr. Smith-Aidoo had for us, and when he started talking it seemed very good to us, but after some few minutes, I realized his message had changed. He said Malgam wanted to do what was in our mutual best interest, and he and his team would like to build a new town they call New Akwidaa, either on the Ezile River or some other place, and tear down Old Akwidaa."

Ackah-Yensu paused, looking as baffled as he must have been at that meeting.

"He said Malgam would pay us for the land and contribute to building the new settlement and the electricity and water. In fact, we were shocked. We never expected something like this. We started to say no, we can never agree to such a thing. Then he told us how much they were offering to pay the elders to do this project, and some of them looked at each other and started to change their minds. To us, it was a lot of money."

"And so what happened after that?" Dawson asked.

"Fighting—that's all." Ackah-Yensu shrugged hopelessly. "The older people in the village say they will never move. The lazy young guys who don't want to follow in their fathers' example as fishermen say they would like to move to a new place. At the same time, the village elders can't agree on any decision to bring to me. Therefore, nothing happened. And now Mr. Charles is dead." He shook his head in regret.

Dawson understood the chief's disappointment: the potential windfall for the village had come to a stalemate and completely flopped. "Please, Nana, after that last meeting with the elders attending, did you see Mr. Smith-Aidoo or talk to him again?"

"By phone," he said, making the universal sign for it. "He said if I could convince the elders and the village it will be good to move, he could give me a little something and make sure I had a very fine chief's house."

Blatant bribery, Dawson thought. If this story was true, his respect for Charles had just dropped a few points. "Did you try to do that, Nana?"

The chief shook his head. "No. Just a few days later, he was killed."

"Do you regret his death, Nana?"

"Of course!" he said with a new intensity. "I think with him, we in Akwidaa had a chance that something good would come if we continued to negotiate."

Maybe, Dawson thought, but he was doubtful. From what he had observed, neither the government nor the private sector was in any rush to change the lot of villages in the country. Urban first, rural last.

"One last question, Nana, if you please," he said. "Do you know of any fishermen or people in Akwidaa who wanted to harm Mr. Smith-Aidoo?"

Nana frowned. "Oh, no," he said firmly, shaking his head and appearing put out by the question. "That's not how we think here. You know, all this type of killing—shooting people and so on—belongs to the ways of the city. I'm not trying to offend you, Mr. Dawson . . ."

"It's no offense, Nana. What about *juju* or witchcraft?"

Ackah-Yensu stared at the ground for a moment and then looked up to meet Dawson's gaze directly. "That one, I can't say. Since my time in Akwidaa, we have only had two witches. One was driven away to a witches' camp, and the other one was killed. I don't think anyone in Akwidaa performed *juju* on Mr. Charles and his wife. Maybe a jealous family member, rather."

Dawson wished he could ask the chief if he thought Mr. Cardiman could have murdered the couple, but obviously he would have to wait for a more discreet moment.

Chapter 20

BEFORE RETURNING TO THE others, Cardiman took Dawson and Chikata up a promontory beyond the mangroves. From there, they could see the bay where Ezile was located to their left, and a second slightly larger bay to their right. The sand was pale fawn in color, the water dark turquoise rolling onto the shore and breaking into white foam.

"It's deserted," Dawson observed in surprise.

Cardiman looked at him, nodding with a smile. "Yes, that's what is so marvelous about it. The most you'll see is one or two people walking along the beach in transit from Cape Three Points village to Akwidaa." He gazed rapturously at the bay. "Unspoiled beauty. I'm not saying don't build anything on the land. I'm saying don't *ruin* it if you do, and that's the vision Charles had—a wholesale raping of the land for commercial purposes. On the other hand, my Ezile is constructed in complete harmony with the environment—no uprooting trees or disturbing the mangroves. Some of our power even comes from solar energy."

Dawson had to admire Cardiman's passion and dedication. For him there was nothing more important than this slice of paradise on earth, and he was going to fight to preserve it. At the same time, Dawson thought, that could make his motive for murder all the more powerful.

On their return, Cardiman went off to supervise the repairs on one of the chalets, and Dawson rejoined Christine and Akosua, who were still at their shady perch on the beach chatting as they watched

Abraham playing in the water with the kids. Chikata and Baah were playing a noisy game of cards at the next table.

When lunch arrived, Akosua beckoned to her husband to come out of the water for something to eat. Sly and Hosiah came running up, wet and exuberant.

"I was swimming, Daddy," Hosiah said jumping up and down.

"Yes, I saw you!" He draped a towel around his son's shoulders. "Good for you! Dry yourself off. How's the water?"

"It's nice," Sly said.

Abraham plunked down in a chair, panting. "My goodness. These kids have made me realize how out of shape I am."

Lunch came. It was a mouth-watering spread of "Red Red"—succulent fried, ripe plantains and black-eyed peas reddened by palm oil; *banku* with tilapia; yam and light soup full of chunks of fish; Jollof rice prepared with chicken and an aromatic mix of spices and tomato sauce; and for Abraham, a plate of fish and chips with coleslaw, a dish he had recently acquired a taste for. After they had washed their hands, they tucked in, eating with their fingers—except for Abraham, who didn't think his meal was made for consumption that way.

"Can we go back in the water, Uncle?" Hosiah asked as he finished his meal.

Abraham looked to Dawson for guidance.

"Only for a little while," Dawson said. "Then we have to go back home."

"Okay."

"Before you kill your uncle," Akosua added, under her breath.

Abraham went gamely back to the water with the boys, although it looked like he could have done with a nap instead.

"You want to go for a walk?" Dawson asked, looking at Christine.

"Where?"

Dawson pointed to the peninsula beyond Akwidaa. "The remains of a seventeenth-century German fort are over there. Let's go and see it."

"But do you know the way?" she said, looking a little doubtful.

"I think there's a path and some signs. I'm sure we can figure it out."

"Hmm. Okay, but if we get lost in there you'll never hear the end of it from me."

"Relax," Dawson said, grinning. "I have a wizardly sense of direction. Come on, it will be an adventure."

He reached out his hand, and when she grabbed it he pulled her out of her seat.

"We'll be back in a little while," Christine said to Akosua.

Before they set off, they went to the water's edge to let Abe know. Hosiah looked immediately anxious. "Where are you going, Daddy?"

"We're just going to walk past the village."

"Is the bad man there?"

Dawson got a knot in his chest. "Come here, Hosiah."

He knelt in the sand and hugged his wet son, giving him a kiss. "The man isn't there, okay? I promise you. We went with Mr. Cardiman and saw the village with the chief and everything, and no one bad was there. Only good people, okay?"

Hosiah nodded mutely.

"We'll be back soon. Play with Uncle Abe and Sly."

He lifted his palm in the air and his son gave him a resounding high five, running back into the water.

Dawson and Christine held hands as they sauntered along the beach a little in front of the farthest point the waves rolled up onto the sand. The sun was high overhead, and the aqua hue of the water appeared more intense.

"This was such a wonderful idea, Dark," she said, her eyes shining as she looked at him. "The boys are having the time of their lives, and they're overjoyed to see you safe and sound. Thank you."

He looked back at her. She was lovely in a loose flowered skirt and a waist-hugging sleeveless teal blouse. She asked him if he had learned anything useful from Cardiman or the chief.

"I don't know," he said. "I have to digest it tomorrow."

He wasn't interested in talking any further about it, and he knew she sensed that.

They crossed a bridge over the Ezile River, passed along the outskirts of Akwidaa, negotiated another clump of rocks, and entered the peninsula forest along a path that twisted and turned through thick undergrowth and palm and banana trees. At intervals, lengths of chicken wire stretched between one bush or tree and the next.

"What are those for?" Christine wondered.

"I think it's to keep goats and sheep out when they plant crops," Dawson said. "And of course, any wild animals."

"Wild animals? What wild animals?"

"You know, forest leopards and things like that," Dawson said casually.

"What?" Christine said, stopping in her tracks. "There are no leopards in Ghana."

"Oh, yes there are," he said, turning to her authoritatively. "People just don't know about them. Just like they don't know we have dolphins and whales."

"Wait a minute," she said incredulously. "There are leopards in this forest? Who told you that?"

"One of the villagers," he replied casually. "He said they stalk people, pounce on them, and devour their flesh. Sometimes the remains of people are found stripped to the bone."

She looked around. "Dark, are you serious?" Her voice shook slightly.

He looked back at her. "Of course I'm serious. Don't worry. It's not very likely we'll run into one of them. They're very secretive."

Her eyes widened. She jumped and swung around as though she had heard something. At that, Dawson couldn't keep his face straight any longer and burst out laughing. "I'm just playing with you."

"*What?*"

"I'm lying. No one told me there are leopards here."

"Okay, that's it," she said furiously, pulling a strip of leaves off a bush. "You're done for."

She charged at him and began whipping him with the flimsy branch. He fell over with laughter.

"Get up and let's go, you bad man," she said. "We're wasting time."

He dusted himself off and took the lead again.

"I thought you said there are signs showing which way to go," she grumbled after a few minutes. "I haven't seen one yet."

"I just said that to get you to come with me," he tossed back.

"I'm beginning to dislike you," she commented. "Besides that, I'm exhausted."

"There!" he exclaimed.

"What? Where?"

"The ruins of the fort." He pointed. "Over there."

"Oh, *yes!*" she exclaimed. "I see it now."

They were looking at segments of crumbled walls constructed from earth-colored bricks. Large trees grew in and among the ruins, wrapping roots around the walls as if trying to strangle them.

"Four hundred years old," she murmured. "Amazing."

They moved closer to the ancient structure, but didn't touch anything.

"I wonder what they're doing to preserve it from further damage," Dawson said.

"Apparently, not much. Aren't the trees and their roots going to eventually split the walls open?"

Dawson circled around to the left edge of the ruins. Here, the ground sloped quite steeply into a shaded depression. He called out to her. "Let's go down there."

"Whatever for?"

"It looks nice and cool. We can relax for a minute." He stooped. "Get on my back. I'll take you down."

HE SPENT A few minutes creating a soft, clean spot on the ground using fronds from a banana tree, and then he sat with his back against the tree while she rested in between his thighs, leaning against his chest.

"You're right," she said. "It's nice here."

He nuzzled her neck, her ticklish spot, and she went into convulsive giggles and tried to get away from him, but he held her fast.

"Darko, stop!" she begged in between paroxysms.

"Okay, okay," he said, grinning and letting her relax against him again.

"You know what I'm thinking?" she said.

"What?"

"I get the feeling this might be some kind of sacred grounds and that we're trespassing."

"Then they should put a sign up that says so."

"The gods expect you to automatically know certain things."

"Oh, really?" he asked innocently.

"Yes, Dark. Which is why you probably shouldn't have your hand in my blouse."

She gave his right hand a firm but playful slap and he withdrew. "All right," he said with a sigh. "I'll be good—even though it's going to kill me."

She laughed and relaxed against him. "You can handle it."

"Barely."

She was quiet for a moment, then, "I hope the kids are all right."

"Abe is taking care of them," Dawson murmured. "For once, don't think about the boys. We hardly ever get to spend time together alone, you and I, so let's enjoy this moment."

"Okay," she said softly.

He wrapped his arms around her and inhaled the sweetness of her skin. They were silent, enjoying each other and the sound of the gentle breeze stirring through the trees of the forest.

Chapter 21

ON SUNDAY MORNING, CHRISTINE, Hosiah, Akosua, and Abraham went to church while Dawson stayed behind with Sly, who was Muslim. They walked over to Chikata at the Stellar. Dawson switched the TV channel from the action adventure he had been watching to something more child-suitable, and Sly settled down on the bed to watch while the two men sat at a table on the balcony to talk about the case. They hadn't had time to discuss Chikata's outing with Baah in detail, but Dawson knew that the trip had turned up little to nothing.

"We went to a priestess in New Amanful," Chikata told him now, leaning back and stretching his legs. "When I asked her about human sacrifice, she got offended and said, 'I don't involve myself with the spilling of human blood.' She seemed very serious about that. Then we found fetish shrines in Kwesimintsim and Anaji—those are some other sections of Takoradi. The priests and healers we saw there wouldn't talk. They mostly shook their heads and gave me evasive answers. They didn't want to reveal any tricks of their trade."

Dawson nodded. "Much of traditional medicine is jealously guarded. It's like companies who don't want to reveal their manufacturing process."

"One possible lead, though," Chikata continued. "The New Amanful priestess told me I should get in touch with a well-known fetish priest called Kweku Bonsa. She said if anyone knows about something like that, it's Bonsa. He works in Kojokrom, a little way out from Takoradi. We didn't have enough time, but maybe I can track him down tomorrow."

"All right. Good job." Dawson looked at his phone. "They should be back from church by now. Let's go to Abraham's house. They're having us for lunch."

AFTER A SUMPTUOUS meal, it was time to say goodbye to Christine and the boys.

"Drive safely," Dawson told her as he saw them off outside Abraham's shop. He gave her a hug and kissed her.

"When will you be back, Daddy?" Hosiah asked, swinging on his arm.

"As soon as I can. Be good. Don't give Mama any trouble."

Hosiah smiled with a hint of mischief. "Okay."

"And remember, Daddy's going to be fine."

He kissed Hosiah and pulled Sly closer for a somewhat quicker embrace. The older boy was less inclined to demonstrations of affection, and Dawson respected that.

"Take care of your little brother, okay?"

Sly nodded and smiled.

"While you're on the way, Mama will give you her phone to call me and let me know everything is all right."

Sly liked taking on responsibility and being in control. "All right, Daddy."

Dawson watched as they pulled away in the car, the kids waving at him for as long as he was within sight. He went back inside thinking what a nice time this weekend with the family had been.

HE JOINED CHIKATA and Abraham to watch a televised soccer match between British teams Manchester United and Arsenal. To Dawson's chagrin, Man U massacred his team Arsenal 3-0, and he had to submit to the taunts.

"Next time," Dawson said, waving the teasing away, "no mercy."

His phone rang. It was Sly calling on Christine's phone. "Daddy, we're passing Saltpond now."

"That's good. Everything okay?"

"Yes, Daddy, everything is fine. We'll get home soon."

"Cool, thank you for calling. Let me talk to Mama."

He exchanged a few quick words with Christine before ending the call. "Cousin Abe, Chikata and I should get back now, so we can prepare for tomorrow."

"Okay, no problem."

With Chikata watching, Dawson sat at the small table in the lodge sitting room with a pencil, eraser, and a large paper pad. He wanted to work out what they had so far on the case, what was missing, and what still needed to be done. Sometimes it helped to do that in dia-grammatic form.

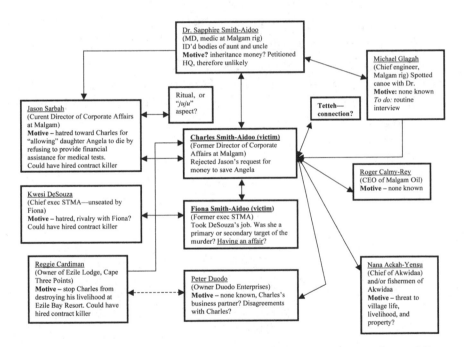

THE SMITH-AIDOO MURDER

Dawson had drawn a dashed lined between Peter Duodo and Reg-gie Cardiman because a direct connection between the two wasn't yet established.

"What do you want to do about Duodo?" Chikata asked.

"Talk to him on the phone tomorrow," Dawson instructed him. "Find out what kind of business arrangement he had with Charles, if any. Were they on good terms, did they have any disagreements, you know, that kind of thing. In other words, could Duodo be a suspect? Get a feeling for if he's hiding something. If so, we might have to interview him in person. Also, check if Duodo ever heard of any threats made to Charles or Fiona."

"No problem. Is that it for today?" Chikata said.

"Why?" Dawson asked knowingly. "Where are you going tonight?"

"There's a private party tonight at the Champs Bar at Stellar. Do you want to come?"

"No, thank you."

"Come on," Chikata said, laughing as he went to the door. "Your wife isn't here."

"I prefer to stay out of trouble." A thought occurred to Dawson. "What kind of party is this?"

"I don't really know. The manager of Champs invited me."

That was typical for Chikata. People invited him to everything.

"While you're there," Dawson said thoughtfully, "keep your ears open for anything interesting. For example, I understand there was a rumor that Fiona Smith-Aidoo was having an affair. See if you dig up anything like that."

"Okay, boss, I will."

"And don't get drunk," Dawson called out. "I need you fresh for tomorrow."

Chapter 22

IN THE MORNING, DAWSON was just out of the shower when Chief Superintendent Lartey called to ask how the case was progressing. Dawson gave him a quick summary of events so far.

"Move it along," Lartey said crisply. "I need you and Philip back as quickly as possible. Cases are coming in all the time, and I want both of you to attend a new forensics course in two weeks."

First he rushes me here to Takoradi. Now he's trying to rush me back to Accra.

"How is Philip doing?" Lartey asked.

"Fine, sir. Very comfortable at the hotel."

If the chief super detected the jab, he didn't let on. "I want you to give him more free rein. Let him take the lead as much as possible. I'd like him to move up to inspector when you get to chief inspector. That is, *if* you do. How you perform on this case might determine that."

Not that you're trying to pressure me, Dawson thought. "Yes, of course, sir."

He was glad to get off the phone with his boss as he answered a knock on the door. It was Chikata.

"How was the party?" Dawson asked as he invited him in.

"I've seen better," Chikata said.

"Did you hear anything useful?"

Chikata dropped into the sitting room chair. "I was talking to a woman who used to work in Smith-Aidoo's corporate affairs department. She says she resigned, but I got the feeling she might have been sacked. Anyway, she was boasting that Takoradi has a much lower crime rate compared to Accra, and I said, wasn't Charles Smith-Aidoo brutally murdered some months ago? I didn't tell her what I do, by the way. She was drinking and her tongue was loose, so I got her to say more. She told me she had heard that Fiona was having an affair with some businessman in town, and maybe it was the businessman that killed her and Charles."

"Oh, really?" Dawson said with interest. "That's the second time I've heard reference to her possible involvement with a businessman. Did she give a name?"

"No. She said she had heard it was a banker, then she changed it to an oilman, then a bookstore owner, and all this time she was leaning on me and giggling and breathing her alcohol fumes on me. I couldn't keep her on the subject. She kept asking me if we could go upstairs to my room."

Chikata pulled a face, indicating just what he thought of that idea.

"Come on, let's go." Dawson said as he heard the sound of Baah's taxi pulling up. "I'm going to introduce you to Superintendent Hammond."

"Ah, right. Is he going to be glad to see me?"

"I doubt that very much."

BAAH PULLED UP in front of the police headquarters, and Dawson and Chikata alighted. They went inside where Dawson knocked on Hammond's door, opened it, and put his head in.

"Good morning, sir."

"Morning. Come in."

Dawson introduced Hammond to Chikata, who received only a curt nod from the superintendent.

"Kwesi DeSouza called me this morning to lodge a complaint against you," Hammond said to Dawson.

"A complaint? Regarding what?"

"You made sarcastic and discourteous comments to him, you insisted on repeating questions that we have already dealt with, and after you saw him in his offices at STMA, you hounded him at TTI while he was supervising exams."

"Questioning possible suspects is harassment? In that case, we might as well do nothing, sir."

"There you are," Hammond said, flipping his palm up demonstratively. "Did you hear what you just said and how you said it? Exactly the sarcasm Mr. DeSouza is talking about. Coming from CID Headquarters doesn't give you any right to insult people. We are a closely knit community here, and we behave differently than people do in Accra. You have to respect that."

"I was in no way discourteous to the man," Dawson said coolly. "He felt insulted because he has an overinflated opinion of himself and thinks that as the chief executive of the STMA, he's somehow above being questioned. He could be the president of Ghana, for all I care. If there's a need to interrogate him fifty times, I will go back and do so fifty times."

Out of the corner of his eye, Dawson saw Chikata freeze and hold his breath. For several moments, Hammond stared at Dawson in consternation. "What about you, Inspector Dawson?" he said finally. "Do you not have an inflated opinion yourself?"

Dawson mentally dismissed the question as irrelevant. "Would you like to hear what I learned from Mr. DeSouza that might be useful information, sir?"

"Go ahead," Hammond said churlishly.

"He said there is, or was, a rumor that Fiona Smith-Aidoo was having an affair, but he could not say with whom. Sergeant Chikata has also heard that from a second source."

"There are all sorts of rumors all the time," Hammond contested. "Doesn't mean they're true."

Dawson remained steadfast. "Yes, but Chikata and I will keep it in the back of our minds and follow up on it. I also interviewed Mr. Cardiman on Saturday."

"And?"

"I agree it's difficult to see how he could have ambushed the Smith-Aidoo's vehicle."

"So you went all the way to Cape Three Points to establish that," Hammond said condescendingly.

"But if there was an accomplice—"

"Who? What accomplice?"

"Well, I don't know that yet, but—"

"Okay, okay," Hammond said impatiently. "Work on that theory, if you like. I don't know what you'll get out of it, but it's up to you. Regarding Mr. Smith-Aidoo's mobile, I went to Vodafone, and they did a trace on the Lawrence Tetteh that Mr. Smith-Aidoo was communicating with. It's not Tetteh, the CEO at Goilco. So we don't need to concern ourselves with that question anymore."

Dawson tensed as a hot streak flashed across his left palm like lightening. He paused a moment to let it subside. "Thank you for finding that out, sir."

"No problem."

Dawson's phone rang, and he picked up the call. It was Jason Sarbah.

"I've spoken with Mr. Calmy-Rey, Inspector," he said. "He will be available to meet with you at nine o'clock tomorrow morning at our offices. He is located on the top floor. You will be escorted there as soon as you arrive at reception."

"Thank you very much, Mr. Sarbah."

"You are welcome, Inspector."

Dawson ended the call. "I have a meeting with Mr. Calmy-Rey tomorrow morning," he told Hammond.

"Okay."

"Were you able to interrogate him back in July, sir?"

"Yes. He had been out of the country at the time of the murder. He obviously thought very highly of Smith-Aidoo—no motive whatsoever to kill him or have him killed. Please, Inspector Dawson, do not antagonize Mr. Calmy-Rey."

"I don't intend to, sir," Dawson said pleasantly. "Just one other thing I forgot to ask before. On the postmortem report by the pathologist Dr. Cudjoe, he didn't mention gunpowder burns around Fiona Smith-Aidoo's entrance wound. Did either of you attend the postmortem?"

Hammond shook his head. "Seidu was supposed to be there, but they gave him the wrong time and performed the autopsy in his absence. I was quite annoyed."

"Do you have any contact number for Dr. Cudjoe?" Dawson asked.

"Yes. I'll text it to you."

"Thank you very much, sir."

• • •

OUTSIDE, AS SOON as they were out of earshot, Chikata looked at Dawson in astonishment. "What is the man's problem?"

Dawson shrugged. "Insecurity? I don't know, but if he's more concerned about hurting people's feelings than he is about finding out who killed the Smith-Aidoos, there's nothing I can do about that. Honestly, I don't care anymore. I didn't come here to make nice."

"Do you want me to call my uncle about him?" Chikata asked, as they got back into Baah's taxi.

Dawson shook his head. "No, it's not worth it." It was a consideration, but he didn't want Chikata to put himself in an awkward position between Hammond and Lartey. "In any case, he might just call your uncle anyway, to complain about me."

"Massa," Chikata said, laughing, "I thought Superintendent Hammond was about to have a stroke when you pulled DeSouza down from his pedestal."

"What I said was true," Dawson asserted. "DeSouza had no reason to react so negatively to me—unless he's the murderer, of course. In that case he has good reason."

That remark set off another round of laughter for Chikata, with which Dawson eventually joined. Meanwhile, he saw he had just received Hammond's text with Dr. Cudjoe's number. He tried the number twice without success.

"Where now, sir?" Baah asked.

"Let's go to the Effia-Nkwanta Hospital Mortuary to look for Dr. Cudjoe." He turned in his seat to address Chikata. "Hammond wasn't telling the truth about Smith-Aidoo's phone. Either he didn't take it to Vodafone at all, or the Lawrence Tetteh in the address book is really the Goilco CEO."

"How do you know?" Chikata challenged. "Is it your *juju* hand again?"

He was one of the few who knew about Dawson's synesthesia and had always referred to it as his "*juju* hand," half seriously and half in jest.

"That's right," Dawson said.

"It's as though the superintendent doesn't want us to succeed," Chikata said. "Why is he trying to hinder us, or is he protecting someone?"

"It could be both."

• • •

TWENTY MINUTES LATER, they pulled into the uphill driveway of the hospital, and Baah parked to the side. Dawson and Chikata went into the waiting area where patients were sitting or lining up at the information booth. A sign pointed to the HIV Voluntary Testing Clinic, but there was no signage for the mortuary. After asking two people in succession, they were directed up a long flight of steps and across the road. The mortuary was in a dismal grey building with odd, inverted U-structures on its roof.

They went in the open front door. At a small receptionist's desk to the left, a man was laboriously writing in a large notebook. He looked up.

"Yes?"

"We're looking for Dr. Cudjoe?"

"Please, you can try the office," the man said, pointing across the hall.

Dawson and Chikata went in and found a tech in a khaki jacket looking through a filing cabinet.

"Very sorry," the man said, in response to Dawson's inquiry. "Dr. Cudjoe has traveled to Ashanti Region."

"Do you know when he'll return?"

"I'm not actually sure. Do you have his mobile number?"

"I have a number for him."

Dawson brought up the number he had for Cudjoe on his phone and showed it to the man to be sure it was correct.

"Oh, no—it's five-six-six at the end, not six-five-five."

Dawson and Chikata exchanged glances but didn't say anything until they were outside again.

"I bet you superintendent deliberately gave you the wrong number," Chikata said.

"Perhaps," Dawson said, inclining his head. "It could be a genuine mistake, though. I can see accidentally switching five-six-six to six-five-five."

"I can't," Chikata said with conviction. "Considering everything else about Hammond's behavior, I don't think he made a mistake at all."

A pretty, young nurse walked past them and Chikata's head turned as if drawn by a cable.

"Nice," he commented.

"Not as nice as my wife," Dawson said.

"Yes, but I can't have your wife," Chikata said with a snort.

"True."

As they returned from the hospital, a thunderstorm began, their first experience of rain in the Western Region. It put Accra's showers to shame, and to the surprise of Dawson and Chikata, everyone seemed to have large, colorful umbrellas at the ready. In Accra, your umbrella was the nearest building you could find.

After hitting a few puddles, the taxi stalled out, and Dawson and Chikata jumped out to push after the ignition failed several times. The car came to life again after a few shudders, and Baah kept the engine revved while the other two men hopped back in, soaked to the skin.

"Let's go home," Dawson said. He didn't like wet clothes.

Thirty minutes after Dawson was back in a dry outfit at the lodge, his phone vibrated. It was Chikata texting him to say he was coming over from the hotel. Dawson went to the kitchen, opened the door, and looked out. The sergeant was walking up in the pouring rain with a large unfurled red, yellow, and green umbrella.

"Where did you get that?" Dawson asked, as he came in.

"I borrowed it from the woman at the reception desk," he said, folding it and leaning it against the wall. "I am now officially a Tako-radian. Do you know I have never used an umbrella in my life?"

Dawson thought for a moment. "Now that you mention it, neither have I. People in Accra don't know anything about them."

They went to the sitting room.

"Yeah, Dawson," Chikata said, sitting down with one leg swung over the arm of the chair. "I just talked to this Peter Duodo guy in Accra."

"Oh, good," Dawson said, brightening. "What did you find out?"

"In fact, I thought the man was going to cry over Smith-Aidoo."

"What do you mean?"

"Very nice, soft-spoken gentleman. His voice started to shake. Seems like he's still in grief. He and Smith-Aidoo grew up together in Takoradi and they had been friends since secondary school. Duodo moved to Accra about ten years ago for his real estate business, but he and Smith-Aidoo stayed in touch."

"Aha," Dawson said, nodding. "So they were close."

"It seems so. When the oil discovery came along, Smith-Aidoo tried to persuade his friend to open an office in Takoradi and buy up some land along the coast while it was still cheap. He told Duodo that Malgam was looking to partner with someone for development in the Cape Three Points area and that Smith-Aidoo was negotiating with the chief of Akwidaa. Smith-Aidoo said he was going to see if he could cut Duodo into a deal. I asked Duodo if Smith-Aidoo would get a kickback in that case, but he denied it."

"He probably wouldn't admit it if it were true," Dawson said, "but if it is, maybe someone at Malgam got wind of Smith-Aidoo's dealings with Duodo and didn't like it."

"That isn't all. Something else came up during my conversation regarding Cardiman. After the meeting, as he and his wife were leaving Ezile, Smith-Aidoo called Duodo to say that he had told Cardiman that if he didn't voluntarily vacate the Ezile property, it would be easy to pay off Nana Ackah-Yensu to kick Cardiman out. Smith-Aidoo said that led to a heated discussion between him and Cardiman."

Dawson sat forward with increasing excitement. "Cardiman didn't say that at all. He said quite the opposite—that he had parted with Smith-Aidoo on good terms."

"Doesn't sound like good terms to me," Chikata said, flatly. "Now listen to this: While he was on the phone with Duodo, Charles said that he and his wife were debating whether to drive up to the lighthouse. Cardiman had told them as they were leaving that the view of Cape Three Points was spectacular and that they must see it before they leave."

"Now you're talking." Dawson exclaimed. "Because Cardiman told us it was about fifteen minutes from Ezile to the lighthouse."

"Yes, that puts the time at twelve forty-five when the Smith-Aidoos get up to the lighthouse. They spend about twenty minutes looking at the view, or who knows, maybe they even go up in the lighthouse. It's now five after one or a little later. Meanwhile, Cardiman has already left Ezile and—"

"Now he has enough time to lie in wait for them," Dawson finished.

"Exactly."

"Good job," Dawson said. He slapped palms with his sergeant, ending it with the customary Ghanaian mutual snap of the fingers. "This means Cardiman is still a suspect, and he has some explaining to do."

Chapter 23

TUESDAY MORNING, THE SUN was hot and bright under a pale blue sky as Dawson and Chikata arrived at the Malgam office. A guard escorted them to the top floor, where the receptionist asked them to take a seat. The first-floor lobby was nice to look at, but this suite at the pinnacle of the building was spectacular. Geometrically placed *Adinkra* symbols, each with specific meanings, alternated with the Malgam logo patterned the gleaming wood floor. Overstuffed leather armchairs were set around the room with studied casualness. A skylight provided bright, airy illumination.

"Imagine what it's like to be king of all this," Chikata said under his breath, so that the receptionist couldn't hear him.

Dawson grunted, but made no comment. He picked up a business magazine from the table and flicked through the pages with passing interest.

They looked up as a white man in a dark suit appeared from the hallway. Dressed in a crisp white shirt, navy tie, and dark blue slacks, he was short, late fifties, and expanding around the middle. His brown hair was thinning on the top and speckled with grey at his temples.

"Inspector Dawson?"

They stood up as the man came around the table with his hand extended.

"Good morning. I'm Roger Calmy-Rey. What a pleasure, Inspector. Jason Sarbah has told me about you. Good to have you here."

"Thank you, sir. This is Detective Sergeant Chikata who is working with me on the case."

"How do you do? Please, do come this way."

They followed him to the right down the hallway to an automatic glass door that silently slid open as they approached. Beyond that, in a carpeted anteroom, an attractive, light-skinned woman sat in front of the computer on her shiny desk.

"Good morning," she flashed a dazzling smile at them.

"Janice, please hold my calls while I'm meeting with Inspector Dawson, would you?" Calmy-Rey said.

"Of course, sir." Her accent spoke of Ghanaian sophistication.

Calmy-Rey opened the last door, which was solid mahogany, and ushered him in. Dawson was sure he had never seen an office as large as this. In the foreground, a set of armchairs surrounded a coffee table. Calmy-Rey's large polished desk was to the left, positioned at an angle. Beyond that was an executive meeting table with room for eight, a flat-screen TV on the wall facing a sectional black leather sofa, and farther still in the background another door. A floor-to-ceiling window offered a panorama of the city and the Atlantic Ocean.

"Do make yourselves comfortable," Calmy-Rey said, gesturing to a couple of the armchairs. He couldn't be more different from the tall, aloof man Dawson had pictured. He was friendly, and his voice was warm.

"Can I offer you anything to drink? A soft drink? Water?"

"Oh, no, we're fine," Dawson said. "Thank you, sir."

Calmy-Rey took his seat in the facing chair, inclining himself not away, but toward them. Perhaps he had learned that with years of practice. Regardless, Dawson found it an appealing gesture that seemed genuine.

"I can't tell you how glad I was when Jason told me you were here from Accra to help with the investigation into Charles's death," Calmy-Rey said. "It deeply and personally affected all of us at Malgam. Not only in Ghana. It had a strong ripple effect in our offices in London and all over the world where Malgam has activity. For me, Charles wasn't simply an employee. I considered him a good friend, and so was Fiona."

"Were you in Ghana when you heard the news of his death?" Dawson asked.

"No, I was on holiday in Crete. Once I heard what had happened,

I flew into Accra the following day. It was important to give moral support at a time like that."

"I'm sure that was appreciated," Dawson said, wondering for a moment what life on Crete was like.

"It was my duty as CEO."

"Did you spend time with Mr. Smith-Aidoo outside of the workplace?"

"As much as time allowed." Calmy-Rey's eyes became softer. "He was outgoing, charming, wonderfully funny . . . just so likeable and good to be around."

"But evidently someone didn't like him," Dawson observed.

Calmy-Rey nodded, his gaze dropping contemplatively. "It's a tragedy. Charles's career could not have been on a better track." He paused, and it seemed to Dawson that he was carefully choosing his next words. "Em . . . I think the state of family was where the trouble was—issues with his sister, Eileen, and his brother, Brian. The only day I ever saw Charles even remotely upset was after he'd had an argument with Brian."

Dawson sat up a little. "When was this, Mr. Calmy-Rey?"

"It could have been in April of this year. Or May, perhaps."

"Did he say what this argument was about?"

"Not really, but I think money was involved." He looked uneasy. "I'm sorry, perhaps it would be best to ask Sapphire about it. I feel uncomfortable that I may give you the wrong facts."

Dawson nodded. "I understand. Are you aware of anyone who might have wanted Charles Smith-Aidoo and/or his wife dead?"

"There are any number of activists and advocates who see the oil companies as dire enemies bent on destroying the livelihoods of fishermen. Charles was our public face and the most accessible. Sure, one or two of these people might like to kill me—" a smile crept to Calmy-Rey's face "—but it's a lot harder to get to me than it was Charles."

"You say 'one or two people' might like to kill you. Are you referring to anyone specific?"

"No, I'm not. I haven't met any of these activist types, although Charles had. I do know that the most vocal is a man by the name of Quashie Quarshie, who is the head of an NGO called Friends of

Axim, or FOAX, as they call it. Mind you, in mentioning him, I'm not directing an accusation at him."

Something clicked in Dawson's brain. "Reportedly, when the Smith-Aidoos visited Mr. Cardiman at Ezile Bay, they were coming from a function in Axim. Could that have been a meeting with the FOAX people?"

"It might have, I don't know," Calmy-Rey said, standing up, "but we can easily find out."

He opened the office door, put his head around it, and asked Janice to look up Charles's calendar for that week in July. She came into the office two minutes later and quietly handed Calmy-Rey a sheet of paper.

"You were right," he said to Dawson. "This shows his schedule for the entire month, and on Monday, the seventh of July, he was due for a meeting at eight o'clock in the morning with FOAX."

He leaned forward to hand the paper to Dawson, who studied it with Chikata looking on. Other meetings during the month seemed innocuous and routine, but the one with FOAX might have been significant. What if there had been acrimony between Charles and the activists, and one or more of them had decided that Charles Smith-Aidoo had to be eliminated? He, or they, could have followed him and his wife to Ezile Bay and ambushed them on their way back.

"Who else in the office, besides you," Dawson asked Janice, "knew or might have known about Mr. Smith-Aidoo's schedule?"

The light from the window framed her face perfectly.

"I don't know of anyone," she said. "I certainly didn't mention it—there was really no need to."

"Thank you for this," Dawson said. "May we keep this copy?"

"Certainly," Calmy-Rey said.

"What about here at Malgam itself?" Dawson asked. "Could anyone have held a grudge against Charles?"

Calmy-Rey shook his head slowly. "Very small chance of that. We all work well together with mutual respect from the CEO down to the housekeepers. Of course, I don't know every employee intimately, but I would be tremendously surprised if we harbored anyone with such murderous intent."

"However, I've heard something a little troubling."

Calmy-Rey looked concerned. "About Charles?"

"Yes. That he was carving out business deals for himself while he represented Malgam."

"I seriously doubt that," Calmy-Rey said, confidently shaking his head. "If that had been going on, it would have been brought to my notice. People say all sorts of things for all sorts of reasons, and I always approach any accusations with great caution. I am not convinced that Charles was operating under any serious conflicts of interest."

"What if someone felt he was doing wrong by the company?"

The CEO flicked his head sideways. "I know of no one. That's all I can tell you, but you're welcome to ask around, Inspector."

"Have you ever heard of someone named Peter Duodo?" Dawson asked. "He's a real estate developer who was a close friend of Charles's."

"No, never. I'm sorry, I wish I could help more."

"No problem," Dawson said. "How have you enjoyed your time in Ghana?"

Calmy-Rey smiled broadly. "It has been inspiring. The work environment in this country is highly attractive. My late father, Ulysses Calmy-Rey, founded the company in 1955. In Malgam Oil, he has left a legacy of 'capitalism with care.' He was always very concerned about the well-being of the people indigenous to the areas of oil discovery. I strive to follow his example and maintain a responsibility to the environment and to the people. I have to care about the people of Takoradi, and I have to care about the fishermen. It's important to me. Ghana is a very important account for us, and we want to be around for many, many years as the country grows and develops because of well-managed oil exploration."

Dawson nodded. The man was very smooth.

"Is there anything else I can help you with, Inspector? I'm at your disposal."

"No. Thank you very much, sir." Dawson stood up, and Chikata followed.

"I'll walk you out," Calmy-Rey said.

Just as they got to the mahogany door, Dawson had a thought.

"Oh, one other thing," he said. "Did you and Mr. Smith-Aidoo know Lawrence Tetteh, the CEO of Goilco?"

"Oh, yes, of course," Calmy-Rey said, nodding. "We both had lots of contact with Lawrence—Charles and our chief financial officer more so than I did, but still, I knew him well, and I made sure I kept in touch with him. Goilco has a ten percent carried interest in the Legacy Oilfield. His death was another tragedy, and just a month or so before the Smith-Aidoos' murder. It's very sad. I understand Lawrence's stepbrother was charged in his murder."

"Yes. Do you know if Tetteh had enemies in the oil industry, or in government?"

"He was a perfectly straightforward, experienced, and knowledgeable gentleman. On the face of it, he shouldn't have had any enemies at all."

"Might you have Mr. Tetteh's mobile phone number?"

"No, I'm afraid not. But I may be able to find it for you."

"If you can, I would be grateful."

"But of course." Calmy-Rey smiled again. "I'm very glad to have met you, Inspector."

In the lift down to the lobby, Chikata said, "He seems to be a very nice man."

Dawson grunted. "A little too much sugar in the cup."

"What do you mean?"

"He 'cares about the people of Takoradi and the fishermen?' Come on."

"You don't trust him?"

"I just question the sincerity, that's all. Do any of these exploiters really care that much?"

They waited until they were outside the building before resuming the discussion.

"Do you suspect him of being involved with the murder?" Chikata asked.

"Not at the moment, but . . ."

Chikata looked at him quizzically. "Did your *juju* hand speak to you?"

"No. Not this time."

"Then what is it you don't trust?"

"I felt like he was putting on a show for our benefit. To make himself appear to be a better man than he really is."

"People do that all the time," Chikata pointed out. "The question is, do you suspect him of murder?"

"No," Dawson admitted, finally. "I can't say I do. Anyway, we've found out one thing, at least. We know what the Smith-Aidoos were doing in Axim that Monday morning. Now we have to follow up with the people at FOAX."

Chapter 24

ON WEDNESDAY MORNING, DAWSON found himself standing at the edge of an outdoor swimming pool at the Regional Maritime University east of Accra. He was about to start the HUET session that Jason Sarbah had arranged, but a voice inside kept telling him that he still had time to back out and join Chikata on much safer undertakings. Today, the detective sergeant would be checking DeSouza's alibi with Susana, his assistant; and Sarbah's alibi with the staff at Sarbah Properties; and then it was on to Axim to meet Quashie Quarshie, the head of FOAX.

However, Dawson knew he couldn't back down now. It would be cowardly. He had spent the day before in a classroom learning the basics of offshore safety and CPR. Now he faced the second and most challenging day. In front of him, suspended over the water, was a blue and white training module that would be lowered into the depths of the pool by a complicated cable mechanism. They would have several practice runs before the ultimate stage in which the module would submerge and rotate 180 degrees. Dawson and the three other trainees would then make their escape. He already had his helmet, orange overalls, and life vest on. His stomach was churning. It was hot and he was pouring with sweat. Some of it was fear.

With a harsh whine of machinery, the module moved level with the edge of the pool by remote control, and Dawson and the others got in. It seated four. Dawson took the right-hand seat of the second row. He could not bring himself to look down as the module moved out to the center of the six-meter deep pool, but in spite of staring fixedly ahead, he could see the blue of the water from the corner of his eye. His stomach clenched, and he began to feel sick.

Agyeman, their instructor, was one of the three divers on hand in case one or more of the four trainees could not get out of the seat belt or otherwise had difficulty. He showed them how to strap themselves securely into their seats.

"First, we learn how to brace ourselves for the water landing, like this."

Everyone followed his lead.

"Okay, good," he said. "Now we will practice that while the helicopter is lowered to the surface of the water. We will not yet submerge. We are just going to become used to the sensation of going down. When I give the command to brace for impact, you do so immediately."

The cabin dropped, not very fast for the first time, and they practiced the brace. The second time, the drop was more rapid, and Dawson felt his insides float up. After the third and fastest drop, they were ready for partial submersion, where Dawson and the other trainees learned how to take a deep breath in preparation for going completely under.

AFTER A BREAK, it was time for the most anxiety-provoking segment of the training: full submersion and rotation of the module. Here Dawson learned the extra step of placing his right hand on the window frame before the rotation began to help keep him oriented once he was upside down.

The module went out to the center of the pool.

This is it, Dawson thought.

The descent began and Agyeman yelled, "*Brace!*"

Dawson gripped the front of his seat with both hands and pushed himself hard against the seatback.

The splash came sooner than he had anticipated, and then the cabin was filling with water fast. Dawson hyperventilated a few times as instructed, and took a deep breath. As the water reached his neck, the module turned upside down.

It felt to him as if they were spinning multiple times. His arms reached out instinctively. He had to get out. *Seat belt*. He was feeling for the clasps on the belt and realized he had shut his eyes tight. He needed to open them. He released the buckle and freed himself. Was he facing up, or down? The window was still to his right, and he pushed against it. It opened, but at the instant he was preparing to swim out, he felt someone clawing at his back. He turned to look and saw the trainee who had been sitting to his left. He was on the wrong side, trying to exit through Dawson's window, and he was in a state of panic. His eyes were wide open and afraid, his arms and legs flailing wildly and provoking turbulence.

Dawson's impulse was to push the man back and make his escape. Instead, he grabbed the frantic trainee by the waist and forcefully propelled him to the window, giving him a final shove to eject him. One of the divers appeared, grasped him, and took him swiftly to the surface. Dawson followed in their track.

Life vest. He tugged at the red hook and it inflated.

He clawed at the water as he rose, his chest about to explode, and then he burst the surface and felt his head free and clear in air. He drew in his breath in a gasp and looked around. He had made it, and now he felt surprisingly calm. Two of the other trainees were floating around freely in the water, but the fourth, the one who Dawson had collided with, was spluttering and coughing as someone helped him out of the pool.

HOURS LATER, DAWSON was lying in bed with Christine. The HUET center wasn't far out from Accra, so he had decided to spend the night. The boys had gone to sleep, and she was dozing with her head in the crook of his arm.

He was thankful the HUET was all over. His certificate was safely next to him on the bedside table. He was surprised that this was one of the proudest moments he could remember in quite some time. His getting through something he had been afraid of almost to the point of paralysis was an achievement. In addition, the diver who had witnessed him push the other trainee out through the window toward safety had given him a special commendation for his actions.

Christine had begun to snore lightly. He smiled down at her. Silly girl. She never believed him or the boys when they told her she snored. He moved her head over to her pillow and rolled over. No need to switch the lights off because there had just been another power cut.

Oh, Ghana, he thought as he drifted off, *what are we going to do with you?*

THURSDAY MORNING, HE saw that he had missed a call from Dr. Smith-Aidoo. He tried her number. She didn't pick up, so Dawson left her a text to say that he would try calling her again later on.

Before returning to Takoradi, he paid a visit to a friend of his at the Vodafone store on Oxford Street.

"Confidential, okay?" he said to Emmanuel in his deliciously chilled office.

"Always," Emmanuel replied, leaning back. With his hefty weight, his executive chair went all the way back with a squeak.

"Do you remember the story of Lawrence Tetteh?" Dawson asked. "The CEO of Goilco who was shot about five months ago?"

"Of course."

"I need the mobile number he was using."

"Was Vodafone his provider?"

"Yes."

"Then I can get it for you, no problem. By the way, what phone service are you using these days?"

Dawson winced. "*Chaley,* sorry. Still with MTN."

"*What!?*"

"Okay, let's make a deal. If you get me that number, I'll switch to Vodafone."

They shook hands on it.

IT WAS LATE afternoon when he got back to Takoradi by bus. Dawson wanted to give Dr. Smith-Aidoo an update on the investigation, but each time he had tried to call, he had gotten an error message that the "subscriber's phone has been turned off." Dawson doubted that very much. It was much more likely a problem with the network. On the off chance that Dr. Smith-Aidoo was at home, he took a taxi to her house at Airport Ridge. Her car wasn't in the driveway. He got out and knocked on the front door. He waited a couple minutes and tried again, but everything was quiet.

Thinking he'd try Charles Smith-Aidoo's home, he had the taxi skirt the center of town, back to Shippers Circle and past Planter's Lodge to Beach Drive. The taxi driver blew his horn, and after a few moments, Gamal opened the gate and they pulled in.

"Good eve'ng, sir," Gamal said, saluting to Dawson as he got out.

"Good evening, Gamal. Have you seen the doctor today?"

"Please, I have not seen her."

"If she comes, can you ask her to please call me? You remember me?"

"Yes, please."

"Thank you very much, Gamal."

Dawson was just about to turn and leave when he realized he would be missing an opportunity.

"How long did you work for Mr. and Mrs. Smith-Aidoo?" he asked Gamal in a conversational tone.

"About fifteen years."

"Really. A long time, eh?"

"Yes, please," Gamal said.

"They treated you very well."

"Yes, sir."

"I'm sorry what happened to them."

Gamal nodded, looking down for a moment and back up. "It pained me. Too much."

Dawson thought he had never seen anyone look so crumpled and sad, and he realized how devoted Gamal must have been to Charles and Fiona Smith-Aidoo.

"You take care of all this?" he asked Gamal, gesturing toward the manicured grounds with hibiscus and frangipani trees.

"Yes, please."

"You do a very fine job. It looks beautiful."

"Thank you, sir," Gamal said, smiling broadly.

"Is there a garden in the back?"

"Yes, please."

"Can you show it to me?"

"Oh, yes sir."

He walked with Gamal around the side of the house toward the rear. "What's going to happen to you now that Mr. and Mrs. Smith-Aidoo are no longer here?"

"Please, I think the doctor will sell the house, and then I will work for her."

"I see. Do you stay here all the time?"

"Yes, please. I dey for boys' quarters."

The high wall enclosing the rear of the house had both razor wire and bougainvillea running along its top edge. The garden was shaded and green, just as well tended as in the front of the house. On its far side was an exit door, which Gamal unlocked and opened inward. Dawson went through and emerged to open space very unlike the confines of the garden behind the wall. The vegetation was wild and free, with hardy scrub in patches down an incline to the beach barely 500 meters away. He stood for a while looking out across the Gulf of Guinea to the horizon. It was a spectacular view. He realized he would love to own a home with a view like this.

"Who uses this door?" he asked.

"Sometimes when people used to come to visit the house, they pass here to go to the beach. 'Specially the white people."

"Which white people used to come here?"

"One Mr. Cal— . . . Cam—"

"Calmy-Rey?"

"Eh-heh, that one. Him and his wife."

"How many times were they here?"

"Anyway, I'm not so sure. Three times or so."

"When was the last time they came here?"

Gamal turned the corners of his mouth down, thinking. "Please, maybe some six months."

"And who else? What about one white man with red hair, they call him Mr. Reggie Cardiman?"

Gamal shook his head slowly and sucked his teeth three times in a row. "No, I don't think so."

"Okay, now, what about the Ghanaians? Do you know one Jason Sarbah?"

Gamal seemed unsure, so Dawson described what Sarbah looked like.

"Oh, yes," Gamal said, nodding vigorously. "I know the one. He too, he come here one time to make argument with Massa Charles."

"You heard them arguing?"

"It was that man Sarbah cause the *palava*. At that time, I was in the kitchen, so I heard what he said."

"Did he threaten Massa?"

He shook his head again. "No, he was just shouting say why Massa don't give him money."

That confirmed Jason's desperate quest for funds to save Angela, his daughter.

"Who else used to come here?" Dawson persisted. He didn't want anyone left out.

"Another man too," Gamal said, "but now I forget his name. One night, I came to the garden to get the water hose. I heard some people talking behind that bush."

He pointed to a large jasmine bush with its fragrant, star-shaped white flowers. "I went there with my torchlight, and I found the man with the madam."

"You say you found the man with Madam. Doing what?"

Gamal looked away, apparently deeply embarrassed. He was squirming with so much discomfort that Dawson decided to move on. "Was Massa Charles at home at that time?"

"No, please."

"But he was in Takoradi?"

"Yes, please."

"You say you can't remember the name of the man who was with Madam. Can you describe him?"

"A little fat. Not so tall. At that time, I didn't know him, but some two months after Massa and Madam die, when I was walking in Takoradi town with my friend, I saw that man again, and I ask my friend if he know who the man is. My friend say the man own one stationery shop in Takoradi."

"Stationery shop. Which stationery shop?"

"They call it Abraham Stationery. It dey for Kofi Annan Road, near Barclays. The man who own that store be the man who was with Madam."

Dawson's blood turned to ice.

Chapter 25

HE SAT IN THE lodge sitting room with his elbows on the table and his head between his hands. *A little fat, not too tall. He owns the Abraham Stationery Store.* The words kept echoing. Gamal had described Dawson's cousin. Two people—DeSouza and Chikata's fellow party-goer—had claimed that Fiona had been having an affair with a "businessman" in town. *Is it Abraham? It must be a mistake,* Dawson thought desperately, but no matter which way he tried to twist it, he came right back to his cousin.

He went to the kitchen as he heard light knocking on the door, opened up, and was surprised to see Dr. Smith-Aidoo on the step.

"Good evening, Inspector. Gamal told me that you came by earlier, so I thought I would return the favor."

"Thank you very much, Doctor. Please come in."

He invited her to take a seat in the sitting room and he sat opposite her. She was dressed in a sleek, all-black pants suit.

"Long day at work, Doctor?"

"Yes, very much so. I just returned from Kumasi yesterday. I'm sorry I missed your calls."

"No problem. I just wanted to update you on our progress."

Not that he had an enormous amount to tell her, but Dawson knew that keeping in close touch with her at each stage of the game was the best way to maintain good relations. He suspected that Superintendent Hammond had failed to do that, perhaps giving the doctor a false impression that he was doing little or nothing in the case. After briefing her for a few minutes, Dawson had a question for her.

"I hope I don't offend," he said, "but my sergeant and I have both heard that your Auntie Fiona might have been having an affair with a local businessman. Do you know anything about that?"

She shook her head. "No. I don't want to be naïve, but I would never have thought it of her. I suppose I'm idealizing her. This local businessman—do you know who?"

"Not yet."

An awkward pause hung briefly in the air. Dr. Smith-Aidoo hurried to fill it. "How's Hosiah recovering from his surgery?"

"Very well, thank you. You've never mentioned a husband or children. I hope you don't mind my asking?"

"I don't mind. No children, never been married, and not attached. I was seeing a fellow physician for a while, but he turned out to be too domineering. Wanted to get married and start me churning out the babies like a factory. I'm not ready for that. I'd like to set up my own practice in Takoradi before that ever happens."

"I wish you the best. I imagine you'll be very successful."

"Thank you."

His mbira, which was resting in the corner by the window, had caught her attention. "Do you play?"

"A little."

"May I see it?"

He gave it to her and sat down again while she examined it.

"It's wonderful," she said, looking up at him. "I love mbiras. Where did you get this one? From the Northern Region?"

"No, I made it."

She looked at him half disbelievingly. "Really?"

"I've been making them since I was a boy."

"Oh my. Intelligent *and* talented." She laughed playfully, and he recognized she was behaving differently toward him. She was more open, less guarded, and she was being flirtatious. He felt a disturbing twinge of excitement and made himself look away from her lovely face, framed by the soft lighting in the lodge.

She held the mbira out to him. "Play something, maestro."

He smiled. "Okay."

He played a lively piece with a recurring rhythmic theme. She sat forward, watching and listening intently, and applauding when he was done.

"Now I'll play something with a different mood," he said. "It's an old tune I learned when I was a kid."

This piece was more melodious, the notes blending with less of the traditional mbira discordance. For a while, he was lost in the composition. When he looked up again, tears were streaming down Dr. Smith-Aidoo's face. He stopped playing.

"Are you okay, Doctor?"

She covered her face with her hands and began to weep. Dawson kneeled beside her, touching her arm.

"What's wrong?"

"I can't stop seeing it . . ."

"Is it the canoe?"

She nodded, trying to say something but choking on the words. Her body leaned toward him, and he supported her as her arms went around his shoulders.

"Something about the melody brought back memories." She was sobbing. "I miss them. I miss them so much."

She held on to him tightly, and he waited for her weeping to run its course.

"Better?"

"Thank you," she whispered.

"It's okay." He made a slight movement to separate, but she wasn't letting go. Instead, she allowed her full weight to push against him. He tried to shift his position but lost his balance and sank to the floor with her on top of him.

Then he didn't know what was happening. He was on his back, and she was frantically kissing his neck and his face, her sweet breath coming fast. Her hand was in his shirt feeling the curve of his pectorals and stroking his abdominal muscles. She opened his shirt, kissed his chest. He thought he heard her whisper, "Please, I need it."

She straddled him so he felt the heat and softness of her crotch against his rigidity.

She unbuttoned her blouse and unsnapped her bra, exposing her round breasts, succulent yet firm with large, dark areolas that were in shocking contrast with her fair skin. She was unforgivably lovely.

Maybe he touched her breasts, maybe he didn't, but he turned his head away and covered his eyes as she opened undid his belt, and unzipped him. He felt like he was watching himself in a dream from a perch high up on the wall. His head was swirling. She tucked her fingertips in his waistband and gave a gentle tug. He lifted his hips slowly, and she eased his trousers and briefs down. She wrapped her fingers around his stiff shaft and gently stroked up to the tip. It responded, surging up to strike her palm and bouncing back to his belly with a soft thud.

Dawson opened his eyes with a vision of Christine standing across the room.

He gasped. *What am I doing?*

"No."

Pushing Fiona off to the side, he scrambled up frantically, hastily stuffing himself back in and zipping his trousers.

"Sorry," he muttered. "Sorry. I can't."

She was lying on the floor, staring up at him in bewilderment.

"I can't," he stammered. "Sorry. Please go, Doctor. Sorry."

He left her, went into the bedroom, and shut the door. He sat on the edge of the bed with his head between his hands. He was hyperventilating and his chest was tight. *What are you doing?* A wave of nausea went through him.

He held his breath, listening for her. Was she still there? For a terrifying instant, he was afraid she would come into the bedroom. Finally, he heard the front door close as she left.

Had he touched her? He might have, but only her breasts. She had made him hard, and he had let her. Was that adultery?

You don't get involved with *anyone* in a murder case.

He sprang up with a sudden desire to take a shower, but as he began to remove his clothes, he heard knocking on the door. No, he thought. Was she back? He stood where he was, paralyzed. His phone rang. It was Chikata.

"Dawson, are you there? I'm outside your door."

What a relief. "Okay, I'm coming."

He opened up the kitchen door and Chikata came in. "What's going on?"

"What do you mean?"

"I just saw a woman leaving in tears."

"Oh," Dawson said, avoiding Chikata's eye. "That's Dr. Smith-Aidoo. We were talking about the case, and she got sad thinking about her aunt and uncle."

"I see," Chikata said, regarding him with some curiosity. "She's beautiful."

Dawson's face was burning as he turned away abruptly. "Let's talk about the case."

"Sure, but first, how was the underwater training?"

Dawson laughed with relief. "I passed."

He gave a blow-by-blow account to exclamations of amazement from Chikata.

"So you're now qualified to visit the rig?"

"Yes," Dawson said. "I'll be going in a couple of days."

They occupied their usual spots at the sitting room table.

"First," Chikata said, "I went to Axim with Baah to meet this Quashie Quarshie. It took us almost two hours to find him. How this guy could have anything physically to do with the Smith-Aidoos' murder is hard to imagine. He's a very small man who had polio as a child. One leg is much shorter than the other, and sometimes he has to use a wheelchair because he's in pain."

"What about his personality?"

"He's very passionate about the organization's mission statement of sustainable living and protecting the coast from oil pollution and all that, and he says he's also a pacifist."

"What about his associates?"

"I thought it was a big organization, but it's only him and his wife and a part-time accountant, and they work out of a very small office. Quarshie says money is hard to come by these days. The wife was there, but not the accountant. I have his phone number, so I can get in touch with him. They meet once a month—sometimes it's well attended by fishermen and environmentalists, but other times they have only a few people coming in."

"Could any of the fishermen or the other attendees have a motive to kill the Smith-Aidoos?" Dawson asked.

"I asked Quarshie that question—I phrased it a little differently—and he said he's witnessed a lot of anger from some fishermen, but he had contact information for only a few. I can try to track them down tomorrow."

"Okay, good work. Did you get to Kweku Bonsa, the fetish priest?"

"Yes, but I didn't talk to him. He was having one of his ceremonies—dancing to the beat of drums, spinning around in a trance while his assistants were sprinkling him with chalk powder. It was going on for hours, and I was told that Bonsa would be too weak afterward to talk to me. They told me to come back tomorrow."

AFTER A LITTLE more discussion, Chikata left and Dawson hurried to the bathroom to finish what he had been about to do before the interruption. He pulled off his clothes and took a shower. He lathered and rinsed three times, trying to wash the sin away.

Chapter 26

His phone rang and he jerked awake disoriented, unsure what was dream and what was reality.

"Hello?" he said thickly.

"Hi, Dark. Sorry. I woke you."

Christine. His heart surged and then plunged as he remembered Dr. Smith-Aidoo.

"Yes, I fell asleep. What time is it?"

"Just past eleven. I shouldn't have called this late."

"No, it's okay," he said, sitting up at the side of the bed.

"How's everything?"

"Okay, doing okay. Thanks."

He sensed a split second pause on her part, and he realized he might be sounding strange.

"The boys are fine?" he asked hastily. "No more nightmares?"

"No, thank goodness. Seeing you in Takoradi did wonders. Still, they can't wait for you to come home."

"Tell them I will as soon as I can."

"You didn't call me today," she said, "so I just wanted to check on you."

"Thanks, love. I should have. I apologize."

"No, it's all right. Get your rest and take care, okay?"

"I will. And I do love you."

"I love you too."

He put his phone down, wondering if Christine had sensed something was amiss. The way he had said, "I *do* love you" was a bit odd.

•   •   •

HE WOKE SOME time before dawn and sat up in the dark. His head was aching because he hadn't had anything to eat in over twelve hours. He felt like smoking some *wee*, but he didn't have the energy to get up and find any. He fell back in bed, a dark, encircling wall of depression beginning to close in.

WHEN HE AWOKE again, the weather was bright and hot. He looked at his phone, which said 9:25. He groaned, rolled to the edge of the bed, and sat up. He was weak and needed some food. The episode with Dr. Smith-Aidoo came hurtling back with the force of a speeding truck.

IT HAD BEEN a struggle to get out of bed, but Dawson was glad he had. On foot to Abraham's store, it felt good to be out, especially after having had a large helping of roast plantain and groundnuts that he had bought at the roadside. Sometimes the simple yet filling meal was called "Kofi Broke Man," because it was dirt cheap.

Dawson was suppressing any memory of his encounter with the doctor. In the light of day, it had an unreal quality. He knew his sex drive had gotten the best of him, but in Sapphire's case, he sensed it was more complex than that—a misdirected need for physical intimacy had been set on fire when he had offered her comfort in her grief. It was possible that she had not ever received the solace she had needed after the death of her aunt and uncle.

He had called his cousin to say he was coming, so Abraham had been expecting him when he walked into his shop.

"I've missed you." Abraham gave his cousin a hefty hug. "You've been busy, eh?"

"Yes, I have. You won't believe I went to helicopter underwater escape training yesterday."

"Serious! How did it go?"

"I did okay. They gave me a commendation for exemplary performance, too."

"Congrats!" Abraham exclaimed. "Let's go and celebrate. There's a nice bar on Appiah Street."

They walked over and took a seat at a table under a canopy. A young woman came to take their orders—a club beer, a Malta, and some plantain chips.

Dawson sat slightly forward. He was dreading this, but it had to be done. "Abe, something has come up in the investigation that I have to ask you about."

"Oh? Sounds serious. What's going on?"

"You know that no matter what, I respect you, right?"

"Yes," Abraham said warily.

"You told me that you and Fiona Smith-Aidoo were classmates."

Abraham nodded, looking anxious. "Yes, that's right."

"If Fiona was not a murder victim," Dawson continued, "I wouldn't care about your relationship with her one way or the other. In fact, it wouldn't be any of my business. However, yesterday, I was talking to Gamal the Smith-Aidoo's watchman, asking him who had visited the Smith-Aidoos at Beach Road. He told me how, one night in the garden, he discovered Fiona with a man who fits your description. What's more, when he saw the man some months later in town, a friend told him that the man owned Abraham's Stationery."

He stopped there because Abraham knew what the question was and it needn't be asked. He had dropped his eyes and was moving his glass around in a slow circle in the condensation pool on the table. From the expression on his face, Dawson knew he was not about to deny anything.

"Okay, yes," he said quietly. "It's true, and Gamal is right. I was with Fiona. Darko, I haven't told you everything. We all have secrets and this was mine. I should have told you, but I was ashamed. Fiona was my girlfriend when we were together at Takoradi Secondary. To be honest, I thought I was going to marry her, and I thought she felt the same way. Until Charles Smith-Aidoo came along. He transferred from another school. I suppose the first time he ever saw her, he decided she was the girl he wanted.

"It sounds silly to say he took her away from me, but he was everything I wasn't—he had a way with words, he was athletic. When she fell for him, I realized she had never really been in love with me. I had been her friend, a very close companion, but she didn't have the fever for me that she had for Charles. I was hurt and bitter, but once

I had met Akosua, none of that mattered anymore. However, that's not the same as saying that I didn't still have feelings for Fiona."

Abraham glanced around as if someone might have been eavesdropping, but no one appeared the slightest bit interested in their conversation. Nevertheless, he sat forward and spoke confidentially. "About eight months ago, Fiona came into the shop to buy some envelopes and we chatted. As she was leaving, she asked me if I'd accompany her outside to her car. She began to talk about things in a strange way—the old days at school, how we used to help each other with lessons, the fun we had. I kept wondering why she was going on and on about this now. She finally confessed that she and Charles were going through a rough patch. Disagreements, arguments, and so on.

"She started to cry, saying that she needed to talk to someone she could trust as a friend, and the first person she had thought of was me, even after all these years. She asked if we could meet somewhere soon and just talk.

"When she told me this, I felt something inside, something like triumph that she had turned to me. You know that feeling you get when an old rival is defeated? Your ego smiles and says, 'you see now? In the end, I had victory over you.'"

Dawson chuckled. "I know exactly what you mean."

"Fiona and I exchanged phone numbers, and a few days later, she called me to say that Charles was going to be at a Malgam function the following evening, and she wanted to see me then. When I got to her place, she let me in through the back gate. We sat and talked. She was full of stress, and at times, she got tearful. She talked about her campaign to be chief exec of the STMA and how she wasn't getting support from Charles. Some of what Charles wanted for Malgam's success ran counter to Fiona's vision for a prosperous Takoradi."

"Did she give you an example of that?"

"Fiona was challenging Malgam Oil over the rule that no fishing canoe can come within five hundred meters of the oil platform. If a navy patrol vessel catches a canoe within that radius, they arrest the fisherman involved and confiscate the canoe."

"How long did you stay with Fiona that night?"

"Two hours. I will swear on a Bible that I did not have sex with her,

Darko. You have to believe me. We went out to the garden from the back of the house, and we were exchanging some last words when she put her arms around me. At that time, Gamal came into the garden with a flashlight and discovered us embracing. I thought I was going to die of embarrassment."

"Did you ever see Fiona again after this incident?"

"No, I didn't. After that meeting, I realized what a terrible mistake I'd be making to go any further. I felt stupid and ashamed. However, Fiona kept calling me to talk. I was avoiding her, not returning her calls, and so she came to the shop. That was a frightening moment, because I thought she was going to make a scene and then the whole story would be out. Fortunately, she didn't do that, but I got the feeling my shop assistants suspected something might have been going on between Fiona and me."

Dawson wondered if a leak by one of the assistants had been responsible for the rumor that Fiona was having an affair with a businessman in town.

"It was at that visit to the shop that I went outside with her and told her that we had to end the relationship," Abraham said. "She never called me again."

He reached across the table and slipped his meaty palm into Dawson's lean one.

"I hope you believe me and trust me, Darko. I had nothing to do with Fiona and Charles's murder. I bore no malice to either one of them. I did something stupid, but it doesn't make me a murderer."

Dawson squeezed his cousin's hand. "Yes, I do believe you, Abe."

His mind very much eased, Dawson ordered a second bottle of Malta to celebrate. His cousin had now been pulled safely away from the brink of the suspect list. With that, Dawson would be able to concentrate on finding the true murderer without having to worry about family conflicts.

Chapter 27

EARLY THE NEXT MORNING, Dawson's phone rang as he was headed to the bathroom. Emmanuel was calling.

"*Chaley*, time to give up MTN and switch to Vodafone," he sang.

Dawson's heart leapt. "You've got my info?"

"The number that the Goilco CEO, Lawrence Tetteh, had is the same one you've got: zero-two-zero one-five-six four-six-seven-six. It's now out of service, however. He purchased a new phone and changed his number."

"My man, you're the best. Thank you.

"When you get back to Accra, come and see me so we can switch you over to Vodafone. Do you have the latest iPhone?"

"You must be crazy. I can't afford that."

"Don't worry, I'll hook you up with a deal, complete with Internet, email, voice mail, everything included."

Dawson laughed. "Always the salesman."

"I'm serious. A CID detective should have only the best."

"I wish CID thought that way. Thank you, Emmanuel."

As Dawson ended the call, he switched from smiling to sober. Emmanuel had now confirmed that the Lawrence Tetteh who had been murdered and the one listed in Smith-Aidoo's phone were the same man. Why had Hammond pretended the opposite? Was he involved in a conspiracy to hide a connection between the murders of Charles Smith-Aidoo and Lawrence Tetteh, and if so, why?

Dawson thought back to the details of Tetteh's case. Reportedly, the day of the Tetteh shooting, his stepbrother, Silas, had stopped by one afternoon to see him at his home in Accra's affluent Labone Estates. Charity, his faithful housekeeper, who knew Silas from previous visits, had opened up the front gate for him. Silas had told her he preferred to leave his car parked on the street. After darkness had fallen, Charity was in the servants' quarters when she heard a gunshot. She looked out of the window, which faced the driveway, and saw a man she identified as Silas fleeing down the driveway.

Fearing the worst, Charity ran inside the house and found Tetteh lying on the sitting room floor in a pool of blood with a devastating head wound. At the pending trial, Silas's defense lawyers were likely to cast doubt on the housekeeper's reliability and truthfulness. Could she clearly have identified the man running out of the house from where she was in the servants' quarters? It had been dark, and eyewitness testimony could be notoriously inaccurate. Since she usually took Sundays off to visit family, why had she stayed at home that particular Sunday?

What bothered some people, and Dawson agreed, was that Silas appeared to be a scatterbrain—a marginal man barely conducting his own affairs. He didn't fit the profile of a murderer who had executed this quick, clean killing. Moreover, if he had come to see Tetteh with a plan to shoot him, why did he stay so long, arriving late afternoon and leaving after dusk?

Dawson tried Dr. Cudjoe again, the pathologist who had done the Smith-Aidoos' autopsy. This time he got through and a male voice answered.

"Are you Dr. Hector Cudjoe?" Dawson asked

"Yes, I am." He had an air of self-importance. "Who is speaking, please?"

"Doctor, my name is Inspector Darko Dawson. I'm investigating the murders of Mr. and Mrs. Charles Smith-Aidoo. I believe you did the postmortem, is that correct?"

"Yes, I did."

"I read your report. It mentioned a gunpowder burn around the bullet entry wound of the man, but not around the woman's entry wound."

"And what is your question, Detective?"

I thought it was obvious, Dawson thought. "Sorry, I didn't make myself clear. The report does not state either way: yes, a powder burn is present, or no, none is present. The reason I ask is that if no powder burn was evident, it could mean a single assailant shot the man at close range and then shot the woman from some distance. It could also mean that the primary intended victim was the husband and not his wife."

"If I did not mention any soot," Cudjoe said crisply, "then there was no soot. I don't understand this line of questioning, Detective. It doesn't seem very useful."

Dawson felt like rolling his eyes. Another pompous one. "I apologize for troubling you, but by any chance, do you have any photographs available from the autopsy?"

"No. I don't usually photograph my postmortems."

"I see. Thank you, Doctor."

He was about to end the call when Cudjoe added, "However, in this case, someone did take some photos—a doctor visiting from the US at the time I was doing the postmortem. His name is Dr. Taryque. He asked permission to take some postmortem photos."

Dawson stood up straight. Now he was getting somewhere. "What was he going to do with them?"

"He is a forensic pathologist with thousands of photographs from all over the world," Cudjoe explained. "He's working with Korle Bu Hospital in Accra to increase the number of forensic pathologists in Ghana."

"Did Dr. Taryque offer to send the pictures to you at a later date, Doctor?"

"We had some discussion to that effect, but I didn't hear from him."

"Is he still in the country?"

"I don't think so. He told me he was going back to the States shortly."

Dawson's spirit dropped. "Do you have his phone number or email so I can get in touch with him?" he asked hopefully.

"I have his email and both his Ghana and United States numbers."

Dawson's heart leapt. Maybe Cudjoe wasn't so bad after all. He jotted the information down and recited it back to be sure he had them correct. "Thank you very much, Dr. Cudjoe. You've been very helpful."

He tried the Ghana mobile number first. It rang multiple times and then stopped abruptly. Dawson tried the US number. After five rings, a sleepy male voice answered.

"'llo?"

Dawson introduced himself and the man muttered in barely a whisper, "I'm in Philadelphia. Do you know what the time is here?"

Dawson felt like a fool. He had forgotten about the four-hour time difference.

"I'm very sorry," he stammered. "I will call you back later."

Kicking himself, he hung up. Perhaps he would try emailing first, and if Dr. Taryque didn't reply, Dawson would call again, this time at a sensible hour.

HE DIDN'T HAVE to make the call. Two hours later, his phone rang and the screen showed the American doctor's number.

"Inspector Dawson?" He was wide-awake and cheerful this time, to Dawson's relief. "This is Dr. Taryque. Were you the one who called earlier on?"

"Yes. Doctor, I apologize for waking you up. I forgot about the time difference."

"No problem at all. Are you in Accra?"

"No, Takoradi. I believe you were here about four or five months ago?"

"Yes, that's right. Nice town. How can I help you?"

Dawson liked Taryque's open, friendly voice. "I'm investigating the murder of Mr. and Mrs. Charles Smith-Aidoo. I don't know if you recall those names."

"The oil guy and wife, right? The case had just started when I was there. It's still unsolved?"

"Yes. Am I correct that you took some photos of these two victims at the postmortem?"

"I asked permission and Dr. Hector Cudjoe, the pathologist in charge, was fine with it. Why, is there some kind of problem?"

"Not at all. I'm working on whether both victims had powder burns at the entry wounds. Do you recall, Doctor?"

"I believe it was only the man, but I can email the pics to you to confirm it, and that way you'll have them for the case record."

"That would be great, Doctor. Thank you very much." Dawson supplied his email and then ended the call.

He sat for a while, contemplating that he had not yet established the exact nature of Charles Smith-Aidoo's association with Lawrence Tetteh. It was vital that Dawson find that out, because two murders a month apart of men connected to the oil industry was too close a coincidence to accept at face value. Figuring out the connection might even provide insight into both killings. Obviously, he could not go to Superintendent Hammond over this, because the man seemed to want him to stay well away from the Tetteh murder. At some point, Dawson would confront Hammond about that, but first he wanted more ammunition in readiness for his attack.

To whom, then, could he turn for help with the Smith-Aidoo-Tetteh connection? He thought of Jason Sarbah, who had extended an open offer to help if Dawson thought there was something he could assist with. Dawson decided to take Jason up on that and he dialed his number.

"I need some assistance, sir," Dawson said, after Jason had answered the call and they had exchanged greetings. "I hope you can help."

"Certainly, Inspector. I'll do my best."

"I'd like you to keep this confidential. Charles Smith-Aidoo was in touch with Goilco CEO Lawrence Tetteh months before their deaths. I'm trying to establish the basis of their association with each other."

"I see," Jason said, with some hesitancy in his voice. "And where do I come in?"

"Would you have any communications between them, either on paper or email, that I could look at?"

"Oh," he said, not sounding terribly enthusiastic about the idea. "If that's available in company records, I'm afraid it's confidential."

Dawson wondered what had happened to all that previous willingness Jason had expressed. Why the sudden reticence? Was there something particularly sensitive about this area, and if so, what did it have to do with Jason? On the other hand, Dawson reasoned, it might just be normal protectiveness of company records.

"Please, sir, you did say you would help me in any way you could," Dawson reminded him.

"That's true." He laughed nervously. "I tell you what—let me ask Mr. Calmy-Rey and get back to you with an answer."

"Okay, that's fair." If Calmy-Rey said no, then Dawson was willing to use some more "persuasive" tactics.

"Can you give me a couple of hours to give you the final word?" Jason asked.

"Yes, that's fine."

"Oh, before I forget," Jason said, his voice lightening. "I wanted to let you know that we can schedule your visit to the *Thor Sterke* rig next week Monday."

Honestly, Dawson had forgotten about that. Having never flown in his life, he was a little apprehensive about going up in a chopper. Did he really need to go to the rig? What if he found a connection between Charles and Tetteh and that enabled him to crack the mystery? But, he argued, that still wouldn't eliminate his need as a good detective to familiarize himself with the surroundings into which the Smith-Aidoos drifted. What about photographs? No, nothing beat being there in person. It's also possible that from talking to people on the rig, Dawson might discover something hitherto unknown. Sure, there was a statement from George Findlay, the oil installation manger with whom Dawson had spoken before the gentleman left for Scotland, but what about other witnesses on the rig?

"Inspector? Are you there?"

"Yes, yes, I'm here. Certainly. Monday will be fine."

"Good," Jason said. "I'll let you know the details. Please remember that your arrival on the rig means some adjustments in the daily schedule, so if you could make every effort to fulfill your plan to visit, as it will be hard to do that in the future."

"Of course. I understand." *Well, that settles it,* Dawson thought as he hung up. *I have to go—fear of flying or not.*

DAWSON HAD SENT Chikata back to Axim to try to track down other members of FOAX besides Quashie Quarshie. By lunchtime he wondered if he was going to hear from Jason about the possibility of looking at any communications between Charles and Lawrence Tetteh. He was surprised when he received a call in mid-afternoon from a number he didn't know, and it turned out to be Roger Calmy-Rey himself.

"Jason told me about your interest in seeing these communications," he said after he'd exchanged greetings with Dawson. He sounded very serious. "It isn't something the superintendent required from us. May I ask why the interest?"

Calmy-Rey sounded as wary as Jason, and suddenly Dawson felt the need to be just as cautious. Both of them were being cagey. Was it just because of company privacy policies, or was there something else—something about Charles's association with Tetteh that adversely involved Jason and/or Calmy-Rey?

"It has to do with the investigation," Dawson said noncommittally while sharpening his voice a little.

Calmy-Rey paused. "Very well. I can provide you with some selected emails, but I can't release everything because there may be proprietary information included."

"Whatever you can do is appreciated," Dawson said.

"Can you meet with Jason around five thirty? I will not be here."

"Thank you very much, Mr. Calmy-Rey."

DAWSON ARRIVED AT the Malgam Office at the appointed time and was escorted straight up to Jason's office.

"Please, have a seat," he said to Dawson. He seemed edgier and more distant. "I'll show you what I've got for you." Jason rolled up a chair next to Dawson and opened up a thin folder. "Mr. Calmy-Rey authorized me to show you these."

Jason passed the first page to Dawson.

"This is an email from Lawrence Tetteh to Charles in September last year, some months after Mr. Tetteh had become the CEO of Goilco."

> Charles, please see attached Goilco's new mission statement. I developed it in collaboration with PIAC.

"What is PIAC?" Dawson asked.

"Public Interest and Accountability Committee. It's a statutory body established to monitor government compliance in the use and management of Ghana's petroleum revenues. Tetteh was a stickler for high standards and accountability. Goilco's role of partnering with international oil companies, enabling the training of Ghanaian citizens in the petroleum industry, and so on are spelled out in the mission statement, but Tetteh added another layer to it, almost like a moral code."

"Do you have a copy of the mission statement he attached to the email?"

"Yes, I included it in the package."

Jason's phone rang from his desk. "Let me get that. Feel free to look through at your own pace."

While Jason was on the phone, Dawson found the mission statement, a ten-point list with lofty goals like *promulgate, elucidate, and maintain the highest ethical standards of operation in petroleum business and trade.* The last item caught his eye:

To divest Goilco from activities unrelated to petroleum affairs.

When Jason got off the phone, Dawson asked him what that statement meant.

"Over the years, Goilco got involved with some ventures outside of oil," Jason explained. "For instance, they acquired an interest in Obuasi Gold some years back. Tetteh wanted to put a stop to all that."

"Seems like that might have antagonized a few people."

"Including several members of the board of directors."

Dawson reflected that if he were going to look into this thoroughly, he'd have to talk to all of those board members: a time-consuming process—maybe even time-*wasting* because if it took him and Chikata down a wrong path, they would end up losing precious ground on the Smith-Aidoo murder.

"You're thinking Tetteh's death is somehow connected?" Jason asked, as if reading Dawson's mind.

"Maybe," he said guardedly. He looked through the rest of the papers in the folder while Jason made some calls. The emails seemed innocuous. There was nothing here and Dawson was very disappointed. He stood up. "May I keep this folder?"

"Yes, Mr. Calmy-Rey said it would be all right to do so."

"I really appreciate all your help."

"No problem at all," Jason said with a smile.

As Dawson left the office suite, he felt as though he had missed something. He remembered what it was as he was waiting for the lift to arrive. He returned to Jason's office, knocked, and opened the door.

He looked up in surprise. "Back?"

"I was wondering—did Charles have a pen drive?"

Jason looked blank. "I have no idea, Inspector."

Dawson nodded. "Well, if you come across one belonging to him, please let me know."

As Dawson walked back to the lift, he reasoned that if Charles had had a personal pen drive, Dr. Smith-Aidoo was the one person who might well know where it was. Dawson was not going to be able to avoid getting in touch with her despite their recent awkward encounter. He would have to put it behind him. When he got outside the building, he called her, his dialing finger hesitating for a moment. She answered and his stomach plunged.

"Good afternoon, Doctor," he said, trying to sound neutral.

"Hello, Inspector. How are you?" Her tone was uncolored as well.

"I'm very sorry to disturb you," he said, "but I would just like to ask if you've come across a pen drive belonging to your uncle."

"I did find one, but I've put it away in one of the boxes, so I'll have to locate it and call you."

"Thank you very, very much."

He felt relieved as he said goodbye. She had made it painless.

DARKNESS HAD FALLEN as Dawson returned home. Chikata called him to say he was on his way back from Axim after a long, fruitless day of looking for leads. He planned to return there in the next two days.

"Call it a day," Dawson had told him. "We'll talk in the morning."

He felt deflated. Nothing was turning up any leads. He felt an urgency to keep moving, however. The spotlight was now on Reggie Cardiman. Dawson planned to make a move in the morning. It would be Sunday, and millions of Ghanaians, the most religious people in the world, would be off to church, but he had never let a day of worship get in his way of an investigation.

Chapter 28

By 10 A.M., DAWSON and Chikata were at the Dixcove District Court trying to secure a search warrant. It required extracting the magistrate from an evangelical extravaganza in which pastors were casting out demons from evildoers. Dawson got the feeling that the warrant was issued with record speed because the magistrate wanted to get back to the spectacle. By one thirty in the afternoon, they were at Cape Three Points. Cardiman was surprised to see them.

"Can we talk in private?" Dawson asked.

"Of course. Let's go to the office."

Cardiman and the two detectives sat facing each other.

"Let's go back to your meeting with Charles Smith-Aidoo," Dawson said. "What time did Charles and Fiona Smith-Aidoo leave you?"

"I think I mentioned it before, didn't I?" Cardiman said, "Twelve thirty?" Now he sounded less certain.

"As far as you know, where was he going next?" Dawson asked.

"Back to Takoradi, I believe."

"Did you suggest to him that he go somewhere else before proceeding?"

Cardiman frowned. "No, why?"

"Think carefully. Did you recommend to the Smith-Aidoos that they visit the lighthouse?"

Cardiman thought for a moment and his puzzled frown cleared as soon as he remembered. "Ah, yes—you're correct. As they were leaving I did recommend they go up there for the marvelous view. I should have mentioned that to you. My apologies."

"*When* did you recommend that?" Dawson asked.

"Around the time Charles and his wife were leaving."

Dawson took out his notebook. "Let me read you what I noted when we first met and talked. 'Cardiman stated: could not have ambushed vehicle if Smith-Aidoos left at twelve thirty and he left almost thirty minutes after—impossible to catch up with them in order to carry out an ambush.' You went out of your way to make that specific point, and now you tell us you just conveniently forgot to mention that you had suggested to the Smith-Aidoos that they take a detour?"

"That's true," he agreed, "but Inspector, this event was four months ago. My memory isn't infallible. And in any case, they probably decided not to go the lighthouse."

Cardiman was thinking ahead, Dawson realized. "Why do you say that?" he asked, even though he was anticipating the answer.

"Because if they spent time at the lighthouse," Cardiman said confidently, "I would have beaten them to the location their vehicle was found abandoned—or perhaps arrived around the same time. Obviously that did not happen, and so I could not have had anything to do with the Smith-Aidoos' death."

But Dawson did not agree. Deliberately or not—and Dawson suspected deliberately—Cardiman was using invalid logic: if A then B, and therefore C. It was clever, but not clever enough.

"You told us that you had parted with Charles Smith-Aidoo on good terms," Dawson said leaning forward and boring his gaze into Cardiman, "but we've learned that in fact you had heated words with him because he told you that if you didn't voluntarily vacate the Ezile property, it would be easy to pay off Nana Ackah-Yensu to kick you out."

Cardiman's jaw slackened. "What? Whoever told you that completely misrepresented our discussion. We did *not* have a big argument, and we did *not* part on bad terms, and Charles certainly never threatened me in the way you or your source claims. I've already told you what Charles said to me: He offered me a stake in a development along the Cape Three Points shoreline, including the Ezile Bay and Akwidaa locations. He showed me the plan, the expected revenue, the environmental impact assessment, and so on. And I said no."

That was true, Dawson reflected, thinking back to their first meeting with Cardiman. That *was* what he had said. No matter. Dawson was not thrown off course. "Mr. Cardiman," he said, "we're giving you a chance to respond now: did you either kill Charles Smith-Aidoo and his wife, or hire someone to do it, or conspire with one or more people to do it?"

Cardiman appeared shocked. "Oh, *God*, no! I would never do that."

Dawson leaned forward and handed the warrant to Cardiman. "The district court has authorized us to search your office and living quarters."

"Oh," Cardiman mouthed, looking shattered as he read the warrant. "This is just awful. What do I have to do?"

"You may stand at the door," Dawson said. "You should closely observe us as we search in order to reassure yourself that we do not plant any false evidence. Anything we remove, we will note for the record, and you will initial it to confirm that it is the item we have removed. Do you have any questions about the procedure?"

"No," he stammered. "No, it seems quite clear."

Appearing pale, Cardiman moved to the door and Dawson and Chikata began the search. They were looking for a firearm and/or any incriminating correspondence between Cardiman and Smith-Aidoo. It wasn't an easy task. Cardiman was a disorganized man, and his office was a jumbled mess.

How does he run this place? Dawson wondered, as he looked in a drawer containing a fertility doll resting on an unruly pile of receipts from two years before. He glanced at Cardiman, whose expression had changed from shock to disgust.

They went on to the bedroom, which was quite unkempt with an unmade bed that smelled of stale sweat. It was not quite as packed with junk, and it took them less time to search it. There was nothing found and nothing to take away. Dawson had mixed feelings. It was not that he wanted Cardiman, specifically, to be guilty, but he had wanted so much to find something to finally get a break in the case.

He turned to Cardiman and offered a handshake, which he accepted uncertainly. "Thank you very much, sir," Dawson said. "We apologize for the inconvenience."

"Not at all, Inspector," Cardiman said dully. "I suppose I should say have a nice day."

ON THE WAY back to Takoradi, they discussed the encounter with Reggie Cardiman.

"What do you think?" Chikata asked Dawson.

"He hasn't proved that he wasn't involved in the murder," he said, "and neither have we. He could be lying that he didn't have a bad argument with Charles, and if he did, why at the end of that would he talk about such pleasantries like going up to the light-house for the beautiful view? So that he and/or someone else would have time to get into position to intercept them on the way back to Takoradi."

Chikata was quiet for a moment. "At this point, Dawson," he said finally, "whom do you suspect most? You have DeSouza who hated Fiona's guts; there's Jason Sarbah who blamed Charles for the death of his daughter Angela; Cardiman who might have felt deadly afraid that Charles was going to destroy his way of life; possibly some Akwidaa fishermen who didn't want to be uprooted by Malgam; perhaps some members of some activist group like FOAX who want to stop Malgam in its tracks . . . have I missed anyone?"

"Yes, you have," Dawson said. "Brian Smith-Aidoo, Charles's bitter younger brother who was jealous of his success and his influence over Sapphire Smith-Aidoo."

"Does he have an alibi?"

"He says he was at home all of Monday, the seventh of July, sick with gout. He lives alone, so it's not confirmed."

Chikata sat forward in the backseat. "Shall we go back to him and interrogate him again?"

"Yes, I think so," Dawson said, "but I've been thinking about the *juju* angle to this case. I don't feel like we have probed deeply enough into it. Baah, please take us to Kweku Bonsa's shrine."

"Yes, sir," Baah said. He adopted a mocking tone. "So-called best fetish priest in Takoradi."

"You don't believe it?" Chikata asked.

"No, he's just *chopping* people's money."

• • •

As THEY ENTERED Bonsa's shrine, Dawson discreetly commented to Chikata that he had expected much less. Three surprisingly modern buildings with four labeled consulting rooms surrounded a clean cement compound. Maybe Baah was right—Bonsa *was* making good money.

"He even has a website," Chikata said.

"Are you serious?"

"Yes, look over there," Chikata said, pointing his chin to a wall emblazoned with the URL.

They found an assistant and asked to see Mr. Bonsa.

"Please, you can wait for him," the assistant said.

"*Mepaakyew*," Chikata said politely, using the word for "please" in Akan, "tell him we're policemen from Accra, and we don't have time to wait."

"Yes, please," the man said, scurrying away.

Dawson looked at Chikata and smiled. "I like that. You asserted yourself well. And beat me to it, too."

Chikata smiled. "I've already missed him once while he was doing his spiritual dance special. I'm not coming back a third time."

The assistant returned. "Please, he says he can see you in ten minutes."

Ten minutes turned out to be thirty, but by general standards, that was very good. Dawson and Chikata took off their shoes at the doorstep of Consulting Room One and entered.

A small pile of cowry shells in front of him, Kweku Bonsa was sitting on the carpeted floor of a slightly elevated stage around which four attendants stood. Bonsa was a slight man with a severe defect in the left side of his face as though it had been gouged out as a child. A pink, rigid scar tugged at the lower lid of his left eye, which watered constantly because it could not close completely.

One of the attendants prompted the visitors to introduce themselves. Dawson spoke on Chikata's behalf, since the sergeant didn't speak Fante.

Bonsa stared at them and nodded. "What problems do you have?" His voice was hoarse and scratchy.

"We are looking for the person who killed a man and his wife last July," Dawson said, deciding on the blunt approach.

"Why have you come to me?" Bonsa asked.

"We want to know if it was a human sacrifice. The man was Mr. Charles Smith-Aidoo. He and his wife were shot, and then he was beheaded. Can I show you the picture?"

"If you want."

He brought up the image on his phone and gave it to one of the attendants, who showed it to Bonsa. He looked at it for a moment with not even a twitch in his expression and then handed the phone back.

"I don't deal in such blood practices," he declared.

"I didn't say you did," Dawson said. "I'm asking your opinion."

Bonsa leaned slightly forward and swept his hands back and forth over the cowry shells, scattering them. One of his assistants picked up the few that had strayed outside of reach and threw them back in the pile. Bonsa studied the shells as he muttered something inaudible. He repeated the cycle of scattering and studying twice, and then he looked up with the good eye narrowed to a slit.

"If someone is saying it is a sacrifice," he said, "the person is uttering a falsehood. It is a killing of a different purpose. The one who did it is trying to make it seem like a human sacrifice."

Dawson wasn't sure if his next ploy would work, but he took the plunge. "I heard that in April of this year, a man came to you asking your help for his dying daughter."

Bonsa stiffened and stared at Dawson for several moments. "Not me."

"Then who?"

"I don't concern myself with imposters."

Dawson wasn't sure what the priest meant. "You're saying that this man consulted a fake fetish priest about his daughter?"

Bonsa blinked slowly but said nothing.

"Was the name of the man Jason Sarbah?" Dawson pressed. "What did that fetish priest instruct Mr. Sarbah? That he should have Mr. and Mrs. Smith-Aidoo killed in order to save his daughter?"

Bonsa maintained his silence. He had closed his eyes and appeared to be in a trance. Abruptly, one of the attendants held the door open for the two detectives to leave. The meeting was officially over.

• • •

DAWSON AND CHIKATA didn't speak until they were back in the taxi.

"Agh," the sergeant said. "That was unpleasant. I don't like that man."

"Strange atmosphere in there," Dawson agreed. He glanced at Baah, who was staying silent.

"Why did you make up that story about a man consulting Bonsa about his dying daughter?" Chikata asked.

"It popped into my head," Dawson replied. "What if, out of desperation during the final days of Angela's fatal illness, Jason Sarbah consulted a fetish priest? From the way Bonsa responded, it seems I hit a nerve. So maybe Jason *did* go to a fetish, but he went to a quack and Bonsa heard the story."

"Then why didn't he want to confirm whether or not it was Jason?"

"Because I don't think he wants to get involved. It's like if a TV reporter or someone like that came to you and asked about a corrupt policeman. Even if you'd heard something about it, you might not want to talk about it with someone like that because of the mess it would drag you into."

"True," Chikata said. "Okay, so, let's say Jason goes to the quack priest. And then?"

"And then this imposter fetish priest recommends to Jason that he perform a human sacrifice on the man who denied him money for the operation Angela needed. There's no way Jason can do this himself, so he hires two or three people to do it."

"So now we have to go looking for a quack fetish priest Jason went to see? That could take us years."

"There's a much easier way," Dawson said, taking out his phone. "We're going to ask Jason himself about it."

BY THE TIME Jason appeared at the Takoradi central police station with his lawyer, it was well past nightfall. Dawson had reached him at a pool party at Planter's Lodge, an upscale hotel not far from Shippers Circle. Jason had sounded annoyed that Dawson wanted to question him.

"Can you give me a couple of hours?" he asked.

"Yes, all right," Dawson replied, but when he had hung up, he began to worry. Why did Jason need a couple of hours? He dispatched Chikata and Baah immediately to Planter's Lodge, instructing them to park discreetly outside the entrance and watch for Jason. Dawson wanted to be sure he didn't bolt.

He didn't. It turned out that he needed time to contact his lawyer and have him accompany Jason to the station. The lawyer, Calvin DeGraft, was contracted with Malgam Oil.

Smart man to come with DeGraft, Dawson thought.

They met in the CID room, Jason and DeGraft sitting opposite Dawson and Chikata.

"What is this about, Inspector?" the lawyer asked. He was a large, imposing man with a razor edge to his voice. "Today is Sunday. This is a considerable disruption of my client's leisure time."

"I do apologize for that, sir," Dawson said. "However, we need to ask your client some questions, if you would allow it."

"Go ahead. Please be brief."

"Mr. Sarbah, we've learned that during or around April, you visited a fetish priest seeking a cure for your daughter's illness."

Jason's eyebrows shot up. "What?"

"Did you go to a fetish priest about Angela's illness, sir?"

"Is this some kind of joke?" Jason snapped. "You brought me here to ask this ridiculous question?"

"Can you please answer?"

"No, Mr. Sarbah is not going to answer this question," DeGraft cut in. "I will not allow it."

"What about a fetish priest called Kweku Bonsa?" Dawson tried again. "Are you familiar with him, Mr. Sarbah?"

"He won't answer anything related to fetish priests," DeGraft said. "Do you have any other questions?"

"Was human sacrifice ever considered in order to save Angela's life?"

Jason flinched and his eyes swelled and moistened.

"You're an offensive man, Inspector," DeGraft said coldly. "You know very well that Angela's death is a painful chapter in Mr. Sarbah's life. These questions are not only unnecessary, they are deliberately cruel."

"It wasn't my intention to offend," Dawson said quietly. "I apologize."

"Is my client under arrest?"

"No, sir."

"Then we are leaving." DeGraft stood up. "Come along, Jason."

They left in silence. Chikata sneaked a glance at Dawson and then meekly returned his gaze to the table.

"Okay," Dawson said. "I admit it didn't go well, but I think it was worth a try."

"Yes," Chikata said slowly, obvious doubt in his voice.

Feeling deflated all of a sudden, Dawson stood up with a sigh. "I'm tired. Let's go home. We have another long day tomorrow."

Chapter 29

THIS IS IT, DAWSON thought.

For the first time in his life, he was going to be airborne. As he took his seat in the first row behind the pilot and co-pilot of one of Malgam's NHV Dauphin helicopters, his nervousness made his stomach churn.

A few minutes past seven in the morning, Dawson and the five other passengers had watched a ten-minute safety video in the helicopter administration waiting room of Takoradi's small airport. Thereafter, they had donned their life jackets and boarded the van that transported them to the helicopter on the tarmac. Dawson had always pictured a helicopter as a smallish machine, but up close to the Dauphin, he realized how mistaken he had been.

Now he was duplicating all the steps that he had seen on the video—fastening the four-point seatbelts, putting on the protective headphones, checking the large exit window to his right, and mentally rehearsing how to release the window seal and push it out in an emergency. He went through the safety leaflet in the seat pocket in front of him, realizing that his hands were trembling. He surreptitiously glanced at the passenger to his right, afraid that his nerves were showing. He need not have worried. The sixty-ish expatriate with an expanding belly was reading a magazine and showing no interest in anyone around him.

The helicopter door closed. Dawson watched the pilot as he pressed buttons and flicked switches on a bewildering console of dials, levers, and screen displays in front of him and overhead.

Dawson was startled as the engine started, a low rumble rising quickly to a high whine and finally a pulsating roar.

On the ground in front of the Dauphin, a man in overalls signaled to the pilot. For a moment, Dawson thought he felt the craft moving, dismissed it as his imagination playing tricks on him, and then realized they were indeed already about ten feet off the ground. The pilot kept the Dauphin there for a few seconds while he and the co-pilot performed some final checks, and then he shifted the helicopter sideways, a maneuver Dawson found disconcerting. The helicopter pivoted and went forward to the runway, where the pilot turned it again, tipped it slightly forward, and accelerated into a climb. Much more rapidly than Dawson had expected, he had a full view of the city: a patchwork of urban construction and green space.

He could already see the Atlantic ahead and then both the Sekondi and Takoradi harbors. They were climbing higher still, and he closed his eyes for a moment. When the vertigo passed, it was replaced by his awe at the magnificence of the ocean beneath them. Stretching to infinity, its surface reflected the golden arc of the early morning sun. He spotted only a rare trawler, canoe, or flat-decked supply ship, but as the Dauphin began to approach the *Thor Sterke* some thirty minutes later, the picture changed. He saw four drilling rigs over a wide area. Dotted around them like worker ants attending their queen were several vessels, some of which Dawson guessed were the fishery protection vessels he had read about in the docket reports.

He had found it difficult to believe that fishermen would venture out this far in their canoes, but now he saw living proof. There they were, keeping a respectful distance from the rigs. How, he wondered, could the Smith-Aidoos' murderer possibly have delivered a canoe containing two corpses to the restricted zone around a rig and then disappear without a trace?

The pilot came on the PA system to let them know they'd be landing in five minutes, although Dawson could barely hear him above the background noise. He double-checked his seat belts as they began to descend. For an unnerving second, he visualized the helicopter crashing and the awful aftermath. Unable to grasp his father's death, Hosiah repeatedly asked Christine, *what happened to Daddy?*

Dawson shook himself and stopped thinking the worst. Ahead, the *Thor Sterke* with its angular appendages and spindly lattice crane booms seemed incredibly small and far below them. They were going to overshoot, surely? Dawson couldn't see how they could possibly touch down on the octagonal-shaped helipad, marked with a large H and perched at the edge of the rig. Could it really hold a helicopter? As they came closer and the helipad loomed, he felt silly. The structure was obviously solid and more than large enough. The helicopter came to a stop in mid-air, hovering over its landing spot for a moment before the pilot set it down with a delicacy Dawson hadn't anticipated. He heaved a sign of relief. He had made it. He was on a real oil rig after having flown for the first time in his life. *And*, he thought, *all because of murder*.

The helicopter rotor blades were still turning as two helipad crew members opened up the compartment beneath the cabin to remove luggage. Then they directed the passengers to the exit staircase directly ahead. To their immediate right was a crane, and another lay ahead to the far left. The derrick was directly in front of them, emblazoned with the name THOR STERKE. In real life and close up, it was massive and towering.

After leaving the helipad, Dawson entered the helilounge in street clothes and emerged transformed in orange coveralls, a green hard hat that marked him as a visitor, regulation steel-toe boots, and safety glasses.

He felt a little strange, but the rig's culture of safety had impressed him. Indeed, the very first man to welcome him and accompany him on the guided tour was the safety officer. Michael Glagah was as tall as Dawson but of much greater girth. He had a rumbling, resonant voice and was deadly serious about maintaining the rig's clean safety record. Before anything else, he made sure Dawson knew the location of the lifeboats on the second level, two each at the forward and aft positions.

The sun was warm, but a cool sea breeze softened its intensity.

"Please, can you show me where the canoe with the dead bodies was spotted?" Dawson asked.

Glagah led him to a yellow railing at the edge of an upper level. From there, they could look down to the next tier, a drop of about ten meters. "That's the pipe deck below us," Glagah said. "Those long metal pipes you see stacked together on your right are called casing joints. We have to use cranes to lift them and other drilling equipment. So, at the end of the deck there, you see two cranes, one each on the port and starboard side—left and right. You can see how the crane operator has a bird's eye view. That morning, Clifford was on the starboard side. He saw the canoe coming from the southwest direction, somewhere over there."

Glagah pointed in a diagonal direction, and Dawson followed his finger. Traveling in an easterly direction, a distant vessel bleak grey in color was moving slowly into view. Dawson made out the name GNS ACHIMOTA along its side.

"Is that one of the naval protection ships?" he asked Glagah, pointing.

"Correct. There are usually one or two of them in the vicinity."

"How did the canoe carrying Mr. and Mrs. Smith-Aidoos' bodies escape their detection?"

"One patrol was busy on a mission to intercept some illegal trawlers, while the other one had gone back to shore for a crew change." Glagah shrugged in regret. "We wish they could be everywhere at the same time, but that isn't possible."

"If one or both of the protection vessels had been around, could the canoe have made it into the restricted zone?"

"It would have been very difficult. It was either very lucky, or someone clever engineered its appearance at the right time."

"How do you mean, Mr. Glagah?"

"A knowledgeable seaman would know in which direction the ocean currents run at a particular time of the day and season," he replied, looking directly at Dawson, "and therefore when to release the canoe and from what distance. He'd also be familiar with the movements of the patrol vessels. It would take quite a bit of calculation, but it could be done."

"So," Dawson said slowly, "an experienced fisherman from any of the coastal communities who is accustomed to coming out this far would fit the grade."

"Yes," Glagah confirmed. "He would know how to navigate at night, what maneuvers to watch for from the patrol vessels, and the sea currents."

Dawson became lost in thought for a while until Glagah inter-rupted his ponderings.

"Come along," he said. "Let's go back to accommodations to change, and then we'll go to Mr. Findlay's office."

Back in regular clothing, they went to George Findlay's office.

"Good to meet you in person, Mr. Dawson," he said, shaking hands heartily. "I hope you've been enjoying your visit with us?"

"Very much, sir. Mr. Glagah has been a very good host."

Glagah smiled. "Thank you, Mr. Dawson, and now I'm afraid I must say goodbye."

Findlay's office was compact. A quick glance around revealed the artifacts of a long career in the offshore drilling business. A chipped coffee mug with a faded company logo offering to drill deeper cheaper shared dwindling desk space with papers, envelopes, and a computer. Framed pictures of oil rigs and gleaming safety-award plaques adorned one wall.

"Well," Findlay said, "let's have a seat, shall we? I was wondering if it would help you to meet Clifford, the crane operator who first sighted the canoe. He's around if you'd like to talk to him. I let him know you'd be here so we wouldn't catch him by surprise."

He crossed to his desk to use the phone. "Hi, John. Can you have Clifford come down? Yes, my office. Thanks."

They chatted a few minutes until Clifford knocked on the door and entered. In his early thirties, he had a stout build, a diamond stud in his left ear, and jet-black hair. The warm weather outside had flushed his cheeks red.

"Hi, Clifford. Thanks for coming down. This is Inspector Dawson, whom I told you about yesterday."

"Oh, yeah." He nodded at Dawson "Hi." He didn't appear inter-ested in a handshake.

Findlay stood up. "Take my seat, Cliff. I need to go next door for a minute. I'll be right back."

Dawson admired Findlay's tact. Clifford might not be as forthcom-ing in the presence of his boss.

"Anything in particular you want to know?" Clifford asked, sitting down as Findlay left. He had a coiled energy, jiggling his right leg up and down in an unconscious, repetitive motion.

"Just the details of that morning when you were working and the canoe with the dead bodies appeared," Dawson said.

"Well, I was unloading a barge on the starboard side, saw the canoe coming in from the southwest, no one paddling it. I couldn't pay too much attention at first because I had to concentrate on the unloading, but as it got closer, it just looked strange."

Dawson had to listen closely to follow what Clifford was saying. His speech was rapid, and he had a thick Scots accent.

"So, I grabbed the binoculars in the cab to get a better look," Clifford continued, "and I saw it. Two dead bodies in the canoe, and the head wedged onto a pole."

"What did you do?"

Clifford snorted. "Told my supervisor, of course. Told him something fuckin' unbelievable was out there."

"You had a strong reaction to it," Dawson said encouragingly.

"Well, yeah, it was disgusting, really. Not used to this kind of thing where I come from."

"Where is that?"

"Aberdeen. Nothing but trouble from these fishermen round here," Clifford continued resentfully. "Hanging about day and night in their fuckin' canoes. They don't even need to be this far out at sea to do their fishing, getting their nets all tangled up with our equipment and running into the service boats."

"Apart from the canoe with the bodies in it," Dawson said, "what did you see? Any other boats or canoes around?"

"Not really. The protection vessels were missing in action—I think one of them had gone back to shore for a crew change or something and another was off somewhere doing who knows what. Another canoe was lurking about, but I didn't pay that much attention to it. Wouldn't be anything new. Like I said, they're always about."

Dawson leaned forward slightly. "Another canoe?"

"Yeah, like a twenty-four footer, about twice the size of the one with the stiffs in it. About six hundred meters away."

"Who was in it?"

"Couple fishermen."

Dawson knew this was something significant. "What were they doing?"

Clifford shrugged. "Nuthin', really. Just kind of hanging about, fuckin' staring."

"What did they look like—the two fishermen?"

"Look like? Didn't notice. They all look the same to me."

"How long were they in the area?"

"Ten minutes, maybe, and then they took off. Outboard motor. Fishing, I suppose."

"They couldn't have been fishing," Dawson said, "because it was a Tuesday. It's taboo to fish on Tuesdays."

"Really?" Clifford asked in surprise.

"Yes. Are you sure you don't remember anything about these two fishermen, Mr. Clifford?"

Now his eyes took on a depth of thought that had not been there before. "I mean they were just sitting there watching, and you're right, now that you mention it. They didn't have any nets or fishing lines."

Startled as it dawned on him, Clifford looked at Dawson directly for the first time. "You're saying . . . those might have been the murderers who cut off the guy's head?"

"That's what I'm saying."

Clifford blinked and fell back in his chair.

"Oh, fuck," he muttered. "What an idiot I am."

Chapter 30

GLAD TO BE BACK on solid ground again, Dawson reflected on his visit to the rig. He thought about the time spent there, going to and from, and the days spent preparing for it. Had the great effort to visit the unique crime scene been worth it? He thought so. Seeing the staggering breadth and majesty of the Gulf of Guinea had impressed on him more than he had appreciated before what Mr. Glagah had emphasized: how essential a fisherman's skill and knowledge must have been to carry off the feat of getting two dead bodies so far out to sea. From Clifford, Dawson had all but confirmed what he had suspected—that there had been two people involved in the execution of the murder, and Dawson thought that at least one of them, maybe both, was a fisherman.

His perspective on the approach to the case had changed. Perhaps he and Chikata should be seeking a *fisherman* with a motive to kill the Smith-Aidoos or a fisherman willing to do it for the money. If they found the fisherman, whoever else was involved—whether it be Brian, DeSouza, Jason, or Cardiman—would become clear.

His phone showed that Hammond had called late that morning. He tried reaching the superintendent without success and decided to grab a cab to Headquarters. Hammond was likely to be there.

Seidu, who was standing outside as Dawson walked up to the building, gave him a surprisingly curt nod and not much of a greeting. *Something's wrong*, Dawson thought. The ASP had been perfectly affable before.

He knocked warily on Hammond's door and entered. The

superintendent paused briefly from a report he had been writing and then returned to the document without a word.

"Sir?" Dawson said cautiously.

Hammond dropped his pen abruptly and looked up, his jaw hard. "What are you trying to do? Infuriate the whole of Takoradi?"

Dawson immediately guessed what this was about, but he played innocent. "Sorry, sir. I'm not sure what you mean."

"What possessed you to confront Mr. Jason Sarbah with the obnoxious accusation that he performed a human sacrifice on Charles and Fiona Smith-Aidoo?"

"I didn't accuse him of that. I asked him if human sacrifice was a consideration to save his daughter's life."

"It's the same thing," Hammond said, gesturing in exasperation. "The accusation is implied. This is a respectable man, Inspector Dawson. You can't ask him such insulting questions."

"He called you about it, sir?"

"No, his lawyer came here this morning to talk to me in person. In fact, I've never seen Mr. DeGraft so furious and upset. You dragged them out on a Sunday when everyone is trying to get some relaxation and just to ask these offensive questions? Oh, *Awurade!*" It was the first time Dawson had heard the superintendent swear in God's name.

"I need to examine all possible angles," Dawson said quietly.

"No, you are examining *impossible* angles. Human sacrifice. Are you crazy? I will have to complain to Chief Superintendent Lartey about you. This is too much."

I can't let him do that, Dawson thought, an alarm going off in his mind like a siren. It was vital that nothing ruin his prospects for promotion, and this just might do it. "Respectfully, sir, before you do that, I have some questions."

"What kind of questions?" Hammond snapped.

"May I sit down?"

The superintendent nodded as if he hated to grant the permission.

"I now know that the Lawrence Tetteh listed in Charles Smith-Aidoo's phone was the same one as the CEO of Goilco," Dawson said. "They were in direct contact with each other before Tetteh's death."

Hammond appeared startled, but kept his composure. "How do you know that?" he challenged.

"A friend of mine at the Vodafone main office in Accra confirmed the number for me, and I have email documents that Jason Sarbah gave me last week showing communications between the two."

Dawson had the folder from Sarbah. He took out the papers and passed them to Hammond. He read them, swallowing hard once and handed them back. "Okay. So what? My contact at Vodafone here in Takoradi must have made a mistake."

"Or is it that you tried to prevent me from finding out the connection between Tetteh and Smith-Aidoo, sir? Have you been instructed by your superiors to suppress any investigation of who killed Lawrence Tetteh?"

Hammond's eyes narrowed. "This is insubordination, Dawson. I will have you up before the disciplinary board if you're not careful, and then you might as well say goodbye to any chances of making it to chief inspector."

That didn't faze Dawson. The balance of power was in his favor. "I don't think you really want me in front of the board, sir, because I'll say what I know and the outcome might adversely affect you."

"You're threatening me?" Hammond asked angrily. "What gives you the right to threaten me?"

"I'm not, sir. I'm not." Dawson sighed heavily. "I don't even understand why we're fighting. It started the moment I first stepped into this office. We're supposed to be on the same side: hunting down killers. I understand you might not like a junior officer from Accra coming here to investigate, but that's how the system works. What am I to do? Refuse Chief Superintendent Lartey's orders? That will have me before the board, for certain. Please, sir, I'm appealing to you. Let's do this differently."

Hammond rubbed his forehead slowly as he tapped the bottom of his pen repeatedly on his desk.

"I wanted to steer you away from the Tetteh affair," he said at last, lowering his voice. "So yes, when I told you that the Lawrence Tetteh in Smith-Aidoo's phone wasn't the same one as the Goilco CEO, it wasn't true. Now I regret handling it that way, but I don't regret the intention behind it. I was trying to protect you."

"Protect me? From whom, or what, sir?"

"The Tetteh murder is a no-go area." His voice dropped even lower. "Someone high up in government is involved."

"Silas is just a scapegoat, then," Dawson said. "He didn't commit the murder."

Locking eyes with Dawson, the superintendent said nothing, but his expression gave the answer.

"Who in the government wanted Tetteh dead?" Dawson asked softly.

"Tetteh was honest to the very last *pesewa*, and he was ready to expose anything he considered immoral or fraudulent. That's why so many people hated him. They say he was intending to blow the whistle on some corrupt dealings between an MP and the oil companies."

"Who is 'they,' and how do you know this, sir?"

"I have a contact. I can't give you a name."

"Who is the corrupt MP?"

Hammond pressed his lips together and shook his head very firmly. "Look, Dawson, I don't need to give you every detail. It's better for you that I don't. All I'm trying to do is make you understand that you should leave the Tetteh business alone. It's too dangerous."

"There's a cover-up, and you want us to go along with it?"

"I didn't say that," Hammond said impatiently, turning his palm up. "I'm saying we don't need to get involved at all. The Bureau of National Intelligence officially has the case, so let's just confine ourselves to the Smith-Aidoo murders. Leave Tetteh's alone. Don't get mixed up in things that can get you in trouble. This is no time to jeopardize your career.

"Now about the other matter. I realize I have been treating you badly. I've never had a case for which a petition was made. My cases solved rate is high, and I suppose I was too prideful. I apologize to you."

He wants to be on my good side now, Dawson thought. What a difference a good threat makes. "It's okay, sir. Thank you."

"Is there anything I or ASP Seidu can help you with?"

"No, sir. Thank you. I'm waiting for Chikata to return from Axim."

"Very good." As Dawson stood up to leave, Hammond said. "Please keep this conversation strictly between us."

Dawson couldn't promise that far. "I'll do my best to, sir."

He left the room quickly to avoid making more of a commitment. He hadn't yet decided what to do. The fundamental question he had been facing about whether the Tetteh and Smith-Aidoo cases were connected was even more pressing because now, there was the smell of a cover-up. If it wasn't possible to solve one murder without solving the other, then Dawson could not avoid "getting mixed up" with Tetteh's case, as Hammond had put it.

Under a flame tree, he stood pondering which MP could be involved in a corruption scheme with the oil companies. Technically, any of them. However, the most likely were those with direct dealings. He began checking off as many ministerial posts as he could remember: Finance, Environment Science and Technology, Lands and Natural Resources, Interior . . . For a moment, he drew a blank until a thought hit him like a brick to the head. Back at the Raybow Hotel when Dawson had met with Sapphire to talk, she had told him that Terence Amihere, the Minister of Energy, was the BNI director's half brother. Dawson now saw a possible scenario. An oil company was paying Amihere a kickback to allow them to bypass regulations and cut environmental corners. When Tetteh took over the leadership of Goilco, he got wind of this corrupt scheme and confronted Amihere, who got scared of being exposed and turned to his brother at BNI. They come up with a plan to quickly and cleanly kill Tetteh. Either Amihere's people or the BNI could carry out the assassination. The BNI director, through some wrangling at the top echelons, takes over the case from CID and pins the murder on poor Silas.

Then where did Charles come in? Suppose Tetteh talked to him as well, telling him what was going on. Would Charles be a danger to Amihere as well? Possibly. If the oil company involved in the kickback is a Malgam Oil competitor, it could be in Malgam's interest to expose the corruption. Or, perhaps Charles tried to blackmail Amihere after having learned about the corruption scheme.

Dawson nodded to himself, so deep in thought that he had become unaware of his surroundings. Questions remained, however. Why was the signature in Tetteh's murder so different from that of the Smith-Aidoos? Did the BNI stage it to look like some kind of bizarre ritual sacrifice?

Second, why didn't the BNI wrestle the Smith-Aidoo case away from the CID the way they had done the Tetteh murder? Probably because they simply couldn't, despite their efforts. Dawson saw Chief Superintendent Lartey's possible hand in this. Lartey detested the BNI director and over his dead body would he have allowed yet another case to go to the Bureau.

Third, who had put pressure on Hammond to stay clear of anything to do with the Tetteh investigation? Most likely a BNI person, but it was possible that someone high up in the police service could be involved in the scenario Dawson was proposing. That worried him, because if he was going to expose the BNI and the web extended into the police force, then he was going up against two very large and powerful organizations that could crush him to pieces.

If someone had been watching Dawson from a distance, they would have seen a worried man with his hands in his pockets and his head bent in concentration. Every once in a while, he nodded or shook his head, muttering to himself. He looked like a madman.

Chapter 31

AS HE RETURNED TO Takoradi in a taxi, Dawson received a call from Chikata. He was back from Axim again and still with no interesting news. He had interviewed three members of FOAX to no avail. It appeared that this was a dead end. Dawson was sorry that Chikata hadn't hit any leads, but it had been a good exercise for him. Dawson told him he would stop by the hotel in about twenty minutes, but as he ended the call, he received a text from Sapphire that she had left a pen drive with Gamal for Dawson to pick up. Instead of going to the hotel, Dawson asked the taxi driver to go straight through Shippers Circle to Beach Road. The gate to the Smith-Aidoos' house was open, and Gamal had the pen drive ready and waiting.

DAWSON WALKED INTO Chikata's room and held the pen drive out to him.

"Massa, what's on it?"

"I got it from the doctor," Dawson said. "I'm hoping it has some information about her uncle that will help us."

They sat on the love seat and perched the laptop on the coffee table in front of them. Chikata opened up the drive and went through the files. One PowerPoint detailed recent oil discoveries in African countries. The rest was a collection of photographs taken at different events focusing on oil production in Ghana.

"'First oil,'" Chikata said, reading the caption below the image of the President of Ghana symbolically turning the wheel that had opened up the valve for the maiden flow of oil. The caption below another photograph described Roger Calmy-Rey and Charles meeting with the local press and the Parliamentary Committee on Energy Policy.

Dawson clicked through, coming to a set of images taken at a black tie event that Calmy-Rey had attended with his senior management team.

"That's the Minister of Energy, Terence Amihere," Dawson said, pointing to a man in the photograph holding a cocktail glass as he conversed with a white woman in an off-the-shoulder black dress.

"You know him?" Chikata asked.

"I've met him once. We'll talk some more about him in a minute."

Chikata shot him a quick, puzzled look, but said nothing.

In the next image, Amihere was in conversation with Charles.

"Who's this guy?" Chikata asked, pointing to someone in the right background, and then referring to the caption. "Oh, it's Lawrence Tetteh, the Goilco CEO. More evidence that he and Charles knew each other."

Dawson peered at the image, first close up and then from a distance. "Tetteh seems to be looking directly at Amihere. How would you describe the look on his face? Questioning?"

"Maybe something like that," Chikata said speculatively, "But to me it looks more on the side of contempt, or disgust."

"That would fit."

"Are you going to tell me what happened today, or just keep me wondering?"

Dawson related his confrontation with Hammond and then the revelation the superintendent had made. As he described the superintendent's description of the MP corruption scandal, Chikata's face reflected the seriousness of the implications.

"What do you plan on doing?" he asked Dawson.

"Well, in the first place, we need to be careful. If we are going to be dealing with thugs who assassinate their enemies and chop people's heads off, then we need to ask ourselves if we want to get in the middle of this. What I fear the most are threats against my family."

Chikata swore under his breath. "Oh, no. Not that. Dawson, I think we have to go straight to Uncle Theo. I'm positive he knows nothing about this."

"We have to go to him, yes, but we need more information in order to make a strong and clear case to him."

"All right, but how?"

"That's the question."

"Do you have the answer?"

Dawson delivered a brisk slap to the side of Chikata's head and the sergeant fell over with laughter.

"Insubordination, Sergeant," Dawson muttered, a smile playing at his lips. He grew serious again. "There's something that connects the Tetteh and the Smith-Aidoo murders. We just haven't found it. I was hoping this pen drive would shed some light, but it hasn't added much."

The two men sat back pondering for a while. Finally, Dawson sighed and shook his head. "I'm not sure about the next step," he said. "Anyway, leaving that aside for a moment, in the time being, I haven't told you about my expedition to the rig."

"Oh, yes!" Chikata said, smiling. "I want to hear about it. Were you scared when you were in the helicopter?"

"At first I was very nervous," Dawson admitted, "but then I quickly got used to it."

He gave the fascinated sergeant a detailed account of the journey to the rig and the time he spent on it, as well as his conversations with Mr. Glagah and Clifford. "What that trip impressed on me, Chikata," Dawson said, getting to his feet and leaning against the desk, "is how impossible it would have been to carry out this murder without involving someone who knows the Atlantic backward and forward. So even though we've been going after possible suspects like Jason Sarbah and Reggie Cardiman who might have had a grudge against Charles—and we *should*—we have to start giving more attention to the strong possibility that there was also a fisherman who might have had something against them."

"Do you mean I should keep searching for connections in Axim?"

"I'd like you to go to Cape Three Points village tomorrow and ask around. You might come up with a possible lead—maybe someone who had a confrontation with Charles. You'll probably have to visit the chief to introduce yourself, just like we did at Akwidaa."

Chikata nodded. "I'll do that." He made a face. "I'll have to buy some gin."

Dawson smiled. "Yes, you will." He returned to his seat and shifted the laptop over. "Let me check if Dr. Taryque has emailed me the postmortem pics."

Chikata reached over to the refrigerator while Dawson logged on and went to his web mail. "Do you want a Malta?"

"Yes, thank you. You sure your uncle is paying for all this?"

Chikata snorted. "He'd better be, because I certainly am not."

"Ah, the doc has sent me a message."

Dawson turned the laptop slightly so Chikata could see better.

Dear Inspector Dawson,

Here are the images you requested. As you will observe, powder burns are present around the head wound of the male but not the female.

Please let me know if you have any questions.

Best,
WT

Dawson opened the file and went through the fifteen slides—seven for Charles and eight for Fiona. Each of them had descriptive captions. Two slides each pictured their full-length bodies lying on the autopsy table. In Charles's case, one was the headless version and the other was with his head placed contiguous with his neck.

"Oh, dear Jesus," Chikata said, shaking his head and clicking his tongue. "Terrible."

Another image was a close-up of the ragged decapitation site. Dawson shuddered. On the close-up of Charles's right side head wound, the ring of soot was visible even against his dark skin.

Even in death, Fiona's body was curvaceous with large, firm thighs. Besides the bullet wound to her head and the ligature lines at her wrists, she was unmarked. Most importantly, in contrast to Charles, no soot appeared around the entry wound at her left temple. She was lighter in color than her husband, so there was no question about it.

"The way I see it," Dawson said, "two men took part in the murder. They ambush Charles's vehicle on his way back from Ezile with his wife. They kidnap them that afternoon and transport them to a spot near a secluded beach somewhere. Night comes, they take Charles and Fiona down to the beach and order them to kneel or lie on the ground." Dawson formed the shape of a pistol with thumb and index and aimed downward. "The gunman stands at Charles's side, presses the nozzle to his temple, and shoots him, but with Fiona, he stands where he is and shoots her from a distance of two or three meters. Then one of them decapitates Charles. It takes a strong stomach and a cold heart to do that. It's not easy, and it's a bloody mess."

"If only we knew what beach the kidnappers took them to," Chikata said, perching on the arm of the sofa.

"Why?" Dawson asked, studying him.

"Then maybe we could locate the place where they held the Smith-Aidoos throughout the afternoon and evening. It might be close to the beach, and it might have been some kind of house or shack or enclosed structure where they could keep them concealed."

"Go on," Dawson encouraged him.

"I asked people in Axim if they knew of any beach that was exclusive—just one or two houses, for example. No one gave me any useful answers."

Dawson snapped his fingers and sat bolt upright. "I'm such a fool."

"What, what?"

"I've been thinking the kidnappers took the Smith-Aidoos to some faraway place like Axim in order to make it harder to track them down, but no. What do you meet on the road just before you get to Axim?"

Chikata thought about it for barely a second. "Oh! I went there twice and didn't think of it. I'm the fool, rather. There's a customs checkpoint. Not even an idiot would take the risk of trying to get through that with two kidnapped people in the boot of the car."

"Exactly," Dawson said, nodding. "In fact, Chikata, it's the opposite. The kidnappers would want a spot as *close* to the ambush point as possible."

"But not Ezile Bay, because there are people there at the resort."

"But remember the spot Mr. Cardiman took us where we had a view of Ezile to the left and a second bay to the right?"

"Yes, yes," Chikata said nodding.

"The second bay is mostly deserted—remember, Cardiman said only occasionally does someone walk along the beach between Cape Three Points village and Akwidaa. We need to go there. Call Baah and tell him to get down here quick."

Chapter 32

AFTER THEY HAD CALLED Baah, Dawson had a brain wave that they should borrow Abraham's 4x4 to tackle the unpaved section of the road to Cape Three Points. He was glad they did because Baah drove at a speed that would have split his taxi in two over the treacherous surface. In spite of his making it in record time, evening was fast approaching the way it always does at the equator. They reached the sign pointing to Ezile Bay Resort, and Dawson instructed Baah to keep going west.

"Slow down, though," he said. "We're looking for some kind of access on the left-hand side that someone could use to get to the beach."

They went past an unbroken sequence of impenetrable bush.

"I don't see any way you can get through this to the beach," Chikata muttered.

They came to the crest of a hill, below which they could see Cape Three Points village in the distance.

"That means we've gone too far," Dawson said, looking at the dashboard clock. It was almost five thirty. "Let's go back, Baah. Maybe we missed it."

They turned around in swirling red dust and slowly retraced their course.

"Oh, there," Baah said, the first to spot a gap in the bush that hadn't been visible from the opposite direction.

"Good work," Dawson said. "Let's turn in."

Not a constructed road, it was more a vehicular path with a track for the wheels on either side of a crest of grass. The three men were silent, not sure what to expect.

"I can go small-small," Baah said, slowing down, "but the bush start to make thick."

Chikata drew in a breath as, after another 300 meters, the shell of a house appeared on the right side of the path as if it had sprung from the bush like a mushroom.

"Look at that," Dawson said, almost not believing it.

The roof was in place, but the doors and windows were unfinished and the brickwork was raw and unpainted. It wasn't uncommon in Ghana to come across a random, unfinished house in a relatively uninhabited area, but this was especially isolated.

"Let's park and walk," Dawson said. "I want to get to the beach first, before it gets dark, and then we'll come back and look at this house."

Wispy clouds glowed orange as the sun began to set. They followed the footpath that led away from the house, noticing mangroves and hearing the sound of crashing waves as they got closer to the beach. They emerged abruptly onto the shore, surprised at how close the water was. The tide was evidently cresting. A few more meters and their ankles would have gotten a soaking.

The beach arced gently, terminating at each end with a peninsula. Dawson pointed to the promontory on their left. "On the other side of that is Ezile Bay, where we were. Cape Three Points village is over the peninsula on the right. This bay here is secluded, and it would be perfect for the killers to launch out to the oil rig in secret."

The three men stood for a while, looking around. No one was in sight, only the beach with its cresting waves, coconut palms and mangroves—undeniably powerful yet soothing. But somewhere here, Dawson thought, a heinous crime may have been committed, the waves washing away the bloody evidence in the sand. "Come on," he said, "let's get back to that house."

The sun was disappearing and light was fading. Both Dawson and Chikata switched on their flashlights as they walked around the rustic building, picking through scratchy brush. All the windows were frameless, open gaps. The interior was empty, although they could deduce which space would become the kitchen, dining area, sitting room, and the two bedrooms in the rear.

The cement floor was dusty. Dawson was intrigued by how engaged Baah was. He had taken out his cell phone and was using its small but respectable flashlight to shine into the window of the smaller of the bedrooms.

"Please, Inspector," he called out, just as Dawson was about to move on. "Come and see."

Dawson and Chikata joined him at the window. Baah's flashlight beam caught three plastic water bottles tossed on the floor. They had a good coating of dust, meaning they had probably been there for a while. That wasn't what had attracted Baah's attention. It was a glint of metal in the right-hand corner of the room.

"What's that?" Dawson said, craning forward. He focused on it with the light.

"It might just be something that fell from the ceiling." Chikata said.

"No be earring?" Baah said. "Those ones which make like big ring."

"An earring," Dawson whispered. He vaulted through the window and crouched down by the object to examine it more closely. Chikata and Baah followed.

"Well done, Baah!" Dawson exclaimed.

"What's special about the earring?" Chikata asked.

"Now we're getting somewhere," Dawson said excitedly. "Fiona Smith-Aidoo was missing one hoop earring on autopsy. I bet you this is it. This is a real find, thanks to my man Baah. I think this is where the Smith-Aidoos were taken. If so, we might be able to track down the killers."

IN THE MORNING, Dawson and Chikata went to the charge office at Takoradi central police station and asked the desk constable for access to the Smith-Aidoos' personal effects. The constable took them down a corridor to the musty exhibit storeroom, where he checked the rows of shelves containing labeled boxes and plastic bags. He located the Smith-Aidoos' box and brought it down to a table in the front part of the room. He opened up the exhibit register to record that the box was moving from its position for examination of the contents.

The constable took out the labeled bags containing Fiona's and Charles's bloodstained clothes, and from the bottom of the box, a silver hoop earring in its evidence bag. Dawson placed it alongside the earring they had found the night before. The two were identical.

"The same," the constable commented.

"Yes," Dawson agreed, looking at Chikata triumphantly.

THE INSPECTOR AND sergeant had a vigorous debate all during their drive to the Lands Commission on Sekondi Road. Dawson thought that there was a chance that the house belonged to or was in some way associated with the killers.

"But it could be anybody's empty house that the killers knew about and just used for their purposes," Chikata pointed out, leaning forward to gesticulate in the space between the front passenger and driver seats.

"So what?" Dawson challenged, turning to Chikata. "Are you saying it's not worth a try?"

"No, I'm saying we might be on the way to arresting the wrong person."

"Like that doesn't happen all the time," Dawson said dryly. "Look, whatever we find, we'll look at it carefully and consider the next steps. We're not going to rush into anything stupid."

After a few minutes, he added, "At least, I hope not."

Chikata guffawed from the back seat.

BAAH PARKED IN the shaded lot of the Lands Commission. Dawson and Chikata weren't sure which of the four buildings to approach, but they tried the one with the sign LAND REGISTRY DIVISION. The young clerk at the front desk looked up as they walked in and put away the phone he had been texting on.

"Good morning, sir."

Dawson told him he was looking for the owner of an area of land near Cape Three Points. The clerk went to the back and returned with an older man who introduced himself as Nicholas and took Dawson and Chikata into a hot, cavernous room with row upon row of paper files.

"You say Cape Three Points?" he asked Dawson. "Do you mean Cape Three Points village?"

"No, east of that—between there and Ezile."

Nicholas grunted and sifted through giant folders hanging vertically on horizontal tracks. After some searching, he pulled one up and rested it on a table, slowly turning the large pages until he came to the correct area map. He leaned over it, studied it for a while and then pointed to a spot.

"Somewhere here?" he asked.

Dawson peered at it.

"I don't know. The map is a little confusing."

"The bay is here," Nicholas said, his finger outlining the area. "This is Cape Three Points village west of the bay. This is Ezile to the east of it."

"Okay, then yes. That's the area I mean."

"You're sure?" Nicholas said, scrutinizing Dawson.

"Yes."

Nicholas nodded and put the map away. "Please, can you wait here one minute? Let me go and check the records."

"Okay."

He was gone for about ten minutes, during which time Dawson and Chikata began to pour with sweat. Despite the open windows, air was barely circulating.

Nicholas returned shaking his head. "No record of any land title there."

Dawson put his arms akimbo, surprised. "Then how is someone building on it?"

Nicholas snorted. "It happens all the time. The Land Title Registry won't register a tract of land without a concurrence certificate from the Lands Commission. The Commission too won't issue the certificate if it doesn't get approval from Town and Country planning. T and C won't give the approval without a confirmation map from the survey department, who says they don't have enough funding for the mapping, and on it goes. Then who knows? Two brothers may be fighting over the land, neither of them has registered it, but one of them is building a house so he can claim the land is his. Utter confusion."

Dawson frowned. "So can you investigate this any further?"

"Investigate what?"

"Who owns that land, and who is building a house on it?" Dawson said, a little impatiently, feeling his endeavor slipping away by the second.

"Well, I can try. It will take several weeks."

Dawson's eyes popped. "Weeks! I'm investigating a murder case—I don't have weeks."

Nicholas gestured with a sweeping motion of the hands. "Do you see any computers around here?"

"No," Dawson said flatly.

"Exactly," Nicholas said, with a sardonic smile. "I will have to cross-check old files and dig through paperwork from as far back as I don't know when. And don't think yours will be the only case I'm working on. I mean, you are a CID detective. You must understand my situation."

Dawson puffed his breath out through his cheeks in resignation. "Okay," he said disappointedly. "Take my phone number. Please, if you find anything, call me."

"I will do that."

Outside, Dawson shook his head. "What a waste of time," he said, irritated. He was probably more annoyed that his brilliant plan hadn't worked.

"We keep hitting on things that we think will bring us closer to a solution," Chikata said, as they got back into the car. "The earring, Smith-Aidoo's pen drive . . . what next?"

"I don't know," Dawson said heavily. On impulse, he called Christine just to say hello.

"You don't sound so good," she said.

"We're stuck," he replied glumly.

"That means you're about to have an epiphany," she said encouragingly. "Happens every time."

"I hope you're right." He told her he missed her and that she should kiss the boys for him and then hung up. A few minutes later, he gasped and buried his face in his hands.

"Massa, what's wrong?" Chikata said, leaning forward with concern.

"*Awurade*, something is the wrong with me," Dawson moaned.

"What?" Chikata said in alarm. "Are you feeling sick?"

Dawson turned to him. "Don't you see? It's not Smith-Aidoo's pen drive we need, it's *Tetteh's*."

Chapter 33

Baah got Dawson and Chikata to Accra in two hours. He didn't know the big, messy capital at all, so they directed him to Labone Estates. The houses here were large and gated. The schools nearby, like Ghana International School, were posh and top of the line. They were looking for 27 Labone Crescent, Lawrence Tetteh's address. After a bit of wandering around, they found it—a relatively short, curved street with a T-junction at either end. Between 17 and 23, no house numbers were evident, but 25 popped up all of a sudden and Baah overshot number 27. Dawson got out and walked back, gazing up at the high security wall, which was painted in rich tangerine. He pushed the button at the side of the sturdy double gate, and after a few moments, a woman cracked it open. She was slight, mid-thirties with coarse features, and hair singed by cheap relaxants.

"Good afternoon." He greeted her with the smile he used when he thought the person he was addressing might prove useful.

"Good afternoon, sir."

"I'm looking for one Charity. Is she here?"

"Yes? I'm Charity."

"Oh, very good. *Mepaakyew*, my name is Darko Dawson. You were Mr. Tetteh's housemaid, not so?"

"Yes, please," she said, a little warily.

"Can I talk to you about what happened to him?"

Fear moved across her face like a quick wave. "Please, are you from the police?" she whispered, glancing surreptitiously behind her.

"I work at CID."

She seemed unsure exactly what that meant. "Please, they told me not to talk about it to anyone."

"Who told you?" he asked gently.

She swallowed and shook her head, backing up slightly. She had already said too much.

"I know you worked for him for many years," Dawson said quickly to avoid losing her. "You were faithful to him until the end, and I admire you for that. We should keep caring about him, even though he is dead. We have to find out who really killed him."

A woman's voice yelled from the house, "Who is it, Charity?"

"Please, I'm coming," she called back and then leaned toward him to whisper, "The Madam is calling me. I can't talk now. I will close at six o'clock to go to my sister's house in La. Wait for me near the Morning Star School, and I will come there."

She shut the gate quickly.

Dawson trotted back to the car to report. Six o'clock was another four hours from then, so they went to the corner and bought some roasted corn from a vendor. They stood under the shade of a frangipani tree.

"Have you noticed," Chikata said, munching hungrily, "that rich neighborhoods always look deserted?"

Dawson nodded, demolishing the last of his corn. "It's because they're all inside counting their money. Come on, let's go to the Internet café."

On the way there, they passed the highly rated Morning Star School, where they were to meet up later with Charity. Dawson prayed she would show up. He and Chikata entered the Danquah Circle Busy Internet and paid for an hour each of computer time. The gigantic, air-conditioned room was full of people furiously surfing at row after row of computer cubicles, including, no doubt, dozens of *Sakawa* boys, the infamous young Internet swindlers who could make as much as two thousand dollars in a good month. Dawson mentally shook his head at the thought of making that kind of money. He logged onto one of the machines while Chikata used the in-house Wi-Fi on his laptop.

Dawson did a search on Lawrence Tetteh and came across a YouTube conversation between Tetteh and TV host David Ampofo. At the time, Tetteh had just taken over as CEO of Goilco after having worked for oil companies in Dallas for a number of years. He looked distinguished and professorial in wire-rimmed glasses and a dark suit. He had a stubborn jaw and a pendulous bottom lip. He said he planned to make Goilco a world-class oil and gas organization. In doing so, he was committed to transparency and honesty.

"Do you believe you have an equitable relationship with your partners—Malgam Oil, for example?" Ampofo asked him with his legendary intensity. "And with your counterpart Mr. Roger Calmy-Rey?"

"Yes, I do. I believe that Mr. Calmy-Rey and I share similar values and goals."

Standard party line, Dawson thought, a little disappointed. He had expected something less conventional, more radical, from Tetteh. He looked up Roger Calmy-Rey and found a short Wikipedia biography.

Roger William Calmy-Rey *(born 1950) is the son of the late Ulysses Calmy-Rey, founder of Malgam Oil, one of Europe's largest businesses.*

Career
Educated at Harrow School in Harrow, northwest London, and London University where he studied Political Science. He joined Malgam Oil in late 1973 at the urging of his father. He became the CEO in 1987 on the death of his father, Ulysses Calmy-Rey.

After that, Dawson found multiple interviews with and profiles of Roger Calmy-Rey by online publications like the Independent.co.uk. Calmy-Rey believed strongly in the future of oil in Africa, he said. He wanted his company to be in the continent for decades to come, while building relations of mutual respect between Malgam and its African host countries like Ghana and Uganda.

Dawson was now on a searching streak. He tried "Sarbah" and got a GhanaWeb.com article about Jason Sarbah's appointment as Malgam Director of Corporate Relations, replacing the deceased Charles Smith-Aidoo. Other links to the Sarbah name were of no importance.

Dawson stared at the screen and brooded as doubts lingered about what he and Chikata were venturing into. How dangerous might it be to delve into a corruption scheme involving the BNI and people in high positions? If Tetteh and Charles were killed for what they knew, was Dawson setting himself up for the same fate? Most of his panic had to do with his family. Was he being overdramatic in thinking he might be about to endanger the lives of Christine and the boys? He didn't think so.

He got up, signaling he was stepping outside to Chikata, who was showing a pretty girl how to log on as she coyly feigned ignorance. Dawson went to the far brick wall of the car park to call his mentor, Daniel Armah, but he didn't pick up. Armah had long retired from the police service, and now ran a private detective agency in the city of Kumasi.

Dawson was tempted to call Christine as well, but she would be able to tell from his voice that he was worried about something, and that would inject anxiety into her. He wanted to see her, but this was not the time.

He caught a whiff of smoke and immediately recognized its sharp sweetness. Someone was puffing on marijuana in the alley behind the wall. Dawson had an intense desire to smoke some himself. He went back inside the Internet café to get away from temptation.

STANDING NEXT TO Baah's taxi, Dawson waited at the north end of Morning Star School. He had sent Chikata to the opposite side of the building when it had occurred to him that he didn't know which of the two approaches Charity would use. It was six o'clock. The schoolchildren were all gone for the day. Four staff cars remained in front of the building. No sign of Charity yet. He called Chikata. "Nothing?"

"Not yet."

By 6:30, Dawson was becoming doubtful that she would show, and by 7:00, he was losing hope. He buzzed Chikata again and told him they would wait until 7:15 and call it quits if Charity did not show up.

Ten after seven, Dawson saw her hovering uncertainly at the corner of Labone Avenue and Cantonments Road. She spotted him and hesitantly began to walk in his direction. He closed the space between them and met her halfway.

"Hello, Charity. Thank you for coming."

"Yes, please."

She was jumpy and kept looking around. Taking a guess, Dawson asked her if she was a Ga. She said yes, and Dawson switched from English to Ga to help her feel more at ease. "Where do you want to talk?"

"Not here," she said firmly. "Rather, let's go to my sister's house."

"I have a taxi."

They swung around to pick Chikata up, and Dawson introduced Charity to him, reassuring her that he could be trusted. Charity suggested Baah avoid the congested Ring Road and directed him through the twists and turns of the side streets, some of which were in a terrible, potholed state. Along the route, vendors sold *Kelewele*— ripe plantain crisply deep-fried with ginger, red pepper, and other spices—by fluorescent light or smoky kerosene lamps.

Charity's neighborhood was relatively close to the beach, separated from it only by Labadi Road. She told Baah where to stop and Dawson asked him to wait, giving him a couple of *cedis* to get something to eat.

It was pitch dark as they made their way to the house, and although Charity knew every inch along the route, Dawson and Chikata thought it best to use their flashlights as they navigated clogged gutters and undulating terrain with sharp outcroppings of rock.

In her own environment, Charity seemed less diffident. Her sister's house was small and square with a corrugated metal roof and hole-ridden mosquito netting on the windows. Outside, a young woman in her early twenties was crouched on her haunches frying fish on a charcoal stove by lantern light. Three small children ran up to Charity to hug her before going back to playing.

"My grandchildren," she told the two men with a smile. "That's my daughter who is cooking. Please, let's go inside the house."

In the sitting room dimly lit by one anemic bulb, a boy of about thirteen was sitting on a lopsided couch watching a small TV with grainy reception. He got up immediately without prompting and turned off the set before leaving with a respectful "good eve'ng" to the two guests.

Charity pulled up some plastic chairs, and the three of them sat down at a slight angle to each other.

"Thank you for bringing me to your house," Dawson said in Ga. "I told you I'm trying to find out what happened to Lawrence Tetteh, and I hope you can help me."

"Yes, please."

"Can you tell me a little bit about him?"

"He was a good man. He always tried to help me. I stayed in the servant's quarters, but every Sunday, he told me to take the day off to go to church and visit my family."

Dawson sat forward with his elbows on his knees. It was a more relaxed pose, which tended to put people more at ease. "Who is living in his house now?"

"His uncle and his aunt, their son, and the son's wife. And another woman too, but I don't even know who she is." She shook her head as if she was talking about a den of thieves.

"How did Mr. Tetteh treat you?"

She clasped her hands together, and her face took on heavy sorrow. "He respected me and trusted me even more than his own family."

"What about his wife?"

"He married some woman when he was in States. She doesn't live in Ghana." Charity looked down at her fingers. "Different women always used to come and visit him."

"What happened that day when he was killed?" Dawson asked her gently. In the corner of his eye he saw Chikata watching with his usual stress-free pose, arms open, legs apart. "It was a Sunday, correct?"

"Yes please," she said, nodding. "He had been in Côte d'Ivoire since Monday of that week, returning on Friday night. He spent the whole of Saturday at home writing something on the computer. On Sunday morning, I came to him to ask him if he needed anything." Charity rubbed her hands back and forth over the top of her thighs, revealing the stress she was feeling telling the story. "He said no and told me I can go to church and spend the day with my family. That was the last time I saw him alive." Charity's bottom lip began to tremble. "When I returned in the evening, I went to check on him and found him dead in the sitting room."

Ah, this is what I want, Dawson thought ecstatically. "So, it's not true that you welcomed Silas to the house in the afternoon or that you were home when you heard a gunshot and saw Silas running from the house?"

She bowed her head. "Yes, please. It's not true."

"It's okay." Dawson didn't want her to feel any shame or embarrassment. He could tell she was the kind of person who easily accepted undeserved blame. "Who told you to say that you were home that day and that you saw Silas?"

"Two policemen," she said softly, almost fearfully. "They came to see me the next morning to ask me what happened. I said to them that I had already told an inspector from the police station what had happened the night before, and they had already taken my statement. They told me that the inspector was not working on the case anymore and that I had to sign a new statement."

Dawson exchanged a glance with Chikata. These two so-called policemen had probably been imposters or BNI guys.

"Did they tell you their names?" Dawson asked.

"No, please. They told me to come with them and they took me inside their car. One was driving and the other one sat with me in the back. They drove me far to somewhere around the Trade Fair site, and they didn't say anything. I was afraid to ask where they were taking me." Charity's voice was shaking with emotion. "They found some lonely place and parked the car there. They told me I was in trouble because since I was the only one who found Mr. Tetteh dead, then probably I was the one who killed him. So they're going to arrest me."

She sniffed, wiping her nose with the back of her hand and brushing tears away.

"I told them I can never kill Mr. Tetteh. I begged them for mercy. Then they said they had to arrest me, and the one who was driving said he was going to handcuff me, and the other one said, 'No, don't do it.' And I begged them, *ofaine, ofaine*, don't take me, please. They said they knew Silas killed Mr. Tetteh, and they could arrest him if I confirm it for them. If I don't confirm, then they have to arrest me rather."

Charity was wringing her hands and curling her feet inward. Dawson could see how much anguish the story was causing her. "They said I should make another statement saying that I saw Silas coming to kill Mr. Tetteh. They would write it for me, and I would sign it. Then when the time came to testify in court, I have to say the same thing as I said in the statement, and they said they will teach me how to say it. So I signed the statement, and they let me go."

She looked up at them almost apologetically. Dawson was angry but not with her.

"There's nothing else you could have done," he said, doing his best to reassure her. "I would have done the same thing if I had been in your position. Did the two policemen ever return?"

"Once, about one week later. They said they had arrested Silas for killing Mr. Tetteh, and they wanted to thank me for helping them but that later they would need me again to make the statement in court."

Dawson's jaw was clenching and unclenching. "Don't worry. You won't have to."

Her eyes searched his face with both hopefulness and pleading, as though she had finally found someone she could lean on.

"Charity," Dawson said, "do you know what a pen drive is?"

"Yes, that small thing to stick into the side of the computer."

"Did Mr. Tetteh have one?"

"Yes, please."

Without warning, she smiled, taking Dawson completely by surprise. He realized he had not yet seen her smile. "Do you know where I can find it?"

"He gave it to me to give to you."

Dawson's heart stopped. "What?"

"You were the one he said would come."

"We don't understand what you're saying," Chikata said, coming so far forward in his chair that it almost tipped over.

"He told me that certain people hate him," she said. "Even, some of them used to threaten that they would kill him. He told me that if he dies, many different detective policemen will come to ask me questions, but only one will really care, and one day—he didn't know when—that one will come to see me and that I should give the pen drive to that one who cares, but to no one else. When you came this morning, and I heard you say, 'We have to care about Mr. Tetteh,' I knew you were the one."

Dawson was reeling. He felt heat and chills alternately in his face. "You have the pen drive here?" His voice almost shook.

"Yes. Please, I'm coming."

She went into another room. Dawson looked at Chikata, speechless in disbelief. Charity returned seconds later. Into Dawson's hand, she dropped a shiny, dark blue 8 GB pen drive inscribed with the word GOILCO.

This has to be it, Dawson thought. This pen drive held the solution to the mystery of who killed the Smith-Aidoos. He tried to curb his enthusiasm. His hunch could easily be wrong—again—he cautioned himself. Still, in spite of his trying to restrain his exuberance, he had a certain feeling, a feeling he had something very hot in his hand.

Chapter 34

THE TIME WAS ALMOST eleven when Dawson and Chikata left Charity. They had spent hours talking and not only about Mr. Tetteh's murder. Conversing with the two men in rapid Ga, Charity had become relaxed and full of good humor. She had then insisted that they join the family for a meal of *kenkey* and fried fish.

No good would come from trying to get back to Takoradi at this late hour, and in any case, they were dead tired. They drove around and finally found a cheap place to stay for the night.

"I can sleep in the car," Baah said.

Dawson and Chikata looked at each other and laughed.

"Oh, why you dey laugh?" Baah asked in surprise.

"*Chaley*, dis no be Takoradi," Chikata said, grinning. "Dis be Accra."

Dawson put his arm around Baah's skinny shoulders. "Come on, you're not going to sleep in the car. It's too dangerous."

Dawson paid for one room. It was all he could afford right now. The accommodations were the lowest of the low: a bare ceiling bulb, two low-set, lopsided beds with thin foam mattresses, and no toilet, bathroom, or even a sink. The public facilities outside were unpleasant. Baah sat in the one plastic chair and dozed off almost immediately.

Chikata looked for an electrical outlet but didn't find one.

"Ah, well," he said, switching on his laptop and sitting on the bed beside Dawson, "we'll run it as long as the battery lasts."

He popped in the pen drive. Dawson was trying to tone down his sense of anticipation so that if nothing on the pen drive turned out to be of interest, he wouldn't feel crushed with disappointment.

The first thing they found on the drive was a set of emails between Charles and Tetteh.

From: Charles Smith-Aidoo
10 April 2012
To: Lawrence Tetteh
Subject: Re: Corporate responsibility

Hello, Lawrence –
I understand your concerns, but Malgam is working very seriously on developing a fund to cover the cost of cleaning up any spills.

Charles

Original Message
From: Lawrence Tetteh
8 April 2012
To: Charles Smith-Aidoo
Subject: Corporate responsibility.

Charles – the lack of serious commitment by Malgam to prevent environmental degradation by oil spills concerns me greatly.

After this exchange, no communication appeared between the two men until 10th May, when Charles sent a brief message:

I've been trying to call you regarding what we discussed. It appears your phone is off. My brother, I'm appealing to you as a fellow Ghanaian and colleague, please, don't do this. This could threaten everything that we've achieved so far. All whistleblowers eventually suffer contempt, and they all come to regret their actions.

Turning to Chikata, Dawson explained. "On the fourth of May, Smith-Aidoo had texted Tetteh to say he would be in Accra in a few days and that they should meet up. He sounded very serious. They must have met, and this is the email after the meeting. So, it seems Tetteh wanted to blow the whistle on something, and Charles was trying to stop him from doing it."

"Maybe it was a corruption scheme," Chikata suggested. "Is it possible Charles had Tetteh killed in order to stop him from exposing it? But then, who killed Charles and Fiona, and why? This is confusing."

Dawson's eyes were closed as he tried to work it out. "It's more likely that Charles told a third party, who decided to get rid of both him and Tetteh because of what they knew. It could be the BNI director behind it, or Amihere, the MP."

"What about Superintendent Hammond?"

Dawson opened his eyes again and looked up at Chikata. "What about him?"

Chikata shrugged. "Maybe he hasn't told you the whole story and he's more involved than we think. How do we know he's not caught up in a cover-up and had a hand in the killings? Why else has he been trying so hard to block our progress?"

"Maybe," Dawson said with a sigh. He was worried that Chikata could be right. "We'll have to keep it in the back of our minds as a possibility."

There were no further emails to be found on the drive.

"He has some documents on here too," Dawson said. "Let's see what they are."

They skimmed quickly through minutes and transcriptions of several meetings with sterile-sounding titles like *Progress on the East Cape Three Points Exploration Block* and *Plans for Monetization of Natural Gas*. Nothing was remarkable about them, but the next one they found had them carefully reading every line.

THE OIL COAST
Why Ghana is Not the Master of Its Destiny in the Petroleum industry
By Lawrence Tetteh

To: TheTimes.co.uk

In 2007, the Malgam Oil Company discovered large reserves of offshore oil at Ghana's Cape Three Points in the Western Region. With the cooperation of the Ghana government, the development of the East Cape Three Points well oil was fast-tracked in record time to first oil in December 2010. A feeling of elation captured the country. People dreamed of working in the oil and gas industry and of the riches that would result.

Of course, much of it was, and still is, an illusion. Most of oil work is restricted to a highly trained few, and the industry itself will never be a huge employer. There are more opportunities in the supportive, service, and hospitality industries, where less-skilled workers have a chance. This explains the massive influx of people moving from other parts of the country to the city at the center of the new oil industry, Takoradi.

Another illusion abides, however, concerning Malgam in particular. Malgam's CEO, Roger Calmy-Rey, son of renowned Ulysses Calmy-Rey, has given the impression that the company is committed to preserving the environment, the fishing industry, and the livelihood of the coastal peoples. With his successful promotion of the highly polished public image of his company, Mr. Calmy-Rey is lauded for aspiring to his father's lofty ideals of humanitarian oil exploration and production.

Yet, last year when an oil spill occurred and killed millions of fish, Malgam showed no interest in compensating fishermen for their losses. They claim they paid for cleanup costs, but the process lacked transparency, and it is not clear how much they spent or how much they actually cleaned up. The two companies refused to pay the Ghanaian government a fine. Malgam is now embroiled in a legal case.

A number of additional disturbing issues have surfaced within the last year:

- Mr. Calmy-Rey has indicated that he seeks to bring local content online as soon as possible. However, the "training programs" that Malgam provides are a token gesture that involve only a small handful of Ghanaians every year.

- Rather than sourcing local food supplies, Malgam imports food for its rig workers from Europe or neighboring Ivory Coast.

- Malgam has preferentially awarded contracts to foreign companies, *e.g. air transportation for executives was awarded to a Dutch company instead of a capable Ghanaian one; heavy lifting equipment was awarded to a British company; and the tug boats used in repositioning offshore oil rigs are operated by an Italian group.*

- *Expatriate engineers are paid three or four times what their equivalent Ghanaian counterparts are and are more likely to get certain perks such as a free car or company credit card.*

Goilco, Ghana's state-owned petroleum company, has a 10% carried interest in the East Cape Points license. That Goilco entered into this agreement is a matter of personal pride for me in the last three years that I have been on board as the CEO. However, I have a wider pride that goes far beyond the boundaries of our offices. I want to see a minimum and not arbitrary pay scale for Ghanaian workers, and I have fought for it. It has been a losing battle.

Malgam CEO Roger Calmy-Rey himself approached me with a proposal that I abet his efforts to achieve certain ultimate goals in return for substantial remuneration to me. The specifics were as follows:

- *Reduce pressure on Malgam to reimburse fishermen in the event of an oil spill.*

- *Strengthen regulations against fishing activities near deep-sea installations.*

- *Work toward avoiding fines on Malgam in the case of an oil spill—they will pay for cleanup only and their own experts will determine the cost.*

- *Establish few or only loose regulations against waste dumping from the FPSO (Floating, Production, Storage, and Offloading) vessel into the Gulf of Guinea.*

- *Firm pressure against establishing a Maritime Law in Parliament.*

- *Avoid any formal, government-determined pay structure for*

Ghanaians, and a "look-away" policy vis-à-vis discriminatory salary policies against Ghanaian workers.

• And above all: collusion in promoting a humanitarian image for the Malgam in general and Roger Calmy-Rey in particular.

Malgam Oil and its CEO now have a problem. I am the problem. In my entire career, I have never been corruptible, and I don't intend to start now. My answer to all of the above proposals is "no." I have sacked the three Goilco officials known to have accepted gifts of cash and expensive trips abroad from Malgam.

In order to achieve the corrupt schemes listed in the foregoing, Malgam is paying off high government officials in the chain of command. The Minister of Energy, the Hon. Terence Amihere, has received a retainer of $200,000, deposited in his Swiss bank account in order to assist Malgam in the ways outlined above. I have this on the authority of a ministry insider.

The time has come for a full investigation of corrupt practices carried out by Malgam and other oil companies operating off Ghana's shores. I call for this because I love my country and I want to see it prosper. This is not about me. In fact, I don't care what happens to me. This is about Ghana, a country whose immeasurable potential can be attained only if honor can triumph over greed and corruption.

Dawson took a breath and leaned back. "Unbelievable."

"Do you think all these accusations are true?" Chikata asked.

"I don't know," Dawson said, rubbing his chin in thought, "but it almost doesn't matter. The point is that the accusations have been made, and they are so serious that they warrant an investigation."

"Why was Tetteh sending it to a UK paper?"

"Because he wanted the biggest impact, I suppose," Dawson said. "He knew the penalties imposed on a UK company for corrupt practices in foreign countries are severe, so he was sending the article to where it really counts. From the *Times* it would immediately be picked up here in Ghana—all over the world, actually, especially online. But let's go back to the beginning and work our way forward to this article. Say I'm Tetteh of Goilco and you are Charles of

Malgam. We've known each other since the beginning of the discovery of oil in Ghana, say, five years—or maybe even before that."

"Okay," Chikata said, nodding.

"Formerly," Dawson continued, "I was an employee of an oil company in Texas, but now I'm back in Ghana and I want to work for the state-owned oil corporation, Goilco. Three years ago, I became CEO, and I'm passionate about making it a world-class oil and gas company. I'm determined to do it. I want to leave that legacy, right?"

"Right," Chikata agreed.

Dawson got to his feet and paced a few steps back and forth. "However, after looking into way the previous CEO ran the company, I'm finding waste, redundancy, missing reports, missing money, and above all, evidence of bribery and corruption. I dig further, and I find this goes wider, deeper, and higher than I'd imagined, and I'm shocked to find that Malgam Oil is paying off people at all levels of government to maximize oil profits and avoid being regulated. So now, what should I do?"

"Well, you—Tetteh—know me very well," Chikata said slowly, leaning forward to rest his elbows on his knees, "or maybe we are quite good friends and you need to talk to someone. I'm in Takoradi, and you're in Accra, so you text me from there asking to meet me to talk about this because you're worried."

"Good," Dawson said, aiming an approving finger at the sergeant. "When you come down from Takoradi, we meet up, and I tell you everything I've found out about this rampant corruption. You, Charles, probably didn't know anything about it—or maybe you did. In any case, you are horrified that I'm thinking of making these allegations public. To you, this would be a disaster. You advise me not to go further, but I'm determined to do it. By phone and email, you try repeatedly to get in touch with me to warn me. You take me as a friend, but you're also a Malgam employee, so your ultimate allegiance is to your company, your boss, Roger Calmy-Rey."

"So I'm going to report to him everything you've told me."

"Yes," Dawson said emphatically. "By all means, you have to make Calmy-Rey aware of such a serious threat to him and his company."

"Then Calmy-Rey is now the one who has the motive to kill you—Tetteh."

"Good, but he's not the only one," Dawson said with a slight smile. "Terence Amihere is also a target. Allegedly, he has taken a bribe of at least two hundred thousand dollars, which is very serious."

"How does Amihere come to find out about the allegations in the article you've written?"

"Because I—Tetteh—go to personally confront him."

"Do you think Tetteh would really have done that?"

Dawson nodded with conviction. "No doubt. Think about the kind of man he was. Straightforward, direct, honest, and incorruptible. He sacked the people in Goilco that he found out were taking bribes. He wouldn't have been diplomatic about this. He would have challenged everyone he believed to be involved in corruption. It was a brave move, but it also got him murdered."

"I can see how that could happen," Chikata said, "but what about Charles Smith-Aidoo? Where do he and his wife fit in?"

"I have always believed that their murder was connected to Tetteh's," Dawson said, taking his seat again. "Now I think I know what happened. After Tetteh's death, Charles must have taken up the cause against corruption. What Tetteh had told him had begun to weigh on his mind. Once Charles began this crusade, whoever killed Tetteh had to get rid of Charles as well. And the message delivered to the Malgam oil rig in the form of a terrible double murder and beheading was, 'Don't even think about challenging the powers that be.'"

"Why kill Fiona Smith-Aidoo as well?"

"That wasn't the original plan. The killer or killers weren't expecting Fiona to accompany her husband to Ezile Bay."

"So who killed them or had them killed?"

"I don't know," Dawson said, suddenly feeling weary. "Tomorrow we'll think again when our brains are fresh."

Chapter 35

THEY HAD TO GET some sleep. Chikata, like Baah, was out within a few minutes, but Dawson, exhausted but bereft of sleep, lay awake on the horrendous mattress, which was giving him a backache. His phone buzzed, and for some reason he thought it might be Christine, but he was wrong. It was Armah. Dawson leapt out of bed as he answered.

"Hello, Daniel!"

"Darko, my dear man, how are you?"

"I'm very well," he said, opening the door to step outside. "Hold on a moment. I want to go somewhere I can talk."

"I hope I didn't wake you."

"No, I couldn't sleep."

"I had the feeling. I saw that you had called and took the chance you were awake. Are you troubled?"

Armah and Dawson had that kind of bond where one could almost sense the other's worry from hundreds of miles away. During Dawson's childhood, then CID detective Armah had doggedly investigated the disappearance of Dawson's mother, Beatrice.

"I am troubled," Dawson said, walking around to the opposite side of the building where the potent ammonia smell of the latrine was less pervasive. He told Armah the story from the beginning, bringing him up to the minute.

"Now I'm starting to have doubts," Dawson said, kicking a large pebble away. "How big is this affair with Tetteh, and should I delve further? Is Amihere or someone else going to come after me, or my family? What if the BNI director has conspired with someone high up in the police service? If I'm going up against them, they're going to crush me."

"Hmm, this is tough," Armah said. He paused for a while. "I don't think you or your family are in any danger yet, so what we need to do is keep it that way. First you need to go immediately to Chief Superintendent Lartey."

"He's going to explode," Dawson said.

"Maybe, but it can't be helped. He has to know about this now."

"I almost hate to pose the question, but no way he could be involved in a cover-up?"

"I can practically guarantee that," Armah replied. "He wouldn't have assigned this case to you if he was, and he certainly wouldn't have included Chikata in the investigation. And in any case, it's not only you in the thick of this, Lartey's beloved nephew is involved as well, so he has to take action over the information."

"Okay," Dawson said, feeling better.

"Now if at any time you receive a threatening note or phone call, you'll know it's the BNI director because that's the way he operates," Armah said with confidence. "Then you know it's time to get out. You're deeply dedicated to your work, but don't sacrifice yourself. You have a family you love and who loves you. If you receive threats, call me immediately, because I have some options. We can discuss them if and when the situation comes up, but I don't think it will. How does that sound?"

"Thank you, Daniel." Dawson felt his eyes pricking. "I miss you. I have to get up to Kumasi soon."

"You really must. Talking on the phone is not enough, and as for all this texting you young guys like to do, I will not abide by it."

They had a good laugh and bid each other good night. Dawson returned to the stuffy, smelly room, and to his surprise, he felt himself drifting off very quickly.

IN THE MORNING, the chief superintendent was so pleased to see his nephew that Dawson might as well not have been present. Finally, Lartey acknowledged Dawson and invited both of them to sit down in the two chairs facing him on the opposite side of his desk. The office was air-conditioned, a relief from the heat outside.

"So tell me," Lartey said, getting comfy in his luxurious leather chair. "Are you close to completing the case?"

He was a small man whose slight stature belied his toughness and effective use of power. He was very likely up for the elevated rank of Assistant Commissioner of Police.

"We believe we are, sir," Dawson said. "I'll bring you up to speed."

Lartey's demeanor remained receptive during Dawson's account until he first heard of the connection between Charles Smith-Aidoo and Lawrence Tetteh. Then his expression began to cloud like a stormy sky.

"Last night," Dawson went on, "we made contact with Lawrence Tetteh's housemaid—"

"*What?*" Lartey bellowed, shooting forward. "What for? What the hell are you doing?"

"We had to," Dawson said bravely. "We're convinced the Smith-Aidoo and Tetteh murders are connected."

"Completely different signatures," Lartey snapped, slapping his palm on the table. "Even a five-year-old could tell you that. This is nonsense."

"Uncle," Chikata chimed in quickly, "the housemaid gave us the pen drive Mr. Tetteh had given her for safekeeping, and we made a discovery you should know about."

His laptop open and ready, Chikata brought it around for Lartey to read, which he did immediately, tapping his middle finger unconsciously on his desk.

"Oh, Lord," he said, when he was finished. He slumped back in his chair. "What have you done, Dawson?"

"It was my idea to get in touch with the housemaid, Uncle Theo," Chikata said. Dawson opened his mouth to protest the lie, but the sergeant sent him a look that said, *don't say anything*.

"You, Philip?" Lartey said in disbelief. "Why didn't you come to me first, eh?"

Chikata looked sheepish and kept his gaze down in submission. "I'm sorry, Uncle," he said meekly. It always worked.

"It's okay, Philip," Lartey said rather gently. "What I'm most concerned about—" he turned to Dawson "—is *you*. You are the senior officer and you take a suggestion from a junior officer without providing him guidance, without showing him the correct thing to do?"

"You asked me to give him free rein, sir—"

"But that doesn't mean you shouldn't exercise some common sense instead of getting up to this foolishness, does it? I'm waiting for your answer, Inspector."

"No, sir. It does not."

"Did you let Superintendent Hammond know about this?"

"Superintendent Hammond has been against us all the way, Uncle," Chikata said heatedly. "He hasn't lifted one finger to help us."

Lartey's expression changed. "Is that so? Why didn't you report that to me?"

"It was pettiness, sir," Dawson said quickly. "Not worth your time at all. Anyway, he has apologized to me and has promised to be more helpful. We also had some, um, worries that maybe he has some knowledge of the conspiracy, but we are not certain how deeply involved he is. I don't want to incriminate him more than I should."

Lartey nodded. "There's time to investigate what's going on in that regard. Let's get to the bottom line. Who do you think murdered Tetteh and Smith-Aidoo?"

"We have three suspects," Dawson said. "The Honorable Terence Amihere, the BNI director, and Roger Calmy-Rey."

"Or all of the above could be involved in some way," Lartey added. "Yes, sir."

The chief superintendent took a deep breath and sighed. "I want to shield you from the BNI, especially. They can be vindictive."

He got up abruptly, sending his executive chair shooting back. He stood at the window for a long time, gazing down at the browning lawn at the front of the CID building. Neither Dawson nor Chikata dared move, but both knew that the chief superintendent was on their side and ready to act. It was just a matter of deciding how.

"Okay," Lartey said finally, turning back to them. "I have to get everything lined up here in Accra before you make any moves on anyone in Takoradi. It can't be the other way around, so you have to wait for word from me before you act. I know two members of the opposition political party who would love to make the party in power look bad with a juicy corruption story. That way, the accusations will appear to emanate at the parliamentary level and keep the two of you safe. Am I making myself clear?"

"Yes, sir," Dawson said. "Thank you, sir."

"Anything else you're hiding up your sleeves? If so, for goodness' sake, speak now. I don't want any late revelations."

"Nothing, sir," Dawson said.

"Good. Now get out. I have a lot of work to do in a very short time."

Chapter 36

BACK IN TAKORADI, DAWSON and Chikata waited for two days, doing nothing while knowing there was so much to be done was a strange and agonizing experience. On each of those two days, Dawson checked that Calmy-Rey was still in town. One of his assistants had mentioned that he would be around for *maybe* another week. Dawson was worried about such vague wording.

He was in Chikata's hotel room when he received the call at 11:35 of the third morning. It was the chief superintendent.

"Everything is set," Lartey said. "Get to work."

"Thank you, sir."

Chikata, guessing that the signal had come, jumped up.

"Let's go," Dawson said.

Having given Baah a couple of days off, they grabbed a taxi and told the driver to take them to the Malgam building, where they went straight to the top floor.

"Oh, I'm so sorry," the receptionist said. "Mr. Calmy-Rey isn't in. He's leaving for the UK today."

No, Dawson thought. "What time?"

"Two o'clock."

It was 12:02, so they were cutting it close.

"He may already be at the airport," Dawson said, as he and Chikata ran down the staircase to the ground floor. "You go there, I'll go to his house. We can't let him leave the country."

They split up, taking taxis in opposite directions.

•   •   •

DAWSON RANG THE bell at the gate and a guard opened up the pedestrian entrance.

"Good afternoon, sir."

"Good afternoon. I'm here to see Mr. Calmy-Rey."

As Dawson went through, a houseboy came out of the house carrying a three-piece matching set of luggage to the waiting SUV, with Roger Calmy-Rey close behind him.

"Good afternoon, Inspector!" he said, cheerily. "To what do I owe this pleasant surprise?"

"Good afternoon, sir."

As they shook hands, Dawson slid his left palm up Calmy-Rey's arm. The Ghana Police regulations manual stipulated that the arresting officer must make every effort to physically touch the suspect. "You are under arrest on suspicion of the murder of Mr. Lawrence Tetteh, Mr. Charles Smith-Aidoo and Mrs. Fiona Smith-Aidoo."

Calmy-Rey turned sheet white.

FOUR HOURS LATER, the charge officer at the Beach Road police station took Roger Calmy-Rey out of his jail cell and handed him over to Dawson and Hammond, who walked on either side of him to the waiting police vehicle.

"Mr. Calmy-Rey," Dawson said as they proceeded, "a warrant has been issued by the district magistrate for the search of your residence and property. You're free to examine the warrant if you wish. You are now accompanying us there, where Detective Superintendent Hammond, Detective Sergeant Chikata, and I will conduct the search. Is that clear?"

Calmy-Rey nodded mutely. He seemed detached, or perhaps he was in a state of shock. He had said nothing more than necessary since his arrest, but he had been polite and cooperative. Just as he had been for Jason Sarbah, Mr. DeGraft was Calmy-Rey's counsel.

Hammond sat in the front passenger seat next to the driver, while Dawson and Chikata sat in the back seat with Calmy-Rey in the middle. They pulled into the driveway of his residence and as they got out of the vehicle, the watchman, houseboy, and gardener watched with wide eyes, aware that something had gone very wrong.

Inside the house, it was obvious that the spotless sitting room was unlikely to yield much in a search.

"Do you have an office?" Dawson asked Calmy-Rey.

"Yes, it's this way," he said softly.

He took them up white marble stairs to a carpeted, immaculate office with a polished desk, a widescreen TV, a love seat, neatly arranged bookshelves, and a scanner and printer in a separate cabinet. Framed photographs of his wife and three children adorned the walls and the desk.

Chikata stood in the doorway just behind Calmy-Rey, who watched as Dawson and Hammond put on their latex gloves and began to go through the drawers in his desk.

The contents of the desk were unremarkable. Calmy-Rey was painfully tidy. Each drawer had designated contents, like printer paper, stationery, or business letters and memos, which Dawson read and found to be of no importance.

"Do you not have a computer?" Hammond asked Calmy-Rey.

"A laptop. It's in my carry-on luggage downstairs."

"Okay, we'll look at that later."

"We'd like to check your bedroom now, please, sir," Dawson said.

Calmy-Rey led them there. As Dawson had expected, the bedroom was a picture of perfection with a mahogany platform bed flawlessly made up by the maid, ornamental rugs on a lustrous wood floor, a matching wood-framed full length mirror, two walk-in closets, a writing desk, and of course, a wide-screen TV facing the bed. The fixtures in the ensuite bathroom gleamed.

Again, Chikata positioned himself in the doorway behind Calmy-Rey, who stood to one side and watched Dawson and Hammond go to work. They shifted the heavy mattress together to have a look underneath. Dawson did not seriously expect to find anything there, and his prediction proved correct.

Calmy-Rey accompanied them now to watch them search the walk-in closets, which were full of business suits. They checked all the pockets, inside and out. The chest of drawers contained neatly folded socks, underwear, and casual wear. Everything was in plain view and neither Dawson nor Hammond could find any hidden spaces or false drawer bottoms.

Calmy-Rey resumed his previous position by the door, and Hammond began to sift through the writing desk.

Dawson went into the alcove of the bedroom. A chaise lounge and coffee table were by the window, which provided a marvelous view of the beach.

A small bookcase with a varied selection stood against one wall. The larger books were on the top and paperbacks were on the lower shelves. Calmy-Rey appeared to enjoy reading detective novels.

The hardcovers on the top shelf were all serious, with titles like *Statistics for Business and Economics* and *Oil Rig Design*, which was the largest of them. Dawson idly wondered how many types of oil rig designs existed. He should have been diligently conducting the search of the room, but he pulled the book from the shelf with some curiosity. Had he never had a tour of the *Thor Sterke*, he probably would not have been the slightest bit interested.

He glanced at Calmy-Rey and noticed he appeared rigid, as though bolted to the ground, as he watched Dawson. He rested the book on the coffee table and opened it to the title page, and then to the first chapter, after which he attempted to turn to the midsection. In fact, no midsection existed. Beyond a certain point, the pages did not turn. They were stuck together like a block. A slim metal lockbox rested in a cavity cut into a block. The book was actually a disguised safe.

"What is in here?" Dawson asked Calmy-Rey in surprise.

He hesitated. "A weapon."

"What kind of weapon?"

"A pistol. I have a permit for it from the Minister of Interior, so it's perfectly legal."

"I'm sure it is," Dawson said. "Do you have a key to open this box?"

For the first time, Calmy-Rey's eyes took on an air of cold hostility.

"Yes," he said quietly. "I keep it taped to the underside of the cabinet in the bathroom."

Hammond went there, found the key, and returned.

"Note that in the inventory, please," he said to Chikata, showing him the small key. "Found affixed with tape to the bottom of the mirror cabinet."

Hammond opened the safe. Cushioned in soft, black velvet, the semi-automatic pistol was the most precisely made weapon Dawson had ever seen, and if such a thing could be beautiful, this was. The grip was matte black, contrasting with the hard shine of the brushed stainless steel barrel and slide, along which was the proud manufacturer's label. SPHINX AT .380-M MADE IN SWITZERLAND.

"And what do you use this for?" Dawson asked Calmy-Rey.

"Self-defense, of course. Have you noticed that armed robbery is becoming rampant in this country?"

"Have you ever killed anyone with it?"

"Fortunately, I've never had cause to."

Dawson's left palm tingled. "I think, Mr. Calmy-Rey," he said, "that we need to talk a little more about this down at the station."

Chapter 37

By daybreak the following day, Calmy-Rey had been in police custody for eighteen hours. DeGraft had agitated for an immediate interrogation the day before, but Dawson had resisted, refusing to allow the lawyer to drive the proceedings. Dawson needed time to digest the case and prepare for the interview. If his questioning was sloppy, Calmy-Rey might well slip from his grasp with DeGraft's wily assistance. In any case, a little bit of detention in jail might urge Calmy-Rey to confess.

Dawson had ascertained that the oil executive had followed procedure and licensed the Sphinx pistol in Accra, filling out the correct forms A1 and A2 and paying the hefty fee to eventually receive the final permit from the Minister of the Interior.

Chikata had returned to Accra to submit the weapon to the forensic lab for fingerprints and ballistics. He was to ask his uncle to pressure the lab's director to expedite the process. Without an incriminating result from the lab, Dawson might not have enough to detain Calmy-Rey much longer. Counsel would certainly press for his release and once Calmy-Rey left local jurisdiction for the UK, any investigation of his involvement would become very difficult, and they might never get the man back.

The inspector's office at the Beach Road station was available for the interview. With a constable on guard at the door, Dawson sat at the desk opposite DeGraft and his client.

Calmy-Rey did not appear to have slept much. With grey stubble growing like nascent plant shoots, he appeared older and more hag-gard, but Dawson suspected that DeGraft had advised him to put on his best face. Calmy-Rey was polite, even friendly as he answered Dawson's preliminary routine questions—full name, date of birth, and places of residence in Ghana, the UK, and Switzerland.

"We are investigating the death of Mr. Lawrence Tetteh, the CEO of Goilco, who was killed last June," Dawson continued, "and the deaths of Charles and Fiona Smith-Aidoo, who were killed about one month later."

"Can you make it clear to my client why you've arrested him?" DeGraft snapped, opening his hands in a *this is ridiculous* gesture.

"We have some new information I will be happy to disclose in short order," Dawson said pleasantly. "But first, I would like to estab-lish one or two facts. Is that okay?"

"Yes, yes, carry on," DeGraft said.

"When did you first meet Mr. Tetteh?" Dawson asked Calmy-Rey.

"About three years ago when he took over as CEO of Goilco."

"Did you have much contact with him over that period until his murder?"

"I make it a point to keep in touch with our partners," Calmy-Rey said, nodding, "even if it's just to say hello or meet for a drink. It's important."

"Why is that?"

"We don't work with companies; we work with *people*. It's our culture at Malgam to maintain close relationships. As the CEO, I set that tone."

"That's laudable. Did you have occasion to visit Mr. Tetteh at his residence in Accra?"

Calmy-Rey shook his head. "No, we always met at restaurants and so on."

"When was the last time you saw him?"

"Last April or May—about two months before his untimely death."

Dawson looked down at his notes and then up again. "You didn't see him in June at all?"

"Not that I recall."

Dawson nodded. "Okay."

He jotted a couple items in shorthand on a plain sheet of paper in the docket. He didn't shield his notes from Calmy-Rey or DeGraft, but his handwriting was almost illegible in any case.

"Mr. Calmy-Rey," Dawson continued, "when and where did you acquire your Sphinx pistol?"

"I bought it in Switzerland several years ago. It's a classic."

"I see," Dawson said with interest. "I understand gun sales and ownership are legal there."

Calmy-Rey smiled tolerantly. "Highly legal. The Swiss people are the country's militia. Gun ownership and training are required."

"So, of course you're very familiar with the use of all kinds of guns, including handguns like your Sphinx," Dawson said, leaning forward slightly.

"Absolutely."

"You're a dual citizen of Switzerland and the UK, correct?"

"Yes, although I spend more time in the UK."

"What is the reason for having the Sphinx here in Ghana?"

"As I believe I told you at the house yesterday," Calmy-Rey said with some impatience, "for self-defense, Inspector. I don't intend to suffer at the hands of thugs attacking me in my home or my car, and on occasions when my wife and children visit me, I make every effort to protect them against marauders."

"Have you ever fired your weapon here in Ghana for any reason?"

"No," he said, quietly.

"I'm sorry, I didn't hear you."

"I said no, I haven't."

Dawson took his time writing that down in quotation marks.

"This morning," he said, putting his pen down, "I was thinking how Mr. Tetteh could have been in many ways like your father."

Calmy-Rey pulled back as if being prodded in the face with a garden fork. "Like my father? Why do you say that?"

"From what I've read, he and your father shared a stubborn commitment to honesty and transparency in all your business dealings."

"Yes, I suppose you could say so."

"Honesty, integrity, making sure everything was above board. In fact, wasn't your father, Ulysses, known as the humanitarian capitalist?"

"Yes, he was," Calmy-Rey said.

"Inspector Dawson," DeGraft chimed in, sitting up to his full height, "this banter is a waste of time. Please get on with something more substantive."

"Sorry, I digressed a little bit. At any point in your career, Mr. Calmy-Rey, did your father ever suggest to you that you had been dishonest?"

Calmy-Rey's face showed a flash of irritation. "No, why? What does this have to do with anything?"

He glanced at DeGraft, who said sharply, "*Please*, Inspector. What is all this?"

"Did Mr. Tetteh?"

"Did Mr. Tetteh what, Inspector?" DeGraft snapped. "What are you asking Mr. Calmy-Rey?"

"Did Mr. Tetteh ever accuse you of dishonesty?"

"No," Calmy-Rey said angrily. "He didn't."

"Did you know of any plans he had to do so?"

"No, Inspector."

"Let me put it another way. Was he going to make an announcement about Malgam Oil falling below ethical standards or engaging in corrupt practices?"

"Not only is that ridiculous," Calmy-Rey said fiercely, "I don't see how Mr. Tetteh would have made that kind of allegation."

"You don't know of any document with such accusations, then?"

Dawson saw that Calmy-Rey was gripping the edge of the table. "*No*, Inspector," he said sharply. "No, I don't."

"I'd like a moment alone with my client, Mr. Dawson. Please excuse us."

"Of course." Dawson got up. "Let me know when you're ready to continue."

He left the room and went out onto the porch of the little police station. Calmy-Rey had been getting a little agitated, and DeGraft was no doubt advising him to play it cool and not to lose his temper. Many factors affected a suspect's ability to withstand an interrogation: the inherent stress, lack of sleep, the discomfort of the cell. Calmy-Rey had undoubtedly never experienced anything as unpleasant as a jail.

The desk sergeant came out to the porch.

"Please, Inspector Dawson. They are ready."

He rejoined DeGraft and Calmy-Rey, who had a determined smile on his face.

"Are you okay?" Dawson asked, taking his seat.

"Just fine," DeGraft said. "Please, try to be as straightforward and forthcoming as possible, Inspector Dawson. Mr. Calmy-Rey has important affairs to attend to."

"Of course, of course," Dawson said, elbows on the table and fingers interlaced. "Mr. Calmy-Rey, what would be the consequences for you and your company if Mr. Tetteh were to make an accusation in the papers both here and in the UK that Malgam Oil was a corrupt, unethical company in bed with several corrupt, unethical government officials?"

"But Malgam Oil is simply not a corrupt company," Calmy-Rey said with forced lightness.

"Do you know Terence Amihere, the Minister of Energy?"

"How would I not know the minister who is the most central government official the oil industry deals with?" Calmy-Rey said haughtily.

"What was your relationship with him? Cordial, friendly?"

"Yes, all of that."

"If I were to say that you arranged for Malgam Oil to pay him two hundred thousand dollars in return for his agreement that the oil companies should not be compelled to compensate fishermen for any oil spills, what would you say?"

"Now just you listen to me, Inspector Dawson," Calmy-Rey said, raising his index finger. "I've held back all along, but I can't anymore. You are a small fry around here. Understand? Rank of inspector? Insignificant. You're nothing. I know many people in the high echelons of the government, and you're going to be very sorry when they hear about this kind of slanderous language you're leveling at me."

"I have something I would like you to read and comment on," Dawson said, taking out a copy of Lawrence Tetteh's letter. Calmy-Rey frowned as he warily took the three sheets of paper and began to read them with DeGraft.

"This is nonsense," Calmy-Rey, sliding the letter back to Dawson. "Utter nonsense."

"Where did you get this?" DeGraft demanded.

"From a pen drive belonging to Lawrence Tetteh. He told Charles that he was about to reveal this corruption scheme along the lines you see in this letter. I put it to you that Charles reported this to you."

Looking mystified, Calmy-Rey shook his head. "Not that I recall."

"Your trusted director of corporate affairs wouldn't immediately let you know about something as scandalous as this?" Dawson challenged. "That doesn't make sense."

"Okay, yes—he did mention something about it."

"What action did you take?"

"Well, I spoke to Mr. Tetteh, and I persuaded him to retract it, which he did, and the matter was resolved."

"When did you speak to him?"

"Three or four days before his death," Calmy-Rey said, as if it should have been obvious to Dawson.

"Did you speak to him in person, or on your mobile?"

"On the mobile."

Dawson's palm tingled again. The man was a liar.

"Is it the same mobile we retrieved from your house?"

"Yes."

Dawson opened his folder again and took out a sheet of paper. "Here is a list of calls you made in the six weeks preceding Mr. Tetteh's murder. Please, would you look at that?"

Calmy-Rey looked coldly at it. "And what of it?"

Dawson slid another piece of paper over to their side of the table. "This is Mr. Tetteh's number. Can you show me where it is on that record?"

"Why, yes of course," Calmy-Rey said, pointing. "Right here."

"Correct," Dawson said. "But that's *twenty-four* days prior, not three or four, as you said. Mr. Calmy-Rey. Why are you lying to me?"

"Please, Inspector," DeGraft snapped.

"I'm not lying," Calmy-Rey exclaimed. He turned to DeGraft. "Calvin, I'm not lying. This is absurd. Why can't you control this man?"

"Why did you say you spoke to Mr. Tetteh on the phone three or four days before his death when you clearly didn't?" Dawson asked.

"I forgot, that's all. It's been several months, Inspector. Evidently I talked to him in person."

"Three or four days before he was murdered, right?"

"*Yes*," Calmy-Rey said, gritting his teeth.

"So that would be on Wednesday or Thursday of that week."

"I don't have a calendar with me, Inspector."

Dawson was ready for him with the calendar on his phone. He pointed out the Sunday that Tetteh had been murdered. "When did you speak to Mr. Tetteh?"

"Well, like you say—Wednesday or Thursday."

"What exactly did you say to him?"

"I asked him if he would hold onto the article a little longer while I order an internal investigation."

"What was his response?"

"He said he would be happy to cooperate with me."

"And all this happened while you were at Tetteh's office."

"Yes."

"I put it to you that you did not talk to him at his office."

"Of course I did," Calmy-Rey said defiantly.

"This is going nowhere, Inspector," DeGraft said. "You have nothing on my client. I demand you release him right away. This arrest has no merit."

"If you had gone to find Mr. Tetteh at his office three or four days before his death," Dawson said, "you would not have found him there."

Calmy-Rey stiffened as if a bolt of electricity had passed through him. "What do you mean?"

"He was away in Côte d'Ivoire all that week. He got home Friday evening and did not go to the office at all. I know this from his housemaid."

Calmy-Rey snorted. "Charity? She's a little liar."

"So you *have* been to Mr. Tetteh's house then. How else would you know Charity?"

Calmy-Rey swallowed. "Okay, yes, I've been once or twice to his home. So what?"

"So, who is the liar, then?"

Calmy-Rey rested his forehead in his palms. "I'm so tired," he whispered.

"He needs a rest, Inspector," DeGraft said. "Please."

"Sure, no problem. I'll have them bring him some water."

Dawson stood outside the room for a while, gazing idly at the road that ran in front of the station. An episodic Benz, Audi, or Japanese SUV went by. His mind was quite serene. He wasn't at all worried.

"Please, Inspector," the sergeant said, "they are ready."

When Dawson sat down again, Calmy-Rey looked a little more refreshed.

"Keep this short, Inspector," DeGraft said.

Dawson reached across and put his hand gently on Calmy-Rey's forearm, deliberately breaching a boundary. Calmy-Rey flinched.

"I understand completely," Dawson said. "The Ghana oil find was your greatest triumph, but you thought, *if I could just squeeze a bit more success out of it, gain a million dollars here, a million there.* You panicked whenever production dropped because of some technical problem. Your excellent engineers would not allow any safety risks, but there were other ways to take shortcuts. Buy off Amihere, as well as members of various committees, and the Goilco people. Save millions of dollars that way. I understand."

Calmy-Rey pulled his arm away. "I don't think you do."

"And neither did Lawrence Tetteh, apparently."

Calmy-Rey folded his arms and became rather smug. "Lawrence was terribly misguided. A sanctimonious attitude in Ghana doesn't get you anywhere, and I'm surprised he could not see that. It's ultimately impossible to defeat corruption in a country where the MO seems to be: steal from the treasury and then turn around and ask for yet another handout from us."

"Who is 'us'?"

He curled his lip—just a hint of it. "The rich countries, of course," he said. "You people constantly beg for more and more aid from us, and what happens? Nothing. You'll never develop this way. And when I hear someone like Lawrence pontificating in language that doesn't match the reality of life in Ghana, I just have to laugh."

DeGraft shot his client a look of astonishment at the outburst.

"Lawrence has the nerve to call *me* corrupt?" Calmy-Rey continued. "It's ridiculous."

"And brazen," Dawson said.

"Yes, it is."

"I would have killed him myself if I was in your situation," Dawson said sympathetically.

Calmy-Rey looked at him in disbelief. "What?"

Dawson shrugged. "Sometimes, murder is the only logical action to take under certain circumstances."

Calmy-Rey's chin trembled with emotion. He was tired, distraught, and no longer holding himself together.

Dawson leaned forward. "The flashbacks can be difficult," he whispered. "Let me help you. Sometimes it's good to talk about it. The impact of the bullet to his skull, him collapsing, all that blood on the floor."

Calmy-Rey was hyperventilating.

"That's all, Inspector," DeGraft snapped. "Stop."

"I'm guessing you didn't plan to kill him originally, sir," Dawson said. "It's just that when you were talking to him, he remained so stubborn, so determined to publish the article, refusing to retract it."

"Don't say anything more," DeGraft said to Calmy-Rey sharply.

"Did Lawrence say anything before you shot him?" Dawson asked. "Did he have any last words?"

"*Stop!*" DeGraft cried.

Calmy-Rey's face crumpled and his shoulders collapsed. "He seemed to smile," he said, "and I couldn't understand why. Then he said the words, 'pen drive.' Seconds after I shot him, I realized I should have found out what he meant."

Chapter 38

IT WAS NO SURPRISE that Dawson could not sleep that night. Like a pendulum, he went back and forth as he thought about the day's events. Roger Calmy-Rey had fully confessed to murdering Lawrence Tetteh. However, he had not killed Charles and Fiona Smith-Aidoo, nor had he contracted anyone to kill them. It was clear. Dawson believed him. Calmy-Rey had cherished Charles and adored Fiona. Charles had been a faithful and resourceful Malgam employee and an asset to the company and Calmy-Rey. The killing simply did not fit no matter what angle Dawson tried.

Even though the hour was late, he called Christine to give her an update.

"I think it's marvelous," she declared.

"You do?"

"As usual, you don't give yourself enough credit," she chided. "You've done several things at once. You've found Tetteh's true murderer and now an innocent man—that poor Silas—will go free. You've uncovered a corruption scheme, and hopefully we can now clean out these thieves at the top."

"Yes, I suppose so."

"You're going to be all right, Dark. You know you get like this during a case. Come home soon, okay? We miss you."

"I will."

HE GAVE UP the idea of sleep and went to the sitting room where he pored over his notes page by page from the very beginning—that Tuesday the canoe containing two corpses drifted into the restricted area around the *Thor Sterke*, and not far away, two men in another canoe watched. They were not fishing—not on a Tuesday. They must have been the murderers, brazenly watching the scene of the crime. Who had the kind of rage needed to behead Charles Smith-Aidoo? Dawson thought about all the people he had met. Beautiful Sapphire Smith-Aidoo, the Sarbahs, DeSouza, Cardiman, Calmy-Rey, Clay, Forjoe, Gamal . . . perhaps even cousin Abe. Yes, he found himself reconsidering that painful possibility. *A sign of just how desperate I am,* he thought. What or whom had Dawson missed? A motive somewhere, an alibi, an opportunity?

He wandered outside wearing only his briefs. The cool night air bathed his skin. He looked up at the sky. The streetlamp on the corner had gone out, but Takoradi's city lights meant it was still not dark enough to see the Milky Way. His favorite secondary school science teacher had once told him, "It's there, but you can't always see it."

Just like this case, he thought. *The murderer is there. I just can't see him.*

How long would it take to travel to one of those Milky Way stars? He didn't know, but it would be a terrific alibi.

"I couldn't have murdered the Smith-Aidoos," he said aloud. "I was traveling to the Milky Way at the time."

And that's when he realized what he had missed.

ON THE WAY, Dawson called Superintendent Hammond to tell him where he was going. The superintendent told him to be careful. Dawson had the taxi drop him off well before Richard Sarbah's house and he walked the rest of the way. When he was close, he ducked behind a neem bush. A single light sat on top of Sarbah's gate. Forjoe was on duty as watchman, sitting not far from the spot the plumbers had been working on the pipe.

A stack of wooden boards stood to one side of the hole that dipped underneath the wall, presumably to cover the pit if it rained. Dawson intended to use it to get into the yard on the other side of the wall, but he would never be able to do that with Forjoe guarding the place.

He was hoping Forjoe would get up and take a patrol around the sides and the back of the house.

For almost an hour, nothing happened. Then Forjoe stood up and stretched.

Come on, Dawson thought. *Move.*

Forjoe went off to the end of the wall to Dawson's left, unzipped his fly, and stepped around the corner to urinate. Dawson moved quickly, sprinting on his toes. He went head first inside the hole. Feet first, he might well end up stuck. Either way, he found little space for both him and the water pipe. He stopped moving as he heard Forjoe's footfall. He was returning. This could be a problem. The next piss break might not be for hours.

In the distance, he heard the rumble of a diesel truck coming closer. It might be a noisy *bola* truck carrying its trash to a dump somewhere. He hoped it was, and that it was coming this way. The ground trembled as the truck transmitted its impact over potholes. The ear-jarring sound of the diesel engine drew closer. Dawson began to move forward. As the truck reached its crescendo, he pulled his way through, coming out on the other side of the wall with dirt in his face and grit in his mouth. His head popped up over the top of the hole and he looked around. No one was in the yard. He pulled himself the rest of the way out and stayed still for a moment, listening for any sign that Forjoe had heard anything. Dawson heard him yawn languidly and mutter something to himself. The coast was clear.

The sitting room was in darkness. Dawson quickly shone his flashlight beam through the window to confirm no one was inside. The glass portion of the window was open, leaving the screen to let in a breeze while keeping out the mosquitoes. One whined in his ear, and he swiped it away. He took out his pocketknife, cut a small slit in the netting, put his hand in and found the latch, which he pulled back. The window opened with a small squeak that seemed loud enough for the whole world to hear.

Dawson vaulted through the window and stayed motionless for a while. He heard a rhythmic, machine-like buzzing, which after a moment he realized was Richard snoring from a room around the corner. *Please be a heavy sleeper.* Dawson slowly shut the window behind him, wincing at the squeak.

Pointing his flashlight beam downward, he moved to the dining area next to the kitchen, where he opened the sideboard door and took out the four hefty photo albums that Richard had shown him on the first visit.

Dawson turned the thick pages of the first book, scanning the photographs as quickly as possible with the flashlight. He shook his head. This could take him half the night.

Each photo in the album was highly posed, some with Richard as a boy—similar to the framed photo on the sideboard—and some without. Also featured was the beautiful Bessie with her radiant skin and dark eyes—all before she married Robert, of course.

Dawson got through the first album and paused listen to the snoring, making sure there was no telltale change in the pattern that might indicate Richard was stirring. For a moment it stopped, and Dawson began to plan an escape if it became necessary. But the drone started up again, so he began on the second album. Interesting black-and-white and sepia photographs of various people . . . but still no sign of what he was looking for.

It was on the second-to-last page, as he was just about to give up, that Dawson found it. The photograph was remarkable for the period in that the two people involved, Richard and his father, Tiberius, were interacting with each other in a way quite unlike the stiff, unsmiling poses of all the other images. Here, Richard, at the age of about seven, was looking up toward Tiberius, who was smartly dressed in a vest and white shirt with long, broad lapels, and a dark tie. Probably around forty at the time, he was in turn looking down and regarding his son with a hint of an affectionate smile. It was far more of a candid shot than anything else Dawson had seen so far—perhaps a moment deliberately captured by a visionary photographer, or quite by accident.

The delight that was so evident on Richard's face was over an item his father was dangling from his fingers. The glinting object was round, made of silver with a dark center.

"There it is," Dawson whispered. "The pocket watch."

Chapter 39

DAWSON HEARD RICHARD GRUNT and then mutter something. Was he having a dream? The mattress creaked as if he were sitting up. Dawson started to move toward the window, but stopped as he heard Richard's footfall because he realized he would never get there without being discovered.

The refrigerator was somewhat pulled out from the wall. Dawson thought he could fit in the space, but for one panicked moment as he squeezed in, he thought he had made a mistake. He pushed out all the air in his chest to flatten himself further and moved all the way into the corner. The loud background hum of the refrigerator drowned out any rustle of his clothing against the wall.

The kitchen lights came on and Richard opened the refrigerator door and pulled something out. Dawson heard his rhythmic glottal sound as he took a drink—Dawson assumed water. He hardly dared to breathe. The heat from the back of the refrigerator was beginning to make him sweat.

The refrigerator door closed and the light went out again. Dawson heard Richard shuffle back to bed, but he stayed where he was for a while to be safe and then moved out from the tight space, his nose tingling from the dust. It was mind over matter not to sneeze.

It was time to get out. He returned to the sitting room window, opened it carefully, and slid out.

To his left stood the toolshed he had noticed the first time he had been here. He kept low while running to it. Shielding his flashlight beam, he examined the door. A padlock hung carelessly open on the latch. He pulled on the door and opened it slightly. It whined and he swore under his breath. His heart was banging hard and fast in his chest. He went in, pulling the door closed behind him and swung his flashlight from right to left. The beam went past something, and he brought it back. A few meters away, a small tarpaulin draped over a bulky object on a wooden stand. He lifted the tarpaulin and looked underneath. An outboard motor.

Dawson put the tarpaulin on the floor. Made by Suzuki, it was a 25 hp model, adequate for a medium-sized canoe. It was old, but it appeared to be well oiled and in good shape. Dawson was about to put the tarpaulin back when the door behind him squeaked. He jumped and turned around. The light came on. Richard Sarbah was standing in the doorway with a raised revolver.

"What are you doing here?" he asked coldly.

"Is this the outboard motor you used on the canoe to take the Smith-Aidoos out to sea?" Dawson said.

"Kneel on the floor with your hands crossed behind your neck."

Dawson got down slowly, his heart thumping, blood rushing through his head.

"How did you get in?" Sarbah asked.

"The dug-out hole under your wall."

"I ought to shoot that worthless Forjoe."

"You shoot a lot of people, don't you?" Dawson remarked.

Richard's lip curled. "You're stupid if you think you'll make it out of here alive."

"Superintendent Hammond knows where I am," Dawson said with confidence, but his legs were trembling. "You'll be facing three counts of murder."

"Three? Where do you get the other two?"

"Count one, Charles Smith-Aidoo. Count two, his wife, Fiona."

"I don't know what you are talking about."

"The silver pocket watch with the onyx center that was stuffed in Charles's mouth and scratched with the message, 'blood runs deep' belonged to your father Tiberius. You put it in Charles's mouth."

Richard froze then tried to recover. "Lies. Inspector Dawson, you're a liar looking for a scapegoat."

"You loved that pocket watch, remember?" Dawson said, raising his eyebrows. "Remember how your father used to dangle it in front of you when you were a boy?"

Richard swallowed hard. "You're going to die, and Forjoe and I are taking you out to sea tonight. Forjoe will do anything for me because he is a fool. He believed me when I told him that his daughter would get better if we offered Charles's head to the sea god." He laughed. "Thank heavens for superstition. He was so petrified that *I*, the old man, had to do the shooting *and* the beheading." He clicked his tongue disapprovingly and shook his head. "These young folks nowadays. Cowards, the whole lot. It was only Forjoe's annoying weeping that stopped me from removing Charles's second eye—even though I knew very well that you should never let a dead man see what you are doing to him, or they will bear witness to the gods when they reach the other side."

Richard came forward and pressed the revolver to his head. "This is going to be just like Charles and Fiona—except there will be no second canoe."

"Why did you do it?" Dawson asked hoarsely.

Richard giggled and stroked Dawson's cheek with the gun barrel. "I like to see you shaking. You're not such a big shot now, are you?"

"Why did you do it?" Dawson insisted. If he was going to die, and there was a good chance he was, he wanted to know Richard's motive before death came.

"I don't have to tell you anything I don't want to, Inspector," Richard said, grinding the muzzle against Dawson's head. It was clear that it gave him pleasure to do so. "Suffice it to say," he continued in a smug fashion, "that now the score between the Smith-Aidoos and the Sarbahs is settled. After generations of their maltreating us, you don't conspire to kill my granddaughter, Angela, and not expect me to take action. Jason would certainly never do it, so I did it for him. I love that boy. He never deserved the loss of his beloved daughter. Say goodbye now, Inspector Dawson. It's all over for you."

Chapter 40

SUPERINTENDENT HAMMOND WAS CARRYING his pistol, but he hoped he would not have to use it because he was badly out of practice. The front gate of Richard Sarbah's house was open and the yard was clear. Ahead, Hammond saw the light from the shed doorway. His stomach plunged when he heard the gun blast. He sprinted, gasping. Oh, God. *Dawson.*

In the doorway, he brought up his pistol and crouched, ready.

Dawson swung around and raised his hand. "Don't shoot, sir!" He breathed again as Hammond lowered his weapon. Forjoe stood next to Sarbah's dead body, looking down at it as if numb. In the few moments before Hammond's arrival, Forjoe had relinquished his firearm to Dawson and offered his wrists for handcuffing. Dawson did not do it.

Forjoe heaved a big sigh. "I heard everything he said. A man like that doesn't deserve to live."

Hammond circled around the growing pool of blood. It was a fatal head wound from Forjoe's weapon at close range.

Hammond looked at Dawson. "Are you okay?"

He checked himself. "It seems so, sir."

"Why was he trying to kill you?"

"Because I found out that he murdered Charles and Fiona Smith-Aidoo."

"Richard Sarbah did?" Hammond said, surprised.

"Yes." He gestured at Forjoe. "And this man saved my life. I would have been dead by now if not for him. Sarbah was just about to shoot me in the head."

Hammond looked at Forjoe. "Thank you, my friend. God bless you."

As he shook hands with the superintendent, Forjoe looked at Dawson with a question on his face. Dawson shook his head imperceptibly. *Do not say anything. You are, after all, a hero, Forjoe. Keep your mouth shut, and I will do the same. No one will ever know the role you played in the death of Charles and Fiona Smith-Aidoo.*

Chapter 41

"PLEASE, UNCLE," CHIKATA HAD said to Lartey in his well-practiced dejected voice, "Dawson has captured not one, but two murderers. Can we be nice to him and bring him home in a nice vehicle instead of him traveling in a State Transport Bus?"

Lartey, who could not resist his nephew's sad eyes, had agreed, if somewhat reluctantly with a lot of grumbling.

Now a satisfied Chikata sat in the back seat of a shiny, dark blue air-conditioned police BMW, respectfully waiting for Dawson as he embraced Abraham and Akosua in preparation to leave the lodge.

"Don't be such a stranger, Darko," Abraham said, shaking his finger with mock sternness. "Come back and see us often and bring Christine and the boys."

"They already want to come back," Dawson said.

"Are they doing okay now?" Akosua asked. "No more nightmares?"

Dawson smiled. "No more nightmares."

He got into the back seat with Chikata and buckled up as the driver started the softly purring engine. The car smelled of sweet, pristine leather.

A glossy, Jaguar pulled up, blocking their exit.

"Wait just a second," Dawson said, alighting.

He walked over to the Jaguar as Sapphire got out. She smiled at him.

"On your way, Inspector Dawson?"

"Yes, Doc."

"I wanted to thank you," she said sincerely. "With all my heart."

He nodded. "I hope you'll find at least a little bit of peace now."

"I think I will."

"I learned something from the experience," Dawson said.

She inclined her head with curiosity. "Really? What?"

"It's all about family," he said, nodding with certainty. "In the end, that's all that matters."

"It is, isn't it?" she said. "Speaking of which, we're having a family reunion of sorts next weekend. My father; my brother, Trevor; and Auntie Eileen will be there, and the twins will join us from the States. You're officially invited."

"Thank you, Doc. I appreciate your kind invitation."

"Not at all," she said, shaking her head. "Listen, if there's anything you ever need assistance with—a medical consultation for your family members, anything at all, don't hesitate to get in touch with me."

"Thank you for the offer," he said. "Please, Doc, actually there is something you might be able to help with, even though it doesn't concern a family member."

"Oh, yes—of course," she said attentively.

"Marvelous, the daughter of the man who saved my life, is suffering from kidney failure and she needs dialysis, which Forjoe cannot possibly afford. Can you see to it that Marvelous gets the right care?"

"Absolutely," Dr. Smith-Aidoo said enthusiastically. "Have him call me today, and I'll get things moving for him and Marvelous." She put out her hand, and he shook it.

"Well, I suppose it's goodbye then. If you'll allow me a hug? A safe one, this time?"

He laughed, hugged her, and returned to the rear passenger seat of the BMW.

As they drove out after the Jaguar, Chikata lowered his voice and said, "By the way, that night I saw her coming out of the house crying . . ."

"That topic is off limits," Dawson said firmly.

"Yes, massa," Chikata said humbly, but he stole an impish glance sideways at Dawson.

The driver moved them through the heart of the city that Dawson had become quite fond of and to the outskirts sprawling with exuberant housing construction.

"Massa," Chikata said, shifting sideways so that he could face Dawson directly, "there's something I don't understand. How did you know it was Richard Sarbah, and how did you know to look for a photograph revealing the pocket watch?"

"Richard told me that on Monday, the seventh of July, he and Forjoe went to Tarkwa together, and Forjoe confirmed that," Dawson said, adjusting his position as well, "but last night, as I was thinking about the case, I remembered that Forjoe had told me that Monday is one of the busiest days of the fishing week and no fisherman misses it. That sparked my suspicion and when I recalled that Forjoe had used the same wording as Richard regarding the trip to Tarkwa, I considered that Richard might have coached Forjoe and that it was possible they were in cahoots. It fit perfectly, because Forjoe was that fisherman we were seeking who knew how to navigate the sea."

Chikata was nodding, and then he laughed happily and exchanged a handshake with Dawson. "You have done well."

"Thank you," he said, smiling. "And as for the pocket watch—well, it was the one clue we didn't pay much attention to, even though its inscription 'blood runs deep' was pointing the way to family ties. I thought that if Richard was the murderer, then the watch must have been handed down to him, most likely by his father. At first I was only looking for a chain on Tiberius's vest that would indicate he used a pocket watch, but there it was clearly exposed—the entire watch, identical to the one found on autopsy."

Chikata digested that soberly for a while. "Why did Richard do it?"

"Revenge," Dawson replied firmly. "But it was revenge on the part of the Sarbah family rather than for himself alone. The Smith-Aidoos have over the generations been like a curse to the Sarbah family. Richard was taken away from Tiberius as a result of Bessie's marriage to R.E. Aidoo; Richard's half siblings, Simon and Cecil, despised him."

"And then there was the accusation by Simon that Tiberius had murdered Bessie and R.E.," Chikata chimed in. "That really ruined his father's reputation, which drove him to alcoholism and suicide."

"Correct," Dawson said, nodding approvingly at his sergeant's valid point. "But the very last, painful straw for Richard to watch his beloved granddaughter, Angela, die. And why did she die in his opinion? Because Charles refused Richard's request for financial aid, and Sapphire turned Jason and his wife away from the private clinic. And as if that tragic death was not anguish enough, according to Richard, Jason came perilously close to the same fate as his grandfather's: suicide."

"He must have been full of anger and pain," Chikata said thoughtfully.

"Yes," Dawson agreed. "He told me he would do anything for his boy Jason, and that's exactly what he did. He took revenge on the Smith-Aidoos on Jason's behalf and that of an entire generation of Sarbahs."

Chikata looked pensively out of the window at the view of the lush forest they were passing. "There is one thing Richard was right about," he said. "Blood really does run deep."

Chapter 42

THE CHRONICLE HAD THE headline:

PROBE LAUNCHED INTO PETROLEUM INDUSTRY CORRUPTION
Minister of Energy Accused

The full text of Lawrence Tetteh's letter was in all the papers and their corresponding websites. The *Daily Graphic* had the sub-headline, *BNI Director Arrested*. In the UK, the dailies had concentrated more on Malgam Oil and Roger Calmy-Rey, whose picture was plastered everywhere as the Malgam stock price plummeted.

Lartey had received a commendation from the Inspector General of Police and was to be awarded some kind of plaque for upholding the values of "service with integrity." He was now almost certain to move up to Assistant Commissioner of Police very soon. *How did he do it?* Dawson wondered. Lartey had turned something that had at first looked like a potential disaster into a bonanza for himself.

Hammond too, was being recognized for heroism in saving another officer's life. Of course, it didn't really happen that way, but it kept away questions about Forjoe and how he came to be in possession of an illegal firearm.

Dawson shrugged. Hammond and Lartey could have their accolades. He didn't care. For him, all that was important was that he, Christine, Sly, and Hosiah were safe, and no one would be threatening their lives. What was more, the prospects for his promotion to chief inspector were now very good.

HE PULLED UP to the front of his father's house on his new motorbike, parked, and went into the yard. A house girl he didn't know was sweeping the front porch.

"Good morning," Dawson said in Ga. "Is my father in?"

"Yes, please. He's sleeping."

Dawson went through the tiny, unkempt sitting room, thinking it needed some fresh air. He knocked softly on the bedroom door and slowly pushed it open.

Jacob was in bed, and the room was dark.

"Papa."

Jacob propped up on one elbow, and with some difficulty sat up and squinted through the dimness. "Who is that?"

"Darko."

"Has something happened? Is it Cairo?"

"No, everything is fine. I came to see you."

"Oh," he said brightly. "You are welcome. Sit down. How are you?"

"I'm fine," Dawson replied, studying his father with curiosity. "Are you sick?"

"No, I was just resting."

"Why do you have all the curtains drawn?"

He shrugged. "I don't know."

Dawson got to his feet again. "This is not good for you."

He thrust aside the window curtains. As the light streamed in and he saw his father in full view, he was horrified by his profound weight loss. The man was melting away.

"Papa," he said gently, "aren't you eating?"

Jacob clicked his tongue resignedly. "Hunger doesn't come anymore."

"What about some *akasa*?" Dawson suggested. "You always liked that."

Jacob grunted. "Maybe."

"I'll go and buy some for you, eh?" Dawson said. "And you can have your bath. Do you have water?"

"I think the girl filled some buckets yesternight. There's none coming from the taps today."

"I can get your bath ready, if you like."

Jacob stood up a little unsteadily. "No, no, it's all right. I can do it myself."

"Okay," Dawson said doubtfully. "Do you want *akasa* or some *kenkey?*"

Jacob grinned, and Dawson winced as he realized that his father had also lost a few teeth since the last he had seen him.

"You can have the *kenkey*, and I'll take the *akasa*," he said, looking hard at Dawson as if he had just noticed something. "It seems you're not so thin anymore. You have muscles now."

Dawson laughed, pleased. What man didn't want muscles? "Really?"

"Yes," Jacob said with a grin. "Have you been doing some exercise?"

"A little. I try to play soccer on the weekends. Lift some weights too."

"Oh, yeah. That's good."

"Okay, well, anyway," Dawson said awkwardly, "go and have your bath and I'll bring your breakfast."

Jacob headed to the door, his gait wavering. Dawson moved protectively closer to him.

"Walking is not so easy for me these days," Jacob complained.

"I'll help you, Papa. I'm sorry I've been away from you so long."

Jacob stopped and looked at Dawson with a smile. "A father never needs an apology from his son. He only needs his love."

"It's true, Papa," he said, his eyes cast downward as he thought of Sly and Hosiah. He looked up again. "Here, hold on to me, and I'll take you to the bathroom."

Jacob leaned against him, and slow step after step, father and son walked together once again.

Glossary

Adinkra: visual symbols originally created by the Akan of Ghana representing concepts or aphorisms. Often used in fabrics, pottery, logos, and advertising.

Akasa: porridge made from slightly fermented corn dough.

Ananse: a cultural figure in Ghanaian folklore taking the form of a spider that is variously cunning, wise, or foolhardy.

Awurade: God, Lord (Fante).

Bola: Trash.

Bra ha: Come here (Fante).

Cassava: starchy tuberous root that can be roasted, boiled, or fried. Tapioca comes from *cassava*.

Cedi: Ghanaian monetary unit, abbreviated GHS.

Cembonit: Fiber cement material used in building and roofing.

Chaley: familiar and friendly term similar to buddy, pal, bro', dude, etc.

Chop: eat.

Fante: language and people mainly in the southwestern regions of Ghana.

FPSO: Floating, Production, Storage, and Offloading. A floating vessel used by the offshore industry for the processing of hydrocarbons and storage of oil.

Fufu: starchy food such as plantain or *cassava* pounded and moistened into a soft, glutinous mass.

Ga: Language and people of southeastern Ghana in and around the capital, Accra.

Juju: used loosely to refer to magical beliefs, witchcraft, spells, supernatural powers and the ascribing of such powers to objects (fetishes).

Kelewele: spicy cubes of ripe plantain deep-fried till crispy.

Kenkey: fermented corn meal.

Mbira: a musical instrument in the lamellophone family with staggered lengths of narrow pieces of metal mounted on a wooden soundboard.

Mepaakyew (may-pah-CHEW): please.

Oburoni: White person or more broadly, a Westerner.

Ofaine: Please (Ga).

Paa: very much, too much.

Palava: An argument, or trouble arising from an argument (corruption of *palaver*, from Portuguese *palavra*, talk)

Pesewa: 100 *pesewas* = 1 *cedi*.

Sakawa: Internet fraud.

Tadi/Taadi: Abbreviated form of Takoradi, third largest city in Ghana (informal).

Tea bread: white bread with a hint of sugar.

Tom Brown: a porridge made from roasted corn flour.

Tro-tro: Van or minivan used for public transportation.

Wee: Marijuana.

Acknowledgments

WHILE WRITING A NOVEL is ultimately a solitary endeavor, an author must often reach out to others for help. In writing this work, I first owe a large debt of gratitude to Well Engineering Supervisor Fraser Lawson of Tullow Oil, Ghana. Without his tireless assistance, I would not have been able to describe the oil rig scenes and related technical details in the novel. Thanks to George Cazenove and Gayheart Mensah of Tullow for giving me the go-ahead to get in touch with Mr. Lawson. It should be noted, however, that the entirely fictional oil company Magnum Oil, its activities, and the fictional operations with government officials in this novel are no reflection whatsoever on Tullow Oil.

I'm grateful to Chief Superintendent James Kofi Abraham of the Ghana Police Service (GPS) in Sekondi-Takoradi for taking time out of his work to explain how police procedures and investigations are organized in his city.

As always, many thanks to my friend Detective Lance Corporal Antwi Boasiako of the Criminal Investigations Department, Accra. He has consistently assisted me in navigating the GPS and making the right contacts.

Rear Admiral Sampa Nuno, Chief of Ghana Naval Staff, helped me with technical aspects of sailing in and navigation of the Gulf of Guinea.

I thank Peter Baah, my driver while in Takoradi, for giving me the benefit of his thorough knowledge of his hometown.

Thanks also to L. Renée Dankerlink for providing me with information on the Roko Frimpong murder case in Ghana, on which some details of this novel were based.

To editor Judy Sternlight, heartfelt thanks are rendered for her perceptiveness and insight. To my Soho Crime editor, Juliet Grames, a big thank you for warmly welcoming Darko Dawson and me to the Soho family.

051770080